Deat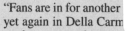

"Fans are in for another ▢▢▢▢▢▢▢▢▢▢▢▢▢▢▢ up yet again in Della Carm▢▢▢▢▢▢▢▢▢▢▢▢▢▢ish on the menu as the ever-delightful, sexy super-cook demonstrates that the proof really is in the pudding. Juggling professional rivalries and a romantic suitor with her trademark self-assurance and wit, Della's sizzling second culinary adventure is a gourmet feast in more ways than one." —Hannah Dennison, author of
Vicky Hill Exclusive!

Praise for

Killer Mousse

"*Killer Mousse* is a treat, a classic culinary mystery played out against the eccentric backdrop of cable TV. Melinda Wells gets it all right, blending an artful plot with engaging characters in a fast-paced whodunit as satisfying as Della's 'Gangster Chicken' Cacciatore."   —Harley Jane Kozak, Agatha, Anthony, and Macavity award–winning author of *Dead Ex*

"*Killer Mousse* is a scrumptious morsel of mystery and mayhem. Take a pinch of murder, a dash of danger, stir it all together . . . Cooking show maven Della Carmichael is poignant and savvy— an amateur sleuth to savor!"   —Linda O. Johnston, author of
Double Dog Dare

"*Killer Mousse* is that wonderful combination of mystery, romance, redemption, and girl-power. Melinda Wells gives you genuine insight into what's really going on behind the scenes."
—Linda Dano, Emmy Award–winning actress,
talk show host, designer, and author of
Looking Great . . . It Doesn't Have to Hurt
and *Living Great*

"Following cable TV–chef Della Carmichael is like a sweet and spicy trip into the fascinating, and often perilous, world of television cooking shows. An appetizing debut!"
—Earlene Fowler, author of the Benni Harper Mysteries

continued . . .

Berkley Prime Crime titles by Melinda Wells

KILLER MOUSSE
DEATH TAKES THE CAKE

Death
Takes the
Cake

Melinda Wells

BERKLEY PRIME CRIME, NEW YORK

THE BERKLEY PUBLISHING GROUP
Published by the Penguin Group
Penguin Group (USA) Inc.
375 Hudson Street, New York, New York 10014, USA
Penguin Group (Canada), 90 Eglinton Avenue East, Suite 700, Toronto, Ontario M4P 2Y3, Canada
(a division of Pearson Penguin Canada Inc.)
Penguin Books Ltd., 80 Strand, London WC2R 0RL, England
Penguin Books Ireland, 25 St. Stephen's Green, Dublin 2, Ireland (a division of Penguin Books Ltd.)
Penguin Group (Australia), 250 Camberwell Road, Camberwell, Victoria 3124, Australia
(a division of Pearson Australia Group Pty. Ltd.)
Penguin Books India Pvt. Ltd., 11 Community Centre, Panchsheel Park, New Delhi—110 017, India
Penguin Group (NZ), 67 Apollo Drive, Rosedale, North Shore 0632, New Zealand
(a division of Pearson New Zealand Ltd.)
Penguin Books (South Africa) (Pty.) Ltd., 24 Sturdee Avenue, Rosebank, Johannesburg 2196,
South Africa

Penguin Books Ltd., Registered Offices: 80 Strand, London WC2R 0RL, England

This is a work of fiction. Names, characters, places, and incidents either are the product of the author's imagination or are used fictitiously, and any resemblance to actual persons, living or dead, business establishments, events, or locales is entirely coincidental. The publisher does not have any control over and does not assume any responsibility for author or third-party websites or their content.

PUBLISHER'S NOTE: The recipes contained in this book are to be followed exactly as written. The publisher is not responsible for your specific health or allergy needs that may require medical supervision. The publisher is not responsible for any adverse reactions to the recipes contained in this book.

DEATH TAKES THE CAKE

A Berkley Prime Crime Book / published by arrangement with the author

PRINTING HISTORY
Berkley Prime Crime mass-market edition / February 2009

Copyright © 2009 by Melinda Wells.
Excerpt from *The Proof Is in the Pudding* by Melinda Wells copyright © 2010 by Melinda Wells.
Cover illustration by Ellen Weinstein.
Cover design by Lesley Worrell.
Interior text design by Laura K. Corless.

ISBN: 978-0-425-22642-1

BERKLEY® PRIME CRIME
Berkley Prime Crime Books are published by The Berkley Publishing Group,
a division of Penguin Group (USA) Inc.,
375 Hudson Street, New York, New York 10014.
BERKLEY® PRIME CRIME and the PRIME CRIME logo are trademarks of Penguin Group (USA) Inc.

PRINTED IN THE UNITED STATES OF AMERICA

10 9 8 7 6 5 4 3 2 1

To Norman Knight

▪ Acknowledgments ▪

I'm grateful to the following:

Editor Kate Seaver, who inspired this series. Thank you for your reactions, your thoughts, and for giving me such a wonderful creative ride.

My gladiators, otherwise known as literary agents Rebecca Gradinger and Morton Janklow. Thank you for everything.

Claire Carmichael, a wonderful writer herself and a brilliant instructor. You've made me a better writer than I would have been without you.

D. Constantine Conte, mentor and treasured friend. I've learned so much from you.

Victor Bardack, Nancy Koppang, Margaret McEldowny, and Ann Talman: Thank you for the recipes you shared with me.

Jane Wylie Daley: Thank you for coming up with the name "Della's Dreamsicle Cake."

Myra Morehouse: Thank you for your recipe that was adapted and turned into the cake Della created for the contest.

To the generous people who read the early manuscript and shared their invaluable reactions: Arthur Abelson, Carole

Moore Adams, Dr. Rachel Oreiel Berg, Christie Burton, Rosanne Kahil Bush, Jane Wylie Daley, Ira Fistell, Nancy Koppang, Judy Tathwell Hahn, Jaclyn Carmichael Palmer, Judy Powell, Ed and Debbie Soloman, Anna Stramese, Corrine Tatoul, and Kim LaDelpha Tocco.

Wayne Thompson of Colonial Heights, Virginia: You're a continuing inspiration.

Berry Gordy: Your place in my heart is, and always has been, unique.

"I hired you a cake coach," said my boss, Mickey Jordan.

Mickey owned the Better Living Channel, the cable TV network where I've been hosting a cooking show for the past three months. There's a flattering caricature of me, Della Carmichael, on the billboard facing traffic just outside the low-tech production facilities in California's San Fernando Valley. My dark hair is a little longer in real life—to tell the truth, I need a trim—and while my waistline hasn't spread yet, it isn't quite so narrow as in the artist's version of me. Whenever I see that drawing, I suck in my stomach.

It was ten thirty on a Monday morning in mid-January when Mickey made his pronouncement. We were in the kitchen of my little two-bedroom cottage in Santa Monica. A third person sat with us at the breakfast table: Mickey's thirty-year-old son, Addison, who had moved from New York to California to work with Mickey.

Introducing us, Mickey had beamed, displaying Addison like a trophy. "Handsome kid, isn't he? Lucky for him, he got his looks from his mother."

If Mickey hadn't announced their biological connection, I never would have guessed it. Mickey was sixty, with a muscular torso, and at five foot five, he was two inches shorter than I am. His hair recently had been cut so close to his scalp that it resembled salt-and-pepper fuzz, but with eyes that could reflect amusement or narrow to intimidating lasers in a second, he looked tough enough that I suspected muggers crossed the street to avoid him.

Addison was six inches taller than his father, with an abundance of light brown hair and aristocratic features. Mickey looked like a fighter; Addison looked like a poet.

Because I'd been pouring coffee and slicing pieces of my sour cream pecan ring, I wasn't sure I'd heard Mickey correctly. "You hired a *what*?"

"Pay attention. This is *big*. I hired a cake coach for you. The guy's a bit of a weirdo, but I checked him out. He'll do the job."

Although I'd known Mickey for several months now, I still wasn't used to his habit of starting conversations in the middle of a subject, so I had to ask, "What job?"

"With what I've got planned, you're going to be the Miss America of Cake!"

I felt a sharp intake of breath. "No. Absolutely not. I won't wear a bathing suit on television!"

He eyed me speculatively. "What's the problem? You still look good."

Still . . .

"If I hadn't read your TV bio, I wouldn't have guessed you're in your forties," Addison said. "Maybe late thirties— but you should think about doing a little glamorizing."

I turned to Mickey. "When you hired me you said it was because I was, in your words, 'down-to-earth.' Natural. I don't even have a regular hair person."

"Don't get ants in your pants," Mickey said. "I'm not talkin' about a *beauty* contest, even though you're pretty hot to be a cook. This contest is a stunt to publicize the show. I'll do the hard thinking. All you have to do is come up with the best new cake in the United States."

At the news that I was supposed to create—invent—an original cake, I stared at him, incredulous. "That's *all*?"

"What's so hard?" Mickey shrugged. "It's not like I'm asking you to cure cancer."

"That certainly puts things in perspective." My tone was wry.

As though I hadn't spoken, Mickey said, "You're one of five contestants and there's a $25,000 prize." Mickey grinned at his son. "My kid is pretty smart. This whole project was his idea—the contest, and that we're gonna tape the match for a TV special."

"Tape it?"

"Yeah, one of those reality shows. I didn't want to tell you this idea before it was a done deal, but Addison talked the owner of the Reggi-Mixx Cake Company into creating the first national Reggi-Mixx Cake Competition."

At the sound of the name Reggi-Mixx, the muscles in my stomach clenched.

Oblivious to my internal horror, Addison seized the conversational baton and started sprinting his lap. "We plan to shoot personal segments about the contestants. Interviews as you five prepare. I've analyzed TV ratings for the last four years and learned the public loves competitions."

"The more trouble somebody has in a contest, the better TV it is," Mickey said.

"But . . . does it have to be *Reggi-Mixx*?"

"They're already committed," Addison said. "It took some fancy convincing, but now the woman who owns the company is thrilled. She thinks this competition could grow to be bigger than the Pillsbury Bake-Off."

"But why Reggi-Mixx? What about some other cake company?"

"I considered going after other companies, but this one needs us as much as we need it. Reggi-Mixx sales have been going downward for a couple of years. That's not good." Addison shook his head and frowned, like a doctor giving a bad prognosis. "But this exciting promotional gimmick will benefit that company *and* it will give a boost to your show. This is a win-win."

Mickey cocked his head and squinted at me. "The contest an' the reality show, it's extra work, but you've got the time right now. You can't teach classes at your cooking school until they finish renovating the building. This project is a big deal, so why are you looking like you just ate a worm?"

I decided to tell him part of the truth. "That cake mix is vile."

Mickey shrugged. "So put stuff in to make it taste better. Problem solved."

But it wasn't solved. It was a lot bigger than the fact that the product tasted like wet cardboard.

Mickey was shrewd enough to have risen from the self-described "fastest kid numbers-runner in the Bronx" to becoming "almost a billionaire." He said, "Spill it. What's the rest?"

"The owner of the company is Regina—Reggie—Davis. She hates me."

"You mean she hates your show?"

"She hates *me*. She's hated me since we were in college together."

Mickey laughed. "Wha'dya do, steal her guy? Hell, that musta been—what, twenty-five years ago? Jeez! Who remembers back that far?"

"She swore she'd never forgive me." *Actually, she'd said something much worse than that.*

"Never forgive you—that's kid stuff." Mickey waved one hand dismissively. "Forget it."

I tried another argument. "You know I'm not a trained chef. I do simple baking on the show, demonstrating things that practically anybody can make if someone shows them how and encourages them to try, but . . ."

"That's exactly the beauty of this idea," Addison said. "It isn't some elitist quiz show where you have to know who Harry Truman's vice president was, or the capital of Finland. It's not a physical endurance test. This will be a show for the millions of *regular* people out there, for anybody who can open a box of cake mix."

Before the discussion could go any further, I heard the front door open, and the sound of four paws and a pair of human footsteps heading in our direction.

First to arrive at the kitchen door was my seventy-pound male black standard poodle, Tuffy, panting from a vigorous morning run. The moment Addison saw Tuffy, he jumped up and stood behind his chair, gripping the top of it as though ready to use it to defend himself.

"Hi, Tuff." Mickey reached out to give Tuffy a friendly scratch beneath one of my poodle's silken ears. Tuffy allowed it, while watching the stranger in the room.

"Sit down, Addison. You can't still be scared of dogs."

"I was badly bitten," Addison said, his tone defensive.

"You were six years old. Get over it. Anyway, Tuffy's not just a regular dog. You haven't seen Della's tapes yet, but he's on her show. Viewers love him—he even gets his own fan mail."

Tuffy left Mickey, came to me for a greeting nuzzle, and trotted to his water bowl to take a few deep slurps.

In that moment, Addison lost interest in Tuffy because he was staring at the vision in my kitchen doorway: Eileen O'Hara, my honorary daughter, a twenty-year-old UCLA business major. Even with no makeup, wearing a faded old Bruins T-shirt and loose sweatpants, with her blonde hair spilling from her ponytail in damp tendrils, Eileen was a spectacular beauty.

She flashed a smile at the three of us. "Ooops. I hope I'm not interrupting."

"It's okay," Mickey said. "We're almost done." To Addison, he added, "This is the brainiac college gal I told you about, the one who talked me into backing Della in a mail-order fudge business."

"I'm Eileen O'Hara," Eileen said to the younger Jordan. "Aunt Della's semipermanent houseguest."

"Addison Jordan." He extended his hand to her and she took it. "I'm Mickey's son, and his new cable TV executive in charge of strategic planning." He added with a self-deprecating chuckle, "Whatever that means."

"It's a floating title," Mickey said.

"I'll do my best not to sink," Addison said. "Anyway, I'm very pleased to meet you, Eileen."

Eileen's response was polite, but enigmatic. "Yes, you, too."

It was hard to tell what she was thinking—if she was as interested in him as he clearly was in her. In that way, Eileen was like her father, LAPD lieutenant John O'Hara, who had turned being enigmatic into a personal art form.

Addison said to Eileen, "We might be working together on the . . . fudge thing." From the enchanted expression on his face, I was pretty sure his mind wasn't on fudge.

Excitement replaced enigma. "That's great! Did Mickey show you my business plan? How soon can we start?"

"Hey!" Mickey held up one hand in his traffic cop gesture. "Cut the fudge talk. Friday morning we'll all discuss that. Eleven o'clock. My house."

Eileen beamed. "I've made improvements in the business

plan. I'll bring that, packaging sketches I worked up, and more specifics about shipping choices and costs."

She took a bottle of water from the refrigerator. "I've got to shower and get to class. Bye, everybody."

After she left, Mickey asked me, "What's your schedule this week?"

"I'm taping the two half-hour shows on Wednesday, then there's the live show Thursday evening."

"Good, so I don't have to rearrange anything."

"What do you mean?"

"Tomorrow morning you're going to meet the other contestants at the Davis Foods Test Kitchens. Eight o'clock. Bring pictures of a couple of the cakes you made on the show. An' wear something that shows off your figure 'cause we'll be taping."

"So soon?"

"Life moves fast, but TV moves *faster*. Addison, give her the address."

Addison took a card from his jacket pocket and handed it to me. A glance at it told me the test kitchens were located on Pico Boulevard, in West Los Angeles, only ten or fifteen minutes from here.

"This is really going to be great for your show," Addison said. "For you, too. More national exposure."

Mickey tapped an index finger against the side of his head and told me, "Start thinking about a *winning cake*."

After saying that he would arrange a time for me to get together with the cake coach Mickey had hired, Addison said good-bye. I saw them both out.

Back in the kitchen, I poured a fresh mug of coffee and sat down at the table with a sigh. I started to slice a piece of the pecan ring, but put the knife down. My session with Mickey had momentarily dampened my desire for anything resembling cake.

Tuffy came over and rubbed the side of his body against my leg. "Good boy," I said, scratching him gently under his chin and stroking the side of his face. "I'm so glad I have you." My smart, handsome standard poodle with the loving heart was giving me comfort at the moment I needed it very much. Mickey had, albeit unknowingly, put me in a trap.

I had to agree to his Reggi-Mixx Cake Contest idea because I was still in the danger zone of debt. If I didn't do everything possible to make my TV show a success and stay employed, I could lose my little cooking school on Montana Avenue. I loved teaching, and that school had been my dream, but it hadn't been the world's smartest investment. Winning that $25,000 prize would solve a lot of problems.

Things had been easier financially since I'd begun working for Mickey's Better Living Channel. At least for now I could sleep through the night again without waking up gasping, wondering how I was going to pay next month's bills. While I wasn't getting a lavish salary by any means, it was enough to start paying off the credit cards I'd had to live on during the months before I'd been hired to replace the previous cooking show host.

In the Kitchen with Della was only two months old and was doing pretty well for a new show hosted by an unknown. But unless the audience kept growing it wasn't likely to stay on the air. My predecessor had been replaced; I could be, too. As fiercely independent as I was—as I'd had to be since Mack died—I could not risk losing this job.

I needed to talk to someone who would understand my concern about Regina Davis. There was no one better for that than my best friend of twenty-odd years, Liddy Marshall. I dialed the number I knew as well as I knew my own.

"Hello?" Liddy always pronounced that greeting as a question.

As soon as I told her that I had a problem, she said, "I'm not working today. When do you want me to come over?"

"I'd like to get out of the house. Let's drive down to the beach and eat somebody else's cooking."

There was just the tiniest hesitation on Liddy's end of the line, but I caught it. "Are you busy for lunch? If so, we can—"

"I promised I'd have lunch with Shannon."

I realized why Liddy was hesitant, but I forced brightness into my voice. "That's fine. Terrific. Let's go, the three of us. Just like we used to."

Just like we used to before my husband died, when John O'Hara and my Mack had been LAPD partners, and during the periods when medication stabilized Shannon's moods.

John and Shannon O'Hara, Liddy Marshall and her husband, Bill, and Mack Carmichael and I had been close friends
for years. During the times that Shannon had been confined to
hospitals, it had been the five us, supporting each other. Now,
thankfully, Shannon was home, and on new medications she
was functioning well, but with Mack's death it became the five
of us again. I could not imagine Nicholas D'Martino, the new
man in my life, as part of our group because John can't stand
him. NDM—as I called him to myself—was a crime reporter
who'd been critical of the police in print.

"I'm glad Shannon wants to go out," I said. And I meant it.
"You two can help me figure out what to do about a woman
who said that if we ever crossed paths again she was going to
kill me."

2

Liddy steered her ivory-colored Land Rover into my driveway where I was waiting for her. When I opened the passenger door I saw lines of worry creasing her forehead. The first words out of her mouth were, "Who is this woman who wants to kill you?"

Climbing in, I said, "Someone I knew in college. I'll tell you about it when the three of us are together."

Liddy's tense grip on the steering wheel eased. "Oh, well, *college*." She backed out of my driveway and headed for Sunset Boulevard. "Don't you think she's forgotten whatever she said by now?"

"I hope so." But, remembering the hatred in her eyes when she swore to do me harm, I wasn't confident. "I'll tell you and Shannon all about it at the restaurant."

It was a chilly gray January day, but Liddy Marshall had arrived looking like early spring. Her pale blue sweater and navy slacks complimented her honey blonde hair and blue eyes. Born in Nebraska, Liddy dreamed of becoming a movie star, but she hadn't been in Hollywood very long when she fell in love with a sweet young dentist who told funny jokes, and she chose marriage and motherhood instead of the life of an actress. With their twin boys in college now, Liddy amused herself by working as an extra in movies and TV shows. "All of the fun of being on sets but nobody cares if I'm over forty, or I've put on a couple of pounds," she'd said.

■ ■ ■

John and Shannon O'Hara lived in a one-story Spanish hacienda in rustic Mandeville Canyon, several blocks north of Sunset Boulevard. They'd bought the house a few months before Mack and I found our English cottage in Santa Monica. Twenty-two years ago it was still possible to buy a home in a nice area of Southern California on the salaries of working people. Mack and John were police officers, I was a high school English teacher back then, and Shannon was a paralegal with a large firm.

It wasn't long after their daughter was born that Shannon started hearing voices. The day she tried to attack Liddy and me with a fireplace poker, John had her committed to a hospital for a psychiatric evaluation. Shannon was diagnosed as a paranoid schizophrenic. For baby Eileen's safety, the child came to live with Mack and me.

After years of being in and out of mental hospitals, Shannon was functioning well, seeing a psychiatrist who monitored her medication, and going to weekly group therapy sessions.

Shannon must have been watching for us through the living room window, because as soon as Liddy pulled up in front of their house, she hurried out. I saw that she'd tamed her mass of red curls into a smooth waterfall that fell just below her shoulders. A symphony in emerald green from headband to shoes, she looked healthy and happy. Shannon climbed into the back passenger seat and strapped herself in.

As Liddy started down the winding road toward Sunset Boulevard, Shannon leaned forward between the two front seats and said, "Okay, Della—I want to hear all about your big heartthrob!"

That surprised me, until I realized that Liddy must have told her. "Oh, you mean Nicholas D'Martino."

"Is there some *other* man in your life?"

"No, of course not. It's just that I haven't seen him for the last two weeks."

"Whyever not? With a macho name like that, don't tell me the sex isn't any good."

The sex was fantastic, but I avoided discussing it by saying, "He's been out of town, working on a story for the newspaper. He thinks a recent double murder up in Utah might have a connection to a cold case down here."

"Ever since I heard about the two of you, I've been going through back issues of the paper, looking for his bylines. I'm impressed—he's a good writer." Shannon's voice developed a teasing lilt. "Cops and journalists—they have the best excuses in the world for disappearing on us. There's always a crime someplace that they've absolutely *got* to go investigate." She gave an exaggerated sigh. "Oh, Liddy, you're so lucky to be married to a dentist. They never leave you to go running off in the middle of the night."

Even though I didn't want to share the specifics of my relationship with NDM, the thought of being in bed with him made me feel warm all over. I missed him and hoped he'd be back soon.

Liddy pulled into the half-filled parking lot beside The Wharf, our favorite fish restaurant just north of Malibu.

Shannon surveyed the weathered exterior of The Wharf. "So much changes, but this place doesn't. It still looks like a shack. No sign outside. Unlisted phone number, and Dominic doesn't take reservations."

Inside, the walls of The Wharf were covered with big nets, shell collections in glass cases, and large photos of fishing boats. But no mounted trophies on the walls. I hated to see anything that had once been alive stuffed and hung up for display.

Dominic, the owner-host who resembled a cement block with legs, greeted us warmly. "Ah, more pretty ladies to brighten my day." He looked first at me and then at Shannon, shook his head and *tsk-tsk-tsk'd*. "You two haven't been here in a long time."

"I've been busy," I said.

"I've been crazy," Shannon said.

Dominic laughed; he thought Shannon was kidding. "Well, you are here now."

"And we're ravenous," Liddy said.

"That's what I like to hear." He led us to a window table at one end of the dining room and passed out menus. "May I bring you ladies something to drink?"

Liddy and I ordered diet sodas and Shannon opted for hot tea. Dominic said he'd have a waiter bring them and take our order.

Shannon and Liddy studied the menu. I didn't need to; as

soon as we'd reached Pacific Coast Highway I was struck with a craving for Dominic's grilled swordfish.

Liddy and Shannon decided to make it three for the swordfish.

After the waiter brought our drinks and a basket of hot garlic bread, and we'd ordered, Liddy said, "Now—what do you need to talk to us about?"

I described Mickey's plan to have me compete in a national cake-baking competition, the purpose being to promote my cooking show.

Shannon said, "I love watching TV contests. What's the problem?"

"I have to use a base of Reggi-Mixx cake batter."

"Yuck. That stuff is awful." Shannon grimaced.

Breaking off a piece of garlic bread from the basket, Liddy nodded agreement.

"That's not the worst of it," I said. "Remember, years ago, when I told you about the girl I had trouble with in college? The one who planted drugs in my room, trying to get me thrown out of school?"

Liddy said, "Lucky somebody saw her do it so you weren't blamed."

"The bitch! What about her?" Shannon asked.

"She owns the Reggi-Mixx company. She's the *Reggie*— Regina Davis."

Liddy put down her garlic bread. "You never told me why she hated you so much."

"Money started disappearing from our dorm rooms. The campus police pretty much shrugged and told us to be more careful with our cash. But the thefts made me mad. Most of us were working our way through and on tight budgets. I got a guy I dated, a chemistry major, to make a dye, something like what banks plant in bags of money when they're being robbed. What he concocted was invisible until somebody touched it. We sprayed it on three ten-dollar bills and left them in a desk drawer in my room. That night the money was gone—and Regina Davis had two bright purple hands. It proved to everybody that she was the thief. Nobody had suspected her because her family was rich—Davis Foods International. She could buy anything she wanted. She didn't need what she stole from us."

"Was she punished?" Liddy asked.

"No. Her father hired a lawyer and threatened to sue the school if she was exposed publicly. A few days later, for revenge, she planted the drugs in my—"

I stopped talking because my attention was caught by two people getting up from a window table at the far end of the room. One was a tall, gorgeous blonde in her early twenties. Just behind her was a man in his forties. He had a boxer's build, and a face that just missed being handsome because of a long-ago broken nose. An unruly lock of his thick dark hair fell onto his forehead just above his black eyebrows.

My pulse started to pound as I stared at them.

Shannon reached across the table and gripped my hand. "Del, are you all right?"

Liddy swiveled in her chair to look in the direction I was facing. "Oh, wow—there's your Italian stallion."

Shannon sat up straighter, followed our line of sight and gasped. "Is that the guy you've been doing . . . *you know what* . . . with? *Yum!* But who's the Miss Universe?"

"I hope it's his sister," Liddy said. But we all knew that the *Playboy* centerfold type with him was no relative.

At that moment, Nicholas D'Martino saw me. The guilty expression on his face made him look exactly like a little boy who'd been caught with his hand in the cookie jar.

3

NDM recovered his composure quickly. Instead of continuing toward the exit, he steered the blonde in our direction.

Arriving at our table, he said, "Hello," with forced heartiness. "This is a nice surprise."

It's a surprise, anyway.

"Hello." My tone was pleasant, but beneath the table, I dug the fingernails of one hand into my palm to keep from showing any emotion in that greeting.

There was a second or two of silence. NDM kept it from lasting longer by introducing his companion. "This is Yvonne Blake. Yvonne, I'd like you to meet some friends of mine: Della Carmichael and Lydia Marshall." He looked at Shannon, smiled, and added, "I'm afraid we haven't met."

"This is Shannon O'Hara. You've met her husband, the police lieutenant," I said. "Shannon, this is Nicholas D'Martino." I was tempted to call him *Nick*, which I knew he hated, but instead I just performed the introduction and kept my expression neutral.

"Hello." Shannon frowned at him. NDM started to extend his hand, but she kept hers folded on the table so he drew his back.

"How was your trip?" I asked him, amazing myself by managing to sound casual.

"Good. I mean, it was *useful*," he said. "The case that took me up there wasn't enjoyable."

Shannon faked a puzzled expression. "Case? Are you a lawyer?" Pretending not to recognize his name was an arrow she shot right into the heart of his ego. I could have hugged her for her loyalty.

The young blonde was peering at Liddy. "I've seen you somewhere," she said. Her voice was nasal, slightly grating, and didn't match her pretty face. I'm ashamed to admit that pleased me.

"Three months ago, on the set of *Malibu Justice*," Liddy said. "You played the slut in the beach house."

The blonde's eyes lighted with recognition. "Oh, right. You were one of those extras in the party scene. I noticed because the dress you were wearing was much nicer than what they gave me." She turned to NDM. "You can be sure the producer heard about it!"

"Perhaps that was why they didn't have me back for the next day's shooting," Liddy said. To Shannon and me she added, "It was my own dress."

During this exchange, NDM was looking at me as though he wanted to say something. I pretended not to notice.

"Well," I said briskly, "it was nice to see you again."

The blonde tugged at the sleeve of his jacket. "Come on, Nicky, or we'll be late."

I couldn't resist giving him a big, bright smile and saying, "Bye, *Nicky*."

His cheeks colored. I wondered if it was from embarrassment or irritation. He muttered good-bye, nodded to Liddy and Shannon, and the two of them left.

Liddy put my thought into words. "That's the kind of young bimbo you told me he went out with before you two got together."

I tried to keep my voice light. "It looks like he's reverted to his real type: pre-cellulite."

Shannon reached across the table and squeezed my hand. "Let's kill him."

Liddy and I snapped our heads around to stare at her.

Shannon laughed. "Just kidding. Jeez, can't the mental patient make a joke?"

Twenty minutes later, while we were having coffee, my cell phone rang. I looked at the faceplate, saw the incoming number, and put it down on the table without answering.

"*Him*?" Liddy asked.

I nodded.

Shannon said, "That's the spirit, honey. Let him sweat."

Ten minutes after that, when we were figuring out how much 20 percent of the bill was so we could leave that amount as a tip, my cell rang again. It was a number I didn't recognize, so I pressed the button. "Hello."

"Don't hang up," NDM said. "I figured you wouldn't answer if you knew it was me, so I'm using a pay phone at a 7-Eleven."

"You shouldn't have gone to so much trouble," I said.

"I wanted to explain about Yvonne."

"Let me guess," I said. "You're interviewing her because she's a suspect in your murder story."

On his end of the line I heard him expel a breath. "I understand why you're upset."

"I'm not upset," I lied. "You have the right to go out—or stay in—with every actress in the Hollywood Casting Directory."

"The truth is . . . I didn't call you as soon as I got back because I think maybe we should take things a little slower."

Hurt swept over me like one of the ocean waves that was trying to swallow the beach outside the restaurant's windows, but I kept the pain out of my voice. "I agree. We had some fun for a couple of months, that's all. Look, I have to go. And good luck on your murder story." I hung up before he could reply. While I still had my dignity.

After Liddy, Shannon, and I sat for a few moments without talking, Shannon said, "I'd suggest that we go to one of our houses and get stinking drunk, but I'm on medication."

We laughed, and I felt better. Having good friends makes up for a lot of life's disappointments.

On the drive back from the restaurant, my cell phone remained silent.

It began to dawn on me that Liddy was silent, too. With a smile and a brief exchange of good-byes, Liddy left Shannon at her house and put the car in gear again to take me home. We'd gone less than a block when I was about to ask Liddy if something was wrong, but before I could speak, she swerved over to the side of the road and cut the engine. She threw both arms around the steering wheel and made a sound that was something between a gasp and a groan.

"Liddy, what's the matter?"

When she turned to face me, I saw tears welling in her eyes. "It's awful. For the first time in twenty-four years of marriage, Bill is lying to me."

"Oh, no!" Her pain hit me like a physical blow. "What makes you think so?"

She pulled a tissue from her purse and wiped her eyes. "Every Tuesday night at seven thirty he plays poker with five of his guy friends. The location rotates—last week it was at Jimmy Dodd's house, in Coldwater Canyon. I called there about nine. I could hear men's voices in the background, but when I asked to speak to Bill, Jimmy started coughing and talking with a kind of wheeze that he didn't have when he answered the phone. And the men's voices stopped, like they'd been shushed. Jimmy told me that he'd come down with a bad cold so the game was moved to somebody else's place, but he said he didn't know whose." Her eyes filled with tears again. "I wasn't checking up on Bill—that would never have occurred to me. My stomach was upset and I just wanted him to pick up some Pepto for me on his way home."

I felt the juices in my own stomach begin to churn with apprehension, even though I couldn't believe the first awful thought that leapt into my head: Bill was seeing another woman. I reached out to squeeze Liddy's hand in comfort. "Honey, there's probably some innocent explanation. Did you try to reach him on his cell phone?"

She shook her head. "It was on the dresser next to the dish of coins. He must have forgotten it when he changed clothes after work. But a couple of minutes after I called Jimmy's house, Bill's cell phone started ringing. I could see that it was Jimmy's number calling him."

"What did Bill tell you when he came home?"

Liddy grimaced. Her voice took on an angry edge. "At ten o'clock I sat by the front window, in the dark, watching the street. About fifteen minutes later I saw a car I recognized—Jimmy Dodd's white BMW—drive up and park across from our house, almost under the streetlight. He just sat there for more than an hour. Bill came home at eleven thirty and opened the garage door with his remote, but before he could go inside, I saw Jimmy come running across the street, waving at him. They talked for a couple of minutes, and then Jimmy hurried back to his car."

Oh, Lord. This looks like Jimmy was telling Bill about Liddy's call.

"I went to the bedroom and pretended to be asleep," she said. "When Bill came in, I faked a drowsy voice and asked, 'How was the game?' He whispered that he'd won twenty-four dollars, then he told me to go back to sleep. He went into the bathroom and took a long shower—probably to wash away the evidence of another woman."

Even though my first flash of apprehension was turning to a cold lump of dread, what Liddy was telling me didn't "compute" with my thousands of mental pictures of Bill and Liddy together. Those two were still so in love they beamed with happiness when they looked at each other, and when we'd gone to the movies together two weeks ago I saw they still held hands.

While I was trying hard to think of a not-so-terrible reason that Bill had lied to her, Liddy went on with her story.

"The next morning at breakfast he mentioned—oh, so casually—that Jimmy had the flu so the guys had to play at Craig's house."

That had to be another lie, or why would Jimmy Dodd have waited all that time for Bill to come home? I was getting the urge to hit Bill Marshall, popular Beverly Hills dentist, with something heavy.

"Tuesday was six nights ago," I said. "You've been listening to my problems and never even gave me a hint of what you were going through. Why didn't you tell me?"

Liddy propped one arm on top of the steering wheel. "Pretending this was an acting exercise was how I've managed to seem normal. I was afraid if I told you what had happened I couldn't help but break down in front of Bill and cry, and accuse him. He'd probably deny he'd been with another woman and then I'd never find out the truth. But I couldn't keep this to myself any longer. I had to tell my best friend."

"I want to go on record as saying I do not believe Bill is cheating on you," I said. The truth was that I didn't *want* to believe it. "It does look as though he lied," I said, "but let's not assume the worst. What can I do to help you?"

"Tomorrow's Tuesday. If Bill says he's going to the game I'm going to follow him."

The inside of my skull felt like a fire station when the alarm bells go off. "No! Please don't do *anything* right now. I'll help you figure this out, but we need a couple days to think about it calmly."

"Calmly! I don't think I'll ever be calm again."

I squeezed her hand again, hard enough to get her attention. "Liddy, this is too important to make a mistake. Promise me you won't try to follow Bill. We'll figure out what to do."

"All right," she said reluctantly. "But not knowing what my husband is up to hurts a hell of a lot worse than childbirth when I had the twins." With tears in her eyes, Liddy turned the key in the ignition and started the car.

While we drove the rest of the way to my house in the heavy silence of shared fear, I thought about Liddy and Bill. If we found out that Bill really was cheating on Liddy, what would she do? Leave him? Or forgive him but forever have a big chunk of her heart ripped out? It was doubtful that things between them would ever be the same. And if there was another woman in Bill's life, was this something serious? Might he actually want to leave Liddy? Years ago, when Mack told me that one of his cop buddies was having an affair, I told Mack that if he ever did that and I found out, he'd better come home wearing a Kevlar vest that went all the way down to his knees.

Discovering NDM and the young blonde in the restaurant. Now Liddy and Bill . . . what an awful day this had turned out to be.

But the shocks weren't over yet.

After Liddy dropped me at the curb and drove off, I heard Tuffy inside the house, barking. He was reacting to the fact that a woman was at my front door, ringing the bell.

Getting no answer, my unexpected visitor turned away and

started back down the path to the street. Her brown hair was long now, and streaked with bold platinum highlights, and she no longer wore glasses, but even after twenty-five years I recognized Regina Davis coming toward me.

4

"Hello," I said. I think I was smiling. At any rate, I was giving it a try.

Regina Davis responded with a huge grin and embraced me.

"Oh, Della, it's so wonderful to see you again. It's been toooooo long."

I returned her hug with a polite squeeze of my own, then stepped back to survey her. She looked elegant in dark chocolate wool slacks, a tan suede jacket, and a cream silk blouse. At nearly six feet tall she towered over me. I straightened my posture to increase my height a bit. I wanted to believe that she had put our college trouble behind her, but I couldn't help remembering the hatred in her eyes the last time we'd seen each other, just before she transferred to another university.

"How are you, Reggie?" I hoped I sounded warm.

"I'm great," she said. "The company is flourishing, and now I'm getting the chance to see you again. By the way, I used to know that boss of yours, Mickey Jordan. I didn't expect him to have a son that gorgeous. The moment Addison mentioned your name I decided to agree to the contest and the TV special, but I let him keep on trying to persuade me because he seemed to enjoy selling so much."

The sky had darkened and the temperature had dropped.

"Come inside," I said. "I'll make you some coffee or tea—"

"Forget that," she said. "I want a serious drink."

After letting Tuffy out into the fenced backyard, I poured Reggie a tumbler of her requested Jack Daniels and gave silent thanks that hard liquor did not go bad; that bottle had been untouched in my cabinet for at least eight years. I filled a glass with ice and Diet Dr Pepper and joined Reggie in the living room, where she'd settled herself on the comfortable old couch

that had been one of Mack's and my first purchases shortly after we were married.

"I didn't know that my old college buddy Della Stewart had
become Della Carmichael until I read an article in *Appetites*
magazine about the new cooking show. It included a brief
biography that mentioned your maiden name and said you'd
married a police officer, but that you're a widow now. . . . How
sad." She sipped at her drink. "Policemen are very noble—I
think they should be paid a lot more. I always vote for bond issues that give them benefits. Was he killed in the line of duty?"

"Mack died of a heart attack," I said.

"That's terrible, too, of course." Another swallow. "I'm divorced. Twice, actually. Both men were darlings. Very sweet,
like big, affectionate puppies. But after that early stage when
you're deaf, dumb, and blinded by love—or lust, or whatever—
I discovered that they didn't have much ambition. Running
the food business Daddy left me, sometimes I've got to put in
eighteen-hour days. The way they wanted to work up a sweat
was by playing tennis, or golf. And they drank."

Another sip of Jack Daniels. "After Tim—my first
husband—I met Rick." She giggled and lowered her voice to a
confessional whisper. "To tell the truth, I was a naughty girl
an' Tim an' Rick overlapped a little bitty bit." She took another swallow and brought her voice back up to normal level.
"The point is, I thought I was marrying a very different kind
of man the second time, but Tim and Rick turned out to be virtual twins, just with different faces. When I realized that, I was
so horrified I went into therapy to discover why I married the
same man twice, when I was so sure they were completely different types."

"What did you find out—in therapy?"

She laughed. "Considering I had to pay two hundred dollars a session, I didn't learn enough." She gestured at the
bottle and I poured a little more Jack Daniels into her glass.
"So let's talk about *you*. I remember reading your wedding
announcement"—she giggled again—"way back in the Dark
Ages. It said you were a high school English teacher. *Ewwww*,
that must have been awful." She shuddered in revulsion, but
simultaneously aimed a lopsided smile at me. "I didn't hear

anything about you for years, and then I read you were going to be on television, starring in your own cooking show. Good for you. I watched your first one, and was planning to write you a note of congratulations . . ." She lowered her voice again. "But then there was that murder—right in front of everyone. I thought congratulating you might be in poor taste, under the circumstances." Her voice went back up in pitch. "Now, only a few months later, fate has thrown us together. After all this time. Isn't this just a kick?"

She held her empty glass out toward me. In a babyish voice, she said, "Can lil' Jackie D come out to play?"

"How about something to eat? I can make us—"

"No, thanks I'm on a diet." She smiled and indicated her glass. "A liquid diet."

By the time Reggie was willing to leave, she could barely stand. She was so wasted I was afraid that if she got behind the wheel of her car she might kill herself or someone else. I picked up her purse—a black Chanel clutch bag that cost as much as two of my mortgage payments—removed her car keys, and told her that I'd drive her home in her car.

When I was behind the wheel of her Jaguar and had secured us both in seat belts, she gave me her address in Beverly Hills. I used my cell phone to arrange for a taxi to meet me at her house.

On the way, Reggie babbled about men. Lurid confessions. Having been married to a police officer, I thought nothing she could say would shock me.

I didn't pay much attention until she started to talk about Mickey Jordan.

"We had a *thing* a few years ago, between his marriages. Short men really are the best lovers," she murmured. "But tall men are good too. My new man is tall. Lots of hair, and beautiful teeth." She yawned. "He's almost perfect . . ."

"Almost?"

She raised her left hand and waved it around. "Gold ring. Third finger."

"He's married?" I heard the disapproval in my voice. "Why don't you find a single man?"

Yawning again, she mumbled, "This is the one I want— because he thinks he loves his wife."

"But if she found out, it could break up their marriage."

As her eyes began to close, she whispered, "Revenge is sweet."

"Reggie, what did his wife ever do to you?"

I didn't get the answer. She'd fallen asleep against her Jaguar's soft leather seat back, and I was left with a feeling of sadness. Regina Davis hadn't changed at all; she was still a thief.

■ ■ ■

Late that night the telephone rang. I was just about to fall asleep with Tuffy stretched out beside me and my little gray and gold calico cat, Emma, curled up on the next pillow.

"Hi," said NDM. "Are you in bed?"

"No," I lied. "I just got home." Let him wonder where I'd been.

Would he wonder where I'd been?

"Ahhhh." It sounded as though he was wondering. "I hope you had a good time."

"Wonderful," I said cheerfully. "Look, I don't want to rush you off the phone, but I have a few things to do before—"

"Oh, right. Why am I calling? Are you free for dinner tomorrow night?"

"No," I said. Pleasantly.

He was silent for a moment, but I could hear him breathing. "Okay. You have to do your show Thursday nights, so how about Friday?"

"Sorry, but I'm busy."

"Are you going to be busy for the rest of your life?" His tone was tight.

"I plan to be," I said.

"Just because I said we should slow things down a little?" I could practically hear him steaming.

"When we were seeing each other, I didn't know you were still going out with other women."

"I wasn't, then."

"You have every right to live your life exactly how you want to live it. But I don't want to be part of a harem."

"That's a ridiculous thing to say. The problem is you were married so long it's obvious you've forgotten how to date."

I thought about that. He had a point. "You're right, but I'm not in high school anymore. I have no intention of getting married again, so don't worry that I'm after you for that, but from now on when I go out with a man, I want to know that he's only dating me—until one or both of us decides we want to move on in different directions."

"Serial monogamy."

"That's it." I made my tone as sweet as his had been sarcastic. "In fact, tomorrow I'm going out to buy new bed linens and some Victoria's Secret lingerie, and put them away for my next relationship."

There was a *click* on his end of the line.

My little performance had worked—I'd deliberately made him so angry he lost his self-control and hung up on me.

It was a Pyrrhic victory; I'd won the battle and lost the war. I refused to be just one of the women with whom he slept, but I was going to miss his touch, his scent, and the excitement I felt in his arms.

So be it. If I didn't have self-respect, it didn't much matter what else I had.

5

In spite of not having slept very well after my conversation with NDM, I got up even earlier than usual, gave Emma and Tuffy fresh food and water, and took Tuffy for a long walk. It was only a few minutes after six AM when I got back home, ready to prepare for another new chapter in my life: TV reality show contestant.

I was unlocking the front door to let us in when I heard three toots of a horn and turned to see a small blue and yellow Better Living Channel transportation van pull up to the curb in front of the house. Behind the wheel was one of the last people I would have expected to see piloting that vehicle. In fact, I'd never seen Phil Logan, the channel's head of publicity, drive anything except his metallic beige Mercedes sedan, which was the approximate shade of his profusion of sandy hair.

Phil alighted from the driver's side at his usual warp speed, his knife-slender frame displaying the agility of Mikhail Baryshnikov and the excitement of a car salesman racing to close a deal. When Phil was out of the vehicle, I saw that a man had been sitting in the passenger seat and was getting out. He was a stranger to me.

"Hey, Della! I called but you didn't pick up."

I gestured to Tuffy on his leash. "We were out."

Phil's companion approached us, carrying a well-worn black attaché case. He was about Phil's age, but shorter with a bright yellow buzz cut and heavily muscled forearms. His face was tanned—the natural darkening of someone who spent most of his free time on the water. I didn't need the deductive gifts of Sherlock Holmes to make that guess: He was wearing a blue canvas jacket with the insignia of a sailing club on the breast pocket. Tuffy watched the man approach us; as long as I was calm, Tuffy remained calm.

I smiled pleasantly and extended my hand to the stranger. "Hello." He took it and mumbled a responding "Hello."

"This is Zachary Blye," Phil said. "He's an artist. Let's go inside. We're on a tight sked."

I unlocked the door and unhooked Tuffy's leash. He went bounding down the hallway toward the kitchen. Phil, following me in, held the door open for his companion.

The gracious hostess, I said politely, "So you're an artist, Mr. Blye. That's interesting. What do you paint?"

"People." He narrowed his eyes and squinted at me.

Phil beamed like an Oscar winner. "Zee's the top independent makeup artist in town. We're here to make you over."

"*Up*," Zachary Blye said. "Make her *up*."

"Sure, Zee—that's your department. I'll do the rest."

"What *rest*?" I asked, with growing apprehension.

"Wardrobe," Phil said. "I'll get the clothes out of the van."

Fifteen minutes later, I'd taken off my shirt and fastened a bath towel around my bra-clad torso. Sitting in my bathroom, in an armchair dragged in from the bedroom, I faced the mirror and watched Zachary Blye study my features from every imaginable angle.

Finally, he announced, "I can do something with this."

"I'm so glad," I said wryly.

Phil was in my bedroom, sorting through the collection of women's clothing he'd brought in on a rack. Through the open bathroom door, he called to Blye, "Remember, she's going to be on camera this morning."

"What kind of lighting?" the face painter asked.

"Reality show," Phil said.

Zachary Blye snorted with disgust. "That's not much more flattering than what the cops use for booking photos. But don't worry, I'll compensate."

His attaché case, actually a makeup case, lay open on the counter next to the basin. It was full of brushes and sponges and puffs, tubes and powders, pencils, blushes, and mascara wands in every shade I'd ever seen.

I heard rustling behind me, looked up, and saw Phil's reflection. "Mickey wants you in something figure flattering, so I put together some outfits to show off the assets and hide the flaws." When he began holding them up, I saw that Phil—who always dressed himself like the cover of *GQ*—also had good taste in women's clothing. "What do you like?"

"I like them all. Do I get to keep any of these?"

"Just what you're going to wear today. The rest go back to the store. After today you'll be in cooking clothes, but for your on-camera introduction and interview, you've got to look great."

From the array Phil had spread out, I chose a pale gray sweater, black slacks, and a black suede jacket.

Phil held the gray sweater up against my face, frowned, and shook his head. "*Uh-uh.* The pants and jacket are fine, but a gray sweater is too mousy for TV." He put it down and took a cherry red cashmere from his stack. "This is the one."

Zachary Blye nodded agreement. "I'll make her up to complement that color. And I'll clip her hair an inch." As though remembering that a human being was sitting in the chair, his eyes met mine in the mirror. He held up a pair of scissors. "Okay to give you a trim?"

"Yes," I said. "I've been meaning to do that but haven't gotten around to it."

By seven thirty, Zachary Blye had finished his work and he and Phil left with the rest of the clothes Phil had brought. Tuffy and Emma were lounging together on the bed, watching me with the fascination they usually reserved for a nature special on Animal Planet.

I surveyed myself in the mirror, and was amazed at how much better I looked. The makeup had been applied with such a delicate touch that I had to lean in close to the glass to be sure it was there. Stepping back to examine the effect of the new outfit in the full-length mirror on the closet door, I had to admit that the combination Phil chose was very flattering—unless one of Mickey's "reality" cameramen decided to sneak around and shoot me from behind to record the fact that I'm a bit full in the derriere.

Oh, well. I'd rather be healthy than perfect.

After checking the contents of my shoulder bag and adding two eight-by-ten glossies of the best cakes I'd made on the show—from the food portfolio that Phil Logan had created for me—I was ready to go.

Giving Tuffy and Emma a few quick strokes and whispering, "Wish me luck," I headed for the front door. A few feet before I reached it, the doorbell rang.

A glance through the living room window showed me who was on my stoop.

I opened the door and said, "Hi, Addison, I'd invite you in, but I'm just leaving for the Davis Test Kitchens."

"This isn't a social call." His gaze started at my hairline, swept down to my shoes and back up again to my face. The intensity of his scrutiny was a bit unnerving.

"What's the matter?" I asked.

"Nothing at all," he said. "Phil's man did an excellent job."

"Do I pass inspection?" I tried to keep irritation out of my voice, but I couldn't resist the impulse to thrust out my hands palms down and then turn them palms up. "See, I've washed. Both sides."

He had the grace to look embarrassed. "That was pretty crude of me, wasn't it, coming over here to check you out. I apologize. You look great."

"Apology accepted. And thank you." To indicate that all was well again, I smiled, but I don't think he saw the smile because he was looking past me into the house.

"Is Eileen home?" he asked.

"She had an early class this morning."

"Oh, well, I thought if she had a few minutes we could talk about the fudge project. Maybe I'll call her later. We can make a stronger presentation to Mickey on Friday if we put our heads together first."

I didn't doubt for a moment that he was eager to put his head together with Eileen's.

"If I get a chance, I'll give her a call later." He aimed a thousand-watt smile at me. "Good luck today. I know you'll knock 'em dead."

As I locked the front door behind me, I said, "I'll do my best." We started walking toward my Jeep.

"It's true you're a long shot," he said, "but once in awhile a long shot does come in."

I stopped in midstride. "Wait a minute, Addison. I won't be any part of it if you or Mickey have fixed this contest."

"Absolutely not! There'll be three independent judges with unassailable food credentials. They'll have no connection to either Reggi-Mixx or our network, or to any of the contestants. All that was thoroughly checked out by Mickey's lawyers." There was such sincerity in his voice that I believed him.

I sighed with relief. "Okay." I unlocked the Jeep with the remote on my key chain.

Addison opened the driver's side door for me. As I climbed behind the wheel, he said, "All I meant was that life is full of surprises."

For the last two years my life had been a series of good news/bad news jokes. I wondered under which column my next surprise would fall.

The Davis Foods Test Kitchens were inside a large concrete block and stucco building on Pico Boulevard in West Los Angeles. Square, two stories high, and painted a yellow brown shade reminiscent of Dijon mustard, it was located a block east of a business offering a service that made me chuckle whenever I passed it: Precision Sandblasting. For years I'd been tempted to stop and ask for a demonstration of the "precision" part, but of course I never did.

Arriving a few minutes before eight o'clock, I followed the "Park in Rear" sign and turned into an alley that led to a large area behind the building. There were already several cars in the lot, including two of the Better Living Channel's mobile vans.

I pulled into a space the right size for my Jeep Compass. One of my pet peeves is seeing big vehicles squeezed into slots marked for compact cars. As I was getting out of my Jeep, I heard the sound of a powerful motor entering the parking lot and turned to see an older model Cadillac, pink and roughly the size of a motor launch, ease into a slot three spaces away from me. It had a California vanity license plate that said "WINNIE" and a woman with a huge cloud of cotton-candy pink hair at the wheel.

She saw me, and a big grin bisected her face. She waved so enthusiastically I thought she believed we knew each other, but I was sure I'd never seen her before. I smiled, lifted my right hand in a return greeting, and started toward the building's back entrance.

"Wait up!" she called.

I stopped and she hurried out of the buffed and polished classic Caddy. She was buffed and polished, too, in a pink silk dress with a short pink jacket and pink high heels. Beneath the halo of pink hair was a smooth, Kewpie doll face with full red lips and dark brows shaped into high arches above large pale blue eyes.

"Hi, honey," she said, waving again as she quickstepped toward me. "You're Della Carmichael!"

"Yes. Hello." I extended my hand and she grabbed it with exceptionally soft fingers. I had thought my hands were smooth until they came in contact with hers.

"I'm Winnie King!" Her voice was breathy, with the slightest trace of a southern accent. "I'm a big fan of your show. In fact, I've been meaning to get in touch with you because the moment I saw you on the air I said to myself, 'Winnie, that's a pretty woman, but she needs to use moisturizer before it's too late!'"

Caught off guard by that statement, I said witlessly, "Moisturizer? I use moisturizer."

She *tsk-tsked*. "Not the right kind, I'm afraid," and opened her big satchel-style designer handbag. I recognized the bag as one Liddy told me cost several thousand dollars. Pulling out a small plastic bottle, she said, "I sell Mary Kay cosmetics, but I'm giving this to you as my little gift." Winnie King nodded in the direction of her pink Cadillac. "That car? It's twenty years old, but I'm never going to part with it! I earned it by being the top Mary Kay saleswoman in Jeffersonville, Georgia, and surrounding territories four years running."

"Congratulations. That's terrific."

Winnie extracted a matching tube from the bag. I wondered if she carried the entire Mary Kay line in there.

"Here's a mask, too, honey. This is absolutely magic for erasing those tiny little lines we get after a certain age." She folded the tube into my hand, lifted her chin, and turned her face so I could view it from all angles. "See, no lines. Every night when I'm reciting my regular prayers, I say God bless Mary Kay!"

"This is very kind of you," I said, "but—"

"Fret not if you don't know how to use these. I'll teach you." She gave a light squeeze to my wrist. "It's the philosophy I live by: Do something nice for somebody and it will make the

Lord smile. It's the least I can do—He has so many things to grieve about nowadays."

Winnie King hooked her arm though mine. "Let's go meet our competition."

Our competition? Was the top saleswoman in Jeffersonville, Georgia, and surrounding territories going to be in the Reggi-Mixx contest?

She must have seen my puzzled expression because she said, "Oh, selling Mary Kay products is just my way to help people, honey. I own the Pink Lady Bakery in Beverly Hills."

"One of my friends always orders her twin sons' birthday cakes from you. The replica of Beverly Hills High School you made last year was spectacular, and delicious." The admiration in my voice was genuine.

Winnie's grin grew even wider. "You must mean Miz Marshall—she's as sweet as buttercream! One of my favorite customers. Isn't this just the smallest world in the whole wide universe?"

Before I could reply, the back door to the Davis building opened and was filled by the tall, slender figure of Regina Davis, standing straight and looking sober. She was "camera ready," as perfectly made up as a fashion model about to shoot a cover for *Vogue* magazine, and wearing a becoming designer suit. It was so short it made her legs look as though they were long enough to go all the way up to her neck.

"Hello, you two. I see you've met."

"Yes, and I've had the pleasure of tasting some of Winnie's amazing cakes."

"Don't you let her skills discourage you, Della," Reggie said. "I'm sure you can learn to be creative, too."

That was a not-so-subtle bit of damning with faint praise. I decided I preferred Reggie when she was drinking.

Reggie stepped back and scanned me from head to toe, settling her scrutiny on my face.

"You've done something to yourself, Della."

"Just a little duct tape here and there," I joked.

"You look better than I'd . . . well, let's go meet the others." Turning her back on us, the majority stockholder and CEO of Davis Foods International led Winnie and me into a spartan reception room with two chairs, a sofa, a coffee table, and a tall, potted fiddle leaf ficus. Two men sat in the chairs; a woman perched on the edge of the couch. I hadn't met any of them, but I recognized all three from appearances they'd made on various television shows. They were a lot better known in the food world than I was. I told myself I didn't have to worry about Mickey fixing the contest so I'd win it. In this race, I was definitely the long shot.

Regina said brightly, "Now that we're all together, I'll perform the introductions." She began by grabbing the hand of a stout man with hair the color of paprika and a matching red handlebar mustache that stretched well beyond the width of his small mouth. "This is Gordon Prescott, the former pastry chef for Governor Ball of Arizona and now executive chef for the Newport Plaza Hotel and Resort."

Reggie moved past Gordon Prescott to drape an arm around an attractive black woman in an emerald green suede pantsuit. This woman had such beautiful posture that I automatically straightened my back.

"Meet Viola Lee," Reggie said. "Vi does the weekly dessert feature for the nation's number one morning show, *Wake Up with GBN*."

"Please call me Viola," she said softly. "Not Vi." She shifted her shoulders slightly, as though trying to dislodge Reggie. I got the feeling she didn't like to be touched—or perhaps she didn't like to be touched by Regina Davis.

Reggie abandoned Viola Lee and moved close to a slender man in his late twenties with a mass of surfer-dude streaky blond hair and the greenest eyes I'd ever seen. They were such a startling color that I looked at him closely, and realized he was wearing green contact lenses.

"This is Clay Sutton," she said, "Hollywood's new celebrity caterer and private chef to the stars. Clay's going to be opening his own exclusive restaurant next year."

After giving Clay Sutton's left arm an affectionate stroke, Reggie introduced Winnie King. "Winnie's Pink Lady pastries are known all over the country. One of her creations was featured on the cover of *Modern Homemaker* just last month."

Reggie turned her attention to me. "And, lastly, this is Della

Carmichael." After two silent beats, she added, "Della hosts a new cable TV cooking show."

As the five of us exchanged polite greetings, I tried to get at least a quick snapshot impression of these people with whom I'd be competing. Gordon Prescott had a mouth that smiled but eyes that did not. He took my right hand with both of his, but instead of looking at my face his eyes focused on my breasts. I withdrew my hand quickly. He responded with an arrogant shrug and turned away to speak to Reggie.

Viola Lee was warmer with me than she had been with Reggie. Her eyes were the color of good cognac and full of light when she smiled. Her handclasp was firm and confident. I felt that I'd like to get to know her.

When I shook Clay Sutton's hand I was surprised to find that his palm was damp. Embarrassed, he stammered an almost unintelligible apology, and wiped his hands down the sides of his khaki trousers.

Reggie cut off any further interaction by striding to the room's interior door. Placing one hand on the knob, she announced dramatically, "Here we go!"

She flung open the door and suddenly we were facing a bank of powerful lights and two cameramen with shoulder-mounted television cameras.

Regina introduced us to the cameras, repeating our contestant credentials for the benefit of a future audience. "Did you all bring pictures of some of your cakes?" she asked.

We produced them, and she passed them to the nearest cameraman. "Photograph these later." Speaking to us, but cheating toward the camera, she said, "Now let me show you where you'll be working for the next three weeks, until you've perfected what each of you think will be America's new favorite cake, created from Reggi-Mixx."

The tour began. The area occupied by the test kitchens took up a good 90 percent of the building's ground floor interior. Regina said, "We have forty fully equipped kitchens where we develop and test new products, always striving for the best in taste and texture." She gestured to the lines of cubicles that stretched before us. "Each kitchen contains utensils, electric mixers, a work table, a small refrigerator, a stove top, and an oven. They are separated by plywood walls six feet high, which I designed to give each of my test bakers the privacy and lack of distractions that make it easy for them to concentrate on their work, but you see there are no doors on these mini-kitchens. This is to encourage interaction and collaboration among the employees. It's my 'several-heads-can-be-better-than-one' theory of management."

The mini-kitchens were divided into four horizontal rows of ten cubicles each. On the wall beside every other kitchen in the line facing us—the line closest to the entrance—were printed signs with each of our names.

"Now for your test kitchen space assignments," Reggie said. "We're going girl-boy, girl-boy, girl. Viola, you'll have station number one. Gordon has station number two. Winnie, you're in the middle. Then Clay. Della, you're down there at the far end, but at least you'll be next to our extensive pantry. I'm sure you'll all be able to find every ingredient you could possibly need in that pantry, but if there's something you want that isn't here, let me know. I'll order the item and have it brought in for you. That rule is an absolute necessity to keep the contest fair." She smiled at the camera flirtatiously. "We can't have anyone smuggling in some other brand of flour or packaged cake mix. Not that I think one would," she added hastily. "Davis Foods makes the very best products in our categories." She frowned at the nearest camera operator and waved at him to stop shooting. "I'll supervise the editing of this footage before it goes on the air—right?"

The camera operator nodded in the affirmative. Reggie switched her bright smile on again and signaled him to resume taping.

As Reggie began extolling the virtues of Reggi-Mixx, I wondered if she'd ever actually *tasted* a cake made from her company's mix. Perhaps not; thin as she was, it didn't look as though she ate cake, or much of anything. When we were in college, she'd been at least twenty pounds heavier, but still slim. No one outside of a fashion magazine editor would have considered her overweight then.

Another question occurred to me. *Didn't anyone ever tell Reggie that her company's mix left a bad taste in one's mouth?*

During the tour, some two dozen Reggi-Mixx employees had arrived and settled into their own cubicles, in the rows behind the line designated for the five of us. As we passed by, I noticed some hostile glares thrown at us, but no smiles of welcome. Before I could think about that, our little parade had moved on.

With the portable TV cameras moving around to catch shots of our faces, we, like little ducklings following their momma, trailed in Reggie's wake. The most interesting part of the tour for me was the immense Davis Foods supply pantry. Except for lacking a butcher section and fresh produce, it was almost as well stocked as a good grocery store.

As I moved along the shelves that held the company's packaged cake mixes, I saw that they came in white, devil's food, strawberry, lemon, banana, orange, angel food, carrot, and spice. I wondered how many I would have to test to find one I might be able to use as a base for the cake I was supposed to create, and how much I would have to do to it before it would taste like a treat.

When we'd finally viewed everything in the pantry, we were back at the line of little test kitchens with our names on them.

Reggie beamed into the nearest camera lens and announced, "Now I have a little surprise for you contestants." She held up five keys on large gold rings. "Because my company operates from nine to six every weekday, and I can't have the work of my employees interrupted, you'll have to create your new, original cakes after business hours, or on weekends. I've had keys made up for each of you. These are the type that cannot be copied, so be careful with yours. I'm afraid that losing a key will mean disqualification from the contest."

Clay Sutton asked, in a tone that was close to a whine, "Do we have to work here? What I mean is, I'm really comfortable in my own setup."

"Your cakes *must* be created on these premises. It's the only way we can be sure that no one uses anything other than Reggi-Mixx products."

Winnie King chuckled. " 'Trust the dealer but cut the cards,' as my gamblin' man daddy used to say."

Reggie signaled the two camera operators to stop taping. They turned off their cameras and took the rigs off their shoulders.

I looked at the key she handed me. "But isn't there a burglar alarm system with a code? Or security guards?"

"Unnecessary," Reggie said. "All the things worth stealing are in our corporate offices in Westwood. Believe me, I have plenty of security there. This building just houses the test kitchens, and the stoves and fridges are bolted to the floor."

One of the cameramen whispered something to Reggie. "Go ahead, leave," she said. "I'll call you later with the taping schedule."

As he left through the outside door, Reggie turned back to we five contestants and said, "Before anyone leaves today, I want your first personal interviews on tape. They'll be done separately, in this order: Della, Clay, Viola, Winnie, and Gordon. Those who aren't taping, wait in the test kitchens until it's your turn. I don't want anyone to see anyone else's interviews until the show is on the air." She aimed a teasing smile at us. "Remember, this will be a family viewing special, so don't say anything naughty."

With a slight incline of his head, Gordon Prescott said—no, *intoned,* in the deep, practiced voice of a radio announcer—"I assure you that I will perform with the utmost decorum. My years of experience in diplomatic circles—"

"Yes, that's fine, Gordon. I trust your impeccable good taste." Dismissing Gordon Prescott, she focused on me. "You're up first, Della. Be interesting."

Be interesting. Thanks a lot, Reggie. If ever there was a command that was likely to freeze an interviewee's brain it was that one.

7

As I put down my bag and smoothed the front of my clothes, the other four contestants filed back into the test kitchens. The camera operator—in his early thirties and as solid as a side of beef—grinned at me, exposing a mouth full of teeth in desperate need of a dentist's attention. He stuck out his right hand. "I'm Ben."

I was surprised to see that his fingers were as long and smooth as those of a pianist. With the body of a wrestler, the rough, weathered face of an outdoorsman, and the hands of a musician it was as though Nature had stapled together three different men.

"Hi," I said. "I'm Della Carmichael."

"Yeah, I know." His tone rose just slightly to a more feminine pitch as he quoted my TV line, " 'Let's get cooking!' " Hefting his taping rig onto his right shoulder, he added, "My wife says that all the time now. She loves you, and she's cooking better."

"That's nice to hear. Is there some part of the show she likes best?"

"Oh, yeah—it's when you drop a pot, or spill something on the counter. She says you make her feel like less of a klutz."

"I'm so glad I can help." I did my best to keep irony out of my voice. After all, no matter why his wife watched the show, she was a viewer, and I needed every one I could get for the show to stay on the air.

He gestured to a straight chair against the wall and in front of a framed ad for Reggi-Mixx. "There. We gotta keep the product in the shot."

I did as directed, and I reminded myself to sit up straight.

"Ben, if I make a mistake—garble my words—can you stop the tape and let me do it over?"

"Nope. Reggie's got us on a strict schedule. But if you goof up, they'll probably fix it in the editing."

I doubted that.

He switched on the red light over the lens. "Anytime you're ready, start talking."

I fought down a moment of panic and managed to smile at the camera. "Hello, I'm Della Carmichael from *In the Kitchen with Della*. I'm here at Davis Foods International, getting ready to compete in the first national Reggi-Mixx Cake Competition." Suddenly my mind went blank. *Think, think! Keep talking.*

"I come from a family of medical people and accountants. My father was a veterinarian and my brother's a doctor in the navy—right now he's on an aircraft carrier. My mother and my two sisters are the accountants. They're in business together in San Francisco: I J K Accounting. The I is for Isobel, my mother's name, and the J and the K are my sisters, Jean and Keely. I'm the oldest of the four kids. Both our parents had to work, so Grandma Nell took care of us. When she was fourteen, she came to America from Scotland, sponsored by an uncle who'd become an American citizen. He got her a job as a servant for the wealthy family where he was the chauffeur. She worked her way up from mopping floors and scrubbing pots in the kitchen to being the cook. Except for one year when her employers spent six months in Europe—and Grandma Nell worked as a cook for a man who turned out to be a famous gangster—she was with that same family for thirty-five years. By the way, that gangster taught her how to make a great chicken cacciatore. I call it 'Gangster Cacciatore' and I've made it on my show. But she quit working for him the night some men sprayed the front of his house with bullets. After Grandma Nell retired, she came to live with us and taught me her kitchen skills. From the time I was ten years old I made our family's meals."

Ben mouthed: *Talk about your cake.*

"I've always loved to bake, but I'm not a fancy baker. I can't spin sugar, or make bouquets of roses out of fondant.

I'm still deciding what I'm going to create for the contest, but my strategy will be to concentrate on how my cake will taste."

Ben shut the camera off. "That's it."

"We're finished?"

"For now. You'll be interviewed several times during the course of the competition. If you want a tip for next time . . . ?"

"Absolutely. Please."

"Maybe you should plan in advance what you're going to say."

He was confirming my fear that I'd just taped the dullest few minutes in the history of reality television.

Disappointment in myself must have shown on my face, because Ben said, "You did okay. Jeez, when some people talk to a camera, it's like punishment to listen."

"But I'm a teacher, and I talk into a camera several times a week. I should have given you something better."

"On your shows you're always doing something with your hands while you talk. Maybe next time you can crack eggs or be stirring stuff in a bowl."

I realized he was right. "I'll do that. Thank you."

He acknowledged with a nod. "I'll call you in the next couple of days to set up a time to shoot some B roll."

"What's B roll?"

"Oh, it's silent footage of you at your house, messing around in your real kitchen, walking your dog, and at the studio getting ready to tape one of your shows. We edit the B roll into your facing-the-camera interviews, to make the talking interesting visually. We'll have some of your voice on the sound track running over the silent shots."

"Okay. Just let me know when." I wondered if I'd be able to get Zachary Blye to glamorize me again.

As I picked up my tote bag and turned toward the exit, Ben opened the door to the test kitchens and called, "Next."

Clay Sutton came in at a trot, simultaneously beaming and fluffing his hair. "I'm going to start with a joke," he said.

Outside in the parking lot, I turned my cell phone back on just as it rang. I recognized the calling number as one of Mickey Jordan's, and stopped next to my Jeep to answer.

"Hi, Mickey."

"How's it going?" he asked.

"I've met the other contestants, had a tour of the place, and now I'm heading home."

"Great. I'll have Kyle meet you there."

"Who's Kyle?"

"Kevin Kyle—the cake guy," Mickey said. "He lives in Westwood and I've got him standing by. I'll tell him to leave now, so he should get to your place about the same time you do."

8

As it turned out, I was stuck behind a traffic accident on Wilshire Boulevard that left the front ends of two sports cars mashed together. Fortunately, no one was injured, but the vehicles were positioned diagonally across the boulevard, blocking traffic in both directions as the drivers screamed at each other. The police arrived quickly, but it required a pair of tow trucks to separate the mangled cars and open up a path so that the rest of us could pass the scene. It took twenty minutes longer to get home than it should have. I wanted to call Kevin Kyle to tell him I was on my way, but I hadn't thought to ask for the man's cell phone number before Mickey went into his meeting.

Pulling into my driveway at last, I saw a man in his thirties—I assumed it was Kyle—sitting on my front stoop, his legs folded onto each other at the ankles. The lotus position, I remembered from a yoga class.

His eyes were closed and his hands rested on his knees, palms up, with index fingertips and thumbs touching. It didn't take an IQ high enough to qualify for Mensa membership to guess that he was meditating. That sight didn't surprise me nearly as much as the *silence*; Tuffy, who must have been on the other side of the front door, was not barking as he usually did when someone was outside the house.

I cut the engine, climbed out of the Jeep, and called, "Hello."

The man opened his eyes, glanced in my direction, and began the process of unwinding his legs. When he was standing he reached down and picked up the object beside him. I hadn't noticed it before. It resembled a salesman's sample case, or what photographers use to carry their equipment.

Striding toward him, I saw that my visitor had pale blond

hair cut short in the back and on the sides but swept up in the front to dip forward like an incoming wave. Emerald green eyes were complemented by what looked like a real emerald stud in his right ear. He wore slacks the color of caramel, and a whipped cream white silk shirt topped with a nut-brown cashmere sweater. Seeing him made me begin to crave a scoop of my homemade maple pecan ice cream in the freezer.

"I'm Della Carmichael," I said, extending my hand. "Sorry I'm late. There was a traffic—"

"Kevin Kyle, pastry chef." He took my hand briefly. "There's no need to apologize. Your delay gave me a chance to talk to your dog. It's a standard poodle, isn't it?"

"Yes. How did you know?"

"I recognized the bark when I came to the door, but then we chatted a bit and he settled down. I used to have a standard . . ." His voice trailed off. I saw sadness in his eyes and knew that look. I'd felt the painful emotions behind it, from having lost a beloved pet to old age death months before Mack brought Tuffy, then a twelve-week-old bundle of black fur, into my life five years ago.

"Come in," I said, unlocking the door. "Meet Tuffy."

As soon as I entered, Tuffy greeted me with his usual whole-body wags of enthusiasm and I returned his welcome with affectionate words and strokes. Turning to the man behind me, I was surprised to see that his eyes were filling with tears.

"Are you all right?" I asked.

"He's black. . . . My big boy was a black standard, too. Derrick—that was his name. . . ." With his free hand, he gave Tuffy gentle scratches beneath one ear.

"What happened to Derrick?"

"Cancer. Inoperable. I took him to three veterinarians to be sure." He barely choked out the words, then he cleared his throat and muttered, "Get a grip, Kevin." To me, he said, "Whenever I see a black standard on the street I just start to tear up. I'll try to make myself get another some day, but it's so devastating when . . ." He couldn't finish the sentence.

"It might help to think of the joy they bring us," I said, "and the fact that we can give them love and good care and happy lives for as long as we have them."

Kevin Kyle nodded, took a deep breath, and shook his head as though to clear it. "You have a competition to win. Take me to your kitchen."

Tuffy loped ahead of us down the hallway. In the kitchen, he sat on his thick pad next to the refrigerator. It was his favorite place to watch me while I cooked.

The pastry chef made a quick survey of my baking utensils. From the expression of disdain on his face I could tell he was not impressed.

"I have all of the basics," I said, a touch defensively. "Round and angel food, a Bundt mould, and cupcake pans."

"How pedestrian. Everyone has *those*. I'd hoped for more from you. Obviously, I'll have to upgrade not just your equipment, but your *thinking*."

I fantasized bopping him on his full frontal blond wave with one of my "pedestrian" pans.

He opened the oven door, and I gave silent thanks that I kept it clean. To my surprise, I heard him grunt with what sounded like satisfaction.

"Good," he said. "You have a stand-alone oven thermometer. Never trust the temp setting on your stove. Too many of them are inaccurate." He gestured to the case he carried and to the kitchen table. "May I set this down here?"

"Yes. Can I make you some coffee? Or tea?"

"Nothing, thanks." He sat and opened his sample case. I saw that it contained two thick photo albums and several cake pans in a variety of designs. He removed one of the albums and indicated that I should sit next to him. "Before we start looking at cakes, tell me about the other people in this contest."

I recited their names and told him the little that Reggie had said about each of them.

Kyle grimaced. "You're in trouble. Three of those are celebrated bakers with years of experience, and one is a lying, cheating poisonous snake of a semihuman."

I felt my eyes widen. "What do you mean?"

He emitted a snarl of distaste. "Clay Sutton, caterer-to-the-stars. He's as phony as a sugar substitute. Phonier—fake sugar doesn't claim to be real sugar. Be sure you lock the door to your kitchen."

"No doors," I said. "We're working in open cubicles, separated from each other on only three sides."

"Then take the ingredients home with you every night and bring them back the next day."

"Nothing is allowed to leave the Davis Foods building or be brought in."

The pastry chef pursed his lips for a few moments. Finally, he said, "You're in even bigger trouble than I thought. That guy will do anything he can to sabotage his competition. On the bright side, maybe he won't think you're enough of a threat."

"That's your idea of the bright side? And what makes you so sure he'll try to sabotage anyone?"

"Because he did it to his former employer. That's how he managed to start his own business—by ruining his mentor."

"What about the others?"

"Gordon Prescott is an amoral bastard. Even if Mickey Jordan wasn't paying me to help you, I'd want to see you beat the confectioner's sugar out of him."

"It sounds as though you two have a history," I said.

"In a manner of speaking. At one point our lives bisected, one might say. He stole the woman to whom I had been engaged." His mouth curved into a wry smile. "When she married Prescott she found herself part of a triangle: She was in love with him and *he* was in love with him. I realize now that she did me a favor by running off with Prescott. I wouldn't have been happy with a woman so shallow."

That was a fascinating chapter of real-life soap opera, but I wanted to learn something useful to my problem. "What is Gordon Prescott like as a baker?"

"All show. He bakes to be admired—spectacle without substance. I have to admit that he's masterful with icing, but his cakes beneath the froufrou are virtually without taste. Inoffensive in the mouth, but lacking the distinction of discernible flavor."

"What about the others? Winnie King and Viola Lee?"

"I know Winnie. All sugar and no spice. Inhaling as you pass her bakery is enough to put a diabetic into a coma, but she's got a devoted following because she specializes in sweet-sweeter-*sweetest*. In my not-so-humble opinion, your toughest competition will be Viola Lee. She bakes cakes so light you think you'll have to weigh them down to keep them from floating away, and she's mastered melt-in-your-mouth flavor." He aimed a deeply sympathetic glance at me. "From what Mickey told me, you've had no experience in the world of competitive pastry."

Competitive pastry. "I never thought of baking as a sport."

"Filmed as a national television special, my dear, it will be a blood sport." A cheerful thought seemed to occur to him because his grim expression eased. "There is one tiny little spot of hope in this gloomy picture."

"Please, tell me."

"While you're up against superior bakers, the fact that all of you have to use that awful Reggi-Mixx could level the playing field just a smidge."

Kyle's "picture" still appeared gloomy to me.

Tuffy stood up and looked at me with that "I need to go out" signal in his eyes. Kyle saw it, too.

"Let's take him for a walk and talk cake," he said.

I don't know if Tuff understood "cake," but he certainly knew "walk." He was trotting toward the front door before I could take his leash from the hook on the kitchen wall.

Kevin Kyle and I strolled around the neighborhood with Tuffy for close to an hour. He took the opportunity to cover the history of baking.

"The first people to show skill in baking were the ancient Egyptians, who sweetened some of their breads with honey." With the enthusiasm of a little boy who'd just won a prize in school, he asked, "Did you know that it was the ancient Greeks who created a form of cheesecake? And that the early Romans developed the fruitcake, with nuts and raisins and whatever other kinds of fruit they could find?"

"Some of the Christmas fruitcakes I received when I was teaching high school English were so hard they might have been made by the early Romans."

He ignored my remark, and continued his eager tutorial. "Wars—although tragedies, of course—have been a great advantage in the spreading of recipes. What I mean is that it was through marauding armies and the sacking of various lands that fruitcakes traveled to fourteenth-century England. Chaucer mentions huge cakes made with barrels of flour and cream and eggs, spices and honey."

"I wish I'd thought of bringing food into the classroom for a kind of *eat-and-tell* when I tried to teach Chaucer. The students might have been more interested."

"Undeniably," Kevin Kyle said, apparently missing the irony. "Historians say that modern cakes—round ones with icing—began to appear in the seventeenth century, in Europe, when bakers started using hoops or round molds to shape their creations. But it was the development of bicarbonate of soda and baking powder in the nineteenth century that was the great leap forward in the epic story of baking. Did you know that it was the Industrial Revolution that gave us dry mixes?"

"No, I didn't."

"Aunt Jemima was born, so to speak, in the 1890s. Then packaged mixes for cakes began to appear in the 1920s, but they didn't become popular until the 1940s." He shuddered with disgust. "That dreadful slogan 'just add water and stir' has led to the debasement of the glorious treat that was: the sifted and creamed, hand-aerated and folded celebration of pure and unadulterated ingredients—the personal *cake*. And the worst offender by far was old Rupert Calvin Davis, creator of the contemptible *Reggi-Mixx*." He emitted a gagging sound that made Tuffy stop and stare at him.

"Sorry, boy," he said to Tuff. "I'll try to control myself."

"I agree that Reggi-Mixx isn't a good product. Who buys those boxes?"

"In my opinion, it's people whose taste buds have been degraded by plastic-wrapped imitation cakes. I'm convinced the reason it exists is that Regina Davis likes to see her name on those boxes."

"The company—or at least that division—can't be doing very well. Why is it still in business?"

"That woman's ego. It's a privately held company so she doesn't have to make stockholders happy. This contest will bring them a lot of publicity, and probably increase sales."

Back in my kitchen, Kyle and I went through his albums of creations. I was dazzled at his imagination and skill.

"But I can't make cakes like these," I said.

"It won't be easy, given that you've never attended pastry school, but I can help you—"

"No," I said.

"What do you mean, 'no'? You can't possibly win this competition without my expertise."

"From what you've said about at least three of my competitors, it doesn't seem likely that I'd win no matter how much you helped. But the point is that I want to try to succeed on what *I* can do. If you help me, then it's as though two of us are competing against the others. That's not fair."

"Without me, you're going to come in fifth out of five."

"I've agreed to be in this contest, so I'm just going to have to accept the consequences of competing on my own. Besides I've been making birthday cakes for my honorary daughter, and the cupcakes she's needed for school events over the years. I've never used a mix and I've never had so much as a crumb left over, so I must be a pretty good home baker."

"Against the competition you're facing, 'pretty good' will get you zilch. Kiss off any hope of winning that $25,000 prize."

"I appreciate your advice—really—but if I won the contest because of what *you* can do, it would be a kind of baking plagiarism. I can't do that."

"Well, I wish you good luck." His tone was pleasant, but it was obvious that he wouldn't be placing a bet on me. He leaned over to give Tuffy some affectionate strokes.

"Maybe I'll drop around to see how you're doing," he said. "Ever since I took the side of the British in a high school debate on the American Revolution, I've been a sucker for lost causes."

9

ठाठ

After Kevin Kyle left, I admitted to myself that I had about as much chance of winning that $25,000 as there was of snow falling in Florida. Then I remembered the trip that Mack and I had taken to visit his grandmother in West Palm Beach. It was during the Easter break one April. Some snowflakes had fallen. . . . Maybe—okay, *probably*—I would lose the contest, but it wouldn't be because I didn't try as hard as I could.

Something besides cake was on my mind: Liddy's problem. It was Tuesday afternoon, a few hours before Bill might—or might not—go to his weekly poker game.

Liddy answered on the second ring. This time she didn't have the usual lilt of an invisible question mark in her voice when she said, "Hello."

"Hi, it's me. How are you?"

"Do you mean have I gone to pieces, screamed, and thrown a vase at Bill's head? No. I'm keeping up the 'I'm-not-even-a-little-bitty-bit-suspicious' act. But it's so hard it's just about killing me!"

"Hang on, honey. We'll find a way to get through this."

"It's Tuesday," she said in a tone full of despair. "Wasn't it a Tuesday when the stock market crashed and the Great Depression started?"

"It might have been." I said that cautiously, even though I knew she was right: Black Tuesday, October 29, 1929.

"My depression started last week. How long did the Great one last?"

I thought: *Until 1941, when the United States went to war.* Instead of answering the question, I tried to comfort her. "Oh, Liddy, you're tormenting yourself. We don't know the truth yet. I still believe that Bill will have an explanation that's not going to break your heart."

As though she hadn't heard me, she said, "It's four o'clock. I don't know how I'm going to be able to keep up the pretense when Bill comes home to change his clothes before he goes to his"—her voice took on such a bitter edge that I could envision her using her fingers to make sarcastic quotation marks in the air—"*poker game.*"

I reminded her that she'd promised me she wasn't going to follow him tonight.

She sighed heavily. "No, I won't do that, but I want to confront him."

"Don't do it *yet*, Liddy. You don't know enough." I didn't want her to damage their years of trust in each other in case she was wrong. Confrontation could wait a day or two. Certainly, lying to Liddy was a stupid thing for Bill to do, but it *might* not mean what she feared. "I'll call you later. Now do something to raise your spirits before Bill comes home."

"Like what?"

"Eat some ice cream. Carbohydrates are a natural tranquilizer."

"I don't want to get fat—I have to be better looking than the other woman."

"You could exercise," I said. "Wear yourself out, then relax in a hot, foamy bath."

"All right . . ." she said.

I tried to make a joke out of how gloomy she sounded. "Eileen was more enthusiastic when she was ten years old and we told her she had to have her tonsils out."

In response, Liddy elevated her pitch to theatrical superbright. "All right!"

I clapped my hands, applauding her performance. "Brava! That's my good actress friend. I'll call you later."

■　■　■

For the rest of the day my mind was divided. I watched the clock, mentally tracking Bill Marshall working in his dental office, and Liddy pacing the dimensions of her house like a captive tiger in a cage. I didn't know what Bill was thinking, but I was pretty sure Liddy was in turmoil, wondering how her life was going to turn out.

I forced myself to shut out those visions and concentrate on my cake problem. Ransacking my memory for Mack's and Eileen's favorites didn't help. Mack preferred a triple layer chocolate-on-chocolate, but it wasn't interesting enough to enter in a contest. Growing up, Eileen usually asked for a banana split cake. Delicious, but it was more ice cream and toppings than cake.

At six o'clock I gave Tuffy and Emma their dinner. As usual, Tuffy ate heartily and then settled down next to the kitchen chair where I was working at the table. Emma, who liked to dine in spaced segments, nibbled delicately and then made one of her amazing leaps to the ledge beneath the kitchen window. There, she stretched out like a sphinx and stared into the mysteries of the night, as though she could see things in the darkness that mere humans could only imagine.

I put aside thoughts of Bill and Liddy and cake to prepare for the three half-hour TV shows I was scheduled to tape tomorrow. At least with taped shows I didn't have to prepare the finished dishes in advance. During taping, when I put something into the oven, we'd stop the cameras and pick up again when the dish finished baking and was ready to come out to be exhibited.

By six thirty I'd decided on the vignettes I'd share while cooking. Whether doing the show, or teaching cooking classes, telling stories about the food is as important as putting together the ingredients in the dishes. Even if the viewers couldn't write everything down while watching, the recipes would be posted on my website, DellaCooks.com. I was sure that my years of teaching were what had made it possible for me to function with ease during *In the Kitchen with Della* broadcasts. The trick was pretending that the TV cameras were my students.

I put away my notes just as Eileen came bounding into the kitchen from her gym workout, all glowing cheeks and tousled hair. As usual, she greeted Tuffy and Emma first, with a few affectionate strokes and kissing sounds. Turning, she started to say something, but stopped to stare at me. "Aunt Del, you look *gorgeous*! What happened?"

I arched one eyebrow. In a wry tone, I said, "Thanks a lot."

Realizing her gaffe, she emitted an embarrassed little giggle. "Ooops! I mean you always look pretty, but . . ." She peered at me closely. "It's a surprise to see you all dolled up at home. Did Aunt Liddy give you a makeover?"

"Remember Phil Logan, the network's head of publicity? He brought a professional makeup man here this morning to apply some glamour for the TV interview today about the cake contest. I've been so busy ever since I got home I forgot to wash my face."

"Don't wash it," she said firmly. "Maybe this will be your magical night."

"What are you talking about?"

Eileen scooted the kitchen stool over beside the table, perched on it and leaned toward me. "This could be the night when Mr. Right's car breaks down outside the driveway, his cell phone's battery is dead, and the lights on the rest of the street are out so he's forced to ring the doorbell and ask to use your phone."

With such a gaudy imagination she should be majoring in creative writing instead of business.

"I'm not looking for Mr. Right," I said.

That didn't discourage her. "Just go with me for a moment. Suppose some wonderful man with car trouble came to the door tonight, with you looking so great—"

I waved my hands to stop her. "I wouldn't let a stranger into the house, and I hope you won't do it, either. Asking to use the phone could be a robber's ploy."

Eileen's expression was so disappointed that I relented an inch. "But if this man you imagine *did* have car trouble and rang the bell, I'd offer to call AAA for him—while he stays outside. That's what you should do, too."

She sighed. "I know."

"Why are you so intent on me . . . connecting . . . with a man?"

"I want you to be happy, Aunt Del."

"I am happy." *Pretty happy. More or less.*

"But I'll bet there is a Mr. Right somewhere for you," she insisted. "Don't you *want* to meet him?"

"No." Eileen didn't know that I'd tried a new relationship with NDM, who turned out to be Mr. *Wrong*. I wasn't going to let myself get hurt like that again. I gave Eileen an affectionate pat on the hand. "My life is fine, sweetie. Mack and I had a good marriage. I don't expect I'll ever fall in love again."

Eileen slipped off the stool and hugged me. Straightening up, she said, "Stranger things have happened. A year ago who'd have thought you'd be starring in a TV show?" Before I could think of a reply, she went to the refrigerator and opened the door. "What can I grab for dinner?"

"I can heat the leftover cacciatore and make us a spinach salad. How does that sound?"

"Fab! I'm going to go get cleaned up."

While dinner was reheating in the oven and Eileen was in the shower, I looked up Phil Logan's number and dialed it. He wasn't home, so I left a message telling him about my first reality TV interview, and asking if he could get Zachary Blye back again when I found out when the silent footage was going to be shot.

Phil called back while I was snapping the stems off the fresh spinach leaves. From the noise in the background I guessed that the Better Living Channel's head of publicity was in a busy restaurant. "I'm having dinner with the biggest talent manager in town, trying to talk him into giving us one of his clients as a 'guest cooker' on your show."

"I didn't know you were thinking about something like that, but I like the idea," I said. "What I called you about—"

"I know—I got your message. As soon as we know when they want to shoot B roll, I'll book Zachary. Since they want you in different locations, it'll take several hours, so block out the time." He must have covered the phone's mouthpiece because I heard him mumble something. When he came back on the line, he said. "Gotta go now."

We said quick good-byes and I went back to making salad.

■ ■ ■

After dinner, Eileen said she was going to her friend Connie's study group and rushed off, carrying her laptop and several issues of the *Wall Street Journal*.

It was nearly eight o'clock. I wanted to call Liddy to find out how things were going with Bill, but I didn't want to talk to Bill and sound awkward if he was at home and picked up, so I dialed Liddy on her cell phone. When she answered I could hear misery in her voice and felt a sharp stab of fear. "Liddy, what's happened?"

"Bill didn't come home to change tonight." She started to cry. "He didn't even call me—he had his nurse phone! She gave me some stupid story about Bill's patients taking longer today than expected so he had to leave for his game right from the office."

Yikes. This doesn't look so good.

"I pretended to believe her," Liddy said. She was making an effort to control her voice, but I could hear anger in it. "I forced myself to sound casual and asked where the game was happening tonight. She said she didn't know. I've always liked her, she's so grandmotherly sweet, but she could be covering for him. Or maybe he's lying to her."

"Are you going to call his cell?"

"No. I'll wait until he comes home and find out what lie he's going to tell me."

"I'm coming over to stay with you."

"Don't!" She said it sharply, then immediately softened her tone. "I'm sorry. I didn't mean to snap at you. I love you for the offer, but I really have to be alone."

"If that's what you want, but call if you need me, no matter how late. When I'm out walking Tuffy, I'll have my cell phone with me."

"Della, I'm so lucky to have you as my best friend. Thank you for being there for me."

"That's what best friends are for," I said.

At nine o'clock, I was giving Tuffy his final stroll of the day. Because there was nothing at the moment that I could do for Liddy, as we ambled our way through quiet residential streets, I made myself think about cake.

What can I put into a package of Reggi-Mixx to give it a better flavor?

If I could find that answer, then I could decide how the cake would look, what shape, what frosting. I wasn't an artist in sugar—my strength as a cook was in making food taste good.

When I got back to the house, the telephone was ringing. I picked it up and heard Eileen's voice.

"Don't wait up for me," she said. "I'm probably going to sleep over here at Connie's."

"Okay. Study hard. Thanks for letting me know."

A little while later I was brushing my teeth when I glanced in the mirror and realized that I was still in Zachary Blye's makeup. With a trace of regret, I picked up my complexion brush and soap and scrubbed my face clean. I wished that I had run into someone I knew this afternoon—someone who would have noticed how good I looked.

Why was I trying to kid myself? The truth was that I wished I'd run into NDM so he'd be reminded that while I might not be one of his twentysomething counterfeit blonde bimbos, I was a damned attractive natural brunette, with desirable qualities that only came with a certain amount of maturity. *Forget NDM*, I told myself sternly. *Think about cake*.

I spent half an hour going through my collection of Grandma Nell's old recipes, but I didn't find anything that inspired me.

At ten o'clock, I was about to call it a night and curl up in bed with a good book to read for a couple of hours, but instead of taking my Lakers' jersey nightshirt out of the bureau, I reached for a sweater and hastily pulled it over my head. Slipping into a comfortable pair of jeans and running shoes, I told Tuffy and Emma—both reclining on the bed, "Be good. I'll be home in a couple of hours."

The lot behind the Davis Foods Test Kitchens was empty of vehicles but full of shadows, dimly illuminated only by the glow from the streetlights on Pico Boulevard. I wished that I could have brought Tuffy with me for protection, but it's forbidden to bring an animal into a place where food is prepared.

I parked the Jeep close to the building, took my big, heavy Maglite from beneath the seat—it was my combination flashlight and defensive cudgel—and headed toward the back door.

Fitting my key into the lock for the first time, I was relieved to discover that even though it had been newly cut it turned easily. The heavy door opened with a creak that sounded loud in the darkness.

I flashed the Mag around until I found the wall switch and turned on the reception room lights. I closed the back door and headed across the narrow room to the door leading into the test kitchens.

As soon as I touched the knob I realized that the door hadn't closed completely. Pushing it open with one arm, I faced total darkness. Using the Mag again, I found the bank of wall switches. Since I was the only one here, there was no need to turn them all on, so I clicked the one closest to me. As I'd hoped, the bulbs in the ceiling lighted the first line of mini-kitchens, those reserved for us contestants.

I put the key back in my jeans pocket, stashed the Mag in my tote bag, took out my notebook, and headed down the line of mini-kitchens toward the pantry, which was on the other side of my end cubicle. It was my plan to stash the tote in my station and then make a list of pantry items that might inspire the creation of a new cake.

A dozen feet from the entrance to my cubicle, my foot kicked an object that went rolling a few inches ahead of me. It was a whisk that someone must have dropped and forgotten about.

Reaching down to pick it up, I felt the *crunch* of broken crockery under the sole of my shoe. Stepping aside, I saw that I'd stepped on a little piece from one of the heavy ceramic mixing bowls that were part of the equipment in each of our little test kitchens. More bits of the broken bowl were scattered across the hallway. Up ahead, in front of the entrance to my assigned cubicle, I saw an empty, discarded box of yellow cake mix. Next to it was a black spike heel from a woman's shoe. Just the broken heel.

What's happened here?

My skin prickled with dread, but I kept going. A few more steps and I'd reached the opening to my kitchen space.

I hadn't counted on the fact that someone had gotten there before me.

A woman's body was sprawled diagonally across the floor in front of the stove. A black Chanel clutch bag lay on the floor a few feet away from her. The heel was missing from the shoe on her right foot. Her left leg was slightly twisted at the knee, making her body look like that of a doll tossed aside by a careless child.

I recognized the long legs in the short skirt, and the familiar cascade of brown hair with the artful golden highlights. But the highlights were partially obscured by the congealed blood that matted the back of her skull as Regina Davis lay utterly still—facedown in a bowl of cake batter.

10

My first instinct was to lift Reggie's face out of the gooey mess, but then what I'd learned in twenty years as a police officer's wife took over. Unless she was still alive, I knew that I must not move her.

Dropping my bag, I quickly knelt beside Reggie. Searching for a pulse, I pressed the tips of my fingers against the side of her throat.

Nothing. Not even the faintest hint of a beat.

Unwilling to give up, I touched my fingers to the inside of her wrist. No pulse—and her skin was cool. There was no doubt that Regina Davis was dead.

Images of the broken bowl, the snapped-off heel of her shoe, and the blood on the back of her skull flashed through my mind. I scanned the area but didn't see any place where she might have fallen, causing that awful wound to the back of her head.

Oh, Lord—Reggie's death was not an accident.

Another thought struck me like a slap in the face: suppose the killer was still in the building . . . I knew I had to get out of there and call the police.

Grabbing my bag, I ran for the door.

Outside in the parking lot, I saw that it was still empty except for my Jeep. I hurried toward the alley next to the building, heading for the lights on the street. Taking deep breaths to calm myself, I fumbled in my tote for the cell phone. Grasping it at last, I willed my fingers to keep from trembling.

I punched in nine-one-one. Miraculously, an operator answered right away. "What is your emergency?"

"There's been a murder . . ."

■ ■ ■

I heard the police siren scant seconds before I saw the red and blue flashing lights of the patrol car racing toward me. It had been three minutes since I'd called. I gestured for the car to follow me through the alley and into the building's parking lot.

First on the scene were two uniformed LAPD officers, a man and a woman. Both young, attractive, and fit, with dark hair and similar slender builds. They might have been brother and sister, or at least cousins. The female officer's ID tag said "Bloom" and the male officer's identified him as "Kraft."

As a cop's wife, I knew what the drill was, and they followed the training. They asked for my identification and I showed them my driver's license. They took down my name, address, license number, phone number, and asked me to tell my "story." I recounted just the facts of my arrival and finding the body. Then I led them into the building so that they could view the crime scene.

As soon as they saw Regina Davis, they tried to find some sign of life. In a few seconds, they determined that she was dead. Officer Bloom called their division to report the situation and ask for a detective and a medical examiner to be sent to this address.

Officer Kraft instructed me that I was not to leave the building and asked me to wait in the reception room while he made a cursory tour of the premises and secured the building until the rest of the investigation team arrived. Officer Bloom stood by the outside door, effectively blocking me from exiting, in case I had the impulse to flee.

She took out her notebook. "Do you know the name of the deceased?"

"Regina Davis. She owns the company that occupies this building." I managed to call up from memory Reggie's home address in Beverly Hills and gave it to her. She wrote it down.

"What is—was—your relationship to the deceased?"

"Friend, I suppose . . . I mean we know—*knew*—each other. We're not related."

"Can you tell me the name of her next of kin?"

"No, I'm sorry. I don't—"

We heard a car driving fast through the alley. It came to a gravel-scattering stop just outside the door.

Anticipating the arrival of the homicide detectives, I stood up.

But through the open doorway strode the familiar figure of Nicholas D'Martino.

Officer Bloom told him, "You can't come in here."

NDM gave her one of his seductive smiles and flashed his press pass. *"Los Angeles Chronicle."*

"All right," she said reluctantly, "but you can't be anywhere except in this room without permission."

NDM wasn't looking at her because he'd spotted me. Almost simultaneously, we said, "What are you doing here?" Under other circumstances, we might have laughed at that, but murder was not a laughing situation.

First it was the shock of Reggie's murder and now the surprise arrival on the scene of NDM. Weren't there any other crime reporters in Los Angeles? Maybe the others lacked the police wavelength scanner in NDM's car.

Before I could say anything, my nervous system got another jolt. Looming up behind NDM, his detective shield on a cord around his neck, was the taller figure of LAPD lieutenant John O'Hara. Mack's old partner . . . and Shannon's husband. Because of a certain discomfort between us, I hadn't seen John for almost two months. It was the longest period in twenty years when we hadn't been in the same room together.

The first thing I noticed was how tired he looked. At fifty, his rangy quarterback's body moved with its usual vitality, but there were new creases around his eyes and deeper lines bracketing his mouth. I knew there was no problem with his daughter, Eileen; I hoped everything was going well for him at home with Shannon.

John shot a hostile glare at NDM, then focused on me. "What are you doing here?"

"I found the body—"

"Don't say another word." He aimed a curt nod in NDM's direction. "Not in front of *him*. And you, D'Martino—out."

Flashing his *Los Angeles Chronicle* press card again, NDM said, "I have the right to be here."

"Not until after the crime scene has been processed. Now you can leave under your own power, or you'll be arrested and charged with obstruction. Pick one."

Anger colored NDM's cheeks, but he didn't try to defy John. Speaking only to me, he said quietly, "I'll talk to you later."

A man in his forties, his detective's shield clipped to the lapel of a jacket that was too tight through the shoulders and didn't look as though it would quite close over his jutting belly, lumbered through the outside door, momentarily blocking NDM from leaving. After a couple rounds of "After you—no, after you," NDM departed and the newcomer came more fully into the light of the reception room. I recognized Detective Hugh Weaver. Or, rather, I barely recognized him. We'd met several times over the years at LAPD events, but I hadn't seen him since Mack's funeral. He'd gained a lot of weight in the last two years, and his once pale face was ruddy now, his cheeks and nose latticed with prominent red veins. It was the face of a drinker.

Hugh raised one eyebrow and squinted at me quizzically. "Della Carmichael?"

"Yes. She found the body," John said.

Hugh started to extend his hand to me, but then drew back and shifted from one foot to the other. I guessed that he was uncomfortable to find the wife—the widow—of a fellow detective at a murder scene and wasn't quite sure how to act.

"Della, I don't know if you remember my new partner, Hugh Weaver."

"Of course I do. Hello, Hugh."

"Hi. I meant to call you after Mack died . . . but, well, you know—*tempus fugit*."

"Yes, time does fly," I said. "How's Shelly? Is she still working at the hospital?"

He shrugged. "She could be an astronaut now for all I know. We're divorced."

"Oh. I'm sorry."

John cut off this awkward stumble down memory lane by addressing Officer Bloom. "Are you here alone?"

"Paul Kraft and I caught the squeal. He's checking the premises. I made sure no one came in or out since we arrived."

"Good. Stay here." To me, he said, "Where's the victim?"

I gestured to the door into the test kitchens just as Officer Kraft came through it. Reporting to John, he said, "The building's secured, Detective. Nobody's in there."

"Take Officer Bloom and canvas the area to see if you can find anybody who might have seen something useful."

Officers Kraft and Bloom left, and I led John and his partner into the test kitchens. The entire floor was blazing with light. In his search, Officer Kraft had flipped every switch in the place.

Stopping in front of the first cubicle—the one assigned to Viola Lee—I explained that the five of us contestants were assigned these small test kitchens and that each of our names designated the one in which we were to work.

"Mine is the last one, at the end. That's where I found Regina. Be careful—there are pieces of broken crockery on the floor."

We proceeded forward, but walking single file, close to the wall to avoid disturbing any evidence.

When we reached the opening of my kitchen, I stepped back to let John and his partner move in close. Positioning themselves on either side of Reggie's body, they squatted down next to her.

"Careful, boys. Look but don't touch."

Hearing a husky new voice, I turned to see a woman striding toward us. Her pewter gray hair was cut very short, and large red-framed glasses were balanced precariously on the bridge of an unusually small nose. She carried a medical bag. As soon as she came close, I could tell she reeked of cigarettes.

"So, Big John, what have you got for me?" She looked down at Reggie. "Well! That's something I haven't seen before."

John and Weaver stood up to greet her. "Hi, Sid. You know my partner, Hugh Weaver."

"Yep."

Indicating me, John said, "This is Della Carmichael. She discovered the body. Della, this is Dr. Sidney Carver, our new medical examiner."

Dr. Carver—I wondered how many bad jokes she'd endured over the years about that name—barely acknowledged me. Instead, she knelt beside the body and opened her medical bag.

Two male Scientific Investigation Division techs arrived wearing identifying Windbreakers and carrying their evidence-collecting kits. They exchanged greetings with Dr. Carver and the detectives, and started documenting the scene in photographs.

"We'll get out of your way, Sid."

"I'd appreciate that."

When John, his partner, and I were back in the reception room, John asked me, "How are you holding up?"

"I'm okay."

"Finding that body had to be a shock. Why don't you sit down?"

I did as he suggested, but chose to perch on the arm of the couch instead of sinking into the cushions. My legs felt a little weak, and I didn't want them to see me struggling to get up again.

"I'm sure you've already told the responding officers, but let us hear what happened. From the beginning."

"Don't leave anything out," Weaver said.

I took a deep breath and told them about being one of five contestants in the Reggi-Mixx Cake Competition. "The Better Living Channel is taping the contest as a reality show special, and Mickey Jordan wanted me in it to promote my cooking show."

"So why are you here at night?" Hugh Weaver asked. "All by yourself."

"Reggie gave each of the five of us keys to the building because we're only allowed to work on our cakes after the test kitchen employees leave at six o'clock."

John said, "How well did you know the victim?"

His expression was impossible to read, so I couldn't tell if Shannon had told him about my old problem with Reggie. If she hadn't mentioned it, I knew I would have to tell him because I couldn't ask Shannon to keep my past encounter with Reggie a secret from her husband. With no time to think the situation through, I made the quick decision to tell John about that when we were alone and let him decide if that long past history needed to be in his investigative report.

"We were in college together," I said, "but until the other day, I hadn't seen her for twenty-five years."

"You're both here in the LA area." Hugh Weaver's tone was on the verge of being hostile. "I thought college buddies kept in touch."

"We were never buddies, Detective." I kept my reaction cool, but thought it best to stop using his name. Hugh Weaver and I weren't buddies either. "Reggie and I just attended the same school."

John and Weaver took notes as I continued my story. I told them about meeting the other contestants this morning and gave them what few details I knew about them. I left out the two items that Kevin Kyle had told me. I didn't mention that Gordon Prescott had married the woman Kyle had planned to marry because Prescott hadn't been the victim, so I couldn't see how Kyle's feelings about Prescott had any relevance to Reggie's murder. Nor did I mention Kyle's belief that Clay Sutton would try to win the contest through sabotage. I thought of that as gossip. It might have been relevant if Reggie had been Sutton's competitor, but she was the contest's sponsor.

Hugh Weaver looked up from his notebook and gave me an assessing stare. "You said the regular workers left at six, so Ms. Davis must have been killed sometime after. Where were you between six o'clock and twenty after ten when you say you found the body?"

I didn't miss his subtle emphasis on the word "say." He wanted to know if I had an alibi. "From the time I left here this afternoon, I was at my home," I said. "During the period from six PM until I arrived here and called nine-one-one, I made and received several telephone calls. I'll give you a list of the people I talked to, and my phone records will confirm the calls. Eileen O'Hara, John's daughter, who stays with me while she's going to UCLA, came home at about a quarter to seven. We had dinner together and then she left at eight thirty to go to a study group. I made and received another couple of phone calls, and at ten o'clock I left my house to come here. Her body was already cooling when I arrived, so she must have been killed closer to seven than to ten."

Keeping his face expressionless, John said, "It looks like Della's in the clear."

"Maybe." Weaver didn't sound happy. I imagined he was disappointed not to have the killer within grabbing distance. "John, you can check the story with your daughter." Weaver returned his attention to me. "Let's have the names of the people you talked to and the times."

After I told him what he wanted to know, and Weaver had written the information down, he and John closed their notebooks and told me I could go home.

Weaver took a card out of his pocket and handed it to me. "If you think of anything you left out, give us a call."

He accompanied us while John walked me out to my Jeep. I could see it wasn't going to be possible to talk to John alone there. I said good night without telling John about my early history with Reggie, but I'd call him later.

As I steered the Jeep through the official vehicles toward the alley, I glanced in the rearview mirror. Weaver had turned to go back into the Davis Foods building, but John was lingering outside, watching me drive away.

Because it was well after midnight, with very little traffic in either direction, I took a chance and made an illegal left-hand turn across Pico's double yellow line. I wanted to get home to Santa Monica as quickly as possible.

A car that had been parked on the street at the mouth of the alley flashed its lights and made the same illegal turn.

The fear of getting an expensive moving violation ticket clutched my heart—but almost immediately I realized that the vehicle behind me was not a patrol car.

At the same time, my cell phone rang. I punched the answer button and heard NDM's voice.

"I'm right behind you. Where can we go to talk?"

11

Where can we go to talk?

"The County Cork is still open," I said. "It's an Irish pub, on Westwood Boulevard, half a block north of Pico."

"I know where it is. Can't we go to your place?"

"The Cork is closer." My tone was meant to shut off argument.

"Okay," he said.

Less than two minutes later, I turned into the lot next to the County Cork. Designed inside and out to resemble an Irish village pub, it had a dark green awning with white letters over the wooden front door and a faded sign that featured a drawing of a shamrock with a leprechaun's hat tilted on one of its leaves. The Cork had been a popular late-night hangout in West Los Angeles for decades. I parked where the valet attendant directed, and handed him the keys to my Jeep.

Glancing around, I didn't see NDM or the prized silver Masarati Quattro Porte that he'd bought for pennies on the dollar at a federal confiscation auction. I was sure he wouldn't park in the Cork's lot because he hated to turn the keys over to a stranger.

I'd almost reached the pub's entrance when I heard heavy footsteps hurrying behind me. I turned as NDM caught up.

"Here, I'll get that." He stepped ahead, opened the door, and followed me inside.

The Cork's lighting was comfortably dim, and the air smelled of fried potatoes and beer. There was a colorful old jukebox opposite the bar, stocked with Irish songs. Mack and I used to come here sometimes. He was Irish on his mother's side and loved those tunes. As NDM and I came in, I heard a cut from *Songs of the Irish Rebellion* sung by Tommy Makem and the Clancy Brothers. It had been a favorite of Mack's.

With one hand cupped lightly beneath my left elbow, NDM steered me past the big mahogany bar with the thick brass footrail and its rows of bottles and glass mugs above the mirror on the back wall. At this hour, close to closing time, there were only a few customers, which left plenty of tables far enough away from anyone else to prevent our being overheard. He chose a secluded booth.

As we settled ourselves on opposite sides of the table, a young blond waiter in a green shirt with a shamrock pinned above a nametag that read "Dennis" came over with two menus and handed them to us. We put them down without looking.

"Do you know what you want?" NDM asked me.

My taste buds weren't craving anything, but my stomach felt hollow. I realized that I should eat something, if only to help calm my emotions. I looked up at the waiter. "A strawberry scone, please."

"A slice of your bacon and egg pie," NDM said.

The waiter scribbled. "And to drink?"

"Two coffees. Mine black. Half-and-half for the lady."

So NDM remembered how I liked my coffee, and that I could drink it late at night without losing sleep.

The waiter nodded and went off to give our order to the kitchen.

When we were alone, NDM crossed his arms on the table and leaned toward me slightly. "You look good."

"You don't have to compliment me."

"I always say what I mean."

You just leave things out—lies of omission. Instead of bringing that up, I asked, "What did you want to talk to me about?"

"A lot of things . . ."

"Let's concentrate on one subject only: murder. Did you hear a police call on your scanner?"

He nodded. "My sources tell me that the victim is Regina

Davis, owner of Davis Foods International. What were you doing there?"

"You're after a story, so where's your notebook?"

"I don't need to write everything down. You know what a good memory I have." A glint lighted his dark eyes and his full lips curved in that slight smile I'd seen so often just before we made love. It sent a little electric jolt of remembered desire to my nether regions, but I fought against reacting to it.

I kept my tone bland. "What do you want to know?"

"Okay, I'll be professional—for now. How did you happen to be at the Davis test kitchens to discover the body?"

I decided that there was no reason why I shouldn't tell him that. "I'm one of five contestants in a baking competition sponsored by the Reggi-Mixx company. We can only work there after hours so we don't interfere with company business, and we were each given a key to the premises."

"How did Regina Davis die?"

I worded my answer carefully. "As far as I know, the medical examiner hasn't rendered her opinion yet."

"But what did you *see* when you found the body?"

"You'll have to ask the detectives on the case."

NDM snorted. "John O'Hara wouldn't tell me what time it was if I was on my way to the gallows. And you know why."

I felt my cheeks flush with embarrassment. "You're a reporter and he's LAPD—natural enemies."

"He dislikes me because of you—because of *us*. Don't play dumb."

"There is no 'us.' " *Not anymore.* Before I could stop myself I added, "Anyway, I thought you liked 'dumb' women. But maybe only if it's *genuine*."

NDM grinned at me. "Meow. So you still care."

I wanted to kick myself. No—I wanted to think of a great comeback, a put-down that he'd never forget, one so clever that it would wither his libido for at least a month. But my brain seemed to freeze and I couldn't think of anything. Fortunately, at that moment, the waiter arrived with our food and coffee.

By the time Dennis had set the plates and cups in front of

us, asked if we wanted anything else, and departed again, enough time had passed that I could pretend the feelings NDM awakened in me hadn't occurred.

On edge in NDM's company, and annoyed at myself for it, I broke off a piece of the scone and, while it was still on the plate, I said, "Delicious."

"You haven't tasted it yet."

Archly, I declared, "The strawberry scones here are always delicious." I put the piece into my mouth and nearly choked. The crust was hard and the inside was dry as chalk. I managed to wash it down with the coffee. That, at least, was excellent.

NDM took a large forkful of his bacon and egg pie, which looked a lot better than my wretched scone. While it had pleased me once, now it was maddening that he was able to eat so heartily without looking gross. Everything about him was irritating me.

After he'd chewed and swallowed, NDM reached into his pocket and took out a small notebook and pen.

"Who are the other people in this contest of yours?"

"The police might not want that information made public yet, so I don't think I should tell you."

"That's ridiculous. I'll find them out through my sources tomorrow."

"Then you don't need to get them from me tonight."

In the tote bag that lay beside me in the booth, I heard my cell phone ring. I fished it out and saw a familiar number on the faceplate. "Excuse me," I said, turning my head away from NDM to answer. "Hello."

"I'm at your house," John O'Hara said. "Where are you?"

"I stopped somewhere. Is Eileen all right? Is that why you're there?"

"Eileen's fine. When are you coming home?"

"Right now," I said. "I need to talk to you. I'll be there in a few minutes."

"I'll wait."

I said a quick good-bye and disconnected.

Across the table, NDM was scowling. "No mystery who that was," he said. "Does Lieutenant O'Hara worry about his wife as much as he worries about you?"

"What a rotten thing to say. John's been one of my closest friends for years. That crack reveals more about you than it does about him." I grabbed my bag and stood up.

"Are you in such a rush to go see him that you won't even finish your scone?"

"I've lost my appetite."

12

John was sitting on the front stoop when I pulled into my driveway and cut the engine. He stood, hurried over to the passenger door, and climbed into the Jeep before I could get out.

"Eileen was coming back from walking Tuffy when I arrived," he said. "Now she's gone to bed. Do you mind if we talk out here?"

"No, but wouldn't you rather come into the house? I can make some coffee—"

He shook his head. "I wanted to be sure that you're really all right, that you got back safely. I need to get home."

The way he said that part about needing to get home caused me a twinge of concern. "Is Shannon all right? We had lunch yesterday and she seemed to be in a fine mood."

"She hasn't been sleeping the last couple of nights. What did you want to talk to me about?"

"Regina Davis. Your partner seemed so hostile to me that I didn't tell you everything back there. It's true that until Mickey Jordan entered me in this cake competition I hadn't seen Reggie since college, but she and I weren't just casual acquaintances back then. We had a serious problem with each other." I told John about exposing the fact that it was Reggie who was stealing money from the dorm rooms, and that when she left to transfer to another school, she said that if we ever crossed paths again she was going to kill me.

John's mouth tightened. "And you agreed to be in a contest she sponsored? What's the matter with you? Do you have some kind of a death wish?"

I bristled. "Don't talk to me like I'm a child who ran outside to play in the street. I repeat: The trouble Reggie and I had happened twenty-five years ago with no contact since—

not until two days ago, when she came to my house and acted as though we'd always been the closest of friends. She told me all about her unhappy marriages, and got so drunk in my living room that I had to drive her home."

"Jeez! How could you let yourself get involved with—"

"John, that's enough. Please. I agreed to be in the contest to promote the TV show. I have to do whatever I can to help it succeed and stay on the air." I wasn't about to admit to him that the show's success was vital to my financial survival.

John was quiet for a moment. He put one big hand on the passenger door handle but didn't open it. Looking straight ahead through the windshield, he said softly, "There was a time when, if you were in trouble, I could give you a hug and tell you everything was going to be all right. But I can't do that now."

"No, you can't . . ." This was the closest that John had come to acknowledging the unexpected—and profoundly unsettling—flash of attraction we'd felt for each other a few months ago. Since that evening in my kitchen I did my best to be sure we saw very little of each other. Those times when we were unavoidably in the same place there was a slight awkwardness on both our parts, and we had been careful not to touch.

The embarrassing realization that I could be attracted to John had driven me directly into the arms of Nicholas D'Martino. NDM had flirted with me, I'd rejected him with what I thought was withering sarcasm, and then I'd thrown myself into his startled but receptive arms. Our romance, or our collision of lust, or whatever that relationship had been, was wonderful for as long as it had lasted. The lovemaking was fabulous, and we discovered that we laughed at many of the same jokes and situations. Except for our arguments over politics—heated but never angry and usually leavened by humor at some point—I had thought NDM and I were a good match.

I must have been the only one of the two of us who thought so, because seeing him with that young blonde yesterday was as big a shock as if he'd flung ice water in my face. On reflection, I knew that I had been foolish and naïve to assume that

our sleeping together had meant some kind of implicit promise of fidelity. While it had been that for *me*, now I wanted to
smack the palm of my hand hard against my forehead and
yell, "You idiot!"

Yanking myself back from my momentary wallow in self-
flagellation, I realized that the silence between John and me
had grown uncomfortable. I had to break it before one of us
slipped and said something personal we might regret. To get
us to the safer subject of murder, I asked, "Are you going to
tell Detective Weaver about my history with Reggie?"

"I'll have to, but I'll also tell him I'm convinced that it
doesn't have anything to do with our case."

"What's the next step in your investigation?"

"Tomorrow morning we'll start interviewing all of the people in her life." He opened the passenger door, but turned to me
as he was getting out of the Jeep. "We don't know what this
case is about yet. Until we do, please don't take any chances."
Turning away from me, he added, "Eileen needs you."

John escorted me to my front door and we said good night,
carefully.

After greeting Tuffy and Emma, with enough stroking and
cooing to satisfy them, I checked my voice mail and found
that an excited message from Liddy had come in at eleven
PM.

"Oh, Del—the most wonderful thing has happened!" She
was breathless and burbling like a teenage girl. "I was *so
wrong* about Bill! He came home a little while ago and told
me *everything*! I can't talk long right now because he'll be out
of the shower in a minute—but he volunteered that he'd fibbed
to me about where he was last Tuesday, and where he was going to be tonight. He said he had to tell me the truth because it
was so painful for him not to. Del, what he was really doing
was working on a surprise for me: He was taking *ballroom
dancing lessons*! You know how I loved to dance but Bill said
he always felt like a three-legged buffalo when he got up to
try? Well, he decided that since it's something I like, he's going to learn so we can enjoy it together. And that's not all! He
bought tickets for us to go on a week's cruise to Mexico on the
Pacific Princess! We'll be dancing to an orchestra every night.

Don't I have *the* most marvelous husband in the *whole world*?"

There was a momentary pause in the message. I thought it was over and was about to push the key to delete it, but then she started talking again in a hurried whisper. "I heard Bill turn off the water in the shower. I'm going to go make love to my wonderful man. Talk to you tomorrow!" The call ended. There were no other new messages.

I sat quietly and stroked Tuffy as I thought about what I'd just heard, that Bill had lied about where he was last Tuesday and tonight because he was secretly taking *dancing lessons* . . . I was thrilled to hear Liddy sounding so happy, but I wondered if he was telling her the truth. With all of my heart, I hoped he was.

Reminding myself that I'd known Bill Marshall for more than twenty years and had never doubted that he was a devoted husband, I tried to banish the feeling of unease that was threatening to envelope me.

I told myself that I believed his story.

Almost.

With one last glance at the phone on the living room end table—ridiculously, as though by looking at the instrument I could learn if Bill was telling Liddy the truth—I stood and took a step toward the hallway leading to my bedroom.

And then the doorbell rang.

I hurried to peek out the front window and saw Addison Jordan on the front steps. He was pale and shifting his weight from one foot to the other.

Good Lord—what now?

Before he could ring again, and perhaps awaken Eileen, I opened the door and ushered him inside. Addison had lost his cool self-possession. He looked as though he'd dressed hastily because his top shirt button was in the wrong hole.

The moment I'd closed the door behind him, he said, "Regina Davis was *murdered*?"

"How did you find out?"

"A reporter from the *Chronicle* called. Guy with an Italian name."

"Nicholas D'Martino?"

"That's it."

"He wanted Mickey, but Mickey was out so I picked up the phone. I'm staying with Mickey you know."

"I didn't."

"The house is so big Iva barely knows I'm there, which is a good thing for Iva. She's polite, but I don't think she's exactly crazy about me. Anyway, when I told the reporter I was Mickey's son and an executive in the company, he told me what happened to Regina Davis."

NDM must have tried to contact Mickey as soon as I left the Cork.

Addison was pacing back and forth behind my sofa. I invited him to sit down, but he declined with a shake of his head. "I'm too upset. D'Martino said you found her—her body. What were you doing at the test kitchens?"

"Trying to get inspiration for a cake. What did he tell you?"

"He just asked questions. He knew you were one of the contestants in the Reggi-Mixx Cake Competition and wanted the names of the others."

"Did you tell him?"

"Yes. There didn't seem to be any reason not to. Jeez, I feel awful." Now he was pacing around the edges of my area rug. "Della, this could be my fault."

"How in the world could it be your fault?"

He paused to straighten one of my already straight lampshades. "If it turns out to be connected to the contest and the reality show. They were my ideas. I talked her into the project— although, when I mentioned Mickey's name she didn't need much persuading." I sat down on the couch, hoping my example would make him light somewhere.

I said, "When did you meet her?"

"November fifth, a few days after I moved out here from New York. I'd started working for Mickey, but he didn't know what to do with me. Going over the channel's schedule, he was most enthusiastic about you, so I thought up the contest as a way to promote the network, and your show. Before I told him what I had in mind, I researched food companies, looking for one that needed promotion as much as we did."

"Reggi-Mixx. That makes sense. I've heard that the company has lost market share."

Addison nodded. "When I had her data and crunched the numbers, I ran the idea past Mickey. I think I impressed him because he gave me the okay to try and set up a deal. Regina Davis went for it, I could tell, but she pretended to make me keep selling her. She asked a lot of questions."

"What questions?"

Addison began to calm down, at least enough to perch on the arm of the sofa. "A lot of them were about you. What were you like to work with? What kind of person were you off the air? Then there was one question she asked that didn't seem relevant to the contest."

"What was that?"

"She said she'd read that you were a widow and she was curious to know if you were romantically involved with anyone. I didn't know anything about your personal life—I hadn't even met you yet—but I didn't want to admit that, so I just told her what I hoped was true: You were a dream to work with, always cooperative. I did know for sure that the viewers liked you and your audience was building. When she agreed to the deal I proposed—that our two companies share expenses on the project and share ad revenue from the TV special—she said that you could be one of the five contestants, but that she would pick the other four to keep anyone from thinking that the contest was fixed because you're on our network. I said, 'Fine.' I didn't care who was in the contest as long as you were."

Addison stood and started pacing again. "Do the police think someone in the contest killed her?"

"I doubt they have any theory yet. It's only been a few hours."

"Mickey told me you're friends with a police detective. When you hear anything at all, will you tell me?"

"I'll share what I can, but until we know what happened, please don't blame yourself just because the contest was your idea."

"You're right. It's just that this was such a shock. I've never known anyone who was murdered."

You've been lucky, I thought.

Addison looked at his watch and sighed. "Mickey should be home by now. If he hasn't heard about the murder, I'll have to tell him." He made an unsuccessful attempt to smile. "I don't know Mickey very well yet. When he gets bad news, does he kill the messenger?"

"Not that I've ever heard."

"Maybe the bodies just haven't been found," he said.

Next morning, when I brought the newspapers in from where they lay in the middle of my driveway I saw that the front page of both the *Los Angeles Chronicle* and the *Los Angeles Times* featured stories about the murder of Regina Davis.

NDM's byline was on the *Chronicle*'s piece, which mentioned that the victim's body had been discovered by "the Better Living Channel's new cooking show star Della Carmichael." The reporter for the *Times* referred to me simply as "a cable TV chef." There were few details in either article, but NDM had managed to learn that the medical examiner's office was going to report that the victim's death was estimated to have occurred between seven and nine PM.

I wondered how—and from whom—he had extracted that information. Dr. Sidney Carver had not looked to me like the kind of woman who would be susceptible to NDM's charm. Then I remembered that the man had a great deal of charm.

Stop it, I told myself. Don't think about how good it felt to be in his arms, or how much you enjoyed the touch of his hands, the taste of his lips . . .

The phone rang, mercifully cutting off that train of thought.

"Hello."

"Della, it's Iva Jordan. Can you hear me?"

"Just barely. Could you speak a little louder?"

"I've got to talk to you." She raised her voice just enough for me to stop straining. I realized that she was crying. "It's a matter of life and death. May I come in?"

"Come in? Where are you?"

"Parked in the alley right behind your house. I don't want anyone to see me."

Now what? I wondered. But what I said was, "I'll come right out and unlock the back gate."

My little one-story English cottage on Ninth Street in Santa Monica, three blocks north of Montana Avenue, has a small front yard but a large back area. Privacy was assured by a chain link fence Mack and I'd screened with rows of young trees that we'd planted on three sides of our lot shortly after we moved in. Now, eighteen years later, the trees had grown to more than six feet high and had filled out in all their year-round leafy glory, making the chain link behind all but invisible.

In the center of the rear property line there was a wooden gate that I kept locked, and usually opened only to put out the trash for the weekly collection. Two dozen rosebushes that I'd grown from bare root packages gave the yard gorgeous splashes of color when they bloomed, but in late December I'd performed the yearly task of cutting them back down to about eighteen inches high. At the moment they held only the promise of future beauty.

Grabbing the key to the back gate from a hook on the kitchen wall, I hurried out the door and down the rear flagstone path. As I pushed the heavy gate open, I heard the hinges squeaking and reminded myself to give the metal a few squirts with WD-40 later.

Iva squeezed inside before I'd had the chance to open the gate all the way. Fortunately, she was slender enough so that her winter white cashmere sweater didn't catch on the rough wooden edges and rip.

As soon as I closed and relocked the gate, Iva sighed in relief. "Thank God you're home!"

"Come inside and have some coffee."

Halfway up the path to the kitchen door, Iva suddenly stopped and looked around at the yard. "Where's your pool?"

"I don't have one."

"No pool?" She said it wonderingly, as though the idea of a house without a pool was a concept difficult to grasp.

Mack and I had wanted to put in that famous California luxury and fitness asset, but we'd never been able to afford to do it. That was not something I was willing to discuss with Iva. Annoyed, I said, "No pool. I'm allergic to chlorine."

She missed my sarcasm and replied in a sympathetic tone, "Oh, I'm so sorry. Have you tried to find a doctor for that?"

I liked Iva, but I'd never counted her among the brightest people I know. I dropped the sarcasm, ushered her into the kitchen, and gestured for her to take a seat at the table. "What would you like in your coffee?" I asked.

"Just black. I have to watch my figure. Being married to a man as rich as Mickey, with so many women after him, is a full-time job."

The mental image of hordes of women chasing short, rough-edged, sixty-year-old Mickey Jordan down the street made it hard not to chuckle, but I forced myself to keep a straight face and poured her a mug of black coffee. I'd already had enough that morning, so I just sat down opposite her. Iva, the much younger and a bit taller fourth wife of Mickey Jordan, wore her pale gold hair in a gamine cut that emphasized her high cheekbones and large brown eyes. Usually, she was attired in some stunning designer ensemble, gilded with at least one piece of serious jewelry. This morning, in plain gray wool slacks, a white sweater, no jacket and no ornaments except her diamond "eternity" wedding ring, she looked—for Iva—unfinished.

"What's the matter?" I asked. "Why did you need to see me?"

She put down the coffee mug without having taken even a sip and clasped her perfectly manicured hands together so hard her knuckles were white. "That woman who was murdered . . . Della, I'm so scared! I'm afraid the police are going to think I killed her!"

That was the last thing I expected to hear. "I didn't know you knew Regina Davis."

"I didn't, not until she came to my house eight days ago to blackmail me."

I couldn't imagine what Iva might have in her past that could be blackmail material, but I'd only known her for about a year and a half. We met when she enrolled in my cooking school, and it had been Iva who had convinced her husband that I would be the right person to replace the show host he had fired a few months ago. I would always be grateful to her for that.

"Did you tell Mickey about Regina's visit?"

"Oh, no!" Both hands flew to her mouth and she flinched. "I couldn't let Mickey know because she was threatening to tell him something about me!"

I handed her two paper napkins from the holder—a plywood dragon that Eileen had constructed and painted in her high school shop class—in the center of the table. Iva used one to wipe her eyes and the other to blow her nose.

"Do you want to tell me about it?"

"No," she sniffed, "but I have to because you're friends with the detective the TV news said is investigating: Lieutenant O'Hara. Please speak to him on my behalf. Beg him to keep me out of this."

Because Iva was so nervous, instead of asking what she had done, I phrased the question more delicately. "Why did Regina Davis think she could exploit you?"

Iva expelled most of the air in her slender body. "Oh, this is so embarrassing. I never wanted anyone to know." She took a deep breath in. "A couple of months before I met Mickey I was having a terribly tough time paying my bills. I was a fit model—you know, one of the girls that designers fit their sample clothes to—but the company went out of business and left us all stranded. Suddenly no income. I don't have any regular skills. I can't do data entry, whatever that is, or operate a forklift. Lots of employers want those people. Then, when I was literally down to my last forty dollars, I saw an ad for a telephone actress."

Yikes.

Iva's lips twisted into a wry smile. "I can see you guessed what that was, but I didn't figure it out until I applied for the job. It was an adult entertainment company—but the people there were all so nice and so . . . *normal*. They explained what I'd have to do on the phone, and gave me some written guidelines, a kind of script. . . ." She shivered. "Oh, this is awful!"

"How long did you work at that?"

"One hour."

"*One hour?* Was there a police raid? I thought the phone sex business was legal. What happened?"

"I was a total failure, Della. Every caller hung up on me in less than a minute. I never even got to the talking dirty part."

Her story fascinated me. I propped my elbows on the table and leaned forward. "Why did they hang up?"

"Well, we're supposed to start off talking about what we do for a living, if we're going to college. The callers were supposed to want sort of girls-next-door. Anyway, I wanted to be really good at this because I needed the money. When the men called, I said my name was Judy, or Betsy, or Diane, and told them that I was going to college part time and studying marketing because I wanted to be a focus group leader. That's when they would hang up. Nobody even stayed on long enough to ask what I was wearing. The switchboard woman unplugged me after an hour."

I couldn't help it—I laughed.

"I guess it's funny, now. But then I was devastated. Anyway, I couldn't pay my rent, so I had to bunk with a girlfriend. Luckily, in a few days I got work modeling for catalogues." She hastened to add, "Regular, ordinary catalogues. That's what I was doing when I met Mickey."

"You weren't involved in anything illegal. In fact, you didn't even work at phone sex, so how could Reggie hold that over you?"

"She had a detective investigate me! I know because she showed me the guy's report. Somehow he got hold of a copy of my employment agreement. It had photocopies of my driver's license and Social Security card, and listed the shift I was supposed to work. It didn't say that I didn't actually *do* any of the work."

"I'm sure Mickey would understand about the situation you were in."

She shook her head and moaned. "Mickey is sort of old-fashioned. He thinks there are only two types of women, and I'm the *good* kind. He thinks you are, too. If he found out what I was willing to do, he might be disgusted and leave me. I really love him, Della. My losing Mickey—the police could think that's a motive for murder."

"You didn't kill Reggie, did you?"

"No, of course not! But I can't *prove* I didn't. Mickey was out at a business meeting and I was just home alone, watching TV. Mickey's driver was with him, but our butler, Maurice, was sick in bed with a bad cold, so I *could* have gone out without him knowing. Please—you've got to help me."

"I'll do what I can, but one thing puzzles me. From everything I've heard, Regina Davis was a wealthy woman. What did she want from you, in exchange for her silence?"

"She told me her arrangement with Mickey about the cake contest was that they split the cost of producing the TV special, but she said she had a 'little cash flow' problem. She wanted me to persuade Mickey to pick up the whole tab."

"What did you tell her?"

"I couldn't say no because I was terrified, so I told her that I'd start working on Mickey. I wasn't going to, Della—I'd *never* do something behind Mickey's back. She called every day, but I kept stalling her, telling her that I had to do it at just the right moment. Her last call, day before yesterday, she told me I'd better hurry, or I'd regret it."

It concerned me that Reggie had called Iva's house several times. When the police checked Reggie's phone records they'd find that number and ask questions, but I thought there was no reason to upset Iva further by telling her that now.

"I'll do what I can to keep track of how the investigation is going," I said. "If I find out that your name has come up, then I'll go with you and help you explain this to Mickey. I'm sure we can make him understand that what you almost did was really nothing."

Iva gave me a grateful hug. I walked her down the path and let her out through the gate to the alley where she'd left her car.

Back in the kitchen I quickly reviewed my notes for today's shows, then checked the wall clock. There was just time to take Tuffy for a thorough morning walk before we had to leave for the TV studio.

As I snapped the leash onto Tuffy's collar, I thought about finding Reggie's body last night. It had shaken me more than I wanted to admit to anyone. While I was still feeling the effects of that shock, I didn't have the luxury of indulging myself by going back to bed and pulling the covers over my head. The common link in such seemingly diverse lives as having been the wife of a police detective, teaching in the public school system, being responsible for my own little cooking school, and hosting *In the Kitchen with Della* was that it didn't matter what I was feeling. No matter what, I had to show up when I was supposed to, and do whatever was necessary.

14

The Better Living Channel's production facilities were located on the corner of Lankershim Boulevard and Chandler Street in North Hollywood, in a converted warehouse that was the approximate size and shape of an airplane hangar. It was nineteen miles from my home in Santa Monica. Barring an unforeseen traffic problem, the trip took me about thirty-five minutes. I'm a conservative driver. In the two or three times when I'd ridden to the studio with NDM, it took considerably less time. He was skillful at the wheel of what I called his "Italian Batmobile," although he refused to believe that speed limits applied to him.

A giant billboard outside the fenced-in studio property advertised the three shows currently produced on those premises: *Car Guy*, *That's Not Junk*, and *In the Kitchen with Della*. We on-air hosts were depicted in caricatures. I liked the flattering way the artist improved my figure, but on that billboard Car Guy—a man so secretive about his personal life that he had his real name changed legally to Car Guy—looked slightly deranged. The artist exaggerated the mechanic's casually unruly hair into wild spikes, and the grin he put on Car Guy's face made him resemble a horror movie's mad scientist.

When I met Car, I was surprised to discover that while he would never be described as movie star handsome, he was not bad looking. In person he was more moody than "mad," reminding me somewhat of *Jane Eyre*'s Mr. Rochester with a grease gun.

The billboard interpretation of Gil York, the channel's cute young Cockney wizard-with-refuse, was little short of adoring. Gil's forty-foot likeness enlarged his big brown eyes, his dazzling smile, and crowned his head with twice as many butterscotch curls as he possessed in real life.

One afternoon shortly after I began doing my show, I heard Gil complaining about the drawing to channel owner Mickey Jordan. "That bloody thing makes me look like a silly ass in one of those boy bands," he'd said.

Mickey's typically diplomatic response had been, "Suck it up. It attracts viewers."

Tuffy, who had been lounging in the backseat of the Jeep for most of the trip, sat up in his safety harness as we neared the studio. His body began squirming with excitement as he looked out the window. It wasn't just the pleasure of going for a ride; his attitude when we approached either the veterinarian or the shop where he was groomed was decidedly unenthusiastic. Tuffy found interesting new scents to explore inside and outside the studio, and he enjoyed sitting on the set, watching me cook for the cameras.

I turned onto the short gravel driveway that led to the locked cast iron gate, pulled up parallel to the call box, and pressed the button.

"Hi there, Miz Della." It was the warm Southern cadence of sixty-something Angie Johnson, who monitored the security cameras and entry access on the day shift. She lowered her voice and sounded as though she'd leaned closer to the microphone. "Mr. Jordan's here. He wants to see you soon as you get in."

"Thanks, Angie."

She pushed the control button and the big gate swung inward. As I drove around the side of the building to the employee parking spaces, I caught a glimpse of Mickey's huge yellow SUV in the "No Parking" lane facing the front door.

I parked a few yards beyond the big double doors of the studio entrance and turned in my seat to unfasten Tuffy's safety harness. No sooner had I stepped to the ground and let him out than I saw Mickey exit the building from the door to the security office. He headed in my direction, followed by his son, Addison. They were a funny sight, because even though Addison was taller and had longer legs, Mickey was barreling along at such a fast pace that he had the younger man hurrying to keep up.

Mickey stopped in front of me so abruptly his shoes raised a small cloud of dust. "I heard you found Reggie's body last night. You okay?"

"It was a shock, but I'm all right."

"She was f-in' murdered." Mickey followed his statement with a stream of even more colorful expletives, then took a breath and calmed down. "I liked her."

Addison asked, "Do they know who did it?"

"Not yet," I said. "At least I haven't heard anything." With a sudden flicker of hope, I turned to Mickey. "With Reggie dead, I suppose you'll cancel the cake competition now."

"Hell, no," Mickey said. "I've spent too much up-front money to toss it away. Anyway, that's not why I came out here this morning. I've got a surprise for you." Mickey nodded at Addison, who had moved up to stand beside his father. "Della, meet your new producer. He's a smart kid. He persuaded me he'll learn to be a producer on the job, if you help him."

With a warm smile, Addison said, "I'll still be involved in corporate strategic planning, but thought I could be more valuable to Mickey if I learned the cable TV business from the ground up."

I admired his ambition, although I hadn't thought of my show as "the ground." *At least he didn't refer to it as "the bottom of the barrel."*

"We can use the help," I said. "Quinn and I have been handling the producing chores ever since George Hopkins . . . since he left." I stopped short of saying that my previous producer had disappeared to avoid paying his huge gambling debts. It wasn't my place to disclose his problem. Wherever George Hopkins was, I hoped he was all right, and attending Gamblers Anonymous meetings as he'd promised to do.

I asked Addison, "Have you met our director, Quinn Tanner?"

He stopped smiling. "Just now."

Having experienced the fact that Quinn did not exactly welcome change, to put it mildly, I asked, "How did that go?"

"Not well."

Mickey shook his head. "She's acting like a cobra with a toothache. I thought English women were supposed to behave like ladies, but she used a word I'd never heard before. Ah, f-it. I'm the boss around here. You two get started." With his right fist, he tapped the left side of his chest. "I got other businesses giving me agita."

Mickey gave us a quick wave and strode back toward the front of the building, where he'd parked his SUV.

I asked Addison, "Did Mickey show you around the studio?"

"He said he didn't have time."

"Then I'll give you a quick tour before we tape the first half hour."

We started toward the studio entrance when Addison looked down at Tuffy. I was glad to see that he didn't flinch.

"Finally, I had a chance to view a couple of your tapes," Addison said. "Mickey was right—that standard poodle is a nice touch. Even though I'm not exactly comfortable around big dogs, I found myself smiling at those shots the camera people got of him watching you cook."

Inwardly, I gave a sigh of relief about my new producer's attitude toward Tuffy. I wouldn't have to fight for Tuff's presence on the set.

"We get a lot of positive e-mail about him," I said. "But he doesn't come Thursday nights when I do my live hour in front of a studio audience. Too many people around."

"Since I saw him in action, I told Mickey that we should have an artist work a drawing of him next to you on the billboards. Do you have a picture of him they could use?"

"Lots of pictures," I said. "I'll have a good one for you tomorrow."

Addison gave me the thumbs-up sign.

We were at the door of the huge, cavernous space that housed the Better Living Channel's West Coast production facility when Addison touched me on the arm lightly and indicated that he wanted me to wait for a moment.

"Before we go inside, I wanted to tell you something. I persuaded Mickey to let me work on your show not just because I want to learn the nuts and bolts of cable TV production.

There's another reason, too. What I didn't tell Mickey is that my mother loves your show. Seeing my name on the screen as producer is going to make her very happy."

Hearing that, and knowing how much I loved my own mother, I said, "I'll make sure that your name goes on the credits right away. If you like, we'll send her DVDs of the shows before they go on the air."

"That would be great!"

One thing puzzled me. "Why didn't you want your father to know why you wanted to work on the show?"

I saw the smile leave his eyes. "Mickey and Mom divorced when I was about eight. He was generous with money, but we didn't see him very often." He shrugged, throwing off the cloak of sadness that had descended on him, and made an obvious attempt to lighten the mood. "Nobody's childhood is perfect, right? I have a great mom, and Mickey's a decent guy. He was certainly a good provider. That's more than you can say about a lot of divorced men."

With a smile that looked a little forced, Addison gestured for me to precede him into the studio. "Now, show me where the magic happens."

Entering, I said, "There are four standing sets. Two in the front of the building and two here in the back. Gil York's furniture repurposing workshop is in the front, along with space for a set when Mickey picks another show to produce here. The wall between the two halves of the studio is soundproof, with a lock on each side to prevent someone from coming in and accidentally interrupting a show."

I raised my free hand to indicate the director's booth overhead. "That's one of the two control booths. There's a duplicate on the other side of the wall. When the schedule requires it, shows can be taped or broadcast in a front set and a back one simultaneously."

Through the booth's glass wall, I saw a familiar wraithlike figure with long black hair framing her narrow face: TV director Quinn Tanner. She glanced down at us, and then looked away quickly. From her cold behavior, I guessed that Quinn would not be coming down to the floor for a pleasant chat before taping. Quinn and I had developed a cordial—if not exactly chummy—working relationship. If she and Addison had started badly, they would have to make peace. I hoped it happened soon. I'd do what I could to help because I couldn't afford to let tension between them affect the job I had to do.

Passing Car Guy's fully equipped garage set, which today had a Buick on the hydraulic lift, Addison screwed up his face. "Phew," he said. "This smells like a garage. Doesn't the odor bother you?"

"I don't mind it. The air conditioning gets rid of most of it while I'm cooking," I said. "Because he often makes a lot of noise demonstrating repairs, we tape at different times. Today, Car Guy's working at two o'clock, and I'll have finished both of my half hours by twelve thirty or one."

In my studio kitchen, on the far side of Car Guy's garage, the lights for taping had already been adjusted.

Addison surveyed my set. "Nice. Homey. It looks like your real kitchen."

"The studio designers liked mine and copied it."

Camera operators Ernie Ramirez and Jada Powell were doing their pretaping checks of the equipment. I introduced them to Addison and said, "Addison is going to be our new producer."

Jada smiled at him. "Great."

"Hey, man, welcome to the family," Ernie said cheerfully.

Our new producer shook hands. "Actually, I'm already family—Addison *Jordan*." With a self-deprecating smile he said, "No surprise how I got my job, is it?"

"We won't hold that against you," Ernie said.

"Unless you make us call you 'Sir,' " Jada added.

Addison laughed. "Not a chance."

Tuffy tugged at my leash, reminding me to let him go. As soon as I unhooked him, he trotted over to his comfy dog bed beside the refrigerator and lay down.

"That's one smart pooch," Ernie said.

As I filled Tuffy's bowl with fresh water, Addison said, "You mentioned the unused studio space up front. I have some ideas for shows that can elevate this network. We don't have to stay on the cable business's equivalent of Skid Row."

"*Owww-eee*, that's putting us in our place," Jada told Ernie, but loud enough for Addison and me to hear.

"I didn't mean that the way it sounded," Addison said quickly. "It's just that we're not exactly the Food Network. Not yet. But I want us to be that good."

"That sounds like my cue to get cooking," I said.

"Now that I'm responsible for this show, I'm going to think about how we can make it better. If the ratings fall—well, I can't do my job for the network by supporting a failure."

I got the message loud and clear: If I didn't do everything I could to keep *In the Kitchen with Della* rising in popularity, my metaphorical goose would be cooked.

15

When "A Festival of Pasta," the first of my two shows that day, was completed, studio personnel converged on the set to help themselves to the dishes I'd made. There was always plenty to go around. I'd put a stack of paper plates and packages of paper napkins and forks out on the prep counter next to the Spaghetti Carbonara, the Penne Pesto, and the Linguine with Sautéed Mushrooms, Garlic, and Lemon.

I asked Jada, who was dishing pasta for herself, "Will you fix a plate for Angie on the security desk? I don't want her to miss out just because she can't leave her post."

"I'll go eat with her," Jada said. She loaded two plates, balanced them deftly, and grinned at me. "I used to wait tables. It's better now that I can eat what I carry."

Addison stared as the big bowls of pasta disappeared. "This is a great thing to do to build team spirit, but what if somebody gets sick? Would the station be liable?"

"Mickey said I could give the food to the staff—let them have a little between-shows party. You can see they're enjoying themselves, and it keeps everybody energized. Why don't you let me fix you something?"

"No, thanks, but would you make a plate for me to take up to Quinn Tanner?" He winked at me. "If we raise her blood sugar, maybe it will improve her disposition."

"Can't hurt," I said.

When I'd dished out generous portions of all three pastas, I handed the plate, cutlery, and napkins to Addison.

With a nod, he indicated the director's booth above us, where we could see Quinn making marks on a clipboard. Grinning, he said, "If I'm not back in an hour, call the police."

Ernie came over for a refill. Watching Addison head toward

the stairs to the director's booth, he joked, "Too bad. That Addison was a nice guy."

As Ernie helped himself to more pasta, I asked, "Which of these did you like best?"

"All of them, but especially the linguine with the mushrooms and garlic and lemon."

"Me, too," I said. "It was created when Eileen unexpectedly brought home a friend who was a vegetarian, and I had to assemble a main dish she could eat just from ingredients I had on hand: pasta, lemons, mushrooms, garlic, and olive oil. The girls loved it, so it went into my repertoire."

"God bless vegetarians," Ernie said.

I decided to make this new recipe for pasta lovers Liddy and Bill, as soon as they had a free night. Maybe seeing them together would relieve my mind. Liddy sounded happy in her phone message, and I wanted to be happy for her.

While the stagehands were cleaning up and placing the ingredients I would need for the soufflé show we'd tape next, I grabbed a plastic bag and Tuffy's studio pooper-scooper. It was time to take Tuffy for a walk around the property, and I wanted some fresh air.

I glanced around for Addison, intending to tell him that I'd be back in a few minutes, but he was still up in the director's booth with Quinn. I hadn't heard a scream, or seen one of them come flying through the booth's glass wall to crash on the studio's concrete floor, so perhaps things were going well up there.

When Tuffy and I returned, I didn't see my new producer. I asked Ernie, "Where's Addison? Is he still up with Quinn?"

Jada shook her head. "He came down just after you went out with Tuff, and asked for the rundown for the Thursday night live show."

Ernie said, "I got him a copy from the production office. Then his cell phone rang and he took the call outdoors. When he came back in he said to tell you he'd see you at the show tomorrow night."

Puzzling, but I had other things to think about. "Thanks, Ernie," I said.

Tuffy drank from his water bowl, then settled down on his bed, and I took my place behind the preparation counter.

When Camera One's red light came on and we were taping, I smiled into the lens. "Hi, everybody. I'm Della Carmichael and today we're going to take the fear out of making a soufflé. A cheese soufflé and a mixed vegetable salad make a perfect lunch or light dinner. If you're entertaining, then a chocolate or a Grand Marnier soufflé for dessert will be very impressive, and your non-cooking friends won't have any idea how really simple it is to make. When I show you in a few minutes, you'll be whisking and folding with the best restaurant chefs. So, let's get cooking—and begin with a cheese soufflé."

I moved to the oven, turned it on, and said to the camera, "We start by preheating the oven to 475 degrees. That's hot, but I'll reduce the heat ten minutes after the soufflé goes in."

Returning to the preparation counter, I indicated and identified the row of ingredients that had previously been set out: one cup of sharp cheddar cheese finely grated, four tablespoons butter, the same amount of flour, a cup of milk, one tablespoon of distilled white vinegar, a tablespoon of water, a little bottle of Tabasco sauce, a third of a cup of freshly grated Parmesan cheese, and six eggs.

Indicating the eggs, I said, "We're going to need six egg whites, but only four yolks. You can store the other two yolks in the fridge to use later—add them to a batch of scrambled eggs and onions or hash, or dilute with a little water and use as an egg wash to brush across the top of a piecrust."

I picked up the first egg, cracked it, and separated the white from the yolk. Explaining the process as I went along, I said, "You may find a recipe that tells you to beat the whites in a food processor, but I don't agree. I like using an electric hand mixer because then you know the exact moment when the whites form stiff peaks. The hardest part of making a soufflé is getting over the *fear* that it won't puff up and stay up." I aimed a sly, teasing smile at the camera lens. "It's the cook's version of performance anxiety. Seriously, what's the worst that can happen if it falls? No one's going to drag you off to the 'flat soufflé dungeon.' You'll just say 'Ooops' and whip up some pasta for dinner. That's why I keep a variety of pastas in the pantry at all times, for those 'ooops' moments we all have. In fact, you don't have to wait for a disaster in the kitchen. If somebody comes over to my house unexpectedly and I need to whip up a quick meal, there's nothing faster than a package of angel hair pasta—which takes three minutes to cook—tossed with five or six cloves of chopped garlic lightly sautéed in three or four tablespoons of extra virgin olive oil, and some salt and pepper. Pasta with oil and garlic—*yum*! It's even better if you have some grated Parmesan cheese and a little flat-leaf parsley to chop up and sprinkle over the dish. Serve that with some crusty bread and a glass of wine, and maybe some fresh fruit for dessert, you'll have a five-star meal on a rock-bottom budget."

After I'd folded the beaten whites into the cheese, milk, butter, flour, and yolk mixture, I tilted the soufflé dish so that the camera could watch my fingers as I buttered the inside, and then dusted the sides with two tablespoons of the grated Parmesan cheese.

"The dry cheese on the buttered insides gives the soufflé something to clutch as it rises. Picture tiny hand- and footholds on the side of a cliff, or on the exercise wall at the gym."

As soon as I'd transferred the mixture into the prepared baking dish, I topped the rim with a stand-up collar of aluminum foil two inches high and tied it in place with string. "This foil collar will keep the soufflé from spilling over when it rises."

Carefully, I transported the dish to the oven and slid it inside. I said to the camera, "After the soufflé's been in the oven for ten minutes, reduce the heat to 400 and continue baking for about twenty-five more minutes. If you don't have a glass-front oven—and as you see, I don't—resist the temptation to keep opening the door to look at your soufflé. Have a little faith, folks."

Through my earpiece, I heard Quinn say, "Della, lead in to the commercial insert."

I smiled at the camera. "We're going to take a little break now while I start putting together the ingredients for the chocolate soufflé we'll make next. Stay right there and I'll be back to walk you through a fabulous dessert."

Taping stopped. I decreased the oven heat to 400 degrees and organized what I'd need for the next segment, hoping fervently that this wouldn't be the time that my own soufflé fell.

Luck smiled on me. With the beautifully puffed-up cheese soufflé out of the oven and photographed for the audience, it was time to make the salad, which would be the final dish of this day's shows.

"The best way to cut an avocado," I said to Camera Two as I held up a ripe green Hass, "is to slice it in half lengthwise and then give it a little twist to separate the two halves. Like this." I held the two halves up to face the camera.

"Now to remove the pit without damaging that half of the avocado, just tap the pit with the edge of your knife, and—*aggh!*" The knife slipped off the avocado pit and I felt a sharp jab. Suddenly blood spurted from the palm of my left hand.

In my earpiece, Quinn said, "Keep going. I'm not stopping tape." I heard her order Camera Two in for a close-up.

I grabbed a handful of paper towels from the roll next to the sink, soaked them with cold water, and pressed the paper hard against my cut. Forcing a grin, I said into Camera Two's lens, "I hope you at home won't do what I just did, but if you *do*, stop the bleeding right away by using clean paper towels and cold water."

I lifted the wad to take a look—and more blood gushed out of my palm. Dropping the soaked towels, I snatched fresh ones, pressed again, and produced a light laugh. "Don't panic if it takes quite a few wet towels before the bleeding stops."

The studio lights were bright but the two cameras and their operators were close enough for me to see them clearly. Ernie Ramirez gagged. Jada Powell pantomimed asking if he was all right. He nodded and took a deep breath and nodded, but he looked queasy.

One more wad of wet towels and when I lifted them from the wound this time, I saw that the bleeding had stopped. Turning my palm to the camera, I said, "Success."

Even though it wasn't bleeding at that moment, I kept light pressure on the wound while I reached up to the top of the refrigerator and took down a blue metal box. "This is my first aid kit. I always keep it on top of the fridge because that way I never forget where it is, and—most important—seeing it reminds me to keep the medications inside up-to-date."

Jada, on Camera Two, followed me to the sink. Explaining

what I was doing, I washed the wound thoroughly with anti-bacterial soap.

"This next part stings a little," I said, as I disinfected the puncture with peroxide, "but just for a few seconds. Then squeeze on some antibiotic ointment. If you don't have any, use hand sanitizer. You can get a dispenser to mount near a kitchen or bathroom sink, and carry a little portable squirt bottle in your handbag for away-from-home emergencies."

With my palm facing the camera to show that it wasn't bleeding any longer, I said, "If it looks like you can't stop the bleeding, keep the pressure on but get to an emergency room. You might need a few stitches. But if you don't, just slap on a Band-Aid, like I'm doing."

In my ear I heard Quinn say, "Lead in to the commercial inserts."

I aimed a bright smile at the future audience. "Okay, excitement over. It's time for another little break now, and when we come back I'll finish making our mixed vegetable salad. The romaine, the butter lettuce, and the spinach leaves I'll tear with my hands, but I promise to be *extra careful* slicing the cherry tomatoes and that slippery avocado."

As soon as Camera Two's red light went off, I opened the refrigerator door, took out three cold sodas—*not* the sugar-free kind, because we needed the lift—and gave one each to Jada and Ernie. I raised my soda can in a mock toast and said to the camera team, "At least this didn't happen on one of the live shows."

Jada glanced up at the control booth above us, covered the mouthpiece on her headphones, leaned forward and whispered, "Quinn's even scarier, now that I know she likes the sight of blood."

Ernie joked, "Maybe she's not British, but Transylvanian. The bride of Dracula. She says she's married, but she's never brought her husband to the studio."

Jada picked up on Ernie's theme. "I'm picturing them sleeping in a coffin filled with earth from their homeland."

In my earpiece, Quinn said, "Della, please figure out how to take the pit out of an avocado without maiming yourself and we'll run that insert as a PSA when we air this near-disaster of a show."

I felt like a ten-year-old who'd just been reprimanded by the teacher, then I remembered a line from a philosopher I'd studied in school: "That which does not kill me makes me stronger." It was one of the rare bits in his writings where I agreed with Nietzsche.

As I was wrapping up the show—careful to keep the blood-soaked paper towels below camera range—I saw John O'Hara move quietly into my line of sight.

"That's all for today, folks. Take pictures of your perfect soufflés, send them to me here at the Better Living Channel in North Hollywood. You'll find the address on the screen at the end of the show. I'll show them on the air and put them up on my Web site, Dellacooks.com."

Camera's red light off. Taping over.

Tuffy, spotting John as he came toward the preparation counter, stood and wagged his tail.

"This is a nice surprise," I said, even as some internal warning signal told me that "nice" might not be the perfect word. "Is everything all right?"

"Pretty much. Are you through for a while?"

"For the day." Without thinking about my sliced palm I brought both hands up above the counter. I saw that a little trickle of blood had seeped out below the Band-Aid.

John took one look at the wad of bloody paper towels and blanched. "My God!" He took hold of my arm. "We're going to the nearest hospital."

I pulled back. "We are not. I'm all right. See, it's stopped bleeding." *Finally.*

"You might need stitches—"

"No, I don't, but I appreciate your concern. Really. I'm okay. I'd go to a doctor if it was necessary." To get him away from the subject of my hand, I said, "Tell me why you came all the way out here."

Glancing about to be sure that there was no one close enough to over hear us, John said, "The Regina Davis autopsy's been completed. There was a surprise in it."

"What?"

"The blow to her head didn't kill her. It rendered her unconscious, but she died from asphyxiation—from her face being forced down into that bowl full of cake batter."

I shuddered. "That's horrible."

"It was ugly. And *personal*. Whoever killed her was filled with rage."

"Do you have a suspect?"

John took two photographs out of his jacket pocket and turned the pictures toward me. "Do you recognize this?"

They were shots of a gold fountain pen, both sides.

Automatically, I smiled. "It's Bill Marshall's. I was with Liddy when she bought it for him, for their last anniversary."

"Are you positive?"

"Of course. See the two hearts engraved on the cap? If you look closely you'll see there's a little 'B' in the center of one heart and 'L' in the other. Liddy had the store engrave it like that. Where did you find it?"

The smile died on my lips when I saw the unhappy expression on John's face.

"It was in Regina Davis's handbag. The engraving is how we knew it wasn't hers," he said. "Can you explain how Bill Marshall's pen happened to be in the murdered woman's possession?"

16

My mind, so often racing with ideas and theories, crashed against a virtual wall of shock. I was stunned into silence at the news that Bill Marshall's pen was found in Reggie's handbag. How in the world could that be?

Ah—I've got it! In my head I sounded as triumphant as Alexander Graham Bell must surely have felt when he discovered that his assistant could hear his voice through the first telephone. "The answer is simple," I said. "Reggie's probably a patient of Bill's. She was in his office recently and needed to write a check to him, but she didn't have a pen, so Bill handed her his, and she forgot to give it back. That sort of thing happens all the time."

In his measured baritone, John said, "That's a logical explanation, Sherlock."

"Just call me Irene Adler—the only woman Holmes thought was his equal." But my enthusiasm began to ebb when I saw the unhappy expression on John's face. "What's the matter?"

"From the times we've all been together, I thought I recognized the pen. However unlikely, the initials *might* have been a coincidence, so I asked Weaver to check out the high-end stores where that kind of pen is sold, and I went to Bill's office."

Apprehension was prickling my skin. "What did Bill say?"

"He wasn't there. His nurse said that he'd called her very early and asked her to reschedule his patients. What he told her was that he decided to take a 'vacation day' with his wife."

John paused in a way that told me more was coming, and that the "more" probably wasn't good news.

Even though I was sure I would not like the answer, I had to know. "What's the rest—the part you haven't told me yet?"

"Regina Davis wasn't a patient of Bill's." John's voice was heavy with concern.

A cold, hard lump of dread filled my chest. "Are you positive she wasn't a patient? Maybe she used to be, but then—"

"No. According to his nurse, Ms. Davis has never been one of his patients. So we're back to the question of how Bill's pen got into the dead woman's purse."

I didn't feel much like the brilliant Irene Adler anymore. "What are you going to do?"

"Tell Weaver what I found out, and then we'll have to question Bill. Do you know where he and Liddy would have gone for his unscheduled 'vacation day'?"

"No," I said.

But that was only the literal truth. While I didn't *know* where they were, I had an idea . . .

■ ■ ■

The first thing I did after John left, and after snapping Tuffy into his safety harness, was climb behind the wheel of my Jeep and dial Liddy's number on my cell phone. Listening to the ringing on the other end of the line, I hoped that she wasn't home, because if she was there, and not away somewhere with Bill, then that would look even worse for him in the eyes of Detectives O'Hara and Weaver.

Voice mail picked up and I heard Liddy say, "Hi, friends and family. We're out of town just for today. You won't really have time to miss us, but I'll be checking for messages. Bye for now!" She sounded so happy; her voice was full of little musical trills. I was afraid that happiness would evaporate once they were found.

As soon as John caught up with Detective Weaver and filled him in, they'd start looking for Bill and Liddy. I was sure they'd first check the airlines to see if the Marshalls were listed on any of the manifests. If not, they'd guess that the couple might have driven across the border to Mexico. John or Weaver would alert the officers in San Diego to check outgoing tourists and stop Bill and Liddy for questioning.

While the detectives were waiting for news from the border, they'd begin to check places in the Los Angeles area where a well-to-do couple might "hide out" for a day. They would theorize that Bill Marshall might seek the anonymity of the huge crowds at Disneyland, Magic Mountain, Knott's Berry Farm, or at one of the other magnets for fun-seekers. After that, John and Weaver and others in the squad would probably canvas the luxury hotels in Beverly Hills and Santa Monica, and maybe even ninety miles north, in Santa Barbara, or a hundred and ten miles south in the resort community of Coronado Bay.

That kind of wide-ranging investigation requires both manpower and the power of a detective's shield. I couldn't compete with that, but I was pretty sure I didn't have to. One advantage I had over the police was that Liddy was my best friend, and had shared her most personal feelings with me. One of Liddy's confidences was the investigative track I was about to follow.

I put the Jeep in gear, drove away from the Better Living Channel's production facility, and headed for Ventura Boulevard. At Ventura, instead of turning right, toward Beverly Glen Canyon and home, I turned left, toward Laurel Canyon, and an area of Los Angeles that had none of the elegance of Bill and Liddy Marshall's usual haunts.

My idea sprang from a conversation I'd had with Liddy a few weeks ago when she shared with me that she and Bill had been acting like honeymooners ever since September, when their twin boys left for college in the east. She said she was feeling really wild again, and giggled about her fantasy of taking Bill to one of those motels along La Cienega Boulevard that catered to people who checked in under phony names and stayed for only a few hours. "It would be like being crazy young again," she'd said.

I'd replied, "I'll bet you never did that even when you were young."

"Well, no," she admitted. "I grew up in Nebraska, and when I met Bill he was already becoming successful, and we were both unattached and had our own apartments. Still . . ." She'd looked wistful for a moment.

When I warned her that those "hot bed" motels might not be perfect models of sanitation, she'd joked, "What's the worst that can happen? We've got great medical insurance."

The conversation that at the time had seemed merely silly ended there, but now I wondered if doing something "crazy young" might be Liddy's way of quashing her fear that Bill had been cheating on her.

As I drove east toward Laurel—the most narrow and winding of the canyons, and the one that connected the San Fernando Valley directly into Hollywood—I thought about Liddy's misery when she discovered Bill had lied to her. Then her unhappiness had been swept away by a tide of euphoria when he'd told her that he'd been taking secret ballroom dancing lessons in preparation for surprising her with a holiday cruise.

I'd wanted to believe Bill's story, and I'm sure my nagging vestige of doubt would have vanished if he continued to be where he told her he would be. But now the question plaguing me was how had Bill's gold anniversary pen wound up in Reggie's handbag on the night she was murdered?

■ ■ ■

After the thrill ride that was twisty-turny Laurel Canyon, I reached Sunset Boulevard and turned right toward La Cienega Boulevard. La Cienega winds south down from Sunset all the way to Culver City, where Metro-Goldwyn-Mayer, once the gold standard of Hollywood studios, used to be located. The land is still there, but now it's the site of an international company called Sony that manufactures movies and all kinds of entertainment hardware and software. Liddy told me that Hollywood used to be called "the dream factory." Now it seemed to be just a *factory*, turning out a lot of movies and television shows that appeared to come off an assembly line.

The first mile or two of La Cienega boasts excellent restaurants and expensive furniture, fabric, and decorators' shops, but once one crosses Wilshire Boulevard the ambiance plunges on the economic scale down into a parade of motels barely more alluring than the one Norman Bates owned in *Psycho*. Few of those I passed had pools, which would have indicated that they catered to families. Most had signs advertising "Cable TV." Some also offered "Free Internet Connection."

I drove slowly past a cluster of them with names like "Paradise Motel," "Motel of the Stars," and "Happy Hours," looking for either Bill's bronze Cadillac or Liddy's ivory Land Rover. There would be no mistaking either car because of their personalized license plates: Bill's was "SAY AHH" and Liddy's proclaimed her "TWINS MA."

The long stretch of motels had nearly ended, and I was about to start criss-crossing side streets, when I spotted what I was looking for. I hit my brakes just in time to turn into the driveway of the "Magic Hour" motel, a collection of one-story pale gray stucco cabins. Parked in front of a door at the far end were both of the Marshalls' cars.

I pulled in next to Liddy's Rover, turned off the motor, and realized that my hands were shaking and my heart was beating fast. To calm myself, I started reciting the names of as many state capitals as I could remember. By the time I'd come up with twenty-three, my heart rate had come down to normal. I unhooked Tuffy and let him hop down onto the pavement. With my curly black friend at my side on his leash, I went to the motel room door and strained to listen.

I heard music coming from a TV set, and recognized the theme from a daytime talk show. Leaning in closer, I could hear a woman giggling. It sounded like Liddy. Without knowing for sure what I was going to say—that would depend on what I saw inside—I knocked on the motel room door.

17

The giggling stopped and the TV show was turned off. A voice I recognized as Bill Marshall's called, "Yes? Who's there?"

"It's Della."

"Della?" Liddy's voice, full of astonishment.

"Please let me in."

"Just a sec," she said. I heard rustling, then what sounded like bare feet coming toward the door. It opened a crack—just enough for me see the surprise on Liddy's face but nothing in the room beyond. "Della! What are you doing here?"

"I have to talk to Bill."

"Now?"

"It's important or I wouldn't have come. I'm sorry, Liddy." She had no idea how sorry I was.

"Okay, if you really must." Liddy scooted around behind the door as she opened it for me. Inside, I saw the reason: Her shoulders were bare, but the rest of her was wrapped in the garish orange and green print bedspread she was clutching around her.

Across the room, on the far side of the rumpled and spread-less bed, Bill buckled the belt on his pants. He stood bare-chested; his shirt, jacket, and tie, as well as Liddy's clothes, were draped across the one chair. The room was furnished minimally, with just a king-size bed, a TV set on a stand, that chair, and a small, round table next to the bed. The surface of the table was covered with the remains of a KFC meal, crumpled paper napkins, and coffee containers.

Bill stared at me with a hybrid expression I'd never seen on his face before: part curiosity, part abject fear.

Liddy's husband was lanky and clean-cut, with light brown hair, eyes the color of maple syrup, and a prominent nose that curved slightly to the right. Examined individually, his features didn't seem to belong on the same face, but the overall effect was attractive. Liddy called him, lovingly, her "irregular weave."

Bill had always reminded me of a big, affectionate mixed-breed dog that was so adorable you couldn't help wanting to adopt it. It pretty much described his personality, too, if the big dog told jokes that would make even a confirmed grump laugh. But he wasn't making jokes now.

"Della, why are you here? Bill and I are having a little *adventure*."

"I'm sorry to interrupt."

"How in the world did you find us?" Liddy asked.

"Well, I remembered—"

Liddy didn't wait for my answer. "Guess who Bill signed in as?" She giggled. *"George Bush!"* Liddy knelt down to pet Tuffy. "I stayed in my car, so I didn't get to see the expression on the clerk's face, but Bill said it was a hoot."

I was looking at Bill's face. He'd scrunched his eyes closed and bowed his head, as though he was expecting to be struck. Unwilling to land that blow, I turned to Liddy.

"It's one of my teeth, in the back," I said, clapping my left hand to my left cheek. "It's hurting something awful. Bill, can you help me? I wouldn't have disturbed you if I weren't desperate."

Bill's eyes snapped opened. He looked as relieved as a condemned man who was about to get that final needle but who'd just been told the governor phoned with a reprieve for him.

"Sure! Absolutely!" Bill trotted around the bed and grabbed his shirt. "We'll go to my office and I'll fix you right up."

"Oh, Del, I'm so sorry you're in pain," Liddy said. "I'll come to keep you company. Just give me a minute to get dressed."

Bill opened his mouth to say something, but before he could, we heard sharp knocking on the motel room door.

We three human beings froze in shock, but I glanced down at Tuffy and saw that he was staring at the door with his tail wagging vigorously. I realized he knew whoever was on the other side.

More knocking. Harder this time.

"I should have rented a bigger room," Bill said.

Liddy laughed, but almost immediately the sound trailed off as she glanced from Bill to me and saw that neither of us were even smiling. For all of her softness, Liddy was a smart woman. "What's going on?"

"Open the door, Della. I know you're in there," John O'Hara said.

Liddy recognized his voice. "*John?* What's he doing here?" She looked at me. "Did something happen between you two?"

"No." I was as puzzled as Liddy.

Bill took a deep breath. "I don't think this has anything to do with Della." Without meeting Liddy's eyes, he strode to the door and opened it. I was glad to see that John was alone, without noxious Detective Weaver.

I must have been holding Tuffy loosely, because he yanked the leash out of my hand and bounded across the room to greet his old friend, John.

John leaned over to give Tuffy a few affectionate strokes. When he straightened again he saw Liddy wrapped in the bedspread and quickly looked away from her.

Bill asked John, "How did you find me?"

John closed the door and nodded in my direction. "I tailed Della."

I felt my face flush with anger. "That was a terrible thing to do!"

"Don't get on your high horse with me," he said curtly. "I knew you were lying when you said you didn't know where they were."

"That wasn't a lie. I just remembered something and followed a hunch."

"Hello, everybody!" Liddy reached up high and waved her free hand. "Remember me? Am I invisible? *What* is going on?" Her tone was a demand, not a question.

Bill scooped Liddy's clothes from the chair and handed them to her. "Get dressed and go home, sweetheart. I'll explain everything to you later." She took the clothes but she didn't budge.

As gently as he could phrase it, John told Liddy, "Bill's

right, you should go home. I need to ask him a few questions so
he can help me clear up something about a case I'm working."

"Case?" Comprehension widened Liddy's eyes. "You're
working on the murder of that woman—Regina Davis."

"Yes." John looked profoundly uncomfortable.

"But Bill doesn't know anything about that." She turned to
her husband. "Pussycat, tell John . . ." Her voice trailed off as
she saw the expression of misery on Bill's face. Liddy's sudden look of fear was painful for me to see.

I moved over to stand beside her and touched her arm, but
she pulled away.

"Bill? Why is John here?"

Staring fixedly at an ugly brown spot on the carpet, Bill
said, "I knew her. Reggie Davis."

My chest tightened. *He called her Reggie, like someone
who knew her well, not Regina, the way a mere acquaintance
would.*

Liddy's attention was riveted on her husband. "But you
didn't say anything when I told you about Del being in her
contest. You acted as though you'd never heard her name."

John cleared his throat and said firmly, "We shouldn't have
this discussion here."

Liddy glared at Bill, at John, and at me. Her voice tight
with anger, she said, "My husband. My friends. You don't
have a toothache, do you Del?"

"No," I admitted.

"Apparently, I'm the only one who doesn't know what's
going on. How long were you three planning to keep me in the
dark?"

Bill reached for Liddy's hand, but didn't look at her as he
said to John, "Can we make a deal? If I don't have to go to
your station house, I'll tell you everything I know about Reggie Davis without 'lawyering up,' as they say in the TV cop
shows. Honestly, I want to help you, but you've got to keep my
name out of the news so our boys don't hear about this."

"If I find out you're involved in her death—"

"I'm not! I swear it! But if I go to your cop shop the fact
that you're questioning me will get out. Police departments
aren't exactly leakproof."

"I can't guarantee your name might not become public at some point," John said, "but it won't come from either Detective Weaver or myself." He frowned in thought for a moment, then relaxed one centimeter and said, "At least there won't be any reporters or news vans at your place."

John used his cell phone to call Hugh Weaver and relay Bill's proposal. I didn't hear Weaver's end of their brief exchange, but he must have protested at first because John said in a firm tone, "I think we'll get more out of him this way." Apparently Weaver capitulated, because John gave his partner the Marshalls' address and ended the conversation.

While John was on the phone, Liddy, dressed now, emerged from the bathroom, and marched in between John and Bill. She was my height, which meant the top of her head came up to John's jutting chin. Liddy squared her shoulders, turned her back on John, and faced her husband. "Did you kill that Reggie woman?"

"No." Bill practically shouted the word, then dialed the volume down a notch. "No. I didn't."

"Okay," she said. "I believe you."

But Bill looked so miserable it wasn't hard to guess that he felt guilty about *something*. If I could see that, I knew Liddy could, too, but she kept her face a frozen mask.

John moved a few steps away from Liddy and Bill and shot a glare at me. "Do I have your word you won't tell D'Martino that we're talking to Bill?"

The implication that I would betray my friends made me so mad I would have liked to smack John, but I reminded myself that I'm a lover, not a slugger. In a frosty voice, I replied, "Of course I won't say anything—and you can save that intimidating scowl for one of your *perps*. It doesn't work on me."

"Besides, she's not seeing him anymore," Liddy said.

I could have done without her help, but she was speaking to me—or at least speaking *about* me. That was a start.

Liddy told John, "I want to be there while you question Bill."

Before I could stop myself, I said, "So do I."

John let out a growl of exasperation. I was sure he was about to refuse, but Bill stopped him.

"Please, I want Liddy there," Bill said. "In fact, I insist. She should hear what I have to tell you. Della, too. She's part of this thing I got myself into."

John didn't like that; I could tell by the little muscle beneath his right eye that had started twitching. Eileen called it his "time bomb tick."

While John didn't say he would allow Liddy and me to be present during Bill's interrogation, his silence was de facto agreement. He yanked open the motel room door and, with a jerk of his thumb, motioned the three of us outside.

"I'll follow you, Bill," John said. He made no reference to either Liddy or me.

Liddy's face was pale and taut, but as Bill started toward his car she took my hand and gave it a friendly squeeze. Now that we were both in the doghouse with Big John O'Hara, it seemed as though I was back in Liddy's good graces.

18

Leaving the Magic Hour motel, we were a four-car convoy headed toward the Marshalls' home in Beverly Hills. Bill's new Cadillac was at the head of our parade, with John's aging black Lincoln so close behind he could have been cited for tailgating. Liddy followed John, and I trailed the three of them like the tail on a kite. I had expected John to insist on taking Bill to the West Bureau's West Los Angeles Community Police Station on Butler Avenue for questioning. Silently, I blessed him for granting Bill's request to tell his story in privacy.

In spite of the increasingly heavy traffic—many citizens of Los Angeles leave work between three and four in the afternoon—we managed to maintain our convoy without any other car getting in between. It helped that we caught only green lights. I hoped that was a good omen.

Liddy and Bill Marshall lived in the seven hundred block of Maple Drive, one of the prettiest streets in Beverly Hills, due to the lush rows of mature maple trees that gave the drive its name. The Marshall home was a two-story white colonial that had been built in the 1960s, when houses were still being set back far enough from the sidewalk to allow for a graceful sweep of soft green lawn. Many of the new and lavish "McMansions" utilized almost every inch of their lots, leaving just enough space between structure and property line for a gardener or pool man to squeeze through to the backyard.

Maple Drive was spotted with parked vehicles of the type used by gardeners and pool men, but it was virtually empty of moving passenger cars when we crossed Santa Monica Boulevard into what is known as "the flats" of Beverly Hills, an area marked by well-kept streets and expensive homes.

Because the seven hundred block of Maple was so clear of traffic, when our little procession slowed half a block short of our destination I saw that a brown Crown Victoria was parked in Liddy and Bill's driveway with its rear to the two-car garage and its nose facing the street. Leaning against the driver's door and smoking a cigarette was Detective Hugh Weaver.

As soon as he spotted us, Weaver crushed out his cigarette on the Marshalls' recently resurfaced driveway—I was sure that sight made Liddy flinch—and stepped away from his car. When he did, I noticed that the paint on the driver's door didn't quite match the front and rear fenders on that side, as though that door had been mashed in at some point.

The sudden mental image of someone ramming a police vehicle took me back to the days when I worried about bad guys trying to hurt Mack. It reduced, by a little, my antipathy to Weaver. Maybe his hostility was a result of the risks cops took every day, when even a traffic stop might mean their death. Different men had different styles of coping. Weaver used sarcasm. John turned inward.

Bill glided to a stop on the street. John, Liddy, and I parked in a line behind him and climbed out of our cars. As soon as I let Tuffy out of his safety harness, he hopped out onto the grassy strip along the sidewalk.

John introduced Bill and Liddy to Weaver. Weaver responded with a nod and a grunt. "You know Della," John said.

"Yeah." He lifted one eyebrow and cocked his head in a silent question that I took to mean, "What is she doing here?"

John must have read it the same way. "She's sitting in, at Dr. Marshall's request."

"Where do you two want to question Bill? We don't have a dungeon." Liddy tried to make that sound like a joke, but I heard the sarcastic edge in her voice.

Weaver must have heard it, too. His lips drew back into the beginning of a snarl.

Before he could say anything I jumped in. "There's a breakfast table and chairs in the kitchen. We'll make a pot of coffee for you. And food." I aimed a smile at Weaver. "I bet you haven't had time for lunch, have you, Detective?"

"Actually . . . no." I sensed just a millimeter's worth of softening in his demeanor. That was a start.

"I haven't eaten either," said John.

Liddy unlocked the front door. "The housekeeper's off today. We'll have privacy," she said.

■ ■ ■

Liddy was too nervous to be of any help preparing food, but I didn't need it. She kept a well-stocked pantry, and I knew where everything was. It didn't take long to find a fresh loaf of dark pumpernickel bread and condiments. Liddy's fridge yielded three kinds of cheeses, some leftover roast chicken, baked ham, lettuce, tomatoes, and a bowl of grapes—all the ingredients for an instant feast.

Bill and the detectives took chairs at the table. Liddy withdrew a Milk-Bone from the special canine cookie jar she kept filled for Tuffy's visits. She gave it to him, and sat next to Bill. They clutched each other's hands.

With the Milk-Bone in his mouth, Tuffy settled down next to John's chair and began to gnaw at it.

While the coffee was perking, I sliced three tomatoes, cut a ripe avocado that I found on the counter—without slicing my hand again—and mashed that with half a cup of mayo and a tablespoon of Dijon mustard. I slathered the bread with the spread I'd mixed, and built a variety of hearty, man-friendly sandwiches, as opposed to the more delicate, crust-off triangles I'd create for an afternoon tea.

My kitchen activity took about three minutes, during which time John and Weaver were consulting their notes and Liddy and Bill clung to each other. The only sounds in the room came from my movements, the bubbling of the coffee, and Tuffy's teeth crunching his treat.

Even though Liddy and Bill had said they weren't hungry, I put plates down in front of everyone, but set the platter of sandwiches closer to Weaver and John. I placed a bottle of crushed red pepper flakes next to John, because I knew he liked to sprinkle them on everything except desserts.

Acting as though he hadn't eaten for two days, Weaver quickly devoured two ham and cheese sandwiches, a chicken sandwich, and two mugs of hot coffee. For a moment it looked as though he was going to burp, but the urge passed.

Weaver wiped his mouth with one of the paper napkins I'd set out, squinted at Bill, and said, "So, Dr. Marshall, how long were you and Regina Davis lovers?"

Liddy gasped and suddenly looked sick.

"That's unnecessarily harsh," I said.

Without looking at her, Weaver nodded toward Liddy. "She wanted to be here."

John put down his second chicken sandwich. "Let's not get ahead of ourselves," he said. "Bill, tell us about your relationship with the dead woman. Start from the beginning, and don't leave anything out."

19

Bill took a deep breath. "I met her—Reggie Davis—in my building. She's a patient of Joe Collins." For John's and Weaver's benefit, he added, "Joe's the periodontist whose office is two doors down from mine."

Weaver said, "Skip the geography. Get to the nitty-gritty."

His manner was so unpleasant I was sorry I'd made the sandwiches he'd devoured. I clasped my hands together under the tabletop to keep from saying anything that might get me ejected from the interrogation.

John said, "When was it that you met her, Bill?"

"About three weeks ago. I was coming out of my office to grab some lunch at the café downstairs when we collided. I guess she didn't see where she was going because she was looking in her purse. When she bumped into me, she dropped it and her stuff went all over the floor." He aimed a nervous smile at Liddy. "Do you women actually use all the things you carry around?"

John held up a hand. "Let's stay focused. First, you said you two collided, then you said she bumped into you. Which was it?"

Bill squeezed his eyes shut. "I'm trying to remember . . . Yes. She bumped into me. Does it matter?"

Instead of answering Bill's question, John said, "What happened then?"

"She apologized, thanked me for helping her pick up the stuff, and said she hoped she wasn't making me late for an appointment. I told her I was just going downstairs to the café off the lobby for lunch. She said that she was, too, and—"

"And offered to treat you to lunch for helping her," Liddy said.

Bill looked at her in surprise. "How did you know?"

Liddy expelled a sharp breath in exasperation. "For a smart man, you can be such an *idiot*."

"Bill," I said, "she was trying to pick you up."

"She succeeded," Weaver said.

Bill looked at Liddy. "*Now* I know I shouldn't have had lunch with her, but then it just seemed like having pleasant conversation for half an hour. A break from my work."

"You had the hots for her," Weaver said.

Bill's cheeks flushed red.

"Tell us the rest," John said. "Liddy and Del—don't interrupt."

I wanted to give John O'Hara of the LAPD a good swift kick for treating us like a pair of naughty six-year-olds, but he was sitting on my target area.

Bill lowered his eyes to stare at the surface of the table. "I admit I was a stupid jerk. In two months I'm going to be fifty years old, and it was bothering me—the realization that there's more of my life behind me than ahead . . . You can understand, John, Detective Weaver."

"Leave me out of this," Weaver said. "My life is a daily delight."

No one hearing his sarcastic tone and seeing the darkness in his eyes could have believed that, but neither Bill nor Liddy paid attention to him.

Bill said, "This woman I just met in the hall made me laugh. For a little while I felt . . ."

Weaver prodded him. "You felt horny."

John shot a frown at Weaver. "Go on, Bill."

I could tell from the anguish in his eyes that *going on* was the last thing Bill wanted to do, but he kept his bargain with John.

"When we finished eating, she said she had one more appointment with Joe Collins, the next day, so why didn't we have lunch one more time? We did. Then she suggested we have dinner," Bill said.

Liddy groaned, but clamped her lips together to keep from speaking.

"Get to the sex part," Weaver said.

Bill stiffened his shoulders and pounded a fist on the table so hard the plates jumped. "No sex! We didn't have sex. I swear."

John said, "What did you have?"

"Dinner. Tuesday night, a week ago."

When he'd told Liddy he was going to his card game.

"In twenty years of marriage, I never cheated. But . . ."

"You thought about it."

"Not exactly. I like to look at women. I like women, as people."

Weaver guffawed.

"I do," Bill said. "Reggie Davis was very witty. We laughed all through dinner. After, she invited me to her house for a drink. I didn't go."

I was relieved Bill hadn't gone to her house, but there was such a guilty expression on his face that it shocked me.

John said, "What *did* you do?"

"I agreed to see her again. The following Tuesday night."

"The night she was murdered." Weaver's voice was triumphant.

John said, "Bill, tell us about that night. What did you do?"

"I didn't do anything," Bill said. "Not really. I mean we met at the restaurant she picked, something Italian, I think, on Melrose near Doheny, but I can't remember the name. I was feeling like such a louse about . . . seeing Reggie, lying to Liddy. My head ached, my ears were ringing, and my guts were tied up in knots."

"Poor baby," Weaver said.

Bill ignored his sarcasm. "Reggie got there first and ordered a bottle of my favorite wine—"

Liddy's eye's blazed. "How did she know your favorite wine?"

John said, "Liddy. Not now."

"It just came up in conversation," Bill told Liddy. "I was surprised she'd remembered. Anyway, I couldn't swallow more than a sip. I told her that I thought she was a terrific person, really great, but I loved my wife, so I couldn't stay for dinner, and I wasn't going to see her again."

"After you told her that, what did you do?"

"Put down some money for the waiter and left the restaurant. I was feeling like a lousy piece of crap, so I drove around for awhile."

"How long?"

"Maybe a couple of hours. I'm not sure. But while I was driving I was thinking of what I could do for Liddy to try to make up for lying to her. That's when I got the idea of signing up for ballroom dance lessons."

Weaver rolled his eyes and said to John, "Do you believe this *dreck*?"

"I'm telling the truth," Bill said. "I stopped at a 7-Eleven and looked in a phone book for places that teach dancing. I found one in West Hollywood and went over there and enrolled."

"At night?" Weaver's voice dripped with sarcasm.

"It's Hollywood," Bill said. "Some dance studios are open twenty-four seven."

"Give us the name of the studio," John said.

"Ballroom Boot Camp."

Weaver's slitted eyes popped open. "*Boot Camp?* Cripes! I was in the army before I joined the cops an' we didn't do no *dancing* in boot camp."

"Well, I can't help what the place calls itself," Bill said.

John used his most calming tone. "Let's back up a little. When you told Regina Davis that you weren't going to see her again, what was her reaction?"

Bill grimaced. "Furious. She made some threats."

"What kind of threats?" John said.

"To tell Liddy. To ruin my life."

"Good Lord, Bill," John said.

"I know this must look bad—"

"It sounds like a motive for murder to me," Weaver said.

"But why would I volunteer all this to you if I was guilty?"

"Like your wife said, smart men can do stupid things." Weaver rose and unhooked the handcuffs from the back of his belt.

Liddy gasped and pressed her knuckles against her mouth.

Weaver said, "Doctor Marshall, you have the right to re-main silent. You have the right to an attorney—"

"Lid, call our lawyer," Bill said.

She threw her arms around me and burst into tears.

20

As we watched Weaver steer Bill into the backseat of the Crown Victoria, Liddy squeezed my arm. Tears streamed down her face. "Oh, dear God . . ."

"It's going to be all right, Liddy," I said.

"How? Bill's been arrested!" She let go of me and pressed both hands against her mouth as though choking back a scream.

I saw sympathy in John's eyes, but he kept his tone professional. He told Liddy, "You have a family lawyer, don't you?"

Liddy nodded. "Ted Duncan."

"Call him. Ask him to get hold of a good criminal lawyer and have them meet Bill at the West Bureau station on Butler Avenue. Della knows where it is."

John hurried to his car to follow Weaver and Bill.

Her whole body trembling, Liddy stared after them.

I put an arm around her shoulders, and turned her back toward the open front door. "Call a lawyer." Inside, I picked up the pad and pen beside the telephone on a living room end table. "Here," I said. "This is the address of the West Bureau station. Whatever you have to say or do, get a lawyer over there. Are you going to be able to drive yourself?"

"Won't you come with me?"

I shook my head. "I've got to go home to find Mack's telephone book. He had a friend who's a bail bondsman. I'm going to contact him, to get him ready to help in case he's needed."

∎ ∎ ∎

Fifteen minutes later I turned north from Montana Avenue onto my street. A few yards from home I saw that another shock awaited me: NDM's silver Masarati was parked at the edge of the driveway. He was standing in front of it, dialing a number into his cell phone, but as soon as he saw me pull to a stop he disconnected and hurried over to my Jeep.

"I've been trying to find you," he said. "Why didn't you answer your phone?"

"It didn't ring." I pulled the little instrument out of my jacket pocket and realized what happened. "The battery died. Why were you calling me?"

NDM propped his arms on the edge of my driver's side window. "Your friend Liddy's husband has just been arrested."

I felt my jaw drop open. "It just happened! How did you find out?"

"A source. So you know."

"I was there," I said. "Who is your *source*—"

"Don't ask. You know I can't say." He reached through the window and put one of his hands over mine that was clutching the steering wheel. "This has got to be hard. Are you all right?"

I found it hard to speak at that moment, so I just nodded.

"How's Liddy? Is there anything I can do for her?"

"Don't put Bill's name in the paper. Please."

He was silent for a long moment. "I think I'm the only one who knows it right now. I'll keep it to myself for as long as I can."

"Thank you." I opened the door and took the hand he offered to help me out, then I turned to release Tuffy from his safety harness and let him out. "I'd invite you in for coffee, but I'm not going to be here very long."

NDM reached down to scratch Tuffy below the ears. "Hi, big guy."

Tuffy acknowledged NDM with a quick nuzzle, then strained against his leash in a way that communicated a need to relieve himself.

"I appreciate your being willing to protect Bill for now. Come with me while I take Tuff for a short walk and I'll tell you what happened—*if* you promise that it's off the record."

NDM held up his right hand in a swearing gesture. "Off

the record. Unless it's information I get from a separate source and another reporter is about to break the story. But if and when I have to write the story, I'll be as fair as possible to your friends."

"All right," I said.

While we walked Tuffy around the block, I began by telling NDM that John had come to the studio to show me photos of a gold pen and ask if I knew to whom it belonged. "I recognized it immediately. Liddy bought it as an anniversary present for Bill. I was with her when she had it engraved. John didn't tell me until after I'd identified it that he'd found the pen in Regina Davis's handbag."

NDM said, "I knew that O'Hara's partner, Weaver, was trying to trace the ownership of a gold pen with special engraving, because the police thought it might be evidence. I was paying special attention because I knew what case Weaver was working."

"John said he needed to talk to Bill, but couldn't find him. He asked if I knew where he had gone. I told John the truth when I said I didn't know. What I didn't say was that I had an idea. Anyway, I found them—Bill and Liddy."

"Where were they?"

"That has no relevance to the case," I said. Bill's and Liddy's romantic trip to the motel was no one's business but theirs. "It doesn't matter where they were. The point is that I inadvertently led John to them because he was following me."

"O'Hara knows you pretty well."

I heard the edge in NDM's voice, but ignored it. "Bill agreed to answer all of John's questions, but he wanted to do it in his own home, instead of at West Bureau because he doesn't want his name in the papers. Bill and Liddy have twin sons who are freshmen at college in the east. He doesn't want them to know about this, at least not through the media."

"If Marshall didn't kill the Davis woman—"

"He did *not*!"

"Then the cops better find out who did damn quick. Once they've taken someone into custody, they pretty much stop looking elsewhere."

"If they won't keep looking for the killer, then I will."

"You don't have to do it alone," NDM said.

I stopped and looked at him. "You're going to help me?"

His lips curled in that wicked smile that had sent little electric jolts of desire through my body when we were seeing each other. "I prefer to think of it as you helping *me*."

"You're willing for us to work together because you want the story," I said.

"That's half of the reason."

Before I realized what was happening, NDM pulled me tight against his chest and kissed me. With my arms pinned against my sides, I couldn't resist. In another moment, I didn't want to. My lips parted . . . and it wasn't NDM kissing me, it was two former lovers melting together in mutual desire.

We were spotted by of a car full of teenagers driving by. They began to whoop and slap the sides of their vehicle. Embarrassed, partly at being seen, and partly because I was angry at myself for responding to him, I yanked myself out of his grip.

"To be continued," he said.

"Not on this planet," I said.

"Want to make a bet?"

"Save your money to spend on your age-inappropriate blondes."

"Ouch. Okay, point made, even though it was a little sharper than necessary. What's our next step?"

■　■　■

Back in my house, NDM perched on the kitchen stool while I fed Tuffy and Emma and filled their bowls with fresh water. When I'd taken care of the pets, I took Mack's small brown leather personal phone book out of the napkin drawer where I kept it and reached for the wall phone and dialed.

"Who are you calling?"

"Somebody I hope can help Bill," I said.

After two rings on the other end, I heard a brusque voice. "Book 'em and Bond 'em. This is Mazzone."

"I'm Della Carmichael. You knew my husband, Detective Mack Carmichael."

"Yeah. Good guy. I was sorry to hear what happened. So, you in trouble?"

"A friend of mine is. I think he might need your services."

"Name?"

"William Marshall. He's been taken in for questioning about the Regina Davis murder."

"What does Marshall do for a living?"

"He's a dentist, in Beverly Hills. Is that important?"

"If he's charged and I decide to go on the hook for bail it is. Give me details of his situation in person. You know where I am?"

"I have the card you gave Mack four years ago. Are you still at the same address?"

"Mazzone Bail Bonds and the building's pigeons—the city'll need flame throwers to get rid of us."

21

Hanging up the phone, I told NDM where I was going.

"How do you know Frank Mazzone? As far as I know, you've never been arrested." NDM aimed his one-eyebrow-lifted quizzical expression at me.

I used every ounce of my self-control not to let it excite me as once it had.

I said, "My husband helped him out a few years ago. On the back of his card, he wrote an IOU for a return favor."

"Let me drive. I'm in that nest of one-way streets every day so I probably know downtown Los Angeles better than you do."

"All right," I said. "Most of the times when I've been in that section of town it was to go to concerts at the Music Center with Liddy and Bill, and then Bill was the one who drove."

"See how useful I am?"

"At times," I said. "But you're coming strictly as a friend, not as a reporter."

"Agreed."

"Then we have a deal," I said.

"Friends again?"

"At least for the duration of this trip."

I strapped myself into the copilot's seat of NDM's "silver rocket" and we zoomed away.

Four freeway mergers and seventeen minutes later, we left US 101 at the Broadway exit and made a left on Temple Street in downtown Los Angeles. No longer flying over the freeways, we had to ease into heavy traffic.

"Frank's place is on First, a block down from the back entrance to the Criminal Courts Building." He gestured to our right. "It's that tall, slablike structure. The front entrance is on West Temple."

"After it was renamed Clara Shortridge Foltz Criminal Justice Center, I never heard anyone use that mouthful. When John and Mack worked together, it was still the CCB."

"At the paper, we call having to cover a story there 'going to Clara's.' "

"Seven years ago I was summoned there for jury duty. I would have been glad to serve, but no defense attorney wanted me the moment I said I was married to a police detective. They never called me again."

"You'd have been a prosecutor's dream and a defense nightmare."

"That's an unfair stereotype. I would have been objective, giving my opinion on the evidence alone."

"Maybe," he said, "but in your heart you'd have been pro police."

I couldn't deny that, even though I knew there were a few "bad guy" police among the thousands of decent men and women who put their lives on the line for a not-always-grateful public.

As we inched our way along First Street, I saw by the building numbers that we were getting close to our destination.

"There's a parking lot on the corner."

"Lots are for wimps," NDM said. "I'll find a place."

"Street parking down here is a fantasy. The joke is that grandfathers spin tales to their children's children about the day they found an open space."

"Aha!" Up ahead, we spotted a black Cadillac pulling away from a meter. NDM zipped the Masarati into the rectangle scant inches behind the departing vehicle.

"Forget the 'luck of the Irish,' " he said. "I've got the luck of the Sicilians. And there's almost an hour left on the meter."

"Miraculous." My tone was wry, but I was amazed that he'd found a space so close to our target.

Mazzone Bail Bonds was on the ground floor of an old five-story building that had, so far, escaped being razed and supplanted by a modern office high-rise or condos. His window facing the street was clean, and the sign was clearly visible, but the glass was latticed with iron security bars.

Through the bars I saw a man with slicked-back hair and a

short, round body balanced on his knees and right elbow. He
was scrubbing hard at a two-foot section of carpeted floor in
front of and just to the left of the desk. It was awkward work
because his right hand was in some kind of a brace.

NDM said, "That's Frank."

Obeying instructions on the brass plate above the outside
bell, NDM rang.

Frank Mazzone glanced at us through the thick glass,
threw a handful of used paper towels into a trash bag, and
struggled to his feet. He moved around to the far side of his
desk and pressed a concealed button. We heard a buzz that unlocked the exterior door.

NDM pushed it open and we were inside a kind of cage
about three feet deep. When the outside door closed behind us,
and the heavy glass door directly in front of us clicked, NDM
pushed that one open.

Inside at last, my first sensation was that the sealed office behind the double doors reeked of alcohol and—much worse—
the contents of someone's stomach. I must have flinched at the
odor, because Mazzone took an aerosol can from a bottom
drawer and began to spray around the area he'd been cleaning.

"It'll smell better in a couple minutes," he said. "I just told
a prospective client that I don't go bail for drunk drivers. As a
parting gift, he threw up."

Replacing the can, Mazzone gestured with his braced right
hand. "Sorry, can't shake. Are you Mrs. Carmichael?"

"Yes. I'm sorry about your hand. What happened?"

"Broke my trigger finger. Excuse the expression. Trigger
finger—it's a medical term." He flashed a cheerful grin at
NDM. "Hey, D'Martino—what kind of a society have we got
that's letting you run around loose?"

"A democracy."

"Yeah, well, no system is perfect." Mazzone tied up the
trash bag tightly, tossed it against the wall behind his desk,
and gestured toward the two matching wooden chairs that
faced it. Other than his leather wing chair, they were the only
places to sit in this sparsely furnished office. The one decora-
tive touch in the room was a large mural of vintage Wanted
Posters that covered the rear wall.

Frank Mazzone took his seat and we took ours. "So, what's the story on your dentist friend?"

Briefly, I gave him the basic details: that Bill met Regina Davis, had a couple of lunches and a dinner with her, that she tried to get him to have an affair with her but that he resisted.

"I saw her picture in the paper." Mazzone made a clicking noise in the side of his mouth. "He's a stronger man than I would have been."

I let that pass. "When Bill said no to her, she threatened to tell his wife that they'd been having an affair. That's the motive the police are hanging their case on."

Mazzone shook his head. "Pretty weak. Does he have an alibi?"

"He left her at the restaurant early in the evening, drove around thinking about what a jerk he'd been, and then he signed up to take ballroom dancing lessons."

"You're joking."

"I know that may sound ridiculous—"

"*May?* It's the stupidest story I ever heard."

I got up. "If that's going to be your attitude—"

NDM took my arm and guided me back down. "Good people do dumb things sometimes. Della's known Marshall for twenty years and believes he's innocent."

"Yeah, well, guilty or innocent isn't my call. I care about whether he'd be a flight risk if he's charged and I bail him out."

"I know Bill wouldn't run," I said.

Mazzone tapped the side of the computer monitor on his desk. "My silent partner, 'Mr. Google,' agrees with you. I checked the guy out. Pretty solid. Big house in the hills of Beverly, wife a former actress, two sons who've stayed out of trouble, big bucks dental practice, some movie star clients, no scandals, nobody's sued him. You want to know where he went to summer camp, who he took to his senior prom, and what he buys on credit cards?"

"You found out all that?"

NDM said, "There are no secrets anymore—just information nobody's looked for yet."

Frank Mazzone took a card from the top drawer of his desk, turned it over, and scribbled something. "This is my cell number. Give it to your friend and have him or his lawyer call me if he's charged."

I was about to leave when Mazzone said, "If I put up bail, he better not start looking up airfares to Brazil. I'm not as nice a guy as I seem."

Outside in the car, NDM said, "Where to?"

I took the cell phone out of my jacket pocket. "I won't know until I call Liddy." I punched in her cell number.

Answering on the second ring, she said in a whisper, "Del?"

"What's happening?"

"Bill's in a room with our lawyer, and the criminal attorney he brought with him. John was here a moment ago and told me an assistant district attorney is on his way. What does that mean?"

"He or she will decide if they have enough evidence to make a formal charge against Bill. From what I heard at your house, I don't think they do."

"I'm praying you're right."

"But just in case, I've got the bail bondsman I told you about ready to help. Have one of the lawyers call Frank Mazzone." I gave her his phone number and heard her fumble for a paper and pen to write it down.

"Got it," she said. "But if it gets so far—a charge and court appearance—what if the judge refuses to allow bail?"

"Don't think about that now. Let's go a step at a time, okay? . . . Liddy?"

"Sorry. John says the district attorney person's here." I heard a catch in her voice.

"Stay calm, Liddy. Take a few deep breaths. Do you want me to come to the station and stay with you?"

"No. I'm all right. Really. But where will you be?"

"I'll go home. Call me as soon as you know something." We said good-bye.

NDM looked at his watch. "It's after seven. Let me buy you dinner."

"No, thanks. I've got to go home to make food for the live TV show tomorrow night. But what if I fix dinner for the two of us?"

"Sounds good. Your kitchen's the best restaurant in town."
NDM started the engine and we were on our way back toward
the 101 freeway.

■ ■ ■

Back at home, Tuffy greeted us with vigorous tail wagging.
Emma sailed up onto the hall table and sat down on a piece of
notepaper. I eased it out from under her and saw that it was
from Eileen. Reading it, I said, "Eileen walked Tuffy and now
she's gone to see an artist friend who's helping her with package designs for the fudge meeting."

I started toward the kitchen, with NDM and the pets following.

NDM said, "What kind of meeting?"

"Eileen's a business major at UCLA. She came up with the
inspiration that I should be in the mail-order fudge business
and she talked Mickey Jordan into backing it."

"It's a good idea," NDM said. "You're building name
recognition, and you're better looking than that man who got
rich making chocolate chip cookies."

In the kitchen Tuffy settled onto his thick pad beside the
refrigerator, and Emma soared up into the box I'd fitted with
soft towels for her on the ledge beneath the window.

Before I had a chance to figure out what to make for dinner,
the phone rang.

"I hope that's Liddy," I said.

It was. Her voice was breathy with excitement. "They're
letting Bill go home!"

I nodded at NDM, mouthed *Liddy*, and said into the receiver, "They're letting him go—that's wonderful. What happened?"

"I didn't hear the conversation, but our family attorney said
the criminal lawyer he works with convinced the prosecutor—
a woman—that she needed a stronger case against Bill or he'd
humiliate her in front of a judge."

"That's encouraging," I said, making my voice bright. I
didn't want to deplete Liddy's happiness, but I knew that the
police didn't like having a suspect released. They'd keep in-

vestigating. John would look for other suspects, but I was sure that Hugh Weaver would concentrate on Bill.

Liddy said hurriedly, "We're going home now. I'll call you tomorrow." She hung up.

Replacing the receiver, I said, "They're letting Bill go."

"You must be relieved."

"For the moment, but we both know he'll be under suspicion until they find the real murderer." I opened the refrigerator door and surveyed the contents. "Let's see what I can make us for dinner before I have to cook for the show tomorrow."

NDM leaned against the sink. "Don't you have an assistant to do that for you?"

"Mickey offered, but it wouldn't be honest. I'm on camera and say that I'm making the dishes, so I've got to make them all."

"Truth in advertising," NDM said.

"Don't mock it."

"I didn't mean to. I guess I'm jealous because in my profession I don't get a lot of people telling me the truth. It's refreshing."

His lips curled up in a wry smile. It made my pulse rate jump. Much to my embarrassment, that smile sent a surge of longing through my body.

He took a step toward me. "Are you blushing?"

"Absolutely not," I lied. "It's the kitchen . . . heat."

NDM advanced another step. "You're standing in front of an open refrigerator."

On erotic autopilot, I moved toward him. Before I could form a thought we were in each other's arms. As we kissed, NDM reached past my head and closed the refrigerator door. He whispered, "I've missed you."

I'd missed him, too. Every muscle in my body was responding to the pressure of his mouth and the touch of his hands.

22

In the privacy of my bedroom we made love. Too hungry for each other to waste time in foreplay, release for both of us came in moments.

NDM was embarrassed at the speed. "Sorry about that. Give me a few minutes and I'll make it up to you."

"I know you will," I said.

We held each other, the length of our bodies pressed together. As we lay in that postcoital glow, our breathing synchronized. Soon, I felt a slight stirring against my thighs. Our lips met. Dreamily, we kissed and caressed, and NDM more than made up for his first quick explosion.

∎ ∎ ∎

I awoke a few minutes after midnight, lying next to NDM, feeling wonderful. I had no idea what was going to happen with the two of us, except that I knew I would not accept being just one of the women in his life. Tonight was either a lustful slip on my part, or a prelude to a monogamous relationship. Only time would answer that question.

While I luxuriated in the warmth of sensual satisfaction, I came fully awake. Real-world problems intruded and I thought about Reggie's murder. Other than random acts of violence, the answer to who killed another person lay somewhere in the tangled skein of human relationships. I could only name a tiny fraction of the people in Reggie's life. John, with or without his partner's help, would make sure the police investigated those closest to Reggie.

But there was something I knew that the police didn't: Reggie had tried to blackmail Iva Jordan. She had gone so far as to have Iva investigated by a private detective. Iva had seen the report, so first thing in the morning, I would call Iva to get the name of that detective. It was a place to start.

Feeling energized, I tried to ease myself out of the circle of NDM's arms without waking him, but when I got out of bed he opened his eyes.

"Where are you going?"

"I still have display food to make for the show tonight. You may remember that you interrupted me last night."

He smiled. "You didn't object."

"Object? I helped you disrupt my schedule."

"Can't you cook in the morning?"

"There are some other things I have to do," I said.

NDM rose on one elbow and looked at the glowing numbers on the bedside clock. "I'd better go. I don't want your neighbors, or young Eileen, to guess what a wild woman you are, luring unsuspecting men into your silky web."

"I'm guessing you haven't been unsuspecting since you were old enough to tell the difference between boys and girls."

"No comment." He swung his legs out of bed and reached for his clothes where he'd dropped them the night before. Tuffy was lying on top of them.

NDM looked at Tuffy, who was awake and looking at him, but not stirring. "I'll either have to leave naked, or move in here," he said.

"Come on, Tuff. The man has to be on his way."

Tuffy got to his feet, remained standing on NDM's clothes for another second or two, and then moved toward me so that NDM could retrieve his things.

A few minutes later, at the front door, NDM said, "You got me here under false pretenses. You promised dinner, then jumped me instead."

"I'm a terrible person, but I agree that I owe you a dinner. Rain check?"

He gave me a tender little kiss on the lips. "I'm a very lucky Sicilian. . . . Call you later."

As soon as NDM left, Tuffy hopped up on the bed and settled down to sleep. Emma, who had been lying on top of the television set, stood, stretched, and made the long leap from there onto the bed. She curled up on my pillow, in the indentation made by my head.

I pulled on a clean sweatshirt and sweatpants from the bureau and went to the kitchen.

Tonight's show featured "comfort foods," two hearty dishes perfect for cold winter nights: my Grandma Nell's Cornish Pasties and Chicken Biscuit Pie, a dish that I'd found in a book called *Famous White House Recipes*.

Both of these were among the foods I'd made over the years for Mack and his police pals, and that I'd taught in some of my one-dish-meals cooking school classes. The mechanics were as familiar to me as scrambling eggs. Here in the after-midnight quiet, while setting out the various ingredients I would need, my mind was free to think about the two calls I was going to make when other people were awake.

■ ■ ■

At nine o'clock, after several hours of sleep, two mugs of coffee, and taking care of Tuffy's and Emma's assorted needs, it was time to make the first call. I flipped through the telephone book until I found the number for Bill's colleague and office neighbor, Joseph Collins, DMD. Having prepared the story I was going to tell whoever answered, I dialed.

"Doctor's office," said a woman's voice on the other end.

"I'm sorry to bother you, but I'm the secretary for Regina Davis and I'm trying to get together a list of any of her outstanding bills so they can be paid. Can you tell me if she owes anything to Dr. Collins?"

"Regina Davis? Is that D-a-v-i-s?"

"Yes." I watched the kitchen wall clock for a full half minute of silence.

"She's not one of our patients," the woman said.

"But I'm sure she had at least two appointments with Doctor Collins, two or three weeks ago? Perhaps she paid through insurance, or by check?"

"There's no one by that name anywhere in our records, but I'll ask Doctor Collins about her. If you'll give me your name and number—"

"Thank you, but I must have made a mistake." I hung up.

Reggie had lied about being a patient of Bill's periodontist neighbor, and therefore had lied about why she was in the hallway when she bumped into Bill. There was no doubt in my mind now that Reggie had set out to lure Bill into an affair. But with all of the attractive men in Los Angeles, why did she target *Bill*?

I sat thinking about that, running my mind back over conversations I'd had with and about Reggie since she'd materialized in my life after twenty-five years. To try to organize and make sense of the bits I knew, I took a marketing list notebook from my kitchen receipt drawer. As though I were creating a new recipe, I started by listing the ingredients—here, information—that I had to work with:

1. Reggie connived to meet Bill Marshall.

2. When I was driving a drunken Reggie home after she'd surprised me by coming to my house, she alluded to a new man in her life, and indicated that he was married. (Bill? It must have been.)

3. Iva said that Reggie had had Iva investigated, and then tried to blackmail her with what the private detective uncovered. (I'll call Iva and hope she can tell me the name of that detective.)

4. When Addison Jordan came to my house after he found out Reggie had been murdered, he told me that several weeks previously, when he was trying to sell Reggie on his TV cake contest idea, she'd asked personal questions about me. Addison didn't have any information about my private life to give her.

5. In addition to Iva, did Reggie have me investigated, too? I'd never thought about it before, but bail bondsman Frank Mazzone had just given me an example of how much personal information one could find out about another if one knew how.

6. If Reggie had had me investigated it wouldn't have been hard to learn that Liddy and Bill Marshall were

my close friends. They'd been mentioned in at least one article written about me since the show began. The channel's publicity man, Phil Logan, was big on human interest stories about the show hosts. In one of them I'd credited my friends Liddy and Bill Marshall and John and Shannon O'Hara with helping me through the awful period after Mack's death.

7. In spite of Reggie's friendly behavior when she came to my house, was it possible that she still hated me enough that she'd try to hurt me by having an affair with Bill in order to ruin the marriage of my friends? That seemed like such a stretch . . . but who knows what Reggie was capable of?

What was it I'd read in one of the Sherlock Holmes stories? Holmes had said something like, "When all other theories have been exhausted, the one that remains, however unlikely, is the solution."

That's a bad paraphrase, but it makes the point.

A glance at the wall clock told me Mickey must have left for his office by now. It would be a good time to call Iva without his hearing the question I had to ask her.

I reached for the phone again.

23

After five rings someone picked up, but dropped the receiver. I heard fumbling and clattering and then Iva mumbled a sleepy "Hello."

"Hi, it's Della. I'm sorry I woke you."

"It's okay. I was about to get up." She yawned, then gasped and lowered her voice to a whisper. "Is everything all right? I mean, nobody's found out about . . . you know what?"

"No, nothing like that but I need to ask you something. Are you alone?"

"Yes. I heard Mickey leave awhile ago. What is it?"

"When you told me Regina Davis had you investigated you said she showed you the report. Do you remember the name of the private detective?"

"I'll never forget it: T. J. Hooker. Oh, no, wait—that was an old TV show. Her detective was T. J. *Taggart*. Taggart. That's it. Why do you want to know?"

"I need to check something out."

"Oh, Della, please don't let Mickey learn . . . you know what."

I assured her that I would never reveal her secret, and said a quick good-bye to get her off the line.

The last of my preparations for the show tonight involved individually wrapping forty Cornish pasties—one for each of the thirty members of the studio audience and the rest for staff and crew that would be there—and securing the Chicken Biscuit Pie under aluminum foil. On an impulse, I picked up an object that had been sent to me as a gift and dropped it into one of the cloth tote bags I used when I went marketing. I decided to try an experiment on the show tonight. The rest of the ingredients I'd need were already in the studio's pantry and refrigerator.

By the time I'd showered and dressed for my visit to Reggie's private detective it was nearly noon, but when I stepped outside I found that the sky was so dark it looked like evening. I viewed the darkness and the heavy air with mixed emotions. We certainly needed the rain after many months of drought, but I hoped it would hold off until after I got home from the show tonight. Well, I couldn't control the rain, but I could try a little of what Liddy called my "personal voodoo" by taking a raincoat and an umbrella—both long unused—from the hall closet before I left the house. My silly theory was that if rain threatened, and I was prepared for it, it wouldn't rain, but if I wasn't properly equipped then the heavens were likely to open up and drench me. Sometimes the voodoo worked.

■ ■ ■

T. J. Taggart, Confidential Investigations was located in a pea soup green two-story building on Westwood Boulevard between Olympic and Pico Boulevards, no more than half a mile from the Davis Foods Test Kitchens. Reggie and her checkbook hadn't had to travel far in order to invade Iva's privacy.

When I got to Taggart's block there were plenty of empty parking spaces. The sky was still dark, but it wasn't raining, so I did a semi-voodoo by draping the raincoat over my arm but leaving the umbrella in my Jeep.

The entrance to the building didn't have a directory of tenants but Taggart's Yellow Pages ad listed his twenty-four-hour phone availability, his street address, and the suite number: 209.

I climbed a narrow, dimly lighted staircase to the second floor and followed the numbers along an L-shaped balcony that looked down onto the tenants' assigned parking spaces. A gray green Buick sedan in need of washing was in the slot marked 209. Presumably, the private eye was in his office.

Suite 209 was at the far end of the line of small businesses, next to a back stairway that led down to the parking area. Taggart's was the only office that had its front window coated with an opaque white substance. That veneer was as effective as a wall in preventing a curious passerby from seeing anyone inside.

The sign on Taggart's door only gave his name—no indication as to what the person in suite 209 did for a living. The door was closed. I knocked.

A man's voice said, "Come in."

In I went.

Taggart's "suite" was a room. A slab of red granite on steel legs served as his desk. On it was a computer with a large monitor, a notebook, a mug full of pens, and a can of diet soda resting on a folded paper towel.

The man behind the desk was one of the hairiest individuals I had ever seen. Thick silver tufts peeked out from the open top button on his shirt. A mass of long, salt-and-pepper curls covered his head, fastened behind his neck in a ponytail. The bushy gray mustache framing his mouth dripped on each side all the way down to his chin. It reminded me of a cartoon character that I'd watched with Eileen when she was in preschool: Yosemite Sam.

He was so distinctive-looking I wondered how he could follow a subject without being noticed. But perhaps he didn't have to. A savvy researcher with Internet access could strip bare a person's life without leaving his chair.

"Sam" stood as I entered. I thought I saw a flicker of recognition in his eyes, but I couldn't be sure.

"Mr. Taggart?"

"Yes."

He extended his hand; the back of it was hairy, too. Walking toward him, I managed to get a mental snapshot of the room: a faded brown corduroy-covered sofa against the north wall. Reading lamp at one end and wooden coffee table in front. A television set on a stand angled to face the sofa. I wondered if Taggart also lived here.

As our hands met in a brief clasp, I was sure about the glint of recognition I'd seen when I entered. In fact, I would have bet my precious KitchenAid mixer that he knew my name.

But he pretended he didn't. "What can I do for you, Ms . . . ?"

"I want to find out about someone."

"Ah." He took a sports jacket from the back of his chair. As he wriggled into it, he indicated with a nod the seat on the visitor's side of his desk.

A quick glance took in the rest of the room. Behind his desk was a door: to a closet, a bathroom, a kitchenette? Or some combination? Next to the door was a metal filing cabinet and a bookcase packed with reference volumes and dozens of telephone directories.

I was intent on fixing Taggart's dreary space in my mind because I remembered the terror in Iva's eyes when she told me that Reggie'd had her investigated. I wanted to diminish this man's ugly power by regarding his surroundings with disdain.

"Who do you want checked out, Ms . . . ?"

"Della Carmichael."

A slight twitch of his shoulders. *"Ahhh."* His intonation was bland, but it was what John and Mack called a suspect's "waiting to see which way the wind was blowing" voice.

"What do you want to find out?"

"Everything," I said.

"Let me tell you what I charge—"

"I don't care," I said.

His shoulders relaxed their stiffness and he flashed a smile at me. "That's good to hear."

"Your fee isn't relevant to me."

Taggart chose a pen and poised it over a fresh page in his notebook. "To do a thorough background check I'll require some information. The subject's name, address, date of birth, Social Security number—"

I feigned a frown of concern. "Do you need all that?"

"Not really. If you can give me the person's license plate number I can run the tag and get the rest."

"All that information's available just through a license plate?"

"For an experienced investigator, it is," he said. "A regular citizen can't get it. Do you happen to know the plate number?"

I recited my Jeep's license plate. He started to write, but stopped after the first three letters and put down the pen.

"I see you recognize it," I said.

He tossed the pen aside and leaned forward with his arms crossed on the desk. "Okay, Ms. Carmichael. What kind of a game do you think you're playing?"

"I guessed that Regina Davis had me investigated and you've just confirmed it. I want a copy of whatever reports you gave her."

"My client's files are not for sale."

"I wasn't planning to pay you," I said. "And Regina Davis is dead so she's not your client anymore. You've already been paid for prying into my life, and the lives of people I know. Please, I want a copy of your reports." In a firm tone, I added, "I'm asking nicely."

Glaring at me, he got up. "No. Get out of here."

I stayed in my seat, meeting his glare without a flinch. "Since you've dug into my life, you must know that my husband was an LAPD detective, and that one of my closest friends is Lt. John O'Hara. What you might not know is that John is one of the two lead investigators on the Regina Davis murder. Within minutes of the time I tell them she hired you to check people out, they'll be in front of a judge getting a warrant to wrench those files loose from you. Heaven only knows what else they might turn up while searching."

T. J. Taggart sat down again. He was trying to act cool, but I'd seen a flash of apprehension in his eyes.

"I haven't done anything illegal," he said. "Every piece of information I gave Ms. Davis was obtained through legitimate research."

"Look, Mr. Taggart, we both know that there isn't any private eye–client privilege. I don't like it one bit that you spied on me, but I'm not interested in making trouble for you. All I want is a copy of the reports you gave to a woman who is dead, and therefore is no longer a client."

He shook his head, hanging tough. "Maybe a judge could make me, but giving up confidential reports to an ordinary citizen wouldn't be good for my business."

Taggart thought he'd pulled an ace out of his sleeve, but I had one more card to play.

I said, "Another close friend of mine is *Los Angeles Chronicle* reporter Nicholas D'Martino. What would it do to your

business if he wrote an article about you turning over your confidential files to the LAPD? How many new clients do you
think a story like that would send rushing up here to hire you?"

He grimaced, went to the file cabinet, and pulled out a
folder labeled "Davis."

My wild card—NDM—had won the hand.

■ ■ ■

Clutching the envelope containing copies of T. J. Taggart's investigative reports, I hurried back down the stairs and climbed
into my Jeep. Too impatient to wait until I got home to see
what was in those papers, I drove to a nearby residential street
and stopped next to a tall hedge that obscured the house behind it. I tore open the manila envelope that Taggart had thrust
into my hands too hard. He was an ungracious loser, but who
could blame him.

There were three detailed reports: one on Mickey Jordan,
one on Iva, and one on me. "Rush" was stamped on mine. The
date Reggie had engaged Taggart was at the top of the first
page: November fifth, the day Addison Jordan had presented
his reality TV idea to her.

As I scanned the material Taggart had dug up on me, I felt
myself going from annoyance to fury. Reggie had learned
where and when I was married, about Mack's fatal heart attack, where I shopped and what I bought, my taping schedule,
what I earned from the show, the name of my doctor, and even
the name of Tuffy's veterinarian. And she'd learned about my
financial troubles. That was my only source of embarrassment.

At least Taggart hadn't found out about the brief time I was
dating NDM. Apparently, we'd flown below his radar. NDM
had been out of town when Taggart started prying into my life,
and he'd given Reggie his report before NDM returned to Los
Angeles.

I found what I was looking for on the last two pages. It was
a list of my closest friends, their addresses and phone numbers. Even Eileen's private phone in her room at my house
was here. The last item focused on Bill Marshall: his office
address and hours and his daily routine. Bill was a creature of
habit, taking a lunch break at the same time every day. Taggart

had even found out about Bill's weekly card game, and listed the names and addresses of the other regular players.

I sat behind the wheel of my Jeep, not sure whether I was more angry or more worried. What I'd learned from reading Taggart's report supported my theory that Reggie went after Bill Marshall because the Marshalls were close to me, but if the police learned about that it might strengthen Hugh Weaver's belief that Bill had a motive for murder. It was the only motive they'd turned up, as far as I knew. I wasn't in the investigation's loop.

In trying to help Bill, all I'd done was add to the weight of circumstantial evidence against him. I remembered an old cliché: "A little learning is a dangerous thing." Then I remembered more of that quote: "Drink deep or taste not the Pierian spring."

I was nowhere near Pieria—Macedonia and its Balkan neighbors being a long way from Los Angeles—and the fabled spring of knowledge only appeared in mythology, but I knew I would have to "drink deep" if I was going to discover an alternative suspect to offer in place of Bill. If I couldn't prove Bill's innocence, at least I could try to shoot the case against him full of reasonable doubt.

After my live show tonight, I would curl up in bed with my notebook and make a plan.

A sudden *splat* of water on my windshield brought me back to the present. It had started to rain.

24

"Comfort food—*yummm*," I said to both Camera One and the studio audience from my opening position behind the preparation counter. I was amazed that all thirty of the seats were filled, given the heavy rain. Before the show started and the lights on the audience were lowered from bright to dim, I saw that crew members had set up three portable clothing racks by the studio entrance. They were loaded with raincoats and plastic capes and hoods that were dripping little puddles onto the studio's concrete floor.

If I'd had a choice, I would rather have stayed home tonight and not driven through the wet mess outside. These hearty souls deserved a good show, and I'd do my best to give them one.

On the back wall counter of my kitchen set were the finished dishes I'd made in the middle of the night: the Chicken Biscuit Pie and the forty individually wrapped Cornish pasties. One extra pastie had been kept unwrapped, to be displayed beside the chicken pie in what the TV people called the camera's "beauty shot."

Faking an exaggerated shiver, I said, "On a cold night there's nothing more delicious and satisfying than old-fashioned comfort food. This isn't elegant fare, but it's warm and filling. Another plus: These dishes are relatively inexpensive. They'll be even more of a bargain if you plan your menu around supermarket sales and newspaper coupons. But before we start making our comfort main dishes, I'm going to demonstrate a comfort dessert made from an object comedians joke about and hardly anyone admits to liking."

From the shelf below the cutting board, I retrieved an object that I held up for the camera and the studio audience to see.

"Yes, it's the dreaded fruitcake," I said. "Available in stores during the Thanksgiving and Christmas holidays, but at various places on the Internet all year long. Because it's three weeks before Christmas, this one arrived by mail today, from a company whose services I use. Normally, they send a calendar, but this year they're under new management. Maybe one of the executives owns a fruitcake company. Or maybe this is one of those regifted gifts."

People in the audience laughed, which was a relief because I hoped I was being amusing.

"I'm not exactly a fan of fruitcake, but with people in the world going hungry I can't stand the thought of throwing away edible food. So I had an idea I hope is going to work. I say 'I hope' because I've never made this before. It's an experiment I'm trying right here, in front of everybody. In a circus, this would be called walking the high wire without a net."

I unwrapped the fruitcake, set it on a cutting board, and went to the refrigerator where I loaded my arms with a carton of eggs and containers of milk and whipping cream. Depositing the ingredients next to the sugar and the mixing bowl that were already on the counter, I picked up my favorite chef's knife. "We're going to turn this thing that weighs as much as a doorstop into a fruity bread pudding."

Explaining what I was doing, I sliced and then tore the cake pieces into large chunks and placed them in a buttered nine-by-thirteen baking dish. Next, I measured the milk and cream, added sugar, and cracked the eggs.

"I'm whisking these ingredients into a custard," I said. "The idea came to me just after the cake arrived in the mail, when I realized I had eggs that were about to reach the expiration date on the end of the carton. This seems like a perfect way to use them up."

I tilted the bowl of custard toward the camera so the at-home audience could see the consistency and to allow those in the studio to view it on the big TV screen next to the set, then poured it over the pieces of fruitcake.

"This goes into a preheated 350-degree oven for about forty-five minutes, which means it will be ready for taste testing just before the end of the show." I raised the first two fingers of my right hand and crossed them. "Wish me luck."

Quickly washing my hands at the sink, I said, "Now for the main dish comforts. First up are Cornish pasties. I learned to make them from my Grandma Nell. They're little meat, potato, and onion pies that workmen in England, Scotland, and Wales used to take to their jobs for a nutritious lunch or dinner. They taste good whether they're eaten warm or cold or at room temperature. After I get a batch of them started, we'll be making a Chicken Biscuit Pie, from a book called *Famous White House Recipes*. According to my friend Victor Bardack, who compiled and published these recipes, Chicken Biscuit Pie was created during the period called the Great Depression when President Herbert Hoover asked his wife, Lou Henry Hoover, to come up with something tasty but economical to serve at the White House. It was such a terrible time for the country that President Hoover wanted to give the people a sense that the government was stable, so they continued to have state dinners, but without lavish meals far beyond the means of most Americans."

As I measured out flour, salt, shortening, and ice water, I said, "To make two pasties, you'll need enough pastry for a nine-inch, two-crust pie. I'm cutting Crisco into the flour for this pastry because we're making a meat pie. I'd use butter if this was going to be a fruit tart. Be sure to use only *ice* water to bind your dough. The colder the water, the flakier the crust is going to be."

After rolling out the dough on a floured board, I prepared the inside ingredients, brushed the tops of the filled and folded-over pastry with a beaten egg, put them on a greased baking sheet, and slipped them into a preheated oven.

"Start your pasties at 400 degrees, but after fifteen minutes reduce the heat to 350 and give them another fifteen minutes."

In my earpiece, I heard Quinn's voice from the director's booth. "Ten seconds to commercial, Della. Nine . . . eight . . ."

"We've got to take a break now while I cut this three-pound frying chicken into pieces." I held it up to show the at-home and in-studio audiences. "When we come back in a couple of minutes, we'll start working on Mrs. Hoover's White House comfort food."

As soon as I saw on the monitor that commercials were going out over the air, I picked up my headphone from the shelf below the counter. It was connected to Quinn Tanner in the director's booth.

"Hi, Quinn—where's Addison? I haven't seen him since I got here."

"He came in at four o'clock but he didn't honor us with his presence for very long." Quinn's sarcastic tone made her British accent sound even more imperious than usual. "The poor baby has a cold and went home to his bed. As any fool can plainly see, the show has gone flawlessly without an inexperienced producer mucking about. You might mention that to Mickey when you see him next."

"Give Addison a chance. He's trying to find out where he belongs in the company."

"The Son—spelled s-o-n—Also Rises," she said.

It was too bad that Addison was sick because I'd intended to introduce him to the audience and have him taste the dishes on camera. I wanted to do it because I thought that seeing him on television would be a nice surprise for his mother.

■　■　■

By the time the show was in its final segment, the Cornish pasties and the Chicken Biscuit Pie had been displayed and sampled by members of the studio audience. Happily, both had been praised by the volunteer tasters. Truth is always a risk on a live show, but sometimes disaster can be even more entertaining than success. I've made enough missteps in my life to know that one doesn't die from embarrassment. My favorite episode of a show called *Clean House* was the time a woman whose rooms they'd cleaned, painted, and refurnished— attractively, I thought—was so unhappy with the result she had an emotional meltdown on camera. I felt bad for the unhappy woman, but that edition of the show injected a refreshing dose of "reality" into reality TV.

With just three minutes left before the final credits started to roll, I picked up a pair of pot holders and told the audience,

"Time to take the fruitcake bread pudding experiment out of the oven. As you here in the studio saw, I haven't even taken a peek while it was baking."

Opening the oven door, I was met by a wave of the most delightful aroma. "It smells good," I said.

I carried the hot baking pan over to the prep counter and set it on a cooling rack. "It's hot, but I can't wait." I removed a spoon from the cutlery drawer and scooped up a little of the pudding, blew on it, and put it into my mouth. "Yes!" I said with relief. As I'd hoped, the audience laughed. They even applauded.

"Who'd like to come and taste?"

Several arms shot up. I chose the first two I saw: a man and a woman who were sitting several seats apart in the front row.

"Please, Nina," I said to Nina Reyes, the floor manager who stood between Camera One and Camera Two, "help these two brave souls over the cables."

Even though something terrible had happened to the "taster" on my first live show—not my fault, as it was later proved—I'd done several live shows since then with only good results. Fortunately for me, the public had short memories and I'd had no shortage of volunteers from the audience.

The man and the woman took the offered spoons. From opposite sides of the pan, they dug into the fruity bread pudding.

I said, "What's the verdict?"

Mouths full, they rendered their opinions with enthusiastic nodding from the woman and a thumbs-up sign from the man.

"Whew," I said.

As the show's end credit theme music began, the camera followed me while I took the wrapped Cornish pasties and passed them out to the audience and the crew.

"Don't eat these driving home," I said. "On a night like this, keep both hands on the wheel."

∎ ∎ ∎

Because strong winds had developed during the afternoon, I'd hoped that by the time the show was over the storm would have blown away, or at least lessened. No such luck; the wind had died down, but the rain was even heavier now. It had been hard enough driving from Santa Monica to North Hollywood, but going home it was worse. The rain was coming down in sheets, and many of the streets were hubcap-deep with standing water.

It was very difficult to see the lines dividing the lanes of traffic. I would have taken the 101 Freeway home, but the on ramp was closed. Seeing the flashing red and blue lights of police cars and fire trucks, it wasn't hard to guess there'd been a bad accident. That crash had increased the number of cars on the surface streets.

Every time I had to cross an intersection on a green light, I held my breath, hoping that other drivers would obey the signals, too. Every time I splashed through the deep water in a speed dip, I prayed that no sinkhole had opened up beneath. Southern California had had a plague of sinkholes in so-called firm ground during the past year. They were the stuff of nightmares.

It took twice as long as it did normally, but I finally reached the turnoff onto Beverly Glen Canyon. This was my favorite of the routes that had been cut through the mountains so that San Fernando Valley dwellers could reach Los Angeles and the westside communities, including Santa Monica.

Beverly Glen was a narrow, twisty road until one reached its peak, the Mulholland Drive intersection. About a mile on the other side, Beverly Glen widened comfortably. Unlike the other canyon boulevards, it didn't have as many teeth-rattling potholes, and was subject to fewer mudslides from the hills that lined the west side of the road.

Visibility was terrible. My headlights seemed to bounce off the lashing rain and back at me. I was still making my way up the tight, coiling Valley side of Mulholland when I heard a driver behind me gun his motor. Through the rearview mirror, I saw the headlights of a car rushing up behind me. With high beams on, the glare they produced in the mirror blinded me momentarily. I almost lost control of my Jeep, swerving toward the sheer drop on my left, but managed to right the wheel just in time to avoid plunging down to my death at the bottom of the canyon.

I swore at the driver who had almost killed me, but of

course he or she couldn't hear me over the rain pelting the tops of our vehicles. In fact, I couldn't see into the car behind me to know whether the driver was a man or a woman. Nor could I tell what kind of car it was, except that its shape was that of some type of ordinary sedan.

My heart was racing, but having dodged disaster, I expelled a sigh of relief and started to calm down as I saw Mulholland Drive up ahead and realized that I was going to catch the green light at the intersection.

I got through it just before the light changed, but a glance in my rearview mirror showed that the car behind me had sped through the yellow light. The way down Beverly Glen immediately below Mulholland is the most dangerous part. The car ahead of me was at a great enough distance that I could increase my speed—as much as I dared. It wasn't much.

The car behind increased its speed, too, roaring up behind me on my right. He almost crashed into me, but at the last split second the driver swerved enough that his front wheels were level with my rear wheels.

Simultaneously, he pounded his horn with such a powerful blast of noise that I nearly jumped out of my skin. At that same moment I realized that he was crowding me toward the sheer drop on my left!

Desperate to escape, before I could form the thought, I stomped down on the accelerator and shot ahead of the maniac behind me. The combination of punishing rain, the slippery roadway, and my dangerous velocity was causing the Jeep to rock from side to side.

Please, God, don't let me turn over!

Then I remembered that the Jeep Compass, while it had a high center of gravity, was also the most compact of the styles I'd considered. That gave me the courage to put on more speed.

The Jeep found its balance—and I found mine.

Able to think again, I realized that about twenty yards ahead of me, after the next curve, was Beverly Glen Circle, a small shopping plaza on a rise overlooking the boulevard.

In order to get there before the driver behind me saw what I was going to do, I put on as much more speed as I dared.

Behind me, I saw the sedan's lights sweep from side to side

as the car fishtailed. It didn't crash, but the driver's momentary lack of control gave me the precious few seconds I needed to put more space between us.

Once around the bend and out of sight of the pursing car, I switched the Jeep's lights off and made a sharp turn uphill into the plaza's parking lot. Visibility through the rain was still bad, but there was just enough illumination from the security lights to prevent me from hitting another car, or, God forbid, a human or an animal.

The far end of the lot, beyond the lights, was in total darkness. A perfect place to hide.

I headed for a spot next to a line of trees, away from the cars that had parked close to the shops, and made a tight swing around, backing into the space in case I needed to get out of there in a hurry. After turning off the motor and checking the doors to be sure they were all locked, I found the big Maglight I kept under the front seat and settled down to peer through the heavy rain at the lights of the cars in the canyon below.

None had made the uphill turn into the plaza after I had.

It was reassuring to have a cell phone, but unless an attacker approached me, I couldn't call the police. What would I tell them? That some driver I couldn't see, in a car I couldn't describe beyond the word "sedan" was driving too fast, trying to crowd me off the road and nearly caused me to crash? The dispatcher would probably laugh and remind me that most Californians drive badly in the rain. We're famous for it. I imagined him or her suggesting that the car I thought was chasing me might just have had bad brakes. If I wasn't hurt there was nothing they could do. End of conversation.

My imaginary dispatcher could be right. Bad driving, bad brakes—those were possible answers.

Except I don't believe it.

I think someone really was trying to harm me. But who? And why?

The car was some kind of sedan . . .

The vehicle in T. J. Taggart's parking space was a sedan. Could it have been Taggart who'd tried to force me off the road? If it had been, would he try something else? We didn't get enough rain in Southern California to be able to depend on it. If he tried something else, might that be more successful?

It took a half hour sitting and shivering in the dark before I felt safe enough to drive home.

If Taggart was the one who'd been trying to force me off the road, he knew where I worked and where I lived.

But I couldn't tell anyone—especially John—what I was afraid of because then I'd have to tell him why I suspected Taggart.

I didn't sleep very well that night.

25

Friday morning the sun was out and all trace of the rain was gone, except for the lovely bright green of the freshly washed grass. I forced myself to forget how frightened I'd been the night before. Still, when I was taking Tuffy for his morning walk through the neighborhood, I paid much closer attention to our surroundings than usual.

Eileen came out of her room. Instead of her usual college attire of jeans and sweatshirts, she was dressed like a young executive in a knee-length pale gray suit, a single strand of good pearls that I recognized as her mother's, and her blonde hair held back with a black clip.

"I didn't know you had a 'power suit,'" I said.

"I bought it after Mickey set our official meeting on the fudge project." She gestured to the black leather portfolio in her hand. "This I borrowed from my artist friend. Tell me the truth, Aunt Del: Do I look okay for the meeting?"

"Right out of the Fortune 500. Seriously, that outfit inspires confidence. In fact, you've inspired me to put on something businesslike, too."

"Your black slim skirt, the red blazer, and the white silk blouse Mother and Daddy gave you last Christmas." Realizing her take-charge tone might have sounded a bit too forceful, she dialed it down and said, "I mean, if that's what you want to wear. It's a great outfit."

I felt such a surge of affection for my "honorary niece" that I wanted to give her a big hug. But I restrained myself; it wouldn't have been businesslike.

■ ■ ■

At ten thirty, Eileen and I, both now dressed to impress, stepped out my front door to go to the meeting at Mickey Jordan's house.

To my surprise, we were met by two familiar figures coming up the walk.

"Hello, John. Good morning, Detective Weaver." I tried to keep the concern out of my voice. Unexpected visitors rarely bring good news.

John looked startled to see Eileen. Or perhaps he was taken aback to see her seeming so *mature*.

John said, "Hi, sweetheart. I thought you'd be in class."

"Our big meeting's this morning—I told you." Suddenly, the smile left her face. "Daddy, is something wrong? Why are you here?"

"Everything's fine. You know my partner, Detective Weaver."

"Yes. Hello, Detective," Eileen said.

Weaver nodded to Eileen, then said to me, "We need to talk. Alone."

"Eileen, go ahead to Mickey's house in your car. I'll follow in a few minutes."

I could see she was eager to get to the meeting, but she said, "Are you sure?"

"I'm sure. Go on. I'll be there soon."

"Okay." She beamed at her father. "This is my first big meeting, Daddy. Wish me luck?"

"Always." John watched Eileen hurry into her car and back down the driveway to the street before he turned to me. "In going through Regina Davis's financial records last night we found checks she'd written to a private investigator. T. J. Taggart. We went to visit him early this morning."

I felt a lump of dread forming in my stomach. Had Taggart told them that I'd been there? Had he given them copies of his reports? To buy time to think, I said, "Would you two like to come into the house? I'll make some coffee and—"

Weaver shook his head vigorously. "Forget that. You went to see Taggart yesterday." It was a statement, not a question.

"Yes." I was afraid to ask the next question, but I had to. "How did you know?"

John said, "A woman in the office next to Taggart's saw you through her window. She recognized you from your show and wondered what a TV cook wanted with a private investigator." He stopped. It was one of a cop's interrogation techniques: stop talking so the other person will fill in the silence with words.

I resisted that impulse.

Weaver reached into his jacket for a package of cigarettes, started to take one out of the pack, then stuffed it back inside. He held onto the package, tossing it from one hand to the other.

John said, "Why were you there, Della?"

He's calling me Della, not Del. Bad sign.

"I had a theory and I wanted to see if it was correct," I said.

Weaver balled up his fist, squeezing the life out of his cigarette pack. "Jeez, ice caps move faster than this conversation. What theory?"

"That Reggie had me investigated when she agreed to sponsor the cake contest."

Weaver said, "What'd you find out?"

"Taggart refused to tell me anything." A limited truth: that had been his initial response.

John said, "What made you think Ms. Davis went to Taggart?"

I responded with another limited truth. "When I looked up private investigators in the Yellow Pages I saw that his address was almost exactly halfway between Reggie's corporate office on Wilshire Boulevard and the Davis Food Test Kitchens on Pico."

Even though that was technically true, it sounded pretty lame, even to me. All Weaver did was roll his eyes, but John watched me with an intensity that made my throat feel dry.

"You said you went to see Taggart this morning." I swallowed and tried to sound calm, almost casual. "Did he tell you anything useful?"

Weaver and John exchanged a quick look that I couldn't interpret.

After a moment of tense silence, John said, "We found him dead."

Stunned, I took an involuntary step backward and almost stumbled over my Wipe Your Paws doormat. "Oh, Lord! What happened?"

"He was murdered," Weaver said.

There was a sudden ringing in my ears from the shock. I barely heard myself ask, "When? How?"

Weaver said, "The murder weapon is classified information."

"The ME hasn't given us an official TOD yet," John said, "but her first impression is that Taggart's been dead since sometime yesterday afternoon."

Yesterday afternoon? If that was true, then Taggart couldn't have been chasing me over the canyon last night. But if it wasn't Taggart, who?

"No one saw the guy after you left there," Weaver said.

I couldn't let his insinuating tone go unchallenged. "You mean you haven't found anyone, Detective. Obviously, the murderer saw him after I did."

"Calm down," John said.

The ringing in my ears faded away as I got a grip on my emotions. I said, "You can't honestly think I killed that man."

"No, we don't," John said.

Weaver scowled at me. "Maybe not, but twenty-three years as a cop makes me think you know more than you're telling."

I wanted to ask him where he kept his crystal ball, but I thought better of it. My head was clearing. "Was Taggart robbed? Was that why he was killed?"

"What the hell do we look like—four-one-one?" Weaver rolled his crushed cigarette package into a ball and threw it on my lawn, where it bounced and came to a stop against one of my rosebushes.

My guess was that Weaver was trying to quit smoking. I pitied John for having to work with him during that struggle.

John watched Weaver's cigarette package come to a stop, then turned back to give me a searching look. "Della, I expect you to tell us anything you . . . find out."

I nodded, unable to say anything. I think John suspected I was withholding information, and was giving me a chance to come clean. But how could I tell him about Taggart's investigation without making the situation for Bill and Liddy even worse than it was already? What a terrible feeling—being torn between two precious friendships.

As I watched John and Weaver leave, I forced myself to push thoughts of Taggart away. I took a few long, deep breaths and expelled them slowly. That always helped me to focus. I had to prepare myself mentally for the meeting at Mickey Jordan's house that had already begun. Eileen had been working so hard on her business plan that I owed it to her to be able to concentrate on what she'd prepared.

26

Mickey and Iva Jordan's English butler, Maurice, answered the doorbell in his usual decorous manner. As ever, his black suit and white shirt were immaculate. He was as perfectly groomed and pressed as a new ambassador about to present his credentials to a head of state. I liked Maurice; he managed to be proper without being stuffy.

To my warm greeting, Maurice replied, "It's good to see you again, Mrs. Carmichael. Mr. Jordan is expecting you."

"I'll go right in, but after the meeting I'd like to see Mrs. Jordan. Is she home?"

"Fridays are Madame's health club and hairdresser days. I doubt she'll return until late this afternoon. May I give her a message?"

"Please ask her to telephone me tonight or tomorrow, when it's convenient."

"Very good."

Maurice ushered me through the foyer arch into the cavernous living room of the Jordans' Beverly Hills mansion. As many times as I'd been here, I've never ceased to admire the original Spanish tiles on the floor and the carved beams above. The stone fireplace was tall enough for a center on the Los Angeles Lakers basketball team to stand inside, and it was so wide it could have burned enough logs to warm King Arthur's Round Table room.

"Come in," Mickey said, waving me toward the nearest of the two matching yellow velvet sofas that sat like outstretched arms on either side of the fireplace. The coffee table between had been cleared of its usual object d'art. Instead, the heavy glass top was covered with sketches. I saw one that looked like me, holding a box of fudge.

Addison, his eyes watering and his nose red, clutched a packet of tissues. Even Quinn might be sympathetic if she were here this morning and could see how miserable his cold had made him. As I came into the room, he was perched on the edge of the sofa on the far side of the table. Next to him, Eileen was kneeling on the floor and pointing to another of the sketches.

I greeted the three of them and said, "Sorry I'm late. Did I miss much?"

"No," Eileen said. "We're just looking at some design ideas."

Addison stood when he saw me. "Great show last night." In spite of having a voice husky with cold, his tone was a little too hearty. It made me wonder if he'd watched it on TV, and hadn't told Mickey he'd come home to bed before we went on the air. If he hadn't, I wasn't going to betray him.

"Thank you," I said. "It was fun."

Mickey had remained seated in what I'd come to know was his favorite spot: on the sofa nearest to the foyer, next to the telephone and lamp table. He patted the cushion beside him and said, "Park yourself."

I moved in past Mickey's knees and took the place he indicated. As soon as I was settled, Addison resumed his seat.

Indicating Eileen with a nod, Mickey said, "This chick wants to market your stuff by promoting crazy birthdays."

"Crazy birthdays?"

Eileen picked up a sheaf of typed notes. "This is a list of about a hundred famous people I looked up. They're born in every month of the year. We can sell gift boxes of fudge, and cookies, and muffins, and cheesecake bars by persuading people to give their loved ones something sweet to commemorate, say, President Benjamin Harrison's birthday—he was the first president to have electric lights in the White House—or Rosa Parks's, or Paul Revere's, Muhammad Ali's, Billie Jean King's, Harriet Tubman's, Elvis Presley's—on and on."

Mickey asked Eileen, "Would somebody like you want to get a box of fudge on Elvis Presley's birthday?"

"I love surprises," Eileen said. "Most women do."

"Men, too," Addison said.

"My idea is that we encourage the public to celebrate famous people who don't have their own holidays with delicious gifts to those they love, or even just like, or want to make smile," Eileen said.

"That could be a big market," Addison said. "Untapped."

"This sample list ranges from Queen Latifah to Mozart, Kahlil Gibran to Thomas Edison and Elizabeth Barrett Browning," Eileen said. "Why should people send presents to each other just on Christmas or Hanukkah or on a person's regular birthday? Sweet surprises say 'I love you.' You taught me that, Aunt Del. Remember how I used to help you make cookies for Dad and Uncle Mack when they were working on a really tough case?"

"Carbohydrates are natural spirit-lifters," Addison said.

"But we should also have a sugar-free line, so the needs of diabetics and weight watchers can be served, too," I said. "I've got some artificial sweetener recipes."

"Fine," Mickey said. "I'm for any idea that moves the merchandise."

Eileen displayed a sample of shiny scarlet paper with a black and white caricature of me holding a plate of whatever was inside the gift box. "This is my favorite packaging design. Your dark hair looks good against the red paper, Aunt Del."

"It's eye-catching," I said. "I really like it."

Mickey nodded approvingly. "It's a known marketing fact that red and gold boxes make a statement: It's *buy me*."

Eileen reached across the table to hand Mickey and me several other drawings. "Here are some possible paste-on labels for our nontraditional holidays. The idea is that these labels can be affixed to the basic package, according to what's being celebrated."

"Clever cartoons," I said. Shuffling through them, I kept coming back to one little animal figure. "This chipmunk is adorable."

"Groundhog," Addison said. "It's a groundhog. For Groundhog Day."

"I love the expression on his face," I said.

"Lemme see." Mickey took the page and squinted at it. "Is that little bastard hungry or horny?" He glanced across the coffee table at Eileen. "Pardon my language."

"I don't mind," Eileen said.

I smiled at Mickey with affection. "You never apologized to *me* for your language."

Mickey shrugged. "Yeah, well, you've been married. You know the score." Remaining focused on the drawing, he tapped the groundhog with a stubby forefinger. "This little guy's got charisma. Use him on all the labels."

Addison looked puzzled. "*All?* But there's only one Groundhog Day a year."

"So dress him up like Presley an' Einstein an' Paul Revere—everybody."

Eileen got up off her knees, fairly bouncing with excitement. "That's fabulous! His image can be the products' unifying theme. With his face and body in different costumes it ties together all of the new celebrations we're trying to market."

Addison dabbed at his nose with a tissue. Through clogged nasal passages, he said thickly, "Basic packaging with paste-on labels to differentiate the products and our faux holidays will save considerable money."

"In theory. Show me some numbers," Mickey said.

Eileen pulled a sheet of paper from her borrowed portfolio. I made a mental note to buy her a portfolio of her own when I got my next paycheck.

"Ad helped me get these figures for printing, packing, and shipping," Eileen said.

She calls him 'Ad'? I realized they must have been spending time together.

Addison cleared his throat. "The prices aren't exact, Mickey. There's a 1 percent variable due to paper quality and the exact weight of the boxes."

Mickey studied the sheet while the three of us waited in suspense.

Eileen's fingers were entwined so tightly her knuckles were white. Addison put his hand on her arm gently. It seemed to calm her a little. She relaxed her hands enough so that color returned to her knuckles.

Is something going on between them? I brought her up for most of her life, but I'm not her mother. Do I have the right to ask? Or should I wait until she talks about him?

I admitted to myself that I'd been so worried about Liddy and Bill that I hadn't paid much attention to Eileen.

After what seemed like an eternity, but probably wasn't more than a minute or two, Mickey looked up from the page of figures. "We'll start with traditional fudge and brownies, with sugar-free versions, too. If this catches on, later you can add muffins an' those whatever bars."

"Cheesecake bars," Eileen said.

"But not regular muffins," I said. "I want us to sell muffin tops."

Mickey looked appalled. "Cut muffins in half?" He shook his head firmly. "We're not gonna waste food."

"There's no waste involved, Mickey," I said. "I've got some special pans that bake only the tops of the muffins. But we'll need more."

"Make a list of what you gotta have," Mickey said. "Prepare for success, is my motto. We got the perfect promotion platform with *Della's in the Kitchen*."

Addison said, "The show is called *In the Kitchen with Della*."

"Whatever. Don't sweat the small things, son."

One point concerned me. "Who's going to make all the fudge and the brownies?"

"Not you," Mickey said. "We just use your recipes. But we'll manufacture locally so I can keep an eye on what's happening."

"How soon can we begin?" Eileen asked.

"Very soon. Weeks ago, right after you started talking about this, my real estate people found a bakery on Hollywood Boulevard that filed for bankruptcy. I picked up the building and all their equipment cheap. It's been cleaned and inspected."

Eileen slipped past Addison and quickstepped over to the back of the sofa where I was sitting. Abandoning her business school cool, she leaned down to give me a happy hug. "We're going into business!"

Mickey said, "This'll be a new company. A small subsidiary of Jordan Enterprises." He pointed to Eileen and me. "You two will be officers. Eileen—you know how Della's stuff's supposed to taste?"

"Of course. I grew up eating it."

"Okay, you're in charge of quality control, and a vice president."

"Vice president!" Eileen practically broke into a cheer.

"Don't get too excited," Mickey said. "Della, you'll be president of whatever we call it. You gals are getting big titles, but I'm not paying you much to start. If the company takes off, you'll do well. If it doesn't, then I'm out my start-up money and you two'll be eating whatever we didn't sell. So, you gonna take this gamble with me?"

Simultaneously, I said, "Yes" and Eileen said, "Absolutely!"

Mickey made a note on the pad next to the phone. "Addison, find out we what gotta do to make stuffed toys of that little rodent. Legal considerations, registering the trademark, cost of manufacturing here in the USA, insurance—the whole *schmear.*"

I stared at Mickey with admiration. "That's a great idea."

He winked at me. "Merchandising. Potential gold mine. Hell, I'd make a stuffed toy out of *you* if I thought it would sell."

"When can we see the bakery plant?" Eileen asked.

"Soon as you want. Get the keys from my secretary."

"I will! Aunt Del, when can we go look?"

"How about four o'clock today?" I said.

"Super! I'll go get the keys and meet you back at the house this afternoon."

A few minutes later, the meeting broke up. I was at the wheel of my Jeep and almost home when my cell phone rang. I pulled over to the side of the street and answered to hear Iva's voice.

"Della, thank God I got you." She was whispering. "It just came over the news—that detective T. J. Taggart—he was murdered. Did *you* kill him?"

"Of course not! Iva, how in the world could you think—"

"Damn—I'd kind of hoped . . ."

"Don't ever say you hope I've murdered someone!"

The fear in her voice was so strong it was like a palpable presence. "Della, I'm not very technical but you've got a computer. What's a hard drive?"

"It's the brains of the machine. Everything in the computer is on it. Why?"

"*Everything?* The newscaster woman said the only thing missing in Taggart's office was his computer's hard drive." She started to cry. "If it's gone, then that means the killer has his detective files—a killer has the file on *me*!"

27

I did my best to calm Iva by telling her that I couldn't believe Taggart would have been murdered for her file. "If his hard drive was the only thing missing, then the killer must have been after some other file."

"Even if that's true, my file is there and people could read it," she said.

"In the media's zeal to be first with a story, sometimes reporters rush on the air using unsubstantiated reports."

"You mean his hard drive might not have been stolen?" There was a tiny hint of hope in her voice.

I spoke carefully, so as not to send her spiraling down into despair. "Maybe it wasn't. The news report you heard about the missing hard drive—did it come from the police?"

"The woman said she was quoting 'a source close to the investigation.'"

"Then it might not be true," I said. "There are some people who make themselves seem important by acting like insiders to try to ingratiate themselves with the media."

"You mean maybe I'm safe after all?"

"Let me find out exactly what happened, okay? Where are you right now?"

"I was on the elliptical machine when I heard the news. Now I'm crouching in the bathroom talking to you."

"Go back to your machine. As soon as I find out what's going on, I'll call you."

She sighed. In the voice of a scared little girl, she said, "All right. But hurry, please."

"I'll get back to you just as soon as I can."

"Thanks." Iva disconnected.

I didn't start the Jeep again, but stayed in the parking place, thinking about whom I could call to find out if it was true that Taggart's hard drive had been stolen.

John? No. I didn't want to call him because if I asked him to confirm a report that probably shouldn't have gotten out, he'd surely ask why I wanted to know. I'd already lied to him by omission, implying that I hadn't learned anything from my visit to Taggart, when the truth was that I'd hidden the envelope with copies of Taggart's three reports to Reggie right here under my driver's seat.

I didn't want to call NDM, even though I was sure he'd have at least one "source close to the investigation." If I asked about Taggart's murder, he'd want to know why I was interested and I didn't want to tell him. He might—

My cell phone rang. I saw on the faceplate that it was NDM calling. Coincidence, or telepathy? I decided on coincidence and answered, greeting him with a cheerful, "Hello."

"Hi, honey. Sorry I didn't call you earlier. I'm on a story."

"Don't worry about it. I'm busy, too."

"You're not mad? It's been thirty-six hours since I left your bed."

"I wasn't watching the clock." My tone was casual and pleasant. I was telling the truth.

"Oh." He sounded disappointed. That pleased me.

"Look," he said, "I know you're upset about the Regina Davis murder—worried about your friends—but there just might be a break in the case."

Was this going to be good news or bad? I felt my muscles tense, but I tried to keep concern out of my voice. "What do you mean?"

"A few weeks ago Regina Davis hired a private investigator, a guy named Taggart whose office is in Westwood. He was murdered sometime yesterday afternoon. I'm pursuing the idea that there's a connection."

"What makes you think so?"

"Four violent deaths in LA in the past week. The first was a gang killing, and the cops got the shooter while he still had the weapon on him. The second was a married couple in a murder-suicide—that one solved itself. And in not quite four days, two people who knew each other are dead."

I was in an awkward spot, because I knew more than he did. I stalled. "Do you have any idea why he was killed? What the motive was?"

"Not yet. Maybe you can help. You told me that Davis came to see you a couple of days before her murder. Did she mention anything about hiring a PI?"

"No." It was a relief to tell the absolute truth.

"She mention anybody in her life she was suspicious of, or worried about?"

"No. Reggie didn't say anything like that." To cut off the questioning, I added, "Sorry."

"No problem. It was a long shot."

"Sometimes long shots come in. Well, good luck with your investigation. I've got to get back to work."

"Hold on a minute. There's something I want to say."

"What?"

"I keep thinking about our night together, all the wonderful details. I reach for a mug of coffee and wish I was reaching for you," he said.

"Pretty words, but we both have a lot to do, so—"

"Yeah, I've got to go, too. Oh, I caught your show last night. If you need any more fruitcakes, my editor has three of them he doesn't know what to do with."

Roiling with mixed emotions—I wanted to be back in NDM's arms and I wanted to smack him with one of his editor's fruitcakes for making me feel that way—all I said was, "If I need one, it's good to know I have a source. Happy investigating." I said a polite good-bye.

It must not have been as polite as I thought because he said, "Why do you keep trying to hang up? Is everything all right?"

"Everything's fine."

"With us?"

"We're friends," I said.

"That's all?"

"We slept together the other night, and it was great, but it's not going to happen again," I said.

"Ever?"

"I told you something and I meant it: I'm not going to be one of the group of women you sleep with."

"I didn't sleep with anyone in Utah, and I haven't slept with anyone but you since I got back. In spite of what you think, and seeing me with . . . that girl . . . at the restaurant."

He doesn't remember her name.

I said, "Is that true?"

"Scout's honor—and I really was a Boy Scout. I'll show you my badges. What's happened is I decided I want to be with a woman who knows the name of at least one of the Supreme Court justices. Del, honey, I'd like us to see each other exclusively. For as long as we both want to."

"I'm not interested in getting married again, and we won't live together," I said.

"Not living together—that's fine with me. We need our separate space."

My heart was thumping and my cheeks felt hot with excitement at the thought of his mouth on mine, of his touch . . . but I managed to keep my voice calm. "One-on-one, so to speak. That arrangement sounds fair," I said.

"Fair? I never even thought about making a deal like this before."

"Don't worry about it. Either of us can bail out whenever we want to."

"Easy for you to say. My problem is I don't think I'm going to want to," he said.

I wondered how he would feel about that if, or when, he learned that I was keeping information about Taggart's files from him.

That thought brought me back to my big problem at the moment: finding out if Taggart's hard drive really had been stolen, and if the police had any clues.

While I couldn't ask John, and NDM didn't seem to know, I realized there was someone else who might be able to help me. Once again, silently thanking whoever devised this handy piece of communication equipment, I picked up my cell phone and dialed.

28

Phil Logan's assistant put me through to the Better Living Channel's head of public relations.

"Della? This is the first time you ever called me. Nothing's wrong, I hope."

"No, not at all, but I wondered if you have time to see me for a few minutes. I can come to your office."

"It's a madhouse around here. Meet me at the Hamburger Hamlet, the original one, on Sunset, right next door to this building. I'll buy you lunch."

"Terrific. What time?"

"Can you get there in fifteen minutes?"

"Easily."

"Park in the garage next to the restaurant," he said. "Do I need to bring anything with me for our meeting?"

"Just your vivid imagination," I said.

■ ■ ■

The West Coast outpost of Jordan Enterprises was located in an office building near the invisible line that divided Beverly Hills 90210 from West Hollywood 90069. Mickey's address was, by a few feet, on the B. H. side of the invisible line. Hamburger Hamlet was on the West Hollywood side.

There are quite a few Hamburger Hamlets around southern California, but the one where I was about to meet Phil Logan was the original, established in 1950 by Marilyn and Harry Lewis. The story goes that on their first date aspiring actor Harry told Marilyn he had two ambitions in life: to own a restaurant and to play Hamlet. She found the location and together they opened the bistro. Harry Lewis didn't become famous as an actor, but their enterprise was a huge success.

Hamburger Hamlet managed to weather a roller coaster economy and public whims. It remained popular over the decades while other all-the-rage dining places vanished.

As Phil suggested, I parked in the garage next door. Perhaps I was becoming paranoid after my terrifying ride through the rain, but before I left the Jeep, I scanned the area carefully. When I was satisfied that no one was around, I got out. Just before I locked the Jeep, I reached under the driver's seat and removed the envelope with Taggart's reports and shoved it into my handbag.

I followed the cement path from the garage to the door of the restaurant, and was almost there when I saw Phil Logan striding toward me from the direction of his office building. He saw me at the same time, waved, and doubled his pace so that we arrived at the Hamlet's glass front door simultaneously.

Phil looked at me and gave a low whistle. "You look sharp," he said.

"I've just come from a meeting at Mickey's about—"

"The new company, I know: Della Sweets."

I wasn't crazy about that name, but tried to keep a neutral tone. "Is that what he's going to call it?"

"Maybe yes, maybe no. It's a place saver, in Hollywood-speak, a 'working title.'"

Phil grabbed one of the thick brass handles, opened the door, and ushered me inside.

"Your name should be on the product, like Mrs. Fields cookies, or the Famous Amos chocolate chips. But if you have any ideas, Mickey's open to suggestions. He's a tough guy, but he'll listen."

"I'll give it some thought," I said.

Inside the Hamlet my first impression was of the delectable aroma of spit-roasting chickens. I'd been so focused on finding out if Taggart's hard drive had been stolen that I hadn't thought about food, but after taking one breath here, I was hungry.

The maitre d' greeted Phil with warm familiarity.

"I didn't make a reservation," Phil said.

"No problem today, Mr. Logan. Your favorite table is available."

"Great. I'm entertaining a special woman. This is Della Carmichael, host of *In the Kitchen with Della* on the BLC."

The maitre d' turned to me. "*Ahhh*, Ms. Carmichael. What a pleasure to meet you." His tone was enthusiastic, but I had the distinct feeling that he'd never heard of me. That was fine. When I started on the show I had this dream that it would be successful and I'd earn enough money to start saving for the future, but that nobody would recognize me on the street.

The maitre d' took two large hardbound menus from his station and asked us to follow. We did, into the restaurant's main room: all dark woods and brass fixtures with the banquettes and the wing chairs around the tables upholstered in wine red leather.

Phil Logan's favorite table was in the center of the room. Phil indicated where he wanted me to sit, and then sat down. The maitre d' gave us the menus, told us he'd send a waiter right over, and went back to his podium station.

"This is the best location because I can see everybody who comes in, and they can see me, and who I'm with. A lot of useful people like the Hamlet—media folks I can go after for stories. The Better Living Channel isn't exactly one of the big alphabet networks—not yet. It's tough to get attention for some of the BLC hosts. Your being at the scene of some crimes has made my life a little easier. Of course, I can't depend on that happening."

"I hope not! Violent deaths aren't my idea of good publicity, Phil."

"That's why you couldn't do my job—you don't see how to make lemonade out of lemons. Oh, bad analogy, you being a queen of the kitchen. What I meant was this: You look at a murder and see *death*. I look at a murder and see it as an unfortunate event that can be turned to something positive, namely publicity for the innocent. Is that better?"

"Good save," I said. "But I'll never be able to see murder as anything but a tragedy both for the victim and for the killer. Two lives destroyed by the same horrible act."

"That's why the world needs both of us types. You're sensitive and idealistic—I'm a pragmatic opportunity grabber."

He picked up the menu and gave it a quick scan. "I'm in a pot-pie frame of mind."

"I don't need to look at the menu," I said. "From the moment I took a breath in here I've wanted the rotisserie chicken."

A smiling waiter appeared and took our orders. As soon as he departed, Phil said, "What did you want to talk to me about?"

"Regina Davis—"

Phil waved his hand dismissively. "Nothing to worry about. The contest and TV show are still going forward."

"I know." I saw that I'd have to be more direct. "My question was about her personally. Have you learned anything from your media sources that might give a clue as to who killed her?"

"You mean like who's in her will?" He shook his head. "The will hasn't been filed yet. Why?"

I ignored that. "There was another murder, sometime yesterday or last night. A private detective named T. J. Taggart. His office was pretty close to Reggie's. I wondered if there might be some connection between the two events."

Phil's eyes lighted up with excitement. "Hey, wouldn't that be great!"

"What do you mean?"

"Two murders are a bigger story than just one. If there's a connection between this Taggart and Regina Davis, then that could mean a lot more publicity for our TV show." His expression sobered. "Unless you killed the two of them. That would be bad for the BLC."

In a firm tone, I said, "I did not kill anyone, Phil."

"I was just joking. Tell me what you know and I'll figure out how we can take advantage of it."

"This isn't to be used for publicity, Phil. I'm asking you for information as a personal favor. Okay?"

Clearly disappointed, he lifted his shoulders in a gesture of agreement. "But you'll tell me when there is something I can use? Right?"

"Absolutely," I said.

"What do you want to know?"

"It's about the murder of T. J. Taggart. Can you find out if his murder was a robbery? He was killed in his office. Was anything stolen?"

Punching a number into his cell phone, he said, "Robbery isn't very interesting, media wise." After a moment, someone answered. "Hey, Nick. It's Phil Logan."

Nick? Could his "Nick" be NDM?

"Buddy, I heard about the Taggart killing . . . Doesn't matter where I heard it. What I'm asking is, do the cops know what the motive was? *Uh-huh.* In his office . . . Was he robbed? *Uh, huh* . . . Just his hard drive? Maybe he was into kiddie porn? You're checking—I should have known you'd be on top of things, Nick. Thanks. Let's get together for dinner soon . . ." Phil nodded at the phone. "Yeah, I know this works both ways. If I hear anything about the Davis murder on this end, I'll give you an instant buzz . . . Gotta go . . . Oh, no, I won't repeat what you told me. My lips are zipped, Buddy."

Phil disconnected. "I hope you heard what I said because I promised not to repeat it."

I held up my right hand in a swearing gesture. "You didn't tell me a thing. By the way, who were you talking to?"

"Nick D'Martino." He entwined his first two fingers. "We're like brothers. You know him. He's at the *Chronicle*, gave you some good ink."

"Oh, yes. He's a talented writer." I tried to keep my tone bland, but inside I was seething. NDM knew about Taggart's hard drive and hadn't confided in me.

But, to be fair, I hadn't told him what I knew, either.

29

As soon as I got back home I took Tuffy for a quick walk, then went into the bedroom to study the reports I'd pried out of T. J. Taggart. Tuffy and Emma followed me into the room.

Reluctantly, I took the envelope from my handbag. I didn't want to pry into the private lives of people I knew. During all the years that Mack and I were married, I never opened an envelope addressed to him, even though he told me I could, and I told him he was welcome to open anything addressed to me. But neither of us ever opened each other's mail. Considering that in all other ways we were as intimate as two married people could be, I suppose it sounds silly, but that's just the way it was.

The first of Taggart's three reports was about me. I'd already read it, so I put the pages facedown on the bed. As soon as I did that, Emma jumped up and curled herself on top of the papers. I'd begun to suspect that sprawling all over a human being's reading material was coded into a cat's DNA, so I let her stay there and began to study the report on Mickey Jordan.

What I read on the first page caused my eyes to pop open.

Mickey Jordan had a police record. According to what Taggart had unearthed, Mickey had been arrested in New York City and charged with Aggravated Assault-GBI. GBI was the law enforcement abbreviation for Great Bodily Injury. Taggart's parenthetical note read: "Because you want information ASAP, I'm giving you raw facts as I learn them. I'm trying to track down details, but the arrest occurred before the NYPD kept records on computers, so what we're after is buried in tons of storage boxes."

Before computer records . . . That meant Mickey's arrest had to have happened at least thirty years ago, maybe more.

Taggart had noted the NYPD precinct but not the name of the arresting officer. I wondered if that officer was still alive, and if so, why hadn't Taggart tried to reach him? Was Taggart an inferior PI? Or had Reggie figured she'd gotten enough information and called Taggart off?

Could there possibly be anything in the old file that would drive Mickey to kill in order to keep it secret? I didn't know Mickey Jordan anywhere near well enough to guess. He'd talked openly about his rough, kid-from-the-streets childhood, but he never gave any specific details. A few months ago, he'd acted pleased when, for a while, he was a murder suspect. He'd joked—at least I'd thought it was a joke—if people thought he was capable of murder it made his negotiations easier. Business opponents were more inclined to give him what he wanted.

After the line about Mickey's arrest, Taggart listed the rest of what he'd uncovered in chronological order. Mickey Jordan had been born Michla Jacoby sixty years ago in New York City. The only parental name on his birth certificate was his mother's: Magda Esther Jacoby. Her age at the time of her son's birth was seventeen years.

In the middle of the third grade at Chester A. Arthur Primary School, Michla Jacoby was abruptly reregistered as "Michael Lewis." In a parenthetical comment, Taggart had written: "If his mother married someone named 'Lewis' there's no record of it."

At age eighteen, Michla Jacoby, AKA Michael Lewis, went to court and had his name changed legally to Mickey Jordan. Shortly afterward came the AGB arrest. Taggart noted that he hadn't found out how the case had been resolved, but within a few months, Mickey Jordan had joined the army and was sent to Vietnam. Two years later he received an honorable discharge and was back in New York.

The rest of the report was pretty much what I'd read in Business Section articles about Mickey. Professional and economic ups and downs, skirmishes with government oversight agencies. He'd survived them all, and his fortunes began to rise dramatically ten years ago. By that time, Mickey had become an expert at spotting the potential in losing companies, buying them at a bargain price, and turning them into profit generators. His cable TV network, The Better Living Channel, had been one of Mickey's biggest challenges, but as of this fiscal year it was beginning to make money.

Under "Personal Life," Taggart reported that Mickey had been married four times and divorced three. His only offspring, son Addison Jordan, was born during his second marriage, to Francine Strayhorn. She had been described in news clips from that period as "a socialite with a wild streak." Another parenthetical note from Taggart said, "The lady drank too much, and drove too fast. Today she'd probably be called a 'celeb-u-tant' and get her own reality TV show."

According to Taggart, Mickey had his wife hospitalized twice. After the second time there were no more speeding or DUI tickets. After she and Mickey divorced, Francine Jordan moved to Connecticut and dropped out of the public eye.

"Their son, Addison, got an MBA from Harvard and currently works for his father. As far as is known, Jordan has no other children," Taggart noted.

The investigator went on to report that discreet inquiries provided information that surprised Taggart. Amazing as it seemed to the detective, none of Mickey's three former wives talked about him with animosity.

Regarding "the incumbent," as Taggart referred to Iva, he reported that Mickey's fourth wife had been born Iva Diane Brody, in Pittsburgh, Pennsylvania, thirty years ago. He added, "Information on the current Mrs. Jordan is attached. It makes for juicy reading."

That was an odd note, I thought. According to Iva, the only embarrassing thing in her past was that at a time when she'd lost her job and was desperate for money, she'd tried to work as a phone sex operator. And she hadn't even succeeded in doing that.

Unless . . .

I began to get a creepy feeling, a little prickle at the back of my neck.

Into the envelope went the report on Mickey. I removed the pages on Iva—and got another shock. Iva Diane Brody had been arrested twice for "solicitation." One need not have been married to a police detective to know that "solicitation" meant Iva had been charged with prostitution.

It was so hard to imagine Iva, with her delicate features, soft eyes, gentle manners . . . I'd never even heard her swear.

But I'd learned in my lifetime that all kinds of people did all kinds of things.

According to Taggart, Iva's second arrest had occurred less than a year before she met Mickey.

It was no wonder she was afraid that Mickey would leave her if he found out about her past. Even though Iva had lied to me about the reason, I didn't doubt that her terror was real.

I couldn't predict how Mickey would react if he learned about it, but one thing was clear to me: Iva had a motive to murder both Reggie and Taggart.

Another possible scenario occurred to me. Suppose Mickey had found out about Iva's past, perhaps from Reggie. Or suppose Taggart had contacted Mickey and tried to be paid for burying the information. If Mickey really loved Iva, as I'd had no reason to doubt, he might have killed to protect her secret. It was already on record that he was capable of violence. Mickey's own long-ago arrest might have been for something bad enough that he would go as far as murder to hide it.

If the contents of Taggart's reports were made known to the police, then Bill Marshall would probably slide down the list of suspects, but either Iva or Mickey would rise to the top.

If I told the police what I knew, it could help Bill, but if Iva and Mickey were innocent of the murders, then exposing what Taggart learned might destroy their marriage. Even worse, I wasn't sure that Iva would be able to recover from the public humiliation.

The Marshalls were much closer and dearer to me than either of the Jordans, but if neither Mickey nor Iva was a killer, how could I ever forgive myself if I set the police onto them for the purpose of diverting attention from Bill?

Somehow, I had to learn the truth.

I picked up Taggart's reports on Mickey and Iva and put them back in the envelope. When I slid his report on me out from underneath Emma, I found those papers had been warmed by her body heat. I gave her a gentle stroke before I added that report to the envelope.

Is the answer to who killed Reggie and Taggart in the pages I held?

I had the strong feeling that it was. To think that two different people had murdered Reggie and Taggart was to believe in an outrageous and bizarre coincidence. I wasn't buying that. The link between the two victims was that Reggie had hired Taggart to investigate *us*.

Does the killer know I have these reports?

If so, my situation could be reduced to an exercise in Logic 101: Here were two facts and a conclusion.

1. The killer knew what Reggie had hired Taggart to do.

2. I knew what Taggart had found out.

3. Ergo, the killer couldn't afford to let me live.

While I contemplated this grim syllogism, the doorbell rang.

30

Tuffy followed me to the front door, wagging his tail and making what I recognized as "friendly" noises in his throat. I was sure he knew who was outside before I looked through the living room window and saw Nicholas D'Martino. He pointed his finger at the bell, about to ring again.

NDM saw me. Instead of ringing, he lifted his hand in greeting. But he wasn't smiling.

When I opened the door, he skipped a greeting and said, "You didn't tell me you went to see T. J. Taggart yesterday."

"You didn't tell me his hard drive had been stolen. We're even."

He reached down to give Tuffy an affectionate scratch behind the ears. Straightening, he said, "Do you want to fight, or would you rather compare notes?"

"If we discuss the Taggart murder, will you keep what I say off the record?"

"I can't promise that."

"Then we can't compare notes," I said.

I moved around him and reached for the knob to close the door. He put his hand on my arm to stop me.

"Okay," he said. "We'll go off the record. "But I have my price." He smiled in that way he had of instantly making me think about sex.

I closed the door and took a step away from him. "What's your price?"

"Coffee, and whatever you have in the cupboard for a hungry man who missed lunch."

"Deal." I nodded in the direction of the kitchen and started toward it, but he took my wrist and drew me close to him. His lips touched mine in the lightest, most gentle kiss. "Let's start all over again. Hello," he said.

Tuffy squeezed in between us. Feeling my big dog's entire back end wagging made me laugh.

NDM looked down at him and grinned. "See, Tuff likes me even when you don't."

"I'll have to have a chat with him about that," I said.

Out in the kitchen, NDM flipped the switch on the coffeemaker and put napkins and cutlery on the table while I heated the Bolognaise sauce I had in the refrigerator, and quickly made a pot of angel hair pasta. With that—and running half a loaf of buttered French bread under the broiler for a few seconds—I'd produced one of the world's fastest meals.

NDM poured two mugs of coffee for us as I ladled angel hair and sauce into a pasta bowl and set it, along with a basket of hot French bread, in front of him.

He saw that I hadn't made a bowl for myself. "You're not eating?"

"I just had lunch, with someone you know."

NDM's fork paused on its way to the pasta. "Ah. Phil Logan. So that's why he called me."

"Eat," I said. And while he did, I studied this man with whom I was having a romantic relationship. It still surprised me that this had happened so quickly. Twenty plus years ago, I had waited until I knew Mack Carmichael very well before we went to bed together. Nicholas D'Martino and I had reversed the process.

"I want to be able to trust you," I said. "What I've found out could be very harmful to people I care about. If I tell you the things I've learned, I don't want them to be made public unless one of those people actually committed murder."

He put down his fork and reached across the kitchen table to touch my hand. "You're smart, and it looks as though you've gotten further in the Taggart case than I have, but I have resources you don't. The best way to save an innocent person is to find out who committed the crime."

"Crimes, plural," I said. "I'm sure you're right about Reggie's and Taggart's murders being connected."

"Let's share what we know, and see where the clues lead. The sooner the better."

I stood up. "Finish your pasta. I have to get something I want to show you."

When I left the kitchen, Tuffy looked up from where he was relaxing on his comfy pad by the refrigerator, but instead of following me, he stayed put. Perhaps it was because I'd talked to him conversationally from the time he was a puppy, but I was sure Tuff understood a lot of what I said and knew that I was coming right back.

When I returned to the kitchen with Taggart's reports I found NDM at the sink, washing his dishes.

"That's nice," I said. "Your mother brought you up well."

"She used to say, 'Nicholas, if you want to be invited back someplace, you need to be a good guest.'"

I sat down at the table and moved my coffee mug away from the middle of the table. "Is that what she called you? Nicholas?"

He nodded. "Yes, and that's what I wish you'd call me. Do you realize that you never use my name when you talk to me?"

"Oh, there's something I call you to myself."

"What? 'That bastard'?"

I chuckled. "Not more than once or twice a day. Truthfully, when I think of you, I call you by your initials, NDM."

"Like FBI or CIA—or SOB?"

More like WD, as in WD-40. Like that handy spray, he'd certainly loosened *me* up, but I knew if I voiced that thought it could lead us right to the bedroom, so I kept it to myself.

He sat, glanced at the envelope I'd placed facedown on the table, but didn't make a move toward it. Instead, he looked at me. "Call me Nicholas. Nobody else does."

"All right—Nicholas." The name felt good on my tongue.

But it was time to get to work. I took the three reports out of Taggart's envelope but held onto them. "At this moment it doesn't matter how I found out, but you're not the only one who learned that Reggie Davis hired private investigator T. J. Taggart. She went to him immediately after she agreed to sponsor the cake mix competition slash TV reality show."

"Do you know why?"

"I suspected it was because of me," I said. "Addison Jordan, who made the deal with her, insisted that I was to be a contestant. He said she'd asked him a lot of personal questions about me, but that he couldn't give her any answers. I was sure I was the reason she'd hired a private investigator when I figured out that she'd deliberately gone after Bill Marshall—one of the people closest to me—to try to lure him into having an affair with her."

I handed Nicholas the pages Taggart had written about me. "Near the end of this 'unauthorized biography' is a list of my closest friends."

"Am I on it?"

"You're on *my* list," I said, "but Taggart didn't find out about us. If he had, I think Reggie would have gone after you—to punish me."

I gave him time to read the report. When he put it down, I told him about my college history with Reggie, and my belief that she still was trying to hurt me any way that she could manage. "I think that if she couldn't break up a relationship of mine, the next best thing in her mind must have been to destroy my friends. My reason is that I remember something Reggie said when I was driving her home from my house because she was drunk."

"What was that?"

"She said something about being interested in a married man because he thought he was in love with his wife. I was shocked, and said that Reggie could break up their marriage. Her answer was, 'Revenge is sweet.' She fell asleep before she said anything else, but when I learned she went after Bill Marshall—my good friend, a man she found out about through investigating me—I made the connection."

"That makes sense, in a twisted sort of way," he said. "I've known women who . . . well, no need to go into that." He indicated the pages I was holding.

"Who else did she investigate?"

"This is the sensitive part. It was Mickey Jordan, and his wife, Iva. After you've read these, please don't jump to any conclusions. I want us to discuss how we can find out more than Taggart did."

Nicholas took the papers and began to read them carefully. I saw his eyebrows rise twice, but he kept his expression neutral.

When he finished the last page, he said, "Who knows you have this material?"

"I haven't told anyone. The police—and you—found out that I'd been to see Taggart. When John and his partner came to question me about my visit to Taggart, I only answered their questions—and narrowly at that. Without Taggart's files, they had no idea what might be missing, so they didn't ask if I'd talked Taggart out of any reports."

"How did you manage that?"

"Professional secret. Let's just say I was persuasive."

Nicholas gave me a wry smile. "You can be pretty damn persuasive. I remember the night you came to my house and persuaded me into bed."

"It didn't take much," I said. "On Taggart all I had to use was words."

"I'd have paid to have heard that conversation," he said.

"It wasn't exciting, but I got the reports, which is all that matters—except he was alive when I left him."

"That reminds me. I found out what the medical examiner's ruled as the time frame of his death."

"When?"

"Based on when he'd eaten last, the ME judges Taggart was struck a fatal blow to the head sometime between five and seven PM."

I expelled a heartfelt sigh of relief. "I'd almost reached the studio in North Hollywood by five, and I was there for the next several hours."

But I had no idea where either Mickey or Iva were.

"What was the murder weapon?" I said.

"Apparently, the police aren't sure yet. Whatever it was, the killer took it away."

"Reggie was struck by a heavy crockery mixing bowl that was in my test kitchen cubicle, which could mean the person who hit her hadn't come there intending to kill her." I thought for a moment. "Taggart's death might have been to cover up Reggie's killing."

"Which brings us back to Taggart's investigation," Nicholas

said. "You haven't told anyone except me that you have these reports?"

"No, and it's hard to believe that Taggart would admit he'd turned them over to someone. He was worried about people finding out."

"The killer must have taken Taggart's hard drive to keep anyone from seeing his files. If no one knows what you have then you should be safe."

Another "if."

Briefly, I considered telling Nicholas about the car that I thought had tried to force me off the road, but I couldn't swear that was what the driver was trying to do. I resisted the impulse to say anything and instead, turned the conversation toward making use of Taggart's reports.

"I know where I'd like to start digging," I said.

"So do I. You first. Where?"

"The officer who arrested Mickey way back in the Dark Ages. Is he still alive? If he is, I want to know what he remembers about the case. What exactly did Mickey do? Was the case adjudicated, and if so, how? And how did Mickey end up in the army a few months later?"

"With a case that's thirty or forty years old, the chances are slim that anyone who knows the facts is either alive or coherent enough to remember the details."

"I'm going to try anyway. Where are you going to start?"

"With Iva Jordan's prostitution busts. The most recent happened four years ago. I've got a friend on a Manhattan paper who hangs with some vice cops."

"You'll be careful what you tell him? You won't let him know that Iva's name came up in a murder investigation?"

He patted my hand reassuringly. "I'll put my questions on the basis of a favor. But if it turns out Iva's a killer, I'll cut him in on the story. That sort of quid pro quo has always been the basis for exchanging information. Do you want me to help you find out about Jordan's arrest?"

"No, thanks. At least not unless the idea I have doesn't work."

He cocked his head and gave me a quizzical stare. "You're not a trained investigator."

"I'm not a trained chef, either, but I'm cooking on television."

"Touché. Okay, let's get to work."

We stood and he drew me into his arms. His lips brushed my forehead and he whispered, "Send this soldier off to the trenches with a kiss."

"It will be my pleasure . . . *Nicholas*."

Several sweet, hot, dizzying moments later, we came up for air, and Tuffy and I walked him to the front door.

31

The first thing I did after Nicholas left the house was go to my bedroom to find the old suitcase I kept in the back of the closet. My closet wasn't nearly as neat as I wanted it to be, nor was it as well organized as I'd kept it when Mack was alive.

I removed several layers of old sweatshirts, a stained floral tablecloth, and washed-out sheets and towels. These were fabrics I'd saved because I used to fantasize I'd sew them into a quilt when I had time. But I never had time, and, to be honest, except for replacing buttons, I was terrible at sewing. But I loved the look and feel of homemade quilts. I'd had to buy the only one I owned.

Finally, I spotted what I was looking for.

It took some tugging and grunting, but I managed to drag the suitcase out into the room. With a mighty heave, I got it up onto the foot of the bed.

Good lord. How young I was to have thought that this college suitcase of mine—this bag with its peeling, imitation leather corners, covered in tapestry fabric with a not-very-artistic depiction of a scene from *The Canterbury Tales*—was grown-up, and even elegant. But that's exactly what I thought back then. With apologies to Carl Sandburg and his poem about fog, as we age cellulite, too, "comes in on little cat feet," but at least our taste gets better as we mature.

I pushed the case's twin locks to the open position, raised the top, and was hit with a wave of grief. Unexpected. I thought I'd gotten past it, but for a moment, it took my breath away. I hadn't opened the suitcase for two years, not since a few days after Mack's funeral. These were his things that I'd packed away: the weights he'd used for endurance training, the college term papers he'd saved, his copy of the penal code, his police academy graduation photograph, a citation for bravery that he'd never let me display, our wedding pictures, Tuffy's "adoption" papers, an often read paperback copy of his favorite Joseph Wambaugh novel, *The Choirboys*—and letters. Lots of letters, four stacks, tied in bundles but not organized.

The letters were what I wanted.

I sat down on the floor with my back braced against the side of the bed and untied the first bunch. Shuffling through them, I discovered the six cards that I'd sent Mack when I'd had to go to San Francisco for my father's funeral. He was on a case and couldn't come with me. I'd only been away from home for seventy-two hours, but I missed him so much I'd sent him two cards a day. I had no idea Mack had kept them. Reminding myself that now was not the time for nostalgia, I put the cards aside and kept searching.

What I was looking for was near the end of the second bundle. It was a letter to Mack from his favorite instructor at the police academy, Sergeant Sean Donahue. I'd never met Sergeant Donahue, but Mack had talked about him often and with affection. My interest in the sergeant at this moment was not what a good instructor he'd been for Mack, but what he did *before* coming to the Los Angeles police academy: He'd spent years as a detective in the NYPD. New York was where he'd begun his long career in law enforcement, and judging from his age, I guessed he would have been on the job when Mickey Jordan was arrested.

The return address was unreadable, but the postmark on the envelope was Tucson, Arizona. Seeing it, I remember Mack telling me that his early mentor had retired to live with his widowed sister in Arizona.

Calling Tucson, I found out that there were several Donahues in the telephone directory, but no Sean. I got the operator to give me the first four numbers, then called again and got a second operator to give me four more numbers. I started dialing.

Each time someone answered the phone, I asked if I'd reached the home of Sean Donahue. When the answer was "no," I asked if the person knew a Sean Donahue, and said that the man I was trying to contact would be in his seventies, and had been a police detective.

None of them had information to give me.

On the sixth Donahue number, an elderly woman answered the phone.

"Hello," I said, "I hope I'm not calling at an inconvenient time, but I'm trying to reach the Sean Donahue who used to be with the Los Angeles Police Department."

"That's my brother," she said.

My grip on the phone tightened with excitement. Now came the hard part, tactfully finding out if the man was alive. I chose my words carefully.

"I'm happy to talk to you. My name is Della Carmichael. Your brother taught my husband at the police academy."

"Oh, that's nice," she said, sounding a little faraway. Then she was silent.

"As I said, my name is Della Carmichael. And you're Mrs . . . ?"

"What?"

From the vagueness in her voice I realized this wasn't going to be easy. I decided to get right to the point. "I wondered if I could speak to your brother?"

"Well, dear," she said slowly, "that's going to be a little hard . . ."

Uh-huh. "I hope Sergeant Donahue is well," I said. What I really hoped was that he wasn't dead.

"Who?"

"Your brother, Sean."

"Oh, Sean. What did you want?"

"I wondered if I could speak to Sean."

"He's sleeping," she said.

Thank you, God.

"I don't want to disturb him," I said. "When would be a good time for me to call later?"

"I don't know, dear. He sleeps a lot nowadays."

Faking a cheerful tone, I said, "That's probably good for him. Could I give you my phone number and ask you to have him call me when he's up?"

"Your phone number? I don't have your number, do I?"

"Let me give it to you," I said, being very careful not to sound impatient. "Are you ready?"

"Just a minute, dear. I have to get a pencil." There followed almost a minute of sounds: drawers opening, contents rustling, drawers closing. Another drawer opened, something dropped.

"I'm back," she said. "Now who did you say you were?"

"Mackenzie Carmichael's wife, Della. Have him call any time at all—I don't care how late or how early."

I gave her my cell phone number. Sean Donahue's sister—I still didn't know her name—asked me to repeat it, two digits at a time, but when she finally read it back to me, she'd got Mack's name and my number right.

"I'll put this note next to his dinner plate, in case I forget to tell him," she said.

I thanked her. As Sean Donahue's sister and I were exchanging good-byes, Eileen burst into my room.

Waving two shiny new sets of keys, she said, "Let's go see our factory!"

■ ■ ■

The two-story, gray stucco building that had once housed the Hollywood Stars Bakery was located a few blocks east of such Hollywood Boulevard landmarks as Musso & Frank's restaurant, the Pantages Theater, where touring Broadway musicals played, and the Church of Scientology headquarters, impossible to miss because of the enormous vertical sign that ran up the side of the building.

I'd seen those landmarks too often for them to be interesting to me, but the closer we got to the building Mickey bought, the more excited I became.

"There," Eileen said. "On the right. Oh, wow! We're really going to do this!"

"Yes, we are," I said.

The manufacturing site of our new business anchored a block that had not yet been gentrified, as had so much of Hollywood Boulevard from Vine Street west to Crescent Heights. That was probably how Mickey had bought the building at a bargain price. Our location was on the southwest corner of Hollywood Boulevard and Baker Street.

"*Baker* Street," Eileen said. "How appropriate."

In more ways than one, I thought. I was "sleuthing," and that ancestor of all sleuths, Sherlock Holmes, lived on Baker Street. I hoped this was a good omen.

This new business venture had started with a chance remark of mine to Eileen and to Phil Logan, while Phil, who'd said he needed a sugar rush, was eating some fudge I'd made. I told them about having whipped up batches of it for friends when I was in college and too broke to buy Christmas presents. That little fact took root in Eileen's imagination and blossomed into a full-fledged business plan. Now her idea and proposal were about to become a reality.

"Look, the building has parking in the back," Eileen said.

But I was already turning into the big lot. There was only one vehicle in it: a dark green Mercedes parked next to the rear door. Judging from its boxy shape, I guessed it was close to thirty years old, but was polished to a high sheen. Clearly, the owner took good care of it.

As the two of us got out of the Jeep, I realized that my emotions were now equal parts excitement and *fear*. What if no one wanted to buy our products? Mickey would lose money, and perhaps even sour on the TV show.

No, stop thinking like that, I told myself firmly. If this business made money, I'd be out of debt sooner and I could begin saving again. *Think positive thoughts*.

Eileen led the way around to the front of the building, walking so fast I had to hurry to keep up with her.

"Can you believe this? We're going to be in business together!"

A small man with a round pink face and a thatch of silver hair was staring at us through the large front window that still bore traces of the gold paint that had spelled out "Hollywood Stars Bakery."

He waved at us.

I waved back. "I wonder who that is," I said.

"Oh, Ad told me about him. He's a retired actor who was the bakery's facilities manager. Mickey kept him on for now because he knows how everything works, but we can hire our own staff."

The retired actor looked to be in his eighties, but his eyes were bright and lively, and his smile displayed very white teeth. As he approached his side of the glass front door, I saw that he moved like a much younger man.

"Unless it turns out that he drinks to excess or is totally crazy, we're not going to let him go," I said. "Think how hard it would be for him to get another job at his age."

"You're right," she said.

Our retired actor opened the door. "I will hazard the guess that you lovely young ladies are here to bring this dead enterprise back to life."

"We're going to do our best," I said. "I'm Della Carmichael and this is Eileen O'Hara."

He inclined his head in a courtly nod. "Walter Hovey, at your service." His voice was strong and mellifluous. Although I didn't recognize his face, there was something familiar about that voice.

Eileen gestured to the front of the bakery. "I'd like us to keep the sell counter that's already here—but with fresh paint and new glass in the display case. For people who live in Los Angeles and don't need to buy through the mail."

I indicated the view through the window. "It's a good location for in-person business. There's a freeway exit ramp over there, and we have lots of room for customer parking in the back."

Walter Hovey said, "Have you chosen a name for the new incarnation of this establishment?"

"Not yet," Eileen said.

I enjoyed listening to him talk, but I also caught a glint in his eyes that made me ask, "Do you have an idea—for the name?"

He took a dramatic pause. "In fact, I do. I was told that your intention is to transform these three thousand square feet into a wonderland of edible delights. Is that correct?"

"Yes."

"Follow my thinking: This is Hollywood, the land of dreams. Yes?"

Eileen and I nodded assent.

"Why not call your business Sweet Dreams?"

"I like it," I said.

"Almost," Eileen said. "How about *Della's* Sweet Dreams? We should use your name to tie in with the TV show, otherwise we'll lose a promotion advantage."

"All right. That makes sense." I turned to Walter Hovey. "Would you show us around? I'd like to see what we have to work with."

Walter Hovey gave us one of his little bows. "Right this way, ladies."

With our silver-haired escort guiding us through the premises, I saw that what had seemed to be a two-story building was really a one-story structure two stories high.

"My little office is way in the back," he said. "That is where I do the ordering of baking supplies, keep the inventory, and schedule regular inspections. I am proud to say that since I joined the bakery and instituted our system of multiple in-house inspections, we have received only 'A' ratings from the health authorities."

"Excellent," I said. "We'll keep up your system."

As we toured the premises, Walter pointed out the long preparation tables and the wall of ovens that we would need for the production of brownies. There was a conveyor belt leading to machines for packaging.

"That marble slab will be good for cooling the fudge," I said, "but I'm going to need it extended to twice that length, with a divider in the middle."

Walter took a small notebook and ballpoint pen from his pocket and made a note. "It shall be done."

Eileen pointed to several large vats. "What are they for?"

"Mixing batters and frostings, I think." I looked at Walter for confirmation.

"Just so," he said. "Those chutes above our heads will, when I place the orders, be filled with flour and sugar. The rigging above allows one to maneuver the chutes, depending upon what ingredient is needed in which receptacle. See the control buttons below the red and blue levers on the wall? They turn the mechanism on. Red for sugar, blue for flour. Pushing the levers to the right swings the chutes over the vats."

Eileen said, "What happens if somebody accidentally just pushes a button?"

Walter shuddered. "We would require a backhoe to clear away the mess."

I was particularly interested in those ovens. "How accurate are the temperature gauges?"

"They had begun to run fifty degrees hotter just before the building was sold," Walter said. "I can have a repairman here tomorrow morning."

"Good," Eileen said. "We can't afford to burn the baked goods."

Before I could ask anything else, the cell phone in my pocket rang. I took it out—and felt a jolt of anticipation when I saw the name on the faceplate.

Sean Donahue was calling me back.

32

I pressed the answer button. "Hello."

"It this young Mackenzie's bride?"

"Yes, I am." At least I had been twenty-two years ago. "Could you please hang on for just a moment?"

"Sure. I got no place to go." Sean Donahue's voice was that of an elderly man, but it didn't have a trace of the vagueness that characterized his sister's conversation.

I inched away from Eileen and Walter, and gestured to the cell phone. "I'm sorry, I have to take this."

"Go ahead," Eileen said. "I'll keep looking around."

I moved toward the front area. As soon as I could speak without being overheard by Eileen and Walter, I said, "Thank you for hanging on. Am I speaking to Sean Donahue?"

"That you are. How is my friend Mackenzie?"

Oh, Lord—he doesn't know. "I'm afraid I have some bad news. My husband had a heart attack. He passed away two years ago."

"I'm sorry for your loss," he said.

It was that automatic law enforcement phrase uttered to the bereaved, but Sean Donahue sounded sincere.

"Thank you, Sergeant. I appreciate that. Mack spoke about you often. He was very fond of you."

"Is that why you phoned, Mrs. Carmichael? To tell me he's gone?"

"Please call me Della. No, but I feel bad that I didn't think to let you know at the time it happened. It was a terrible shock, and I wasn't thinking clearly for quite awhile afterward."

He cleared his throat, and then it sounded as though he was sipping something. When he spoke again the slight rasp in his voice was gone. "So, what can I do for you?"

"I wanted to ask about an arrest that happened in New York City, around forty years ago."

He chuckled. "I'm glad you didn't ask me what I had for dinner last night. My short-term memory is shot. Is this about one of my old cases?"

"Probably not." *I couldn't be that lucky.* "I don't know who the arresting officer was, but the name of the young man, who would have been somewhere between eighteen and twenty at the time, was Mickey Jordan. Does that name mean anything to you?"

I heard a *hmmmmm* on the other end. "Doesn't ring a bell. What else do you know about the case?"

"He was arrested for Ag-Assault GBI. A private detective found out that much, but apparently didn't learn the name of the arresting officer, or any specifics about the charge. The only other information I have is that Mickey Jordan was born Michla Jacoby, but he was reregistered in grade school as Michael Lewis, and then when he was eighteen he had his name changed legally to Mickey Jordan."

"Jacoby–Lewis–Jordan . . . No, I'm sure he wasn't one of mine. Sorry."

"It would be too bizarre a coincidence if the only person I knew who'd been with the NYPD at that time just happened to have been the arresting officer. What I'm hoping is that you might have heard something about it, or know someone who might have been involved, or even just remember, the case."

"Forty years back? Not many people I knew in my New York days are still alive, even though some of them were younger than me." I heard the note of sadness in his voice. "Stress kills a lot more of us than the bad guys pick off."

I knew that sad fact from the stories Mack and John had told me over the years. In fact, I believed it was the emotional toll of his job that had led to Mack's heart attack. I said, "Police have to deal with the worst things human beings can do."

"Yeah, that's true, but now and then we get to put something right. Keeps us going. You tell me something, Della. What's this about? Why are you interested in a case from so far back?"

"It might possibly have some connection to the recent

killing of a private detective here in Los Angeles. The man's name was T. J. Taggart. He'd been investigating people for a woman who was murdered shortly before he was. Mickey Jordan was one of the people whose history Taggart was looking into."

"I thought Mackenzie married a pretty little schoolmarm. You on the job now?"

"No, I'm not, but a good friend of ours is a suspect— someone I'm sure is innocent. I'm trying to learn anything I can that might help find the real killer."

"You shouldn't be getting involved in a murder case, Della." His tone had switched from affable to stern. "If I told you something that got you hurt, when my time came to cross over, Mackenzie would chase me all the way down to hell."

I felt a flash of anger. Sean Donahue was treating me like "the little woman" who was supposed to stay home and knit while the big, strong men went out to face danger. I couldn't keep the edge out of my voice as I said, "I'm not that 'schoolmarm' you imagined Mack married. The man who's under suspicion, whose life could be ruined by false accusations, was one of Mack's two closest friends in the world. If Mack were here, you know he'd be doing everything he could think of to save him."

"Whoa. Sounds like I stepped on the tail of a wildcat."

"Not quite," I said. "But I do need your help—anything you can find out. I promise that I won't take any unnecessary chances, and I'll tell the police if we discover anything useful."

"I like that 'we' part." He chuckled; our little storm was over. "Okay, Mrs. Mack." He was quiet for a moment but I heard him open a drawer, then close it. "I'm writing this down: Jacoby– Lewis–Jordan, kid, Ag-assault GBI forty years ago. That it?"

"Yes."

"I'll make some calls, see who's still standing, and nose around a little."

"Thank you," I said. "I'm very grateful."

"Yeah, well, remember that it's not very likely I'll find anything out after all this time. Don't count on it."

"I won't, but I appreciate your trying to help. I know Mack would, too."

I slipped the phone back into my pocket, knowing how small the chance was that Sean Donahue would be able to find out the details of Mickey's arrest. But I had to start somewhere.

I didn't look forward to seeing Mickey, knowing that I was trying to dig into his past. It was going to be especially hard tomorrow morning, when we would both be at the site of Reggie's murder. The four other contestants and I were gathering at the test kitchens of Davis Foods International for the first day of filming our experiments in creating a brand-new cake.

Cake. Cake batter . . .

With a sudden chill I remembered what John had told me about Reggie's murder. She'd been struck on the head with a heavy mixing bowl. That was a weapon of opportunity, indicating that the killer probably hadn't gone to the test kitchens that night with murder in mind. Something must have happened to provoke the initial blow. If the confrontation had stopped there, Reggie probably would still be alive, and at most the person who'd struck her would have been arrested for assault. But the killer hadn't stopped there. He—or she—hadn't just committed murder, but had taken the time to humiliate Reggie by drowning her in a bowl of her own cake batter.

In contrast to the impulsiveness of Reggie's murder, Taggart's was premeditated; the killer must have gone to his office with a weapon. Reggie and Taggart were linked because she'd hired him to investigate three people: Mickey, Iva, and me.

I was convinced that the perpetrator had killed to keep hidden something that Taggart had learned. That had to be why the detective's hard drive had been stolen. If the killer didn't know that I had a copy of the reports, I'd be safe.

But if he or she did know . . .

The chill I felt suddenly got colder.

33

When I guided my Jeep into the parking lot behind the Davis Foods International building at the appointed time Saturday morning, I was still uneasy, but I decided that I had to concentrate on the job at hand. And, being in this location again, perhaps I could get an idea, or even some hint, as to who besides Bill, Mickey, and Iva might have been driven to kill.

At least a dozen vehicles were already there. Among them, I recognized the big pink Cadillac that belonged to Winnie King, the Mary Kay saleswoman and owner of the Pink Lady Bakery in Beverly Hills; two TV equipment vans from the Better Living Channel; Mickey Jordan's sunflower yellow Range Rover that I secretly thought of as his gigantic bumblebee; and several cars I'd seen the day I met the other contestants and toured the facility for the first time.

Three of the cars were sedans in dark colors. The sight of them produced a sudden flashback to the night a dark sedan chased me in the rain and tried to force me off the road. I'd suspected T. J. Taggart, but after I'd learned Taggart had been killed before my terrifying race through Beverly Glen Canyon, I had no idea who might have been behind the wheel.

Briefly, I wondered if one of the other contestants had tried to kill me but I quashed that thought. It was just too ridiculous. This was a *cake* contest, with a prize of only $25,000. That amount of money meant a great deal to me, but it wasn't one of the million dollar prizes the broadcast networks offered on their reality competitions. We bakers weren't being made to live in jungles and build our own shelters, or eat revolting things, or let slimy creatures crawl all over us. In my opinion, those people earned the big prizes, and I hoped they'd used some of the cash to pay for therapy.

Besides, I told myself, if anyone thought of eliminating a contestant in the Reggi-Mixx baking contest, it wasn't likely that I'd be the target. Handicapping this race, I'd be ranked as the hundred-to-one shot.

It was hard to imagine the people I was up against, or their surrogates, trying to get rid of *me*. Every one of them was a better bet to win. Gordon Prescott had been pastry chef to a governor, Winnie King had owned her own successful bakery for fifteen years, Clay Sutton—the chef who looked like a surfer—had been described by Reggie as Hollywood's hottest new caterer, and Viola Lee did the weekly dessert feature on the top-rated TV show *GBN in the Morning*. GBN, the Global Broadcasting Network, was on a par with ABC, CBS, and NBC. It had millions of regular viewers and made Viola the most famous of the five of us.

By contrast, I was on cable TV, the underdog of show business. Although the cable networks were growing more popular every year, most of their shows still had audience numbers in the hundreds of thousands, not the millions.

I parked my Jeep near the end of the row of spaces, where there was no car on either side. Extra walking was good for me, but my choice of spot was an attempt to avoid getting little dents in the sides from vehicles whose owners weren't careful about opening their doors. Touching up chipped paint wasn't in my budget.

Entering the building's small reception area, I saw a cameraman checking his equipment. It was Ben, the young man whose wife watched the show and enjoyed seeing me drop things. He had taped my first interview for the contest.

"Hi, Ben."

He looked up at me and grinned, revealing that he still hadn't taken that needed trip to a dentist.

"I got you again," he said. "I was afraid I was going to have to cover Chef-in-Love-with-Himself, but my pal Freddie got stuck with Prescott."

"Is Gordon Prescott hard to work with?"

Ben grimaced. "He thinks he's a movie star. When I did his personal interview, he demanded special high key lighting to make his complexion look smoother, and then he threw a fit until I stood on a stool and shot him from a slight high angle so his double chin didn't show." Ben glanced at the closed door leading to the kitchens, and winked at me. "Freddie told him that we're using a special 'slimming lens' on him."

Hope rose in my heart. "You have a lens that makes people look thinner?"

"Nah. Freddie just told him that so he wouldn't have to stand on a stool, or twist himself into a pretzel trying to get a flattering angle on Prescott." The cameraman hefted the rig onto his shoulder. "You ready to get started? Want to powder your nose or something before we start?"

"I'm fine," I said.

He gave me an impish smile, and in parody of my line on the show, he said, "Let's get cooking."

Inside the Davis Foods Test Kitchens there were camera people with portable equipment everywhere I looked. Stationary TV lights were aimed at the five cubicles assigned to the contestants. The rows beyond our line of kitchens, where the Davis employees worked during the week, were dark, but the aisle leading from the office at the front of the building back down to the reception area was lighted.

As I'd learned on my first visit, there were forty test kitchen cubicles, divided into four rows of ten each. The little kitchens were separated from one another by six-foot-high plywood dividers that went three-quarters of the way around, and left the back part open.

We five contestants had been assigned the first row, the one closest to the outside entrance. There was an empty kitchen between each of us. Viola Lee had been given kitchen number one; Gordon Prescott was assigned number two; Winnie King would be in the middle; Clay Sutton would be between Winnie and me. My cubicle was at the far end, next to the pantry.

A faint wave of nausea swept over me as I looked down the line of assigned kitchens. I was supposed to work in the space where Reggie Davis had been murdered.

"No, I can't do it," I said.

"Can't do what, sugar?"

I hadn't realized that I'd spoken aloud until I heard Winnie King's voice behind me. I turned. Her hair still looked like a cloud of pink cotton candy, her cheeks were contoured with a deep pink blusher, and when she raised her right hand to brush away an invisible piece of lint from the shoulder of her pink silk tracksuit, I saw that she was wearing a pink diamond ring. That stone was almost as big as an ice cube.

"Sugar, are you feeling woozy?" She leaned closer to me and whispered, "If it's your time of the month, I've got a little somethin' in my bag that's a guaranteed tummy settler."

I shook my head. "It's not that, but thank you." I drew back enough to keep from being smothered by her perfume. "Regina Davis was killed in my kitchen," I said.

"Oh, is that all?" She made a dismissive gesture. "Don't you worry about it. I'm sure the blood's been washed away by now."

For a second I thought I might throw up, but I got control of myself in time to see Mickey Jordan coming down the aisle toward us. Beside him was a woman I'd never seen before. The two of them were followed by Gordon Prescott, Viola Lee, and Addison. Addison was carrying a garment bag.

The stranger with Mickey was about my age, but taller and stockier. Her hair was the shiny black of patent leather, and she wore it pulled back from her elongated face, tied in one long braid that she'd anchored in a circle on top of her head, like a crown. She reminded me of someone, but I couldn't think of whom.

Mickey performed introductions. "Della, Winnie, this is Hedda Klein, vice president of Reggi-Mixx. She'll be supervising the contest now."

Now. He means in place of Reggie, who was murdered thirty feet from where we were standing, chatting so casually. But I didn't say what I was thinking. Instead, I said that I was happy to meet her and extended my hand.

Hedda Klein took it in a grip so firm it was just short of painful—and I remembered who she reminded me of. It was my high school PE teacher, the woman some of the girls referred to as Bone-crusher Bradley.

Clay Sutton hurried in from outside, carrying a package wrapped in brown paper under his arm. It was about the size and shape of a pillow.

"Sorry I'm late," he said. "I was in Beverly Hills. A delivery van hit a Jag and I got stuck behind—"

"Forget it," Mickey said. He introduced Clay to Hedda Klein.

Addison stepped forward and indicated the garment bag. "Do you want me to give these out now, Mickey?" His voice was still husky with a trace of his cold.

Mickey said, "Yeah."

Working together, Addison unzipped the bag and Hedda Klein removed an array of colored smocks on hangers and displayed them for us. On the front of each were the words "Reggi-Mixx Contestant."

"*Ooooo*," Winnie squealed. "Dibs on the pink one!"

Addison handed it to her.

Clay reached for the dark green smock. "That's my color," he said.

"Why don't we let Viola and Della choose first," Addison said.

"Let Clay have the green one, " Viola said.

Without a word of thanks to her, Clay took the green smock and his package and scurried to his assigned cubicle.

Viola turned to me. "If you want the blue, I'll take the burgundy."

"That's good." I reached for the blue smock. With Viola's cognac-colored eyes, she would look great in the burgundy.

Addison tried to hand Gordon Prescott the remaining smock. "Is the black okay for you, Gordon?"

Prescott put both hands up, palms out, in an "I'm not touching that" gesture.

"No, it is not," he said. "Must I remind you that I am a Cordon Bleu chef? There is no way I will even consider donning one of those silly advertising billboards. I insist on wearing my proper white chef's jacket."

Addison looked at his father. "Is that all right, Mickey?"

Mickey shrugged, but I could tell he was irritated. "Prescott can wear spandex if he wants."

Tap, tap, tap, tap, tap.

That sound caught my attention. I turned in the direction it was coming from and saw Clay nailing up a length of heavy green fabric over the entrance to his kitchen. The paper wrapping lay on the floor at his feet.

Mickey yelled, "Hey! Hey! What do you think you're doing?"

"I need privacy while I work." Clay's voice was set on "whine."

"You're gonna be on a TV show—who wants to look at a curtain? Take it down."

Clay screwed up his face and pointed to Prescott. "You let him wear a different coat."

Hollywood's hottest new caterer looked like a child who was about to throw a crying tantrum. I didn't want this dispute to turn into a fight that could delay the start of our work because there were things I wanted to do as soon as I finished here.

"Mickey," I said, "don't you think that the curtain over Clay's space could add a little mystery to the show?"

Mickey frowned in thought. "Somethin' different, huh? Yeah, okay. Keep the curtain."

Clay beamed like sunshine after rain. He threw his arms out wide in a way that made me think he was about to embrace Mickey. Mickey must have thought so, too, because he backed up.

"Let's everybody get to work," Mickey said. "Time is money. *My* money."

I'd wanted to speak to Mickey about my using a different cubicle from the scene of Reggie's murder, but he was already through the door into the reception area. Mickey moved fast. I knew he'd be outside and into the Range Rover before I could catch him.

Hedda Klein tapped me on the shoulder. "Put on your smock. Everybody else has already begun to get supplies from the pantry."

"I'd like to use a different kitchen—"

"No. I'm sorry. The stationary lights have already been set up."

"But do you know that Reggie was killed in the space I'm supposed to use?"

"All the more reason not to change spots," she said. "If you aren't in the same row with the other contestants, it will raise questions as to the reason. We certainly don't want to remind people that a woman was murdered on these premises. *Do we*?"

Hedda Klein's imperious tone—like Bone-crusher Bradley's when she'd threatened to send me to the principal's office for disobedience—signaled that argument would only lengthen the hours I'd have to spend here today.

"I understand," I said, and gave her my best imitation of a good loser's smile.

Deciding to tough it out, I headed for my assigned space. I felt a lurch in my stomach as I carefully skirted the spot on the floor where I'd found Reggie. As soon as I did enough experimental baking to satisfy the cameraman's needs, I'd get back to what I really wanted to do: find a killer.

34

When I got home that afternoon, Eileen was just returning from walking Tuffy. My curly-haired fella wagged enthusiastically. As soon as she let him off the leash, he raced across the lawn to greet me. I knelt down, scratching and petting Tuffy while Eileen unlocked the front door. She was smiling, but I knew her so well I could tell she was unhappy about something.

"How'd it go at the cake place?" she asked.

"I spent hours baking mixes to find out which one has a taste I can make into something I'm not ashamed to serve."

Emma trotted up from the back of the house to meet us. She and Tuff touched noses, as they always did when Tuffy returned from a walk or a drive. I wondered if he was giving her news from the outside world.

In the kitchen, I gave Tuffy and Emma fresh water and began preparations for their dinner.

"The baking didn't sound like it was fun," Eileen said.

"No, but it was necessary. I had to discover which flavor of mix ignited a creative idea in me."

"Did you find one?"

"By cutting and tasting little pieces after I baked them, I was able to eliminate chocolate, white, banana, and spice. Those flavors were pretty hopeless. I didn't get a chance to try the strawberry mix because Winnie King—the Pink Lady baker—grabbed all the boxes in the pantry. But I think the lemon and orange mixes have potential. I just have to figure out how to make something from one of them that's good enough to enter."

"I'm glad I don't have that job," Eileen said.

I watched her pour herself a glass of orange juice. She was

trying hard to be interested in my day, but I knew she was thinking about something else.

"What's on your mind?" I said.

She flashed an eager smile at me and sat down at the kitchen table.

"It's Ad. Addison. I like him—a lot—and he's giving every sign that he really likes me."

I sat down opposite her. "I'm sure he does."

She shook her head. "No, this isn't like when I was a teenager and had a crush on a guy. I'm hoping Ad might turn out to be *the one*."

It startled me to think she was considering getting serious at twenty. "There's a significant age difference between you two."

"He's only thirty," she said.

"I know, but there's a much bigger maturity gap between twenty and thirty than there is between thirty and forty."

"Older men are more interesting than the *boys* I meet at UCLA. Besides, it's not as though he's really old, like forty."

"Hey, be careful, or I'll cut you out of my will."

She realized I was teasing and grinned. "I didn't mean that *you're* old."

"When I was in college, I read a collections of letters written by the English humor writer, P. G. Wodehouse. When he was in his eighties, he wrote to a friend that it was amazing how our perceptions change as we grow older. He said that now when he's reading a novel and a new character who is sixty years old is introduced, he thinks to himself, 'Ah, the young love interest.' " Eileen laughed.

I gave her hand an affectionate pat. "There are a lot of men in this big world, and you'll have tons of choices. Don't be in a hurry."

"Oh, Aunt Del, Ad is so smart. He has great ideas about our business, and about Mickey's company, too. I guess it's hard for parents to think of their kids as grown-ups—as equals—but I know he's going to impress Mickey. I can tell how important it is to him. He told me how generous Mickey's been to him."

She finished her orange juice and got up. "I'm going to

take a shower and change. Ad and I are working together tonight, going over color schemes for the front of the store.
There's going to be a picture of you from the TV show in the
window. Oh—I almost forgot: Mickey approved the name
'Della's Sweet Dreams.' He's giving Walter a bonus for coming up with it."

■ ■ ■

Nicholas and I were going out to dinner that night. In a way,
we were starting our relationship all over again.

I took a hot, foamy bath with lavender body wash and
dabbed on a little of the perfume Nicholas had given me for
Christmas. It was good perfume. I was glad I hadn't poured it
down the sink after I saw him with the blonde and told him I
wasn't going to see him again. I'd only put the bottle away in
the cabinet, behind the bathroom cleanser.

Just as I finished getting ready, my cell phone rang. I answered it to hear, "Hey, Mrs. Mack."

"Sergeant Donahue." Hoping he had some news for me, I
felt a catch of excitement in my throat. "How are you?"

"Not as good as I was twenty years ago, but I'm still here,
so I put that in the 'win' column."

Forcing myself to make a little small talk before I asked
what I was burning to know, I said, "I'm glad that I finally
have a chance to speak to the man my husband looked up to."

"You cook on TV, but you don't need to grease me up like
a raw chicken."

"How did you know I had a cooking show?"

"Before I did any nosing around I checked you out on
Google. Wonderful thing, the Internet. Wish we'd had it when
I was on the job. Would've saved us all a lot of time. I found a
Della Carmichael, read the articles, and saw Mackenzie men-
tioned, so I knew it was you. Funny thing was I'd watched your
show a few times but I didn't connect your last name to Mack.
Hey, I made the chili and the chicken cacciatore. Real good.
Best thing is you can make the stuff once an' eat it for days."

Something I hadn't expected when I started was that men
would watch the show, but network research proved that many
did. I said, "Do you like to cook?"

"Necessity. My sister can't tell salt from sugar anymore. Enough of that. Let's get down to business 'cause this is your cell number so I know the call is costing you."

"Were you able to find out anything about Mickey Jordan's old arrest?"

His chuckle had a distinct note of pride. "It was as hard as I thought it would be, but then I got lucky. The kid's three names—Jacoby an' Lewis an' Jordan—that was what rang a bell in one of the old guys. He didn't recall details of the case, but he remembered it was pretty ugly. He was able to tell me who the arresting officer was."

"Could you locate him?" I was really asking if the man was still alive.

"Took some detective work, but I tracked him to an assisted living dump in Palm Bay, Florida. The Palmetto Lodge. From what I could find out, it's not a place you'd go to if you had a choice. Anyway, he's in a wheelchair—shot by a woman who'd called the cops on her husband who was beating her up. When they got there, she wouldn't let them arrest the bastard. She grabbed a gun an' shot Eddie. That's his name, Eddie Cochran."

I groaned in sympathy. "The poor man. That's terrible. Mack told me the calls he dreaded most were domestic disputes. He never knew what they might turn into. Did Officer Cochran remember Mickey Jordan?"

"His legs don't work, but he's as sharp as I am. Little Mick, that's what he called Jordan 'cause he said the kid reminded him of old movies with that short actor, Mickey Rooney. He said Little Mick was one of his success stories."

"That's interesting. What did Officer Cochran tell you?"

"Using a man's title—Mack trained you well." I heard a smile in Sean Donahue's voice. "Eddie told me he arrested Little Mick for beating a man half to death with a baseball bat."

I flinched at the mental image of Mickey being so violent.

"The victim was the kid's common-law stepfather, a scumbag with a record named Bernie Lewis. Lewis had been pounding on Mick and Mick's mother for years. Mick put a stop to it, permanently."

"This Bernie Lewis. Did he die?"

"Probably by now. Back then Mick just pulverized Lewis's knees and blinded him in one eye."

"What happened to Mickey?"

"When Eddie heard the story from the kid and his mom, he planted a throwaway on Lewis an' persuaded the ADA to call the beating self-defense. It helped that Lewis was a foot taller and sixty pounds heavier than the kid. After, Eddie suggested Little Mick join the army and stay out of sight for a couple years."

"What happened to Mickey's mother?"

"Don' know. But does this help you?"

"Yes, it does," I said.

"Good. Now maybe you can help Eddie Cochran."

"How?"

"I checked out that place he's in. It's filthy, and the food is crap. Doesn't pass state inspections, but somehow it stays in business. Felons get better care."

"That's awful."

"You're in TV. People in TV have some juice. Eddie was too good a cop to end up in a place like the Palmetto just because he's crippled an' broke. He doesn't have any family."

"I'll try to think of something," I said.

"You do that, Mrs. Mack."

As we said our good-byes, Tuffy began to bark. A second later the doorbell rang.

Nicholas was here to pick me up.

35

When I opened the front door, Nicholas's first act was to bend down and greet Tuffy with a few scratches under his ears. "I've got to stay friends with your protector so he'll let me near you."

He stood up and gave me a light kiss. "You look pretty," he said. "I like that red dress."

I wasn't surprised—this was what Liddy called "a man's dress." It had a tight waist and a V neckline, and had been Mack's favorite dress of mine. Miraculously, it hadn't gone out of style. Or maybe it was back in style. The truth was, if I liked something I hardly paid attention to what was in or out of style. Even though I hadn't worn it in two years, it still looked fresh.

"I have a suggestion about your baking contest," he said. "If the judges are men, you'll win if you wear that dress when you display the cake."

"Thank you, but I have to wear a Reggi-Mixx smock."

He arched an eyebrow and grinned mischievously. "*Just* a smock? That could work, too. I know what's under it."

I felt my cheeks flush. "Are you taking me out to dinner or are you going to keep talking like that?"

"You're blushing. That's cute."

He ran one index finger down along the V of my dress, lightly caressing my skin beneath the fabric. It produced such a rush of physical excitement I gave an involuntary little gasp.

"Hold that thought," he whispered.

■ ■ ■

After we took Tuffy for a walk and settled him back in the house, we drove to Amalfi, the small, homey Italian restaurant in Brentwood where he'd made a reservation. I'd heard about Amalfi, but had never been there. The moment we walked in the door we were treated to the most wonderful aromas. The lush strains of a Puccini opera issued from hidden speakers, pleasantly underscoring the quiet chatter of people who were well into their meals.

About two-thirds of the room's twenty or so tables were occupied. Their red, white, and green striped cloths were littered with platters and plates and glasses of wine. Nicholas exchanged a few quiet words with the waiter who greeted us, and slipped a bill into his hand. The waiter smiled and led us to a table as far away from other diners as he could, next to the wall that was covered with a mural of the dramatic cliffs and beautiful coastline of Amalfi, Italy.

The waiter seated us and took our drink orders: a glass of merlot for each of us. He left menus, but Nicholas didn't open his.

"I'm going to have the Spaghettini alla Caprese. Have you ever tasted it?"

"No."

"Pasta with pureed tomatoes, anchovies, tuna, and black Sicilian olives, topped with mozzarella."

"Sold," I said.

Dinner was as good as the restaurant's enticing cooking smells had suggested. While savoring the mellow wine and the flavors in the pasta, I told Nicholas what I'd learned from Sean Donahue.

Nicholas stared at me in admiration. "I'm impressed you found him, and amazed that he tracked down the arresting officer from a forty-year-old case. How did you do it?"

I smiled. "Professional secret—or, rather, an amateur's secret. The problem is that I haven't helped Bill's situation any. All I accomplished was to prove that Taggart didn't have anything to hold over Mickey, so Mickey didn't have a motive to kill Taggart."

"Not necessarily," Nicholas said. He drank the last of his wine and indicated the empty bottle. "Shall I order another?"

"No, I've had enough. What did you mean—not necessarily?"

"Maybe Jordan doesn't have anything of his own to hide himself, but what about Iva? You told me he's in love with her. He might have killed Taggart to keep Iva's past from being exposed."

"What did you find out about her?"

"Those two solicitation busts were just the tip of the iceberg. Your friend Iva was a full-fledged pro, but she wasn't street trade. A vice cop gave my source the details. Iva was on the books of a Manhattan madam who ran a high-priced call girl ring, Charming Escorts. She was a big earner for several years, but one night Iva had a client who got off on hurting women. He sent Iva to the hospital. When she healed up she quit the business. The madam didn't hold a grudge. In fact, she got her the catalogue modeling job Iva had when she met Mickey."

"Iva's terrified Mickey will divorce her if he finds out she wasn't just the hard-working model he thought she was. When she gave me the story about being a failure as a telephone sex performer, I thought it was a pretty silly thing to panic about, but her fear got to me because it was real. Now I understand why she was so scared."

"Do you think she could have killed Davis and Taggart?"

"I can't imagine it," I said. "Maybe, with a gun, but Reggie was smashed on the head and then smothered in a bowl of cake mix. Taggart died of blunt force trauma. I don't know what the murder weapon was."

"A hammer," Nicholas said. "The ME's certain that's what was used. The cops didn't find it, and there weren't any tools in Taggart's office, so their theory is that the killer brought it with him. Or her."

"It wouldn't have been hard to conceal," I said. "It was raining that afternoon. Even though it hadn't quite started when I was in his office, I was carrying a raincoat, and so were people I saw on the street."

Nicholas started to reply, but something in his peripheral vision caught his attention. He swung around to face the restaurant's entrance. "Well, look who's here." His voice had lost its warmth.

I followed his line of sight and was surprised to see John and Shannon O'Hara. As the waiter began leading them to an empty table that was near where we were sitting, John spotted me. He started to smile, but then he saw Nicholas and his mouth tightened. Shannon saw us, too. In vivid contrast to John's glare, Shannon waved at us gaily and hurried forward, squeezing past the waiter on her way to our table.

"Hi, Del!" She grinned at me and then winked at Nicholas as she said, "How come hell froze over and it wasn't on the TV news?"

Nicholas rose gallantly and extended his hand to Shannon, who took it. "Mrs. O'Hara. Nice to see you again."

"It's a heck of a lot more pleasant than *last* time." Shannon withdrew her hand from Nicholas's and leaned over to give me a kiss on the cheek. She whispered, "Congratulations. I want details."

Behind Shannon, John's posture was stiff and his face frozen as he glowered at Nicholas. I was grateful Shannon couldn't see the expression on her husband's face.

Nicholas aimed a bland smile at John. "Hello, Lieutenant." He did not offer his hand.

I greeted John with what I hoped was my usual warmth. His response barely managed to be polite.

Nicholas said to Shannon, "If you two are by yourselves, why don't you join us?"

"We'd love to," Shannon said.

"We can't," John said.

Shannon turned to look at him curiously. John saw her surprise and altered his manner a little. Forcing civility into his voice, he said, "They've already finished dinner, Shan. We'd just be starting."

"But they haven't had coffee yet."

"We didn't want coffee," I said. It was a lie, but I didn't want to stay there a minute longer with John freezing me with his eyes. "We have to go."

"Maybe we can all have dinner together another time," Nicholas said. I wanted him to stop taunting John and gave him a sharp nudge. Nicholas signaled the waiter for the check.

I said to Shannon, "I'll call you tomorrow."

"First thing." She was positively bubbly. I knew she was happy that I was with Nicholas, but the look on John's face made me so uncomfortable I wanted to run out of there before Shannon realized how upset he was, and wondered why.

The waiter seated John and Shannon, and brought Nicholas his check.

Nicholas pulled a money clip out of his pocket and tossed bills onto the table. "I could use a credit card and deduct you as a business expense, but cash is quicker," he said.

Outside, we walked briskly up the block to where Nicholas had parked the car. Before he opened the door he pulled me against him and kissed me, hard. "Your place or mine?"

"Yours," I said.

■ ■ ■

Twenty minutes later, just inside Nicholas's front door, we kissed again. Our hands explored each other's bodies as frantically as they had the first time we made love. Clothing was discarded on the floor as we made our way to his bedroom, until, at last, we were naked in each other's arms.

Gone was the languid pace at which we'd made love so often before he went to Utah. Tonight we were fierce lovers again, our bodies uniting with a passion that was more than sensual. We were equals, claiming each other, partners on a mission we couldn't discuss. I needed Nicholas to drive thoughts of John out of my mind, and I knew he was determined to do just that.

■ ■ ■

Happily sated, we held each other. My head rested on his chest as he caressed my shoulder. We fell asleep.

When we awoke an hour later, Nicholas looked down at me and smiled. "Hello there."

I lifted my chin and smiled back. "Hi."

"How do you feel?"

"I've never felt better," I said.

"If that's a challenge, I'd like to take it."

"Be my guest," I said.

And I shifted my position to welcome him.

36

Later, while Nicholas was driving me home, I told him what Sean Donahue had said about the bad place where retired cop Eddie Cochran lived. "Could you use your press connections to get media in Florida to investigate the Palmetto and help the people who have to live there?"

"I can," he said, "but investigations like that take months, and in the meantime the conditions are the same for the inmates—excuse me, residents."

"Sergeant Donahue told me inmates are better off."

"There's some truth to that, except people in places like the Palmetto are free to leave. If they have someplace to go."

"According to Donahue, Eddie Cochran doesn't have any other option."

"I used to work with a guy who's now an editor at the *Miami Herald*. I'll call him tomorrow. Maybe he'd be willing to get something started."

"Let me know," I said.

When Nicholas slowed his silver Batmobile and came to a stop in front of the house, I saw Eileen's little red car in the driveway. Except for outside lights, my house, and the ones on either side of me were dark. Nicholas and I whispered our good nights and I got out of his car quietly.

A glance through my front window showed that the only inside light was coming from the hallway, so when I let myself into the house I was surprised to find Eileen curled up asleep on the living room couch.

Tuffy was sitting on the floor beside her and bounded over to greet me. That woke Eileen, who switched on the lamp next to the couch. I saw that Emma was nestled beside her.

I greeted my honorary daughter and my two furry companions.

"I was worried, Aunt Del. It's so late." Eileen stared at me with the intensity of Sherlock Holmes searching for a clue. "Where have you been?"

That made me smile. "You were waiting up for me? All three of you?"

"Don't joke about it." She looked at her watch. "It's one o'clock in the morning. Where were you all this time?"

"I went out to dinner."

"I know—with that reporter who likes Playboy bunnies. But you had dinner hours ago."

"How—? Oh. Your father must have told you."

"No, Mother called from the restaurant's restroom. She was all giggly about you having a date, but when she told me what kind of a man he is . . . And when you didn't come home at a reasonable hour, I was worried about you!"

"A 'reasonable hour'? Eileen, you're twenty and I'm forty-seven. I'm the one who's supposed to worry about *you*."

"But that man . . . Did you go to his place after dinner?"

For a moment, I considered telling her that we went to a movie, but that would have been ridiculous. I had nothing to be ashamed of. More important, I'd never lied to her.

"We went to his place," I said, but I felt oddly embarrassed about it.

A spectrum of emotions played across her face. I identified shock and disapproval.

She said, "Did you . . . you two . . . *you* know?"

It was time to draw the line. "Eileen, I couldn't love you more if you were my biological daughter, but I'm not going to discuss that with you."

"Then it's true, what Mother said. You're sleeping with him. Didn't you love Uncle Mack?"

That was a shock. "How could you ask such a thing? You lived with us for much of your life. Don't you remember how we were together? Besides, not long ago you were urging me to find a man. What happened?"

"This is *real*. Is that writer going to move in here?"

"No, of course not."

"Are you going to spend the nights at his house?"

"Not entire nights. No, I have Tuffy and Emma. I can't leave them that long. And I want to be here for you."

What was going on here? Why was she suddenly acting like an angry twelve-year-old?

I moved Emma enough so I could sit on the couch next to Eileen. I reached out and took her hands in mine. Her fingers were cold. Now that I could see her up close, I realized there were tears in her eyes. "Sweetheart, please tell me why you're so upset."

Fat drops began sliding down her cheeks. "I'm going to lose you."

"Lose me? Come on now. You know that will never happen."

"No, I don't. I love my real mother, but she's more like a relative. You're my mother person."

Finally, I understood what was going on with Eileen. She'd become a frightened child again—the four-year-old girl I'd rescued during one of her mother's violent episodes, when Shannon's psychiatric medication had stopped working. I'd taken Eileen to safety with me, and now she had the irrational idea her refuge was about to disappear.

"I'll always be here for you, in any way you ever need me to be. Nicholas is . . . well, I'm not sure I have a label for it yet, but we like to spend time together."

"Was he over here—the nights I was gone?"

"Sometimes he was, but that's the last question of that type I'm going to answer."

She scooted backward on the couch to make enough room so she could bend forward and put her head in my lap. I stroked her hair, as I had so many times when she was growing up.

"I haven't slept with Ad yet," she said. "Kissing, but that's as far as it's gone. We've both been too busy to have a real date."

"You haven't known him very long." I felt like a hypocrite. I hadn't known Nicholas very long, but the two situations were totally different. I'm a mature woman.

Am I? Didn't it hurt like a knife in my heart when I thought Nicholas was sleeping with someone else? I was sure I'd left that kind of pain behind with my teenage years, when the boy

I had a crush on asked somebody else to the graduation dance.

I smoothed a lock of hair back from Eileen's face. "Don't rush things, sweetie. You and Addison will be working together while our business is getting started. By the time it's running smoothly, you two might be in the same place emotionally."

"But that could take months," she said.

"Months go by pretty fast when people are as busy as we'll be."

She gave a deep sigh that turned into a yawn. "You're right, Aunt Del. I'm sorry I got so upset about you and that reporter."

"Nicholas," I said gently. "Use his name. He's not your enemy."

"I know. I'm sorry." Eileen yawned again. Her breathing deepened and I realized she'd fallen asleep.

37

I awoke at eight o'clock to the delightful smell of coffee perking. I gave Tuffy and Emma a few "good morning" strokes, put on a robe over my Los Angeles Dodgers T-shirt, and went to the kitchen. Tuffy and Emma trotted behind me.

Because it was Sunday, I was surprised to see Eileen dressed for business, in a smart new pant suit with a cashmere sweater under the jacket.

As soon as she saw me come into the kitchen, she gave me a hug.

"Oh, Aunt Del, I'm so sorry about last night. I acted like a bratty kid!"

"It's all right, sweetie. I understood how you felt."

"Well, you'll be happy to hear I'm a grown-up again. Can I pour you some coffee?"

"In a minute. I want to feed Tuff and—"

"Already done." She indicated Tuffy's food and water mat on the floor, and Emma's similar mat that I kept up on the back counter, where Tuff couldn't get to her meals. "I set out their breakfasts and gave them fresh water. Now sit down and I'll bring you the coffee."

"Thank you."

Eileen passed me a full mug and said cheerfully, "I'm off to do some work on our project—and on my own project."

"What do you mean?"

"I'm going to look at the window displays of the high-end candy shops and bakeries, meet with the designer Ad hired, and then, perhaps . . ." Her eyes twinkled mischievously.

It was clear she wanted me to ask, so I said, "And then, perhaps . . . what?"

"I'm going to try to maneuver some alone time with Ad."

I wanted to tell her to let their relationship develop slowly, but I restrained myself. At her age I wouldn't have listened to my mother, or to a "mother person," either.

With a cheery, "See you later," Eileen was on her way.

■ ■ ■

Shannon didn't wait for me to call her; she phoned before I'd finished drinking my first mug of coffee.

"Soooooo? Tell me all!" The salacious lilt in her voice was unmistakable, and it made me a little uncomfortable.

"I'll tell you *most*," I said. "Nicholas told me he hasn't been sleeping with any other women since we first got together, and that he won't as long as we're seeing each other."

"And last night you rewarded him for his promise of fidelity?"

"I wouldn't put it exactly that way, but we had a wonderful time together." I hoped that would end this discussion. "Did you and John enjoy your dinner?"

"Frankly, I don't remember what we ate. I got so hot imagining what you and the Sicilian were doing that I jumped John as soon as we got home."

I couldn't think of anything to say except, "*Ahhh.*"

"John rose to the occasion, so to speak." She giggled, and expelled a sigh. "Confession time. I've been worried about us. John's been treating me like some delicate piece of crystal. Before I started getting sick, everything was great between us. We were so right together—especially in bed. Then I was afraid . . . well, forget what I was afraid of. Today is the first time in a long while that I really think we're going to be all right."

"I'm so glad," I said, meaning it with all of my heart.

"I have you to thank, Del."

"What do you mean?"

"Maybe seeing you with that guy snapped him out of the weird mood he's been in for months. Inspired him. Last night he acted like my husband again."

"That's great." I didn't want her to tell me anything else, so I steered her in another direction. "Has John told you anything about the progress of the case against Bill?"

"Only that he's trying to find another viable suspect. I hate that word, 'viable.' It sounds so clinical, and this is our old friend he's talking about. Liddy filled me in on Bill's *almost* being a bad boy. Well, lying to her was bad, but sleeping with another woman would have been a thousand times worse. Did you ever worry about Mack cheating?"

"Early in our marriage I told him that if I ever learned he'd been unfaithful they would find me standing over his bleeding body, asking, 'How do you reload this thing?'"

Shannon laughed. "I remember John telling me that. I told him, 'Della and I think alike, so keep that in mind, buster.' Hey, it's Sunday—why don't you and I pick up Liddy and go have a damn-the-calories ladies' lunch?"

"I can't, but you two should go. I've got to work on figuring out what to do with the least-bad flavor of Reggi-Mixx."

"John's got to work, too. I was disappointed we wouldn't have the day together, but he told me he has a lead on the murder of that private detective."

My pulse quickened. "Did he tell you what the lead was?"

"Yesterday he found out from the man's landlord that he had a girlfriend. They went to her place, but she wasn't home. They're going back this morning."

"I hope she can tell them something useful."

"Me, too," Shannon said. "You know, even though you're busy, I think I'll take Liddy and Bill out to lunch. He's got to be worried about things. Maybe I can make him laugh a little."

"If anyone can do that, it's you," I said.

Shannon chuckled. "Yeah. I've got a few new mental patient jokes from my group therapy sessions."

■ ■ ■

I'd just stepped out of the shower, and was trying to figure out what I would say to Mickey Jordan when I phoned him this morning, when he called me. It was the second time in an hour that people I meant to speak to reached me first. I'd have to study my incomprehensible phone bill this month to see if I was being charged for telepathic communication.

Assuming I'd recognize his voice, Mickey didn't bother

to identify himself. He said, "How'd it go yesterday with the filming?"

"My part went fine, to judge by how hard your cameraman laughed when I accidentally pulled the electric mixer out of a bowl of banana cake batter before I turned it off. It sprayed my face and the smock with yellow goo."

Mickey chortled. "I like that. What'd ya do?"

"Looked into the camera lens, said 'Ooops,' then cleaned myself up with cold water and paper towels. I admitted that at home I use a lot of paper towels."

"That's good TV. If you mentioned the brand of towels maybe I can get the company to kick in a few bucks."

"I didn't notice the brand. Maybe Ben did—the cameraman."

"I'll call him, have him take close-ups of the roll, an' talk to the company tomorrow. If they bite, you can dub in the product name. Okay, next subject: You come up with a new cake yet?"

"No, but I've narrowed down the possibilities." I took a deep breath and plunged in. "Mickey, there's something important I want to talk to you about. It's personal."

"What?"

Glancing at the caller ID I realized that Mickey was speaking to me from his house, where either Iva or Addison might pick up an extension and hear our conversation. "I'd rather not discuss this on the phone. Why don't I meet you for lunch or coffee? Hamburger Hamlet? Or a Starbucks?"

He was silent for so long I was afraid he'd hung up on me. "Mickey?"

"I'll catch up with you later." There was a note of tension in his voice that I hadn't heard before.

"Where?"

"Somewhere," Mickey said. He hung up.

That vagueness—from a man who was never vague—left me a little uneasy.

Why was Mickey acting out of character? If I'd seen a sudden shift in behavior from anyone else involved in a criminal investigation, it would have been a red flag, a signal for me to be on the alert. But this was Mickey Jordan. Idiosyncratic, yes, but in spite of what I'd learned about the violence in his background, I couldn't believe that I had anything to fear from him.

Still, two people with whom he had some connection had been murdered.

On the back of my neck, I felt little prickles of apprehension.

38

For the next hour, while doing rudimentary housework, I kept glancing at the clock, wondering if Mickey might suddenly show up at my door. It seemed strange that I hadn't heard from him again when he knew that I wanted to talk to him. Mickey could be unpredictable, but I'd never known him to avoid things.

My mind was full of conflicting emotions. I didn't believe that Mickey was a murderer, but his icy tone when we spoke was unsettling.

I jumped when the phone rang, but calmed myself before I answered.

"Hi, babe." It was Nicholas. He did a couple of puffs of exaggerated heavy panting and whispered, "What are you wearing?"

I laughed.

In his normal voice, he said, "That's not the reaction I was hoping for."

"If this is supposed to be an obscene call, you don't understand the concept," I said. "It's the middle of the morning, with sunshine flooding through the windows. You're supposed to phone late at night."

"I'll save the naughty talk until we're together. So forget what you're wearing, but if you're naked I'll be right over."

"I'm in ratty old housecleaning clothes."

"That was the kind of thing you were wearing the day we met, when I surprised you by coming to your house too early. You're turning me on."

"I think breathing turns you on," I said.

"Lucky you."

"Lucky me. Are you calling for some reason, or are you just trying to give me a quick thrill?"

"Okay, I get it. You're all business during the day. If we ever get a chance to go away together, I'm going to take you someplace where the nights are six months long."

"Stop it," I said. "I'm supposed to be thinking about cake, not sex."

"I've been thinking about murder, and I found out through a confidential source that the cops have a forensic accountant going through both Taggart's and Davis's financials, looking for someone with a motive to murder either or both of them."

"Have they turned up anything to take attention away from Bill Marshall?"

"Not yet. Your dentist friend is still their number one suspect in the Davis murder. His story about signing up for ballroom dance lessons checked out, as far as that went, but he still had plenty of time between leaving Davis at the restaurant and learning to tango to have killed the woman. The best thing going for him is that he's clean on the PI's murder. He was with his wife during the time frame when Taggart was killed."

I was almost afraid to hope. "They believed Liddy?"

"No, but they had Marshall under surveillance from the time he left the Butler Street station."

I was both relieved and annoyed. "It's wrong to spy on innocent people, but for once, it turned out to be a good thing. Going back to what you said about their examining financial records. Taggart's should tell them who else he did work for."

"The only thing we know it will prove is that he worked for Regina Davis."

"Which will bring them back to the theft of his hard drive," I said. "They'll be sure the killer was desperate to keep something in those files a secret."

"We've gone over your copy of his reports on you and the Jordans, but based on what's there, the ugliest secret Taggart uncovered was that Iva Jordan used to be a hooker. California's a community property state. If he divorced her, she'd come away with a big chunk of change. That's unless she signed a bad prenup. I'll see if I can find out about that."

"I appreciate your helping Bill and Liddy."

"Partly I'm doing this for you, but if this case is solved it'll be a big story for me."

"What do you mean, 'if' it's solved? Don't you think it will be?"

"A lot of cases aren't," Nicholas said. "According to the Bureau of Justice statistics, in 1979 79 percent of murders in this country were solved. But in 2005, which is the last year they have figures for, that rate fell to 62 percent."

"This case has to be solved," I said. "Until it is, Bill will spend the rest of his life under a cloud of suspicion. He's been kept out of the media glare so far, but at any moment that could change."

"I'm detecting as fast as I can," Nicholas said.

"That reminds me. Did you talk to your friend at the *Miami Herald* about looking into the situation at the Palmetto?"

"He said he'd have one of his guys check it out. Maybe it's a scandal to be exposed, but as I told you, a story like that takes months of snooping before a paper gathers enough solid facts to run it."

"In the meantime, good people have to live in bad conditions," I said.

"The wheels of justice don't turn as fast as I'd like them to, either."

"I keep thinking about an old line: 'Justice delayed is justice denied.' "

"This isn't a perfect world," he said.

Even though he couldn't see me, I shook my head. "Of course it's not, but that doesn't mean we shouldn't try to make it better."

After Nicholas and I said our warm good-byes, I took Tuffy for a walk around the neighborhood. I half expected Mickey Jordan to pop out at me from behind one of the big old elm trees that lined the street, but he didn't. I felt pretty silly.

Two hours later I still hadn't heard from Mickey, but at last I was beginning to form an idea about the cake I was supposed to create.

I'd gone through the scrapbooks where I kept my own recipes that I'd developed over the years, and then I'd searched through the book of recipes from old friends. There was nothing I could use.

The last scrapbook was only about a quarter filled, and those recipes were from people who watched the show and had graciously shared with me some of their own favorite dishes. It was in this book that I found the page where I'd pasted the e-mail from Myra Morehouse of Depew, New York. Myra had sent me her recipe for her Orange Creamsicle Cake.

The moment I started reading it, my salivary glands woke up and rushed into action. That cake had been inspired by the frozen orange creamsicles on a stick that I remembered fondly. When we were children, my sisters and my brother and I used to have them on hot summer days. They were so delicious, and refreshing.

My only problem with this discovery was that it was Myra's recipe. I couldn't use it as my own, but as I studied the ingredients, I began to imagine changes and additions I could make. If my version turned out well, I could, legitimately, enter my adaptation in the contest.

I checked my pantry and found that I needed a few items before I could make a test cake. After quickly scribbling a grocery list, I grabbed my wallet and keys, told Tuffy and Emma that I'd be back shortly, and rushed out of the house.

My favorite neighborhood market was a Ralph's only a few blocks away. The lot was crowded, so I had to park quite a distance from the entrance. I didn't mind; I needed every bit of exercise I could get.

Even though the grocery store was full of shoppers, I only needed eight items, so I qualified for the express lane.

The brunette checker at that register, Ginny, was one of my favorite people at the store. She always had a smile for her customers, and was sweet and helpful.

Ginny paused before price scanning one particular item and said, "Are you sure you want to buy Reggi-Mixx? The Duncan Hines cakes are better."

"Thanks for the tip, but for what I'm doing it has to be Reggi-Mixx."

She shrugged, but as she ran the box across the scanner, she lowered her voice and said, "Use a lot of frosting."

Out in the parking lot a few minutes later, I was within a few steps of the Jeep when I got such a surprise that I almost dropped the bag of groceries.

Mickey Jordan was standing beside the front fender. Waiting for me.

39

Irrationally, I felt like the heroine in an old film noir. I held the bag of groceries against my chest like a shield, even though I knew a bullet or a knife could cut through containers of Cool Whip, cream, orange Jell-O, vanilla pudding, and cake mix.

Both of Mickey's arms were visible. He wasn't holding a weapon, but the fingers of his thick hands were slightly curled under. If this were a movie, those hands might become fists, or grasp my neck and crush my throat before I could scream.

I shook off that idiotic fantasy and asked, "How did you know where I was?"

"After our little talk, I sent one of my security guys to watch your house an' let me know if you left an' tell me where you went."

"Why?"

"You wanted us to meet in public. Isn't this parking lot crowded enough for you to feel safe when you try to blackmail me?"

Blackmail?

I said, "Mickey, what are you talking about?"

He gave a snort of disgust. "I figured you for one of the good gals, but, hey, I've been wrong about women before. Okay, let's have the pitch. What are you gonna threaten to do, and how much do you want to make the threat go away?"

"Mickey, I think we're speaking to each other in two different languages and I'm thoroughly confused. What in the world makes you think I could, or would, blackmail you?"

"It's been tried on me before. *Tried*, not succeeded. I gotta say, I admired your grit, making a new life after your husband died, but I never thought you had the chops for murder."

He thinks I committed murder. The realization almost made me laugh.

"You're wrong, Mickey."

I became aware that my grocery bag had gotten heavy and shifted the weight of it from one arm to the other.

I said, "I was not intending to blackmail you. I wanted to talk to you about a man you knew a long time ago, Officer Eddie Cochran."

"So you do have that scum Taggart's files." His "Ah hah-gotcha" expression morphed into a puzzled frown. "But even he didn't know Cochran's name."

"This conversation is a little bit like a bowl of spaghetti. Let's sort it out one strand at a time. You're admitting that you knew T. J. Taggart."

"I saw him once, when he tried to blackmail me. I told him he wouldn't get a penny, and if he went through with what he threatened to do, I'd kill him. Then somebody saved me the trouble. Hey, if it was you who off'ed the bum, I don't care. Just don't get caught an' ruin my network schedule."

He saw me shifting the weight of the bag again and gallantly reached to take it from me. I let him.

Indicating the grocery bag, I said, "Some of those things need to be refrigerated. Why don't we go to my house and straighten out this misunderstanding."

I unlocked my Jeep and opened the door so that Mickey could set the Ralph's bag inside.

■ ■ ■

In my kitchen, I put the groceries away while Mickey poured mugs of coffee for us from the fresh pot I'd made just before I went to the market. As usual, Tuffy was friendly to Mickey, but he sat next to my traditional chair at the kitchen table.

I moved aside the recipe scrapbooks to make room for Mickey on the opposite side of the table.

Before he sat, he used both hands to hold his jacket open. "I'm not wearing a wire," he said. "And to look at that sweater you're wearing, you couldn't conceal one. So, this conversation is private. Time for cards on the table."

"Okay, Mickey. Did you kill Reggie Davis or T. J. Taggart?"

"Nope. Did you?"

"No," I said. "But I did learn that after Reggie agreed to Addison's proposal about partnering on the contest and reality show, she had us investigated."

"Did Taggart try to put the squeeze on you, too? Is that how you found out?"

I evaded that question by saying, "Remember, when you surprised me with this contest, I told you Regina Davis hated me. You were sure she'd gotten over our problem by then, but it turned out that she hadn't. I think she hired Taggart because she was trying to discover a way to hurt me. She found out whom I was closest to, and then went after my best friend's husband. It's been kept out of the media so far, but he became the detectives' number one suspect. I was afraid they'd stop looking for anyone else, so I went to Taggart and forced him to give me copies of the reports he'd compiled for Reggie. After I left his office, someone killed him and took the hard drive out of his computer. Obviously, that person wanted Taggart's files. I'm sure Reggie's death and Taggart's are connected. The thing linking them is that she hired him to investigate us."

"If you read his reports, you know what he thought he could use against me."

"Please understand that I wasn't trying to pry into your private life, Mickey, but I needed to know if Taggart uncovered something that might . . ."

"Give me a motive to kill him? Yeah, I get that."

"Your arrest, when you were eighteen. I had to find out what that was about."

"If you managed to dig up Eddie Cochran's name, I guess you did."

"Yes, and I couldn't imagine you would have killed anyone to cover that up."

"If the circumstances were the same, I'd do what I did all over again." He was silent for a moment, staring off into space, perhaps replaying the old event in his mind. I didn't say anything.

Finally, he focused on me again. "Did you talk to Cochran?"

"No, but I spoke to an old NYPD colleague of his."

"I haven't thought of Eddie in years. He saved my skinny butt way back when. Is he still alive?"

"Yes, and that's what I wanted to talk to you about, where no one could accidentally overhear us."

" 'Accidentally,' I like that. Iva an' Addison—they both got a phone Jones. Can't hear one ring they don't pick it up."

"Officer Cochran was crippled in the line of duty. I don't know any details, but he's confined to what I'm told is a really bad assisted living place. He doesn't have any family to help him."

Mickey took a pen and a small notebook out of his pocket. "What's the name of the place, an' where is it?"

He wrote down what I told him, put the notebook away, and looked at me again.

"We gotta clear the air about something," he said.

I waited, not saying anything.

"Good," he said. "You're a dame who knows when to be quiet." He took a deep breath and said, "Three times I faced a preacher an' said 'I do' when I shouldda said, 'Not on your life.' I didn't want to make the same mistake with number four, so I had Iva checked out before I popped the question."

"You did?"

He gave me a stern look. "Don't play dumb. If you got Taggart's reports, you must know what I found out about Iva. Look, what she did was what she *did*—it isn't who she *is*. You might find this hard to believe, but I'm not an easy guy to love."

I forced myself to keep a straight face, but he must have caught the glint of amusement in my eyes.

"Okay," he said, "I'm a little rough around the edges, but Iva really loves me. I know that as much as I ever knew anything in my life. I love her. I never knew exactly what that felt like until I met Iva. She's a good woman. Forget that old technicality."

"Does she know that you know about . . . the technicality?"

"No. I don' want her to. She'd be embarrassed. Maybe it'd change her personality, an' I don' want her to change. Don't you tell her what I know."

"Of course not."

He looked at me as though he expected me to say something more, but I didn't have a clue.

I said, "What?"

"I've emptied the bag. Your turn. How did you find out about Taggart?"

Because he knew Iva's secret, there wasn't any reason not to answer that question. "Iva told me about him. She knew Reggie had her investigated because Reggie tried to force her to persuade you to fund the entire cost of the reality show."

"Iva never brought the subject up."

"She wasn't going to do it, but she said she kept stalling Reggie because she was terrified you'd find out about . . . the thing in her background and divorce her."

"I love her. Tell her that. Tell her I don't care about anything except having her back with me."

"Why are you asking me to—" I was struck with a sudden, frightening premonition. "Mickey, don't you know where she is?"

"No." The color drained from Mickey's face as he realized what I was saying. "You mean you don't know where she is either?"

"No, I don't."

The pain in his eyes was so intense that I wanted to reach out and give him a comforting hug, but Mickey Jordan was not a man one hugged.

In the air between us hung the unspoken question: *Where was Iva?*

Mickey got up. "If you hear from her, tell her I don't care if she killed those two creeps. I can afford to hide her anywhere in the world. I just gotta know she's okay."

"I will. Mickey, with what's going on, do you want to cancel the contest?"

"No. As far as you're concerned, everything stays the same. Figure out a cake. If anybody asks, I'll say Iva went off to one of those women's spa places. Back me up."

"We could go to John O'Hara, tell him in confidence that she's disappeared—"

"I don't care how good a friend you think he is, that guy's still a cop. No. I want your promise: lips zipped."

"All right, but is there anything I can do for you?"

"Invent a cake ASAP. I'm moving the contest schedule up."

"When is the new deadline?"

"Tomorrow," he said.

"Tomorrow?" I couldn't keep the anxiety out of my voice. "Mickey, that's—"

"Don't argue. I was counting on you knowin' where Iva is. Since you don't, I gotta get this project over with an' start lookin' for her before anybody figures out she's gone and starts askin' questions."

I fought back my apprehension and told him I understood.

"I'll arrange to pay Reggie's workers to stay home tomorrow so we can film the baking in the test kitchens all day. At six PM I'll have the three judges there. Everybody involved will haf'ta sign a high-penalty agreement not to spill the results, 'cause the show won't be broadcast 'til Valentine's Day and I'll be promoting the hell out of it as a contest. Phil Logan's gonna get a Las Vegas bookmaker to lay odds on who's gonna win."

Mickey took his cell phone out of his jacket pocket. "I gotta call Addison and have him contact the other contestants and the tech crew. I'm going to get my lawyer off his tennis court to draw up the confidentiality papers."

He flew out of the house.

I reached down to give Tuffy a few strokes then straightened up. To myself, I said, "Let's get cooking."

40

Before I started baking, I called Nicholas to tell him that I wouldn't be able to see him tonight or tomorrow because Mickey had moved up the contest schedule.

"Is there going to be a studio audience when the contestants display the cakes? If so, I'd like to come to applaud you. Strictly as an impartial journalist, of course."

"Impartial? Yeah, right. But there won't be an audience. The results have to be kept a secret until the show is broadcast on Valentine's Day."

"Okay, so we'll celebrate your triumph on Valentine's Day."

"Don't bet money on me. You work too hard to earn it," I said. "Besides, what makes you think we'll still be seeing each other on Valentine's Day?"

"I'm an optimist," he said. "Good luck tomorrow."

"Thanks."

"I'll see you soon."

I told him I looked forward to that.

■   ■   ■

My first attempt at a new version of the orange creamsicle cake was too dry. The second was too sweet. I still liked my *concept* for the cake, but I was getting the proportions wrong. In the late afternoon I had to rush back to Ralph's for more ingredients.

Eileen came home in time to taste version number three. I cut a small piece for her and watched her face as she ate it. Her frown was not what I'd hoped to see.

"What do you think?"

"It's almost good," she said. "Don't get me wrong, it's not bad, but it's a little bland."

I cut a piece for myself and tasted it. "You're right," I said. "But the good news is that now I think I know what's missing."

"What kind of a cake is it? I mean, don't you have to call it something?"

"I hadn't thought of having a name for it. It's based on those frozen pops called orange creamsicles. Any ideas?"

Eileen beamed with excitement. "Yes! Call it your Orange *Dreamsicle* Cake. That'll be a perfect fit with our company name, Della's Sweet Dreams. Maybe we can get Mickey to let us sell the cakes there, with the fudge and the brownies."

"Let's see how I do in the contest. I don't know if anyone will want to buy a cake that comes in fifth out of five contestants."

"Think positively," Eileen said. "That's what you always told me when I was about to take a test."

"Okay. Positive thoughts." *Maybe I'll come in third out of five—if Prescott drops out at the last minute and Winnie King gives the judges toothaches with her pink concoction.*

While I scrubbed and dried my favorite mixing bowl preparing to begin another cake, Eileen told me about her day.

"I've been all over town with my artist friend, checking out the best candy stores and bakeries. We made a bunch of sketches, but I kept coming back to the same idea. Della's Sweet Dreams shouldn't be elegant—that's not you."

"Thanks a heap," I joked.

"You know what I mean. Your TV image is *homey*. Nonthreatening. Budget-friendly. That'll be the visual style of the walk-in part of the factory. Clean, bright, minimal decoration. The goodies will be the star."

I nodded while I began measuring portions for cake experiment number four. "That sounds good."

"Ad thought so, too," Eileen said. "I didn't get to spend much time with him because just after he agreed with my favorite sketch, Mickey called him and he had to rush off. He said there was an emergency."

"There is. Mickey's moved up the date for filming the cake contest to tomorrow."

"Tomorrow?" Eileen looked as shocked as I had been

when Mickey told me. "Yikes. Are you going to be ready with the right cake?"

"I'll have to be, even if I have to bake all night."

"Working for Mickey Jordan is kind of like riding a roller coaster. I was going to spend the evening with the artist, but I'll stay here and help if you need me."

"No, but thanks for the offer. Go ahead and do what you planned."

"Good. My plan is that my friend and I will do the painting and design work. He agreed to the small fee I offered him. By doing it ourselves, I'll save most of our décor budget for a future emergency. If we've miscalculated costs somewhere, the last thing I want to do is go to Mickey and ask for more money."

As she hurried off, I was practically glowing with pride in her. I knew that she wasn't really my daughter, but my relationship with Eileen was the closest to motherhood that I would ever come. For more than fifteen years, she had filled that hole in my heart.

■ ■ ■

Phil Logan phoned while I was waiting for version number four to come out of the oven.

"Zachary Blye will be at your house at eight o'clock tomorrow morning to do your makeup," he said. "I don't need to bring you clothes because you have to wear one of those Reggi-Mixx *schmatas*. I'll be over at the kitchens during the day to see how the filming is going. Don't let my presence distract you."

"I won't," I said.

"You come up with the winning cake yet?"

"I've created *a* cake. Beyond that I can only hope."

"Just to let you know, I've posted security guards inside the building tonight, watching the kitchens. In case one of the contestants gets the idea to tamper with somebody else's equipment," he said.

"Do you really think one of them would try to cheat?" Then I remembered the warning from Kevin Kyle, Mickey's cake coach. Kevin had said that Clay Sutton had a reputation for sabotage, and couldn't be trusted.

"Cheat?" Phil laughed. "I could tell you some stories . . . Let's just say that some reality show contestants have been known to go to great lengths to win a prize. Anyway, I've been busy all day, taking care of that problem."

"What do you mean?"

"Sorry. Can't tell you." He paused, and lowered his voice. "But here's a little tip. Don't do anything in your kitchen tomorrow that you wouldn't want other people to see."

41

After Zachary Blye used his magic palette and brushes to glamorize me, I was ready to face the biggest test of my career in food.

Because both Eileen and I would be away from the house all day, I left plenty of fresh food and water for Emma and took Tuffy and some of his food over to leave him with Liddy, who had happily agreed to "Tuffy sit." She had adored him since his puppyhood, and referred to herself as Tuff's "Aunt Liddy."

I turned Tuffy over to Liddy and asked her, "How's Bill doing?"

"He's afraid that at any moment they're going to charge him with murder, but he's putting up a good front. Oh, Del, I'm so afraid they won't find that Davis woman's real killer and Bill will go to trial and everything will come out."

"The police think Reggie's and Taggart's killings are linked, and they know Bill didn't kill Taggart, so he's in no immediate danger."

"Yes, but what if they decide he hired someone to kill Taggart?"

"Don't speculate," I said. "No 'what if.' Stay with what *is*—that Bill is free." *At least, for now.* I didn't want to remind Liddy that the LAPD is the smallest police force in any major city, and yet it has to function in one of the most violent places in the country. Some years ago, during a shoot-out in the San Fernando Valley—on a street not far from the TV studio where I did my show—the police had to go to a gun shop to borrow weapons that were as powerful as the ones being used against them by the bad guys.

But this wasn't the time to remind Liddy of LAPD understaffing and lack of funding. Instead, I gave her hand a comforting squeeze. "John and his partner are working hard on the case. So is Nicholas. You've got to have faith." I was working on solving the puzzle, too, but I didn't expect that fact to inspire confidence in her, so I left it out.

Liddy forced a smile. "We went back to church yesterday morning and prayed. Afterward, I told Bill I'm ashamed that we haven't been going regularly since the boys went off to college. We shouldn't pray just when we need something. Would you like to start coming with us again? Maybe next Sunday?"

"Yes, I will," I said.

I was about to leave when Liddy grabbed my hand. "Oh, I have one happy thing to tell you. Bill and I had our first ballroom dance lesson last night."

"Was it fun?"

"As I think you can imagine, Bill wasn't exactly born to dance, but by the end of two hours we were both loving it. We were pretty stiff this morning, but we're going for another lesson Wednesday evening."

"That's great. I have to get going now or I'll be late. Thanks again for taking care of Tuffy."

"The only hard part is that I hate to see him leave. I wish we could have a dog of our own, but with Bill going to the office every day, and my studio extra work, I wouldn't want to leave it home all day when I get a call."

"You're right. That wouldn't be fair to the dog."

"Maybe when Bill retires, or I get tired of being on movie sets." She gave me a peck on the cheek "Good luck today. Or, is there something special you're supposed to wish bakers? Like they say 'break a leg' to actors, or 'break a pencil' to writers. How about 'break an egg'?"

I laughed. "Thanks for the good wishes. I'm going to need them."

■ ■ ■

Cameras had been set up in the parking lot behind Davis Foods to film the arrival of the contestants, to record each of us parking, getting out of our vehicles, and assembling in the reception area.

Inside the building, more cameras whirred. Hedda Klein collected the women's handbags and put them into the reception room closet. Next, she checked the things that all five of us were carrying. We were allowed to bring to the contest only the cake plates or trays or dishes on which we were going to display our creations. No wrapped packages were allowed, nor were tote bags that Hedda hadn't looked through.

I didn't know what was in Gordon Prescott's large tote, but I heard pieces of metal clanging together as Hedda Klein pawed through the contents. Whatever he had passed inspection because she nodded, and moved on to look through Winnie King's carryall.

Viola Lee, standing next to me in the inspection line, whispered, "If she tries to do a body cavity search, I'll treat her to a cake pan full of whoop-ass."

I chuckled. "I'll help."

Being checked out like suspicious-looking airline passengers was a bit annoying, but we had been told it would be necessary to insure the honesty of the competition. Our entries were to be made *only* with Reggi-Mixx batters and grocery items supplied by Hedda Klein, the executive who was supervising the contest for Davis Foods.

Before I went to bed the night before, I'd e-mailed the list of ingredients I would need for my cake to Hedda. Also, as we contestants had been instructed, I included a detailed description of the cake I was going to make. This disclosure was required of us because during times when our cakes were in the ovens, or cooling, we would be free to walk around and see what our competitors were creating. By stating our own plans in advance, we could not "be inspired by"—meaning we couldn't *steal*—ideas from what the other contestants were doing.

When the inspection was over, she distributed our smocks, and Gordon Prescott's chef's coat. They'd all been cleaned and pressed. As soon as we put them on over our clothes, Hedda Klein picked up a large stopwatch from the desk, faced the wall clock, and said, "In thirty seconds it will be eleven AM. At that moment you will have exactly seven hours to prepare your cakes for judging."

The countdown began. As Hedda Klein's flat voice droned through the seconds, we five tensed like track runners at the starting line.

"Five . . . four . . . three . . ." Hedda Klein opened the door to the test kitchens. More TV cameras and lights were aiming at us from inside.

"Two . . . one—begin!" Hedda stepped aside and allowed us to enter.

Gordon Prescott gestured for the women to precede him, but Clay Sutton rushed past all of us and sprinted to his kitchen, which was still covered by the heavy green fabric of the privacy drape he'd put up.

Viola, whose kitchen was closest to the reception room entrance, made the "thumbs-up" sign and said, "Good luck, everybody."

"Why, you sweet thing," Winnie King said. "But no matter what happens at six o'clock tonight, because we're here, we're really winners already—just like every woman who uses Mary Kay cosmetics." Even though I wasn't thrilled with her continual attempts to sell, I had to admit that Winnie King's delicate skin was an effective advertisement for her products.

Clay Sutton had already vanished behind his curtain.

Gordon Prescott nodded curtly, and entered his cubicle without a gracious word.

I thanked Viola, wished her good luck in return, and continued to my station at the far end of the line. Stepping inside, I told myself that until my cake was made, I had to focus single-mindedly on that task. I could not allow myself to think about Iva, or where she had gone, or if she had committed murder.

As Hedda Klein had promised, the items I'd requested were waiting for me on the preparation counter. Two sets. She had said she would give each of us a duplicate set, to allow for any mistakes we might make due to the nervousness of competing. It had been made clear to us that only one "do-over" was allowed, and that had to be accomplished within the allotted time. Our cakes had to be baked, cooled, frosted, and ready to cut by six PM, when the judges would taste each of the competing entries and decide on the winner. Anyone who missed the six PM deadline would be disqualified.

We would know who had captured the $25,000 prize by seven o'clock tonight. Our reaction interviews would be filmed then: words from the happy winner and from the disappointed losers. Even though we and others there knew the contest's outcome, we all were legally compelled to secrecy until the show was broadcast on February fourteenth, at which time the triumphant cake would be displayed, and the check, or a two-by-six-foot poster board replica of it, would be presented to the winner. Immediately afterward, the winning recipe would be posted on the BLC's Web site. It would also be available to people without Web access who wrote to the channel requesting a copy.

The first thing I did in my kitchen was check the oven to be sure it was working properly. It was. One of my requests was a separate oven thermometer, and Hedda had provided it. I turned on the oven to preheat it to 350 degrees. Next, I opened the small refrigerator beneath the counter. Encouraged by the cool air inside, I double-checked by peering at the temperature gauge. I was relieved to find it was working perfectly. A vital part of creating my cake was that it had to chill in the refrigerator for at least an hour before I could add the topping.

My own tote bag contained two nine-by-thirteen baking pans, my sterling silver cake server—which had been a wedding present from John and Shannon—and three presentation plates on which slices of the cake would be provided to the judges.

I organized the equipment and the ingredients that had been supplied, buttered one of the baking dishes, and opened a box of "Sun-drenched Orange Reggi-Mixx." Ignoring the directions on the package, I used the recipe I'd written at home, and proceeded to blend the ingredients in the proportions that I had worked out in my experiments. After measuring, stirring, blending, and adding a touch more of pure orange extract, I beat the mixture to incorporate the elements into a smooth sheen. Then came the moment of truth: I dipped a small spoon into the batter.

"*Yummmm*," I said to myself, pleased that I had managed to defeat the sawdustlike taste that resulted when one followed the directions on the box. I shook my head in silent wonder.

Here I was, standing in one of the test kitchens at Davis Foods International. What were the employees doing during their work hours? Had any of them actually made cakes from their mixes? If so, I wondered if anyone had spoken up and said, in effect, "The emperor isn't wearing any clothes."

Maybe none of the employees had the courage to tell Reggie's father, or Reggie, the truth about the product.

Relieved that my version of the batter tasted good, as soon as the cake went into the oven, I decided to make a second cake, in case the oven temperature suddenly spiraled up or down. If they both came out well, I'd ask Hedda if the second cake could be served to the camera crew, which was what we did after the TV shows were taped.

■ ■ ■

Thirty minutes after I put the first cake in the oven, it was ready to come out. I was removing it carefully when Cameraman Ben appeared at the entrance to my cubicle and aimed his lens at me.

Explaining what I was doing for the camera, I tested the cake to see if it had finished baking. First, I checked to see if it was separating from the side of the pan. It was. Then I touched the surface lightly with the pad of my index finger to see if it sprang back. It did. The last test was the most important. I inserted a toothpick into the center of the cake. When I removed it, I saw that the toothpick had come out clean.

"The cake's done," I said.

I put the second pan of batter into the oven and picked up the wooden pastry brush from the counter. Using the tip of the round handle, I began poking holes in the baked cake, pushing it all the way down to the bottom of the pan.

To the camera, I said, "People who've been baking a long time will probably recognize this as a 'poke cake.' I'm making the holes before I pour my hot orange Jell-O mixture over the top. When the cake is chilled, frosted, and finally cut into slices, you see all these little columns of orange Jell-O streaking the inside."

Ben shut off the camera and took the rig off his shoulder to rotate the muscles of that arm.

"You should see what's going on down the hall," Ben said. "I'm not sure what it is, but it's going to be pretty spectacular."

He looked at my orange sheet cake. I thought I heard sympathy in his voice when he said, "But I'm sure yours is going to *taste* good."

42

Ben's remark, which I was sure he had meant kindly, didn't exactly fill me with hope for my chances in the contest. It made me recall a line Liddy had quoted to me about an actress who was trapped in a catastrophe. She was supposed to have said, "Who do I have to sleep with to get *off* this picture?"

My situation was like being on a nonstop flight from Los Angeles to New York; it was impossible to deplane in the middle of the trip. So, while cake number one was chilling in the refrigerator, and cake number two needed twenty more minutes in the oven, I came out of my cubicle to stretch my legs and see what the others were doing.

Next door, Clay Sutton's curtain was still up, making viewing his activity impossible.

On the other side of Clay's kitchen, Winnie King was making pink spun sugar.

I'd never tried to spin sugar, but I knew that it took a great deal of skill. I said with admiration, "That's impressive."

"I'm making a strawberry dome-shaped cake with little pink spun sugar clouds around the top," she said.

"It's going to be beautiful, Winnie."

Viola, who had just come out of her kitchen, was gazing, wide-eyed, into Gordon Prescott's. When she noticed me in the corridor, she gestured for me to come and take a look.

When I reached Prescott's workspace and saw what he was doing, I felt my own eyes just about pop. Prescott was fitting little round cups into a metal structure nearly three feet high. Braced on four short legs, it was wide at the base and rose to a narrow point at the top. It looked like a big metal Lego contraption.

As Viola and I watched, he took a pan of cupcakes out of his oven.

Viola asked Prescott, "What's that going to be?"

"Isn't it obvious? I'm making a replica of the Eiffel Tower out of cupcakes."

I said, "*Ahhhh*."

Viola said, "Wow." She turned to me. "Shall we kill ourselves now, or later?"

I drew her away from Prescott's kitchen and whispered, "Remember, what he's making has to taste good, too."

That cheered her. "Then maybe we're still in the game."

■   ■   ■

By four thirty that afternoon, I'd frosted both cakes and put them back into the refrigerator to set. They'd be ready for slicing at six o'clock.

All of my muscles ached, partly from the work on the cakes and partly from the tension of the day. But now I had done everything I could, including preparing the presentation plates by garnishing them with sprigs of fresh green mint and slices of red blood oranges.

Grateful to have some time to rest before I had to smile for the camera again, I made my way to the lounge area that Hedda Klein had set up for us in the reception room. Two couches and three overstuffed chairs with ottomans had been crowded into the space.

I had hoped to be alone, but Clay Sutton was already there, curled up on one of the couches. He was sound asleep, so it was almost like being by myself.

Choosing a spot as far away from him as I could manage, I settled into an overstuffed chair and put my legs up. How good it felt to get off my feet!

I closed my eyes, but as soon as I started to relax I began to think about the problem of who killed Reggie Davis and her private detective. I'd read and reread Taggart's reports on Mickey and Iva so many times I knew them by heart. And yet, I was sure that I was missing something significant.

What was in those pages that I had overlooked?

Nicholas had learned that Iva was hiding her arrests for

prostitution, so I concentrated on recalling the information in the report on Mickey.

■ ■ ■

For nearly half an hour, the words in Taggart's pages had been running in my head like a scroll on a movie screen. Suddenly my attention zeroed in on one particular paragraph, something that I'd been passing without thinking about.

It was the part about the troubled life of Addison's mother, Francine Strayhorn Jordan. According to what Taggart had found out, she had been a beautiful, unstable socialite from a wealthy family, a family that disapproved of her marriage to rough-hewn Mickey. Francine's drinking and wild behavior reminded me of what I'd read about the tragic life of F. Scott Fitzgerald's wife, Zelda. Like Zelda Fitzgerald, Francine Jordan had been confined to institutions at least twice. I thought about how terrible those years must have been for Francine's young son. I thought about Addison's polite coolness toward Mickey, made most obvious by the fact that Addison called his father by his first name . . .

But suppose what I had thought was coolness really masked a deeper emotion in Addison. Something ugly.

No longer able to relax, I sat up straight in the chair. Muscles in my stomach began to tighten as I tried to take the separate fragments I had and fit them together into a coherent picture.

Pieces: Addison had picked up the phone at Mickey's house the night Nicholas called to tell Mickey about Reggie's murder. Might he also have picked up the phone on one of the occasions when Reggie called Iva and threatened to tell Mickey what her private detective had learned? Had Reggie mentioned that she'd had Mickey investigated, too? If Addison had heard one of those conversations, then Addison would have discovered what Taggart was doing.

In spite of Eileen's belief that Addison wanted to impress Mickey, what if Addison hated Mickey? Did he blame Mickey for Francine's troubles? If Addison did hate Mickey, was it powerful enough to . . . ? Assuming that theory was true, and Addison didn't want Mickey's love, but wanted to avenge his mother, how would killing Reggie and Taggart accomplish that?

Did Addison want to harm Mickey somehow? If so, letting Taggart's reports become public knowledge would do that. Or . . . would Addison stop at nothing to protect his mother's mental problems from media exposure?

"When all other theories have been exhausted, the one that remains, however unlikely, is the solution."

Thank you, Sherlock Holmes, but all theories hadn't yet been exhausted. There was still the mystery of Iva. Had she pulled a disappearing act out of fear of having her past exposed, or out of guilt because she'd committed murder?

"Della?"

I felt a hand touch my shoulder.

"Della, did you go to sleep sitting up?"

Shaken out of the trance I must have fallen into, I looked up to see Hedda Klein standing over me.

"Sorry to disturb your rest," she said, "but you have a telephone call from a woman who said her name is Eileen O'Hara. I wanted to take a message for you, but she insists that it's urgent. You can take the call over there, on the reception desk."

I saw a light on the phone console blinking and got up. "Thank you."

"Talk softly, unless you want to wake up Sleeping Beauty."

With a frown at Clay Sutton's prone form, Hedda went back through the doorway into the test kitchens.

"Hello, Eileen?"

"Aunt Del, something terrible has happened." Eileen was whispering. "I found—I can't tell you what on the phone, but you've got to get over here right away!"

"Where are you?"

"At our store, the factory. You've got to come right away and see what I found. I don't dare touch it."

"What is it?"

"Something that belongs to Mickey. I think it's evidence about who killed those two people. I'm afraid it was Mickey! Please come over here right away and tell me what we should do."

What she said was such a shock I was trying to think clearly. "Is anyone there with you?"

"Walter Hovey, but he's in the front of the store, hanging your picture. He didn't see what I found. I don't know what it means, and I don't want us to call Daddy until you see what it is. If I'm wrong, I could do something terrible to Mickey."

"All right. Keep calm. I'm leaving now."

Before I was able to replace the receiver on the phone console, I heard Viola Lee's voice behind me.

"You're *leaving*? How can you go before—?"

"It's an emergency." I glanced at the wall clock; it was 5:15. I yanked open the closet door and retrieved my handbag. "I'm last in line for judging. I'm sure I'll be back here before they get to me."

"But what if you *aren't* back?"

"Oh . . . Look, Viola, would you present my cake for me? Just cut the pieces. I've already decorated the plates."

A frown of concern creased her features. "All right. I'll do that. Whatever has happened, I hope it's going to be okay."

"I hope so, too." I squeezed her hand in a gesture of appreciation. "Thank you."

■ ■ ■

It was getting dark when I tore away from the Davis Foods Test Kitchens. Halfway to my destination I dialed Eileen's cell phone to tell her to be sure to keep Walter Hovey away from whatever she had found. The number didn't answer. After six rings voice mail picked up and I heard Eileen's recorded request that the caller leave a message. I left that message, and added that I was on my way and would be there in just a few minutes.

It bothered me that Eileen didn't answer her cell. A few minutes later, when I was stuck at a red light, I tried calling her again.

Still no answer. I hung up before her voice mail message came on again.

The last light of evening had passed quickly into a black, starless night by the time I neared the corner of Hollywood

Boulevard and Baker Street. I eased up on the gas pedal and turned into the parking lot behind the building where we would manufacture and sell our fudge and brownies. Indeed, a large banner had been strung along the side of the building to be seen by traffic heading east on Hollywood Boulevard. In big letters it announced: "Opening Soon! *Della's Sweet Dreams!*"

Two cars were in the lot: Eileen's old red VW Rabbit, and Walter Hovey's elderly dark green Mercedes. I was relieved to see that Mickey's big yellow SUV wasn't there. All the while I drove here, my belief in Mickey's innocence fought with the tone of dread in Eileen's voice. She was convinced that she'd found evidence against him. Fond of Mickey as she was, I knew Eileen's greater concern was that her dream of our having a food business together could be destroyed if Mickey were arrested for murder.

I parked the Jeep, but didn't get out immediately. Instead, I took my phone from the cup holder where I'd put it while driving and dialed Eileen's cell number one more time.

Six rings . . . Seven . . .

There was a tap on my driver's side window that made me nearly jump out of my skin. I turned my head to see Addison's face on the other side of the glass. It startled me so I dropped the phone.

Before I could reach down to pick it up, Addison wrenched open the Jeep's door.

"Get out," he said, bringing the barrel of the pistol in his hand up to the level of my heart.

43

Using the barrel of the pistol, Addison prodded me in the direction of the back door to our factory.

The thought pounding in my head was, *Please God, don't let Eileen be dead.* I was terrified about what might have happened to her, and knew that if he had killed Eileen he would surely kill me.

I forced myself to stay calm.

Talk. Get him to talk. Give him an excuse to let you go.

"Addison, this must be some kind of a joke. Okay, you got me. I'll probably find a hundred new gray hairs when I go home."

"You won't be going home."

That's not what I wanted to hear.

Addison shifted the pistol to his left hand while he used his right to insert a key in the back door lock.

He's right-handed.

Mack and John always said that in dangerous situations they concentrated on details because they never knew which detail might save their lives.

Okay, now I have a detail—but he has the gun.

Addison opened the door and gave me a shove inside that was so hard my teeth rattled. I stumbled and almost fell onto the concrete floor. I just barely managed to stay on my feet and found myself facing the interior of our huge commercial kitchen.

"Keep going." He pushed me forward, into the center of the room. I saw the preparation counter was on my left, and the huge mixing vats on my right.

Only a few of the work light switches that lined the wall

were in the "On" position, but there was enough illumination for me to see Eileen and Walter Hovey. They were sitting on the floor, secured with duct tape, back to back against one of the four big columns that braced the ceiling. Eileen's mouth was covered with a wide strip of tape. She was making little whimpering sounds, but as far as I could see, she was uninjured.

Walter Hovey's condition was a different matter. His mouth wasn't taped because he was unconscious. He was leaning forward, his chin almost touching his chest. Blood from a scalp wound had poured down one side of his face to stain his white shirt. Even in this light, and several yards away from him, I could tell that he'd lost a lot of blood.

"Forget the old man, look at me," Addison said. "I got here while Eileen was talking to you."

He used his weapon to gesture toward an object on the preparation counter. "She found that, before I wanted it to be found."

"That" was a shirt wrapped around a hammer. I could see the hammer's head, and that it was crusted with dried blood. I had no doubt that the blood would prove to be T. J. Taggart's. And I recognized what the hammer was wrapped in: one of Mickey Jordan's signature yellow shirts.

"I'm sorry Eileen found that, but three more killings added to the two charges the authorities will file against Mickey are just cherries on the sundae."

Trying to give Addison a way to let us go, I said, "If Mickey killed two people that's enough to get him at the very least life in prison without the possibility of parole. But all you've done is hold Eileen and Walter and me here for a little while. Let us go and we won't have any need to mention this."

"I hit the old man pretty hard," Addison said. "He could die. Nobody can prove that I killed the Davis bitch and Taggart, and I can't afford to leave any loose ends. That's why I'm going to hide the hammer and Mickey's shirt under the stuff in the dumpster, where the cops are sure to find it. And then I'm going to burn this place down."

Eileen started making frantic little cries from beneath the tape over her mouth.

"Stop that noise," Addison said.

She was silent.

"Don't worry, Della, I'm not going to let her suffer," Addison said. "I'm not going to let any of you suffer. I have nothing against you or Eileen, and I don't even know the old man. I'm going to knock you out before I splash the paint thinner around and light the fire. You'll die of smoke inhalation before the flames get to you, so it'll be a painless way to go. My beef is with Mickey. I've waited twenty years to pay him back for the hell he put my mother through."

"Addison, you're not thinking clearly. If you burn this building down how do you know the police will connect it to Mickey? He might be with a hundred people right now, with an airtight alibi."

"He's on the road, alone, driving north toward Santa Barbara, because that's where I told him Iva went. And he won't be able to prove it beyond a reasonable doubt."

"Iva's in Santa Barbara?"

"I don't know where she is. That was just what I told Mickey to get him out of town. She ran away when I told her I knew her secret, and that I was going to take enormous pleasure in telling Mickey all about it. She turned as white as that phony platinum hair of hers."

Stalling, I asked, "What secret?"

"About her life as a whore."

"So you did kill Taggart, and took his hard drive to get the files."

Addison cocked his head slightly and stared at me with an expression that looked like respect. "When did you figure that out?"

I attempted a rueful little laugh. "Not soon enough—less than an hour ago. You confirmed my suspicion just now when you admitted you knew what was in his files." Faking a sympathetic tone, I said gently, "It must have been very painful for you, reading about the times your mother was taken away and put into the hospital."

Addison's voice softened. "The hospital changed her. Mickey said the doctors were going to help her stop drinking, but they gave her electric shock treatments. Electric shocks!

Damn him to hell—she was never the same after that. She's alive, but not really . . ."

"I'm so sorry," I said. This time my sympathy was genuine, and he seemed to realize that.

"I really think you are. And I'm sorry I tried to run you off the road in the rain. I wasn't trying to kill you. Putting you out of commission so you couldn't go back on the air would have been enough."

I heard Eileen groan beneath her tape.

To keep his attention away from Eileen, I said, "Why in the world did you want to hurt me?"

"Injuring you was a way to hurt Mickey. Your show is getting popular. Losing you would have been a big blow to him. I'd already killed that Regina Davis because she taunted me about Mother, saying that mental problems were sometimes inherited and didn't I worry about ending up like—I hit her to shut her up. Then I stuffed her vicious, dirty mouth in a bowl of her mix. She had told me about the detective's report, but I didn't find out who the detective was until I overheard Iva tell you his name."

I heard a moan. Addison and I both turned to see Walter moving his head. He moaned again.

"Thank God, he's alive," I said.

"For the moment, anyway. The old guy's tougher than a ten-year-old turkey."

Walter mumbled something, then raised his head and looked at me. He cleared his throat. His voice was a rasp. "*The Wizard of Oz* . . . I was going to be in *The Wizard of Oz* . . . but I grew up."

Addison said, "He's out of his head."

Walter's eyes focused on me. "I got the supplies for you . . ." His voice was weak, but he was staring at me as though willing me to read his mind. "*All* your supplies."

I didn't know what to say except, "Thank you, Walter."

He cleared his throat again. "All . . . all your sugar . . . and your flour . . ."

Details.

Details! At that moment I knew what he was trying to tell me.

Walter must have realized that I got his message because he started babbling.

Addison swung around and pointed the pistol at him, "Shut the hell up!"

With Addison's attention momentarily diverted to Walter, I knew I had scant seconds to act. Balling my hand into a fist, I darted to the red and blue control buttons on the wall, and smacked the first button so hard a lightning bolt of pain shot up my arm.

The big aluminum chute above Addison's head opened—and down on top of him gushed hundreds of pounds of white flour! The force of it knocked him to the concrete floor and the gun flew out of his hand. He yelled as he was buried in an avalanche of flour. I snatched his pistol from the floor, but I could see it was clogged with the powdery substance and would be useless.

Addison was moving beneath the white mound, clawing to get out from under it. Operating on autopilot, without conscious thought, I threw my weight against the second control button, and out of that chute poured a cascade of granulated sugar. Beneath that new deluge, Addison stopped moving. *The icing on the cake*, I thought.

Walter coughed and rasped, "In the middle oven—get my rifle out of the oven." He was covered with a fine mist of flour. So was Eileen. When I looked at my hands and arms I saw that I was, too.

There was no time to wonder why anyone would keep a rifle in an oven. I raced to the middle oven, opened the door, and there it was: a beautiful, highly polished Winchester, an old piece, but serviceable. Walter kept his ancient rifle in the same perfect condition in which he kept his decades-old car.

"It's loaded," he said.

"Good." I pulled the tape off Eileen's mouth. She flinched at the pain, and licked her dry lips.

"There are some sharp knives in that cabinet by the counter," Walter said.

I hurried to find them, at the same time keeping an eye on the enormous mound of sugar and flour under which Addison lay.

As soon as I found the drawer full of knives, I removed two and gave one each to Eileen and to Walter. Luckily, Addison had bound them with their wrists in front, not behind their backs. "Cut the duct tape on yourselves. I've got to call for help."

"My cell phone is on the shelf behind you," Eileen said. "Daddy's on speed dial. Press One."

Walter freed himself first. I handed him the Winchester. "Point this at Addison as soon as I'm able to dig him out. I don't want him to suffocate."

Using Eileen's cell phone, I pressed One.

■　■　■

We heard the shrieking of the police cars and the ambulances while Eileen and I were binding Addison with strips from the same roll of duct tape he'd used earlier on Eileen and Walter.

John burst through the door ahead of the medics, Hugh Weaver, and several uniformed officers. He saw Eileen and folded her into his arms in a fierce bear hug. Over Eileen's head he stared at me and silently mouthed "Thank you."

As I'd requested when I called John, there were two teams of medics. One of them examined Addison, while the other tended to Walter Hovey's head injury.

The younger of the two medics with Addison swabbed the coat of sugar and flour from his face and the other clasped an oxygen mask over his nose and mouth.

Weaver replaced the tape the medics removed from Addison with handcuffs. He stepped back as the medics loaded the man who murdered Reggie Davis and T. J. Taggart onto a gurney.

I asked Weaver, "Where are they taking Walter? What hospital?"

"They're both going to St. Clare's. Why?"

"I want to see Walter, and find out if he needs anything."

"He got a pretty bad bang on the noggin. They probably won't let anybody see him until tomorrow. We'll talk to him first, to get his statement." Weaver looked me up and down. "You're a mess, but it'd be better for us if you come to West

Bureau an' fill us in before you go home and clean up. Do you mind?"

Do I mind? "Detective Weaver, this is the first time you've been polite to me since the night Reggie Davis was murdered."

"Yeah, well, I'm not warm and fuzzy. I get paid to suspect everybody."

"There's something I'd like you to do. Mickey Jordan is on the road somewhere between here and Santa Barbara." I gave him the make and vanity plate of Mickey's SUV. "Put out an APB to have him stopped. He needs to know what's happened here tonight."

"You got it. Now are you coming with me?"

"I'll go to the station," I said, "but I have my own car outside."

Eileen extracted herself from her father's embrace and came over to give me a hug. John followed close behind her.

"I'll drive you two," he said.

"No, I have my car. You take Eileen."

She nodded agreement. "I'm too shaky to drive."

John said, "Sweetheart, give me your key. I'll have somebody take your car to our house. I want you to come home and stay with us tonight. Your mother will have to see you or she won't believe you're not hurt."

"Okay," she said.

John took Eileen's car key and gave it, with instructions, to one of the uniformed officers on the scene.

John turned back to me. "Del, are you sure you won't ride with us?"

"I'll meet you there." I smiled. "You called me 'Del' again. Are things all right between us?"

"They always were," he said softly.

After Walter and Addison had been taken away in the ambulances, Weaver helped Eileen into the back of their car while John walked with me to my Jeep.

"I've got to call Liddy and Bill," I said. "They need to know he's in the clear now. And I want to ask Liddy to keep Tuffy overnight. I don't know what time I'll be home."

"I'll call them from my car," John said.

He opened the Jeep's driver's side door, but before I could climb inside John took my right hand. He pressed it flat against his heart until I felt its strong beat. Then he let go, turned, and hurried back to his car without a spoken word.

44

Before I turned on the ignition, I found my cell phone where I'd dropped it on the floor when Addison surprised me. According to the information on the faceplate I had four unheard voice mail messages. I didn't have the energy to play them at that moment, so I put the phone in its dashboard holder and drove out of the lot behind the car carrying John, Eileen, and Weaver.

Within a block, I remembered that I had promised to give Nicholas the story. I plugged the hands-free device into my right ear and dialed his cell phone.

He picked up immediately. "Del, where are you? I left two messages. How did the contest go?"

"Oh, gosh—the contest! I forgot about it!"

"What do you mean, you forgot? Honey, what's going on? *Where are you?*"

Briefly, I told Nicholas what had happened during the last hour. I could feel him listening intently and I imagined him taking notes.

When I finished, he said, "This is great. I don't write headlines, but I'm going to suggest one: 'Cook Cooks Killer's Goose.'"

"No, please don't do that. Make it clear in your story that the hero is Walter Hovey. He's a darling man, a retired actor." I spelled Walter's last name for him. "He's the one who thought of burying Addison in flour. If he hadn't reminded me of the chutes above our heads, I don't think I would have thought of it."

"That's good for a sidebar: 'Actor a Real-Life Hero.' What hospital is he in?"

"Walter and Addison were both taken to St. Clare's."

"I'll get over there right away. Where will you be?"

"At West Bureau with Eileen, giving our statements."

"Call you later," he said, and disconnected.

I studied the numbers on the phone's faceplate. As Nicholas had said, two calls were from him. The other two calls were from the same unfamiliar number. I guessed they were from Hedda Klein, demanding to know where I'd disappeared to.

I dialed the number and knew I was right when I heard Hedda answer. As soon as I identified myself, she said, "Where the hell did you disappear to?"

"It was an emergency. Did Viola—"

"Viola told me, and she fixed your plates for the judges."

"What happened?"

"You didn't win," Hedda said. "Clay Sutton did. But you and Viola tied for second place. Hers was an ice cream cake roll, with three flavors of ice cream wrapped inside a thin crust of lemon cake with lemon zest and chopped walnuts added to the batter. There's no money prize, but you two have each earned silver medals in this first annual Reggi-Mixx Cake Contest. Next year, I think we'll open the contest to the public. No professionals."

"That's a very good idea," I said, relieved that I wouldn't have to be part of it again.

"I'm sorry you lost," Hedda said.

I was disappointed, of course, even though I hadn't expected to win. But something puzzled me. "What about Gordon Prescott's Eiffel Tower and Winnie King's spun sugar clouds? Those were both pretty amazing."

"Too amazing," Hedda said. "The judges felt that ordinary people wouldn't be able to duplicate things like that."

"What was Clay Sutton's winning cake like?"

"Absolute heaven." Her tone was practically orgasmic. "Clay made an angel food layer cake—an angel food cake that he sliced into horizontal sections. Then he covered the layers and the top with the most luscious frosting. As a final touch, he filled the hole in the center with a mixture of fresh raspberries and blueberries, and scattered more of them around the base of the cake. Beautiful."

"It sounds as though he deserved to win," I said.

"That's the spirit. You can congratulate him tomorrow at ten. That's when I'll have a cameraman here to film you admiring Clay's cake. We'll edit that into the show so no one will know that you went AWOL tonight."

I thought, *Oh, they'll know, when the story of Addison Jordan's capture hits the media.* But I was too tired to tell her about that. Instead, I promised I'd be at the test kitchens tomorrow morning, ready to be a gracious loser.

Just as we were saying good-bye, Hedda added, "By the way, I meant to tell you that while your cake wasn't spectacular-looking on its surface, it was *delicious.*"

■ ■ ■

Hours later, after I'd recounted the events in the bakery to John, Weaver, an assistant DA, and their stenographers, and then signed the statement they had typed up, I finally walked out of the Butler Street station into the cold night air. I'd taken in my first refreshing gulp of it when I saw Nicholas leaning against the right front fender of my Jeep.

He hurried forward and started to kiss me, but I put up one hand to hold him off. "I'm a disgusting mess," I said.

"A mess, yes, but not disgusting." He leaned down and gave me a light kiss on my eyelids.

I asked if he'd filed his story.

"Yep, complete with a picture of your Walter Hovey with his head in bandages."

"How did you get in to see him? John and Weaver haven't been there yet."

"I know a nurse," he said. Then he quickly changed the subject. "I kept in touch with my guy at the *Miami Herald.* He told me that retired officer Eddie Cochran is no longer a resident of the Palmetto Lodge."

I felt my heart lurch in fear. "Did he . . . pass away?"

Nicholas shook his head. "Mickey Jordan took him out of· there."

I sighed with relief about Cochran. "That's wonderful, but what about the other people stuck in that place?"

"My friend said that Jordan put some heat on the authorities. He thinks there'll be some big improvements right away. Anyway, I'll keep track of that story."

"Thank you."

"Come here." Nicholas drew me into his arms.

"Your clothes—I'll get flour all over them."

"We'll clean up together. Your place or mine?"

"Mine," I said. "Eileen is spending the night with her parents."

"Is your shower big enough for two?"

"Absolutely," I said.

■ ■ ■

Later, clean and wrapped in each other's arms, we were awakened from a deep sleep by the insistent ringing of my phone. I leveraged myself up on one elbow and reached across Nicholas's chest for the receiver.

"Hey, baby!" It was Phil Logan.

I squinted at the glowing number on my bedside clock. "Phil, it's three o'clock in the morning."

"I didn't call for a time check. Are you sitting down?"

"I'm lying down."

"Then sit up for some big news—you won the baking contest!"

I did sit up, abruptly, accidentally hitting Nicholas in the chest with my elbow.

"Ouch," he said.

I whispered, "Sorry."

Phil was still talking. I tuned in again to hear him say, "It's not as good as a total victory, but isn't this great?"

"I missed part of that, but I'm awake now. What are you talking about, Phil?"

"You won—well, actually, you and Viola Lee tied for first place. You don't have to split the money because I'll make sure you each get the full twenty-five thou."

"But I thought Clay Sutton won."

Now Nicholas was sitting up, too, with his ear pressed close against the receiver, listening with me.

"The little bleached blonde twerp cheated. Fortunately, I

had each of the kitchens outfitted with hidden cameras. Remember, I gave you a hint—I told you not to do anything in there you wouldn't want people to see. When I played the tapes tonight, I saw that he'd had contraband under his clothes, taped to his chest."

"What, drugs?"

"Not that kind of contraband. He'd concealed cut layers of gourmet angel food cake—not from Reggi-Mixx—and Paula Deen frosting in plastic wrap and Baggies. To make everybody think he'd been cooking, he turned on the oven and whipped up a batch of cake mix, baked it just until he got the aroma, then poured the batter down the sink. I swear, could this story get any better?" Before I could reply, he added, "But you can't say anything about this. What he did is going to be exposed when the show airs."

"I'm speechless. Does Viola know?"

"Hedda's calling her now. Tomorrow, you and Viola will be told on camera that Clay cheated and you two tied for first. Act surprised."

"I will," I said. "Thanks, Phil."

"Oh, one more thing. I got a message for you from Mickey. He said to tell you he found Iva and everything is going to be okay."

"Where was she?"

"At the Belle Chateau Hotel, in Bel Aire. Actually, I'm the one who found her, even though I wasn't looking. Somebody I know on the staff told me she had checked in. That hotel is so discreet he could have lost his job for telling who was there, but a maid tipped him off that she hadn't left her room and wasn't ordering room service. He called me at midnight tonight, saying he was worried about her maybe doing something to herself, so I told Mickey and he went there and took her home. I guess they had a little bump in the marital road. Awhile ago when I called him about you tying for first, he gave me the message for you. Said to tell you everything was all right with them."

"I'm so glad," I said. Glad and *relieved*. Phil and I said good night and ended the call.

"Congratulations on your triumph," Nicholas said.

"Thanks, but you can't tell anybody you know what happened."

"I won't." He kissed me gently. Teasingly. "But will you allow me to congratulate the winner in my own special fashion?"

"I wouldn't have it any other way," I whispered.

Recipes

▪ Della's Orange Dreamsicle Cake ▪

Butter or margarine
Flour
1 package orange cake mix
3 eggs
1 cup sour cream
⅓ cup vegetable oil
⅔ cup water
1 teaspoon orange extract
Zest of one large orange
1 package orange Jell-O

Preheat oven to 325 degrees. Using butter or margarine (*not* cooking spray) grease and lightly flour a 9×13 cake pan.

Take 1 box of orange cake mix (I prefer Duncan Hines) and pour the contents into a mixing bowl, but *don't* follow package instructions. Instead add eggs, sour cream, vegetable oil, water, orange extract, and the zest of an orange to the dry mix.

Mix for 30 seconds, until ingredients are moist. Then beat on medium for 2 minutes, occasionally scraping down the sides of the bowl with a rubber spatula.

Pour into the prepared baking pan. If using a dark, coated metal pan, bake at 325 degrees for 30 minutes. If using a glass or a light metal pan, bake at 350 for 30 to 32 minutes, until the cake begins to separate from the sides of the pan.

When the cake is out of the oven, poke holes in it. (I use the small round end of a pastry brush.) Now, mix 1 package of orange Jell-O with 1 cup boiling water. Add ½ cup ice water. Dissolve Jell-O thoroughly and then pour the mixture over the cake. Refrigerate until completely cooled, about an hour.

FOR THE TOPPING

> *1 package orange Jell-O*
> *1 package vanilla pudding mix*
> *1 cup cold whole milk*
> *Zest of one large orange*
> *1 teaspoon orange extract*
> *2 teaspoons pure vanilla extract*
> *8 ounce container Cool Whip*
> *1 cup cold whipping cream*
> *2 tablespoons powdered sugar*

Mix 1 package orange Jell-O and 1 package vanilla pudding mix with 1 cup of cold whole milk. Add the zest of 1 large orange and 1 teaspoon orange extract. Mix until thickened. Add 2 teaspoons of good (pure) vanilla extract. Then gently fold in 1 container (8 ounces) of Cool Whip.

In a separate bowl, beat until stiff: 1 cup of cold whipping cream and 2 tablespoons of powered sugar. (Add a little more powdered sugar if you like it a bit sweeter.) Gently fold the sweetened whipped cream into the Orange Jell-O and Cool Whip mixture. Immediately spread this combination over the top of the cake. It will form a topping about ½ inch thick.

Refrigerate the cake for 2 or 3 hours before cutting into pieces to serve. Keep cake refrigerated between times you cut and serve. Serves 12–15.

■   ■   ■

▪ Della's Chocolate Cheesecake ▪

16 ounces of plain chocolate wafers
1 teaspoon cinnamon
¾ cup melted butter
¾ cup granulated sugar
3 eggs
3 eight-ounce packages of cream cheese (softened
    to room temp.)
12 ounces melted semisweet or German chocolate
2 tablespoons good quality cocoa
1 teaspoon pure vanilla extract
3 cups sour cream
¼ cup melted butter (this is in addition to the butter
    listed above)

FOR THE CRUST

Put the chocolate wafers into a plastic Ziploc bag and crush them with a rolling pin into crumbs. With a fork, mix crumbs with the cinnamon and blend in the melted butter. Press this mixture firmly against the bottom and sides of a well-buttered 10-inch springform pan and chill for about an hour.

FOR THE FILLING

Preheat oven to 350 degrees. Beat the granulated sugar with the room temperature 3 eggs until mixture is light. Gradually add the softened cream cheese. Beat until smooth. Stir in the melted chocolate, cocoa, and vanilla extract. Beat in thoroughly the sour cream. When smooth, fold in ¼ cup melted butter. Pour this batter into the chilled shell. Bake the cheesecake for 45 minutes. *Do not overbake*. When cheesecake is removed from the oven, it should seem quite liquid. Chill the cheesecake for at least 4 hours. To serve, remove the springform circle and put the cheesecake onto an attractive cake plate, with the bottom of the pan underneath.

A FINAL TOUCH

I like this cheesecake plain, but offer whipped cream on the side for your guests.

■ ■ ■

■ Ann Talman's ■ Lemon "Funeral" Cake

Actress Ann Talman's Grandma Richardson passed this recipe down the generations. She called it her "Funeral Cake" because when anyone in her circle passed away she would make it up fast and take it over to the family. Annie was eight years old when she began helping her grandmother make this cake.

> 1 package yellow or lemon supreme cake mix
> 2 eggs
> ¾ cup vegetable oil
> ¾ cup water
> 1 package lemon instant pudding mix

Preheat oven to 350 degrees. Put cake mix and instant pudding mix into a bowl, add water and oil and mix. Add eggs, one at a time, and beat well after each addition.

Grease and lightly flour either a Bundt pan or an angel food cake pan. Pour batter in and bake for 55 to 60 minutes. Remove from oven and leave in pan for 10 minutes. Turn cake out onto a plate. While still hot, pour glaze over top.

FOR THE GLAZE

> 1½ cups orange juice
> 4 tablespoons melted butter
> 2 cups confectioner's sugar

Whip the three ingredients in small mixing bowl.

Punch 100 holes with an ice pick into the top of the warm cake. Pour the glaze mixture over the cake, into the holes. It will run off the sides, but just keep scooping it up and putting it onto the top until glaze is mostly absorbed.

■ ■ ■

■ Nancy Koppang's ■ Black Russian Cake

This luscious recipe is from my friend, Nancy Koppang. It's both simple to make and impressive when it's served.

> 1 package of your favorite chocolate supermoist
>   cake mix (anything from devil's food to double
>   chocolate fudge)
> ¾ cup water
> 4 eggs
> ⅓ cup oil (I prefer canola)
> ⅓ cup vodka
> ⅓ cup Kahlua or Tia Maria (or other coffee-
>   flavored liqueur)

Preheat oven to 350 degrees.

Grease and flour a fluted tube pan (a standard Bundt, or one of the pretty new designs. If you use one of the more complicated patterns, I find it best to use a baking spray with flour. PAM makes a good one, and there are others.)

In a large mixing bowl, combine cake mix, eggs, and liquids. Mix per package directions. Pour into prepared pan and bake for 45–50 minutes, or until it tests done. (I find a wooden toothpick is pretty reliable)

Cool 10 minutes in the pan, then invert onto a baking rack. Cool completely.

This cake is very tasty, and it can be sliced and served plain or with whipped cream or Cool Whip.

My favorite way to serve is to make a thin powdered sugar glaze: powdered sugar, a little butter, a little water beaten well, about the consistency of heavy cream. You'll want to slip strips of waxed paper under the cake because there will be drippings. Spread the glaze evenly over the cold cake and let it set thoroughly. Melt 2 or 3 squares of unsweetened chocolate with 1–2 teaspoons of butter. Let it cool a bit, but it still must be really runny. Pour it over the cake as completely as you can so the white glaze isn't showing. Once you're happy with it, remove the strips of waxed paper and let the cake set completely.

■ ■ ■

■ Della's Fruitcake Bread Pudding ■

Comedians joke about fruitcakes, but one year my husband received three of them as gifts from crime victims that he'd helped. That's when I came up with the idea of turning fruitcake into a fruity bread pudding. Here's the recipe I concocted, but I'm sure you can come up with variations to make this dessert your own.

1 fruitcake, approximately 2 pounds, sliced and
   broken into pieces
8 large eggs
1¼ cups granulated sugar
1½ cups heavy (whipping) cream
1½ cups whole milk
1 teaspoon good vanilla extract

Preheat the oven to 350 degrees. (Don't let the oven get hotter.)

Lightly butter the bottom and sides of a 9×13 baking pan.
Arrange the fruitcake pieces in the dish.

In a large bowl, whisk the eggs, sugar, cream, milk, and vanilla
to blend. It becomes a smooth, thin custard. Pour the custard
over the fruitcake pieces. Press the pieces of fruitcake down
gently so that all of them are submerged in the custard mixture. Let stand for 30 minutes, checking from time to time to
press the fruitcake pieces into the custard.

Bake the pudding for about 40 to 45 minutes, until it's set in
the center. The pudding should puff slightly. It can be served
warm, slightly cooled, or cold. Serves 8.

■ ■ ■

■ Margaret McEldowny's ■
Apricot Raisin Loaf Cake

Margaret is the wife of Brooke McEldowny, the award-
winning newspaper cartoonist who draws *9 Chickweed Lane*
and *Pibgorn*. She's also a gifted operatic soprano.

1 cup boiling water
1½ cups dried apricots
½ teaspoon baking soda

   1 cup granulated sugar
   2 eggs
   1¾ cups all-purpose flour
   1 teaspoon baking powder
   1 cup chopped walnuts
   ½ cup golden raisins

Preheat oven to 350 degrees. Chop dried apricots into quarters. Pour the boiling water over them and soak for 15 to 20 minutes, just until tender. Drain off the liquid. You should have 1 cup. If you have less, add just a little more water. Put this cup of liquid into large mixing bowl. Add baking soda, sugar, and eggs. Stir with wooden spoon until well mixed. Add apricots, raisins, nuts, flour, and baking powder and mix well again.

Butter and flour two loaf pans (9×5×3 loaf pans). Pour equal parts of the mixture into the two pans. Bake for about 45 minutes, or until loaves have risen, are dark in color, and the blade of a sharp knife comes out clean when inserted in the center. Cool on racks and serve. Makes 2 loaves.

NOTE: Slices can be served with a festive breakfast. For dessert, serve slices beneath scoops of your favorite ice cream.

If you wrap it securely in heavy aluminum foil, you can freeze one of the loaves to bring out when you need an emergency treat for unexpected guests.

■ ■ ■

■ Della's Tuscan Potato Cake ■

On our only trip to Europe, Mack and I stayed at a little inn in Tuscany. The elderly woman who ran the inn made a cake unlike any I'd ever tasted. She was kind enough to show me how to make it. It's delicious, easy, and inexpensive.

1 lb baking potatoes, scrubbed but not peeled
¼ cup all-purpose flour
¾ cup granulated sugar
1 stick butter, softened
4 large eggs, separated
1 tablespoon lemon zest (1½ to 2 lemons)
1 teaspoon grated nutmeg (fresh grated is best)
1 teaspoon almond extract
¾ cup golden raisins
½ cup pine nuts
Approximately ½ cup of powdered sugar for
    dusting the top before serving

Preheat oven to 350 degrees.

Boil the potatoes (in their skins) in salted water until fork tender. Peel off the skins and put the hot potatoes in a bowl with the flour. Mash potatoes and flour together until mixture is smooth. (*Don't* let the potatoes cool before mashing.) Now set the mixture aside to cool for 20 minutes.

Butter a 9-inch cake pan and line with waxed paper.

Beat the sugar and softened butter in a large bowl with a hand-held electric mixer on High until creamy. Turn mixer down to Medium speed and add 4 egg yolks, one at a time, until just blended after each addition. (Don't over beat.) Now turn the mixer speed to Low and beat in the potato/flour mixture, lemon zest, nutmeg, and almond extract. Stir in the golden raisins and pine nuts.

In a separate bowl, beat 4 egg whites on High speed until they form stiff peaks. With a rubber spatula, fold the stiff whites into the batter. Pour the batter into the prepared cake pan.

Bake for 35 to 45 minutes, until golden brown and a toothpick inserted into the center comes out clean.

Cool the cake for 20 minutes, then turn out onto a cooling rack. Carefully remove the paper and let the cake cool completely. Just before serving, dust with the powdered sugar.

■ ■ ■

■ Della's Chocolate ■ "Mt. Kilimanjaro" Cake

Turn a "mix" into a special delight.

> 1 box Duncan Heinz Moist Deluxe Devil's Food
>   cake mix
> 3 large eggs
> 1/2 cup vegetable oil
> 1 1/3 cups water
> 1 1/2 cups mini marshmallows
> 1/2 cup mini semisweet chocolate chips

Preheat oven to 350 degrees. Prepare a Bundt pan by greasing the sides and center, and then lightly flouring it, tapping away excess flour.

Combine the first 4 ingredients according to package directions: in a large bowl blend them with a mixer on low speed for 30 seconds. Then beat on medium speed for 2 minutes. (DO NOT OVERBEAT)

With a wooden spoon, stir in the mini marshmallows and the mini semisweet chocolate chips. When thoroughly combined, pour the batter into the prepared Bundt pan. Bake for 50 minutes. When cake is done, remove and set on a wire rack to cool. When cool, turn it upside down onto a cake plate.

FOR THE GLAZE

Over hot water (top half of a double boiler or in a heat-safe bowl) melt:

> *1½ cups regular size semisweet chocolate chips*
> *2 tablespoons honey*
> *1 teaspoon pure vanilla extract*

When these are melted together, add: ⅓ cup whipping cream (this is to thin the chocolate enough to pour over cooled cake).

Just before serving: Take 1 tablespoon sifted powdered sugar and dust top of cake for the "snow" atop the "mountain."

■ ■ ■

▪ Della's Cornish Pasties ▪

FOR THE PASTRY

> *1 cup Crisco shortening (from the can, NOT Crisco oil)*
> *3⅓ cups self-rising flour*
> *¼ teaspoon salt*
> *Several tablespoons of ice water (1 at a time)*

FOR THE FILLING

> *1 large brown or sweet onion, chopped*
> *2 large potatoes, peeled, quartered, and sliced thinly*
> *2 carrots, scrubbed and thinly sliced (I don't peel carrots, I just scrub them clean)*

    1 tablespoon Crisco shortening (from the can, NOT
        Crisco oil)
    1 pound top round or chuck, fat trimmed off, diced
        pretty small (pieces should be roughly fingertip
        size—from length of nail to tip)
    1 tablespoon Worcestershire sauce
    ½ teaspoon dry English mustard
    Salt & pepper
    1 large egg, beaten for a glaze.

Preheat oven to 400 degrees.

Make the pastry first: Sift together flour and salt. Cut in the shortening, then sprinkle the ice water, 1 tablespoon at a time until you can shape the mixture into 4 balls of dough. One at a time, roll each ball out between pieces of plastic wrap into the size and shape of a 9 inch pie shell. Make all four pastry rounds before you cook the filling.

Cook onions, potatoes, and carrots in the Crisco shortening over Medium heat until vegetables are starting to soften. Add the diced beef and cook over Medium heat, stirring until the meat is browned evenly. Turn the heat to Medium-low, season with the salt and pepper, Worcestershire sauce, and mustard. Cook for about 30 minutes, stirring frequently, until everything is tender.

Divide the filling into 4 parts. Put a quarter of the filling onto one side of a pastry circle, fold top of pastry over, curl the edge of the pastry inward, and crimp them like a pie to seal. Do this with all four circles of pastry. When you've made the four pasties, beat 1 large egg with a fork. Using a pastry brush, brush top of each pasty, including the crimped edges, to glaze.

Place the pasties on a baking sheet and bake for 15 minutes. Then turn the oven down to 350 degrees and bake for 15 minutes more.

Cool just enough so that you don't burn your tongue. Serve with chunky applesauce or apple chutney, or whatever spiced fruit appeals to you.

■ ■ ■

■ Mrs. Herbert Hoover's ■ Chicken Biscuit Pie

Herbert Hoover was U.S. president from 1929 to 1933. This dish is from *Famous White House Recipes*, reprinted by permission of my friend, Victor Bardack, publisher.

One 3-pound frying chicken
½ cup shortening
1 cup carrots, peeled and finely diced
½ cup celery, finely diced
3 cups water
¾ teaspoon salt
¼ teaspoon pepper
1 teaspoon paprika

Preheat oven to 325 degrees. Cut chicken into pieces; wash, and wipe with a clean cloth. Melt shortening in a deep frying pan. Fry chicken in the shortening until browned on all sides. Remove chicken from pan and place in a casserole with carrots and celery. Bring water to a boil. Pour over chicken. Sprinkle salt, pepper, and paprika over chicken. Bake covered 45 minutes. Remove the cover and increase oven heat to 450 degrees. Arrange unbaked cutout biscuits over top of chicken. Bake 20 minutes or until biscuits are golden brown. Serves 6–8.

BISCUIT DOUGH

1¾ cups all-purpose flour
2 teaspoons baking powder

½ teaspoon baking soda
½ teaspoon salt
5 tablespoons chilled butter
¾ cup milk

Sift together flour, baking powder, baking soda, and salt. Cut
in butter. Stir in milk all at once and mix lightly to form a
dough. Turn out dough onto a floured board. Knead lightly.
Roll out to a thickness of ½ inch. Cut out biscuits with a
floured biscuit cutter.

Turn the page for a preview of the
next book in the Della Cooks
Mysteries by Melinda Wells . . .

The Proof Is in
the Pudding

Coming soon from
Berkley Prime Crime!

"You're going to love what I've done to promote your show!" said Phil Logan, as soon as he finished gasping for air.

Phil, head of publicity for the Better Living Channel where I hosted *In the Kitchen with Della*, had spotted me walking with my black standard poodle, Tuffy, along the grassy area at the far end of the cable network's North Hollywood production facility. He'd waved wildly and burst into a sprint to join us.

Because the property was surrounded by a security fence, I had let Tuffy off the leash. He had been sniffing happily at scented trails that no human could follow, but he stopped and looked up to watch Phil dashing toward us.

What with Phil's abundant mane of sandy hair and his unlined face, he looked a decade younger than his thirty-two years, but he wasn't in as good shape as his reedy frame suggested. By the time he covered the fifty yards that separated us he was red-faced with exertion and looked ready to collapse.

I reached out to steady him. "Lean forward, Phil. Put your hands on your knees and take deep breaths."

After a few gulps of cool air, his complexion lost its unnatural crimson shade and resumed its normal color, which was somewhere between parchment and the ivory keys on a piano. A workaholic, Phil Logan was definitely an indoor man.

He straightened up. "You're just what every guy needs—a good-looking woman who's a nurturer. Unfortunately, my ex-wife was only good-looking." He shook off that rare moment of melancholy and aimed a triumphant grin at me. "Wait 'til you hear my news!"

I admired Phil's zeal for his job, but I had every reason to be wary when I saw that "I've got a great idea" expression on his face.

I said, "Your last stunt almost put a Los Angeles Dodger on the disabled list."

Two weeks ago, as a tie-in to the show I was preparing called "Cooking for the Ball Game," Phil convinced me to put on a Los Angeles Dodgers' baseball uniform and be photographed "practicing" with the team.

I'd warned him that I wasn't even remotely athletic. "In school, the only team I was ever chosen for was Debating."

"You don't have to *play*," he'd said. "Just take a couple swings with the bat while my photographer gets some shots."

One of the new Dodger pitchers, a polite young man who told me that his mother loved my show, threw an easy one toward me. I swung. Miraculously, the bat connected with the ball, but cheers turned to gasps when the ball struck shortstop Tony Cuervo on the ankle. His yelp of pain brought the team's medic running. In addition to feeling awful that I'd hurt him, I had a horrible vision of the team's owner suing me for the player's astronomical salary.

Luckily, Cuervo wasn't injured. He claimed he just cried out because he was surprised "the girl" could hit a ball. The picture that landed on the sports page of the *Los Angeles Chronicle* showed me gaping in horror, like that Edvard Munch painting, "The Scream."

Nicholas D'Martino, the man in my life, now calls me "slugger."

The *Chronicle* headlined the story "Cook Conks Cuervo." Phil got it picked up by the wire services and published all over the country.

"National publicity," he said proudly.

"You mean national humiliation."

"They spelled your name right, *In the Kitchen with Della* got a bump up in the ratings, and people all over the country who only read the sports section now know about you."

In a gesture of fondness, Tuffy leaned against Phil's thigh. Phil responded by reaching down to give him an ear scratch, but at that moment Tuffy spotted a squirrel a few yards away and took off after it. Tuffy was five years old, and try though he might, had never caught a squirrel. I presumed that by now he gave chase just for the exercise.

Watching Tuffy, Phil said, "Your big guy gets fan mail. My secretary answers it for him, on paw print stationery I had made."

"Isn't that going a little far? Too cutesy?"

"It's good public relations," Phil said. "Speaking of which, our crazy Dodgers' story opened the door to this new opportunity, which I grabbed like a mongoose grabs . . . whatever they grab."

"Cobras," I said.

Phil's lips retracted in a grimace. "I hate snakes. Sorry I brought it up."

"I'm almost afraid to ask, but what opportunity are you talking about?"

The happy grin returned. "You've heard about the Celebrity Cook-Off Charity Gala at the Olympia Grand Hotel this Wednesday night."

"Of course. All the entertainment news reporters have talked about it. But the celebrities who'll be participating are major movie and TV stars. I'm not in that league."

"True," Phil said, "but what I got you is even better. There'll be twenty celebs, but you're going to be one of only three *judges*."

"How can that be? Wednesday is day after tomorrow. The names of the judges were announced weeks ago."

"Ahhhh, but one of them had to withdraw this morning." Phil's tone was positively gleeful. "It's the retired chef who runs that wildlife sanctuary north of Santa Barbara. One of his endangered species bit him."

"That's terrible! Is he all right?"

Phil gave my question a dismissive shrug. "He just got a scratch on that big red drinker's nose of his, but he's acting like he'll need major plastic surgery before he can appear in public again. Frankly, I think he wants to use this as an excuse to have some work done. In a few weeks he'll emerge from seclusion looking—as they say—*rested*. Anyway, the point is that as soon as I heard he'd backed out of judging, I rushed over to the charity's PR office and offered you as a substitute. You're still hot from the Tony Cuervo story, so they said yes. I called my secretary, dictated the press release announcement over the phone and had her do a blast e-mail to all the outlets."

I stared at Phil in astonishment. "You told everybody I'd do it before you asked me?"

"Well, yeah. The national story I sent out doesn't just mention your TV show, I also promoted that mail-order fudge business you started up—Della's Sweet Dreams. A second release went out to the local outlets that also mentions you teach cooking classes in Santa Monica."

Two vertical frown lines suddenly appeared between Phil's eyebrows. "Jeez, this came up so fast I forgot to check. You still teach cooking, don't you?"

"Yes, on weekends."

"That's a relief." Phil's face relaxed, but he didn't look happy. "Not making sure about the classes first—that was careless of me. I pride myself on the fact that anyone can take a Phil Logan press release right to the nearest bank."

Take a press release to the bank . . . Hearing another of those semimetaphors I'd come to think of as Logan-isms made me smile with affection for Phil.

Seven months ago Mickey Jordan, owner of the Better Living Channel, out of desperation had hired me as a replacement host. The desperation was both his and mine. He'd fired the previous host and had to fill vacant time on his cable network, and I was on the verge of drowning in debt trying to keep my little cooking school going. Now I was probably on the second lowest rung of the "celebrity ladder," but the fact that I was known to anyone at all beyond my immediate circle of family and friends was because of Phil Logan's passion for his work.

Phil pulled a folded sheet of paper from his inside jacket pocket and handed it to me. "Details about what criteria you're supposed to use for judging, and how many points you can give any particular dish. When you show up Wednesday night you'll each be given your judging cards and a clipboard. Hey, this'll be the easiest gig in the world. All you'll have to do is walk around in an evening gown and watch other people cook."

Perhaps remembering my notorious lack of interest in fashion, his eyes narrowed and he frowned at me. "Do you have an evening gown?"

"I used to . . . but it's been years since—"

"Never mind. I know some designers—I'll get you a loaner. Try not to spill anything on it."

Phil started to leave, but stopped after taking a single step. When he turned back to me I saw an expression on his face that I'd never seen before: Embarrassment.

"Look," he said, glancing down at the ground, "you know by now that I don't get involved in other people's sex lives, but I think in this case a kind of warning is necessary."

Instantly on the alert against criticism of my relationship with Nicholas D'Martino, I bristled. "Hold it. We're not going to discuss my personal life—"

His head came up and he met my eyes. "Not *you*—it's your friend I'm worried about."

Nicholas? "Oh, Phil, what in the world do you think I could do to a grown man?"

That produced a sly little smile. "I'll bet you could do plenty, and I'm sure ol' Nick wouldn't mind a bit, but that's not what I mean."

"Then what are you talking about? Do I need a translator?"

I saw comprehension dawn in Phil's eyes. "You don't know, do you?"

"Apparently not."

"It's your fudge partner, Eileen O'Hara. I know she's kind of your unofficial daughter, but do you know who she's been having a *thing* with?"

"No."

"It's one of your fellow Celebrity Cook-Off judges, Keith Ingram. Della, when it comes to women—especially the kind that are young and haven't been around much like your Eileen—this is a bad dude."

I'd met Keith Ingram once, four months ago, when he interviewed Eileen and me in order to do a story in his syndicated food column about our just-launched mail-order sweets business. "I think you're mistaken, about her being involved with him," I said. "Since the day the article about us came out she's never mentioned him to me."

"Do you thinks she tells you everything?"

She used to, when I wasn't so busy . . .

"The piece he wrote was so over-the-top favorable, especially to Eileen—'the beautiful UCLA business major with a great idea'—I suspected he had the hots for her," Phil said, "but then I forgot about it."

"How do you know they're seeing each other?"

"I hear things . . . which leads me to the reason I brought this up. I know you're a mother figure to her. She's going to need you to be there for her when he dumps her."

"But if he and Eileen actually are involved, what makes you think—"

"When I was at the charity's PR office signing you up for the Cook-Off gig, I found out Ingram's getting it on with that flaky heiress who's the tabloid's flavor-of-the-month."

"Tina Long?"

"That's the one. A few years ago she couldn't make the grades to graduate from a fancy private high school, so her father bought it. Suddenly Tina's the covaledictorian. Poppa Long hired a novelist to write her speech for her, but the guy forgot to tell her how to pronounce some of the words."

Photographs that I'd seen of Tina Long on gossip magazine covers flashed into my mind. She was a generically pretty girl with blonde hair arranged in a dizzying number of styles, but beneath each new coif there was always the same vapid expression on her face.

Phil's voice interrupted my thoughts. "Ingram's making money with his column and his TV guest shots, but he likes to live big. You know how I got him to do the column on your business?"

In a tone full of irony, I said, "Because we make *really* good fudge?"

He snorted. "I wish that's what it took. I had to arrange a free trip to New York for him on Warner Brothers' private jet."

"Phil, I know you mean well, but I'm not comfortable talking about Eileen behind her back." Sensing that it was getting late, I checked my watch. "It's four o'clock. In a few minutes I've got to start taping the last of today's three shows." I whistled for Tuffy. He looked up from his explorations and came trotting back toward me.

Phil escorted us to the door to the studio and opened it.

I said good-bye and was about to go inside, but the touch of his hand on my arm stopped me.

"What is it, Phil?"

"Publicity is a very *personal* job," he said. "And I usually love it. Seven-day weeks, twenty-hour days—I thrive on building or enhancing careers. But we try to protect our clients, too. The people I work with are family to me. Better, really, because we're close by choice, not an accident of blood. I told you about Ingram because I feel an obligation not to let you get blindsided. Eileen's going to be hurt, but the facts are that her father is a cop. Tina Long's is a billionaire, and she's his only child. You do the math."

Melinda Wells was born in Georgia and grew up wanting to be a writer. She wasn't interested in cooking until she was living in New York City and engaged to marry a talent agent. "Most of the time we went out to dinner with his clients, but one night we were home and I made dinner for him: Beef Stroganoff. He raved about how good it was, and how impressed he was. I was embarrassed to tell him that it was the only dish I knew how to make, so the next day I enrolled in a cooking school." Melinda's black standard poodle (the original "Tuffy") passed away after sixteen happy and healthy years. Currently, Melinda Wells lives in Los Angeles with rescued pets and enjoys cooking for friends. You can visit her website at www.dellacooks.com.

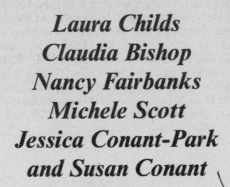

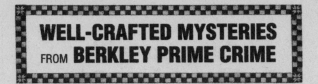